RAGS TO ROYALS

ROYALS GONE ROGUE

ERIN NICHOLAS

ROYALS GONE ROGUE

The Series

Reluctantly Royal (Torin & Abigail)

Reluctantly Rogue (Jonah & Linnea)

Rags to Royals (Cian & Scarlett)

Recklessly Rogue (Henry & Ruby)

ABOUT THE BOOK

A small-town single mom like me has no business believing in fairy tales.

But the very handsome, charming, dirty-talking *prince* (yes, seriously) I met nineteen months ago now has his fine ass and panty-melting grin planted on my front porch.

He's been searching for me ever since I snuck out after our hot, fantasy-filled weekend together.

And, dammit, that's a little romantic.

Now that he's found me, he wants to pick up where we left off. Because he thinks he's in love with me.

Oh, and because he needs to get out of the marriage his grandfather, the king, has arranged for him.

Right. Even if I hadn't lied to him about everything but my first name, the carefree, adventurous woman he burned up the sheets with for three days doesn't exist.

I'm actually a stressed-out mechanic back in my small hometown, raising a sassy fifteen-year-old daughter, and trying to make amends for my mean girl past.

I just don't think my grease-streaked work boots scream *princess material.*

Of course, he won't take no for an answer.
Shocking, I know.

Instead, he proposes a deal: I give him nineteen days to get to know the real me.

Then he'll either get over me, go home, and marry someone else.

Or I'll walk down that aisle.

Author Note and Content Advisory

 I know you have lots and lots and lots of books to choose from and that your time is incredibly valuable. That you've chosen to spend some of that time on this book means so much to me!

Here's what you can expect besides a heart-warming, fun modern-day romance about a prince who falls first and hard for a feisty, stubborn single mom:

- steamy, on-page, open-door sex scenes
- graphic language
- religious trauma
- neglectful parenting
- bullying

If any of that is something you do not want to read, close the book now and return it. No worries! Your mental health and happiness matters!

I hope you love Cian and Scarlett's love story and the time you spend in this fictional world!

xo

Erin

A Brief History of Cara & The Royal Family

In 1848 Tadhg O'Grady was an Irish sailor accompanying King Frederick VII, of Denmark to the Faroe Islands. Their ship was attacked by pirates, and the ships were sunk. Fifty people perished, but Tadhg rescued three men, including King Frederick.

The King was so grateful that he gave Tadhg the southern-most island where they were pulled to shore.

Tadhg named the island Cara, the Irish word for friend. The O'Gradys have ruled the small island, that is just a bit bigger than Rhode Island, in the North Atlantic ever since.

The Modern Royal Family

King Diarmuid took the throne when he was 39 and his father died suddenly of a heart attack.

He has ruled for 43 years. But he has now had three heart attacks and is 82 years old.

His son was in line and ready to ascend to the throne but was tragically killed in a car accident 21 years ago, leaving Diarmuid's eldest grandson, **Declan**, next in line.

But at age 18, Declan abdicated, moved to the US, and cut ties with the family. He has not returned to Cara since. He has built up a multi-billion-dollar company and become a playboy billionaire celebrity of sorts. Americans celebrate the rich as if they're royalty, so he's getting a taste of what he could have had in Cara, but with *far* fewer rules. At least he's charitable with his money.

Next in line then, is the second grandson, **Torin**. At age 19, Torin approached the king with a plan to transition the monarchy to a representative government over a 10-year period.

Diarmuid refused.

So Torin followed in his older brother's footsteps, abdicating and leaving Cara for the US.

His sister, **Fiona**, third in line, and the youngest, their brother Cian, both went with him.

Fiona has become an animal advocate, rescuing, rehabilitating, and rehoming abused, neglected, and displaced animals. She ran a wildlife park in Florida, with her very own tower of giraffes, before falling in love and moving to Louisiana. (She'd argue that the move to Louisiana happened before the falling in love, but no one—not even the guy she fell for—really believes that.) The giraffes and her oops-out-of-wedlock-baby-daddy-isn't-involved daughter, **Saoirse**, moved with her, and she now helps run an even larger sanctuary there.

Cian, the youngest, has become…well, Cian's still finding himself. But he'll get there. Eventually. Probably. He's also in love with a woman he met nearly two years ago and who he has been searching for ever since.

While he was in the US, Torin traveled the world, studied other cultures and traditions, went to college where he was able to immerse himself in ecology, and history, and politics, and economics, and every other subject he could think of. He'd been happy. But duty called, and his conscience finally got the better of him after his grandfather's third heart attack. He returned to Cara, and rescinded his abdication to keep Saoirse from having the burden of the throne. He is now ready to step into his new role, and even has a new princess at his side.

Which simply leaves one "little" issue to resolve…

Who will marry and unite the O'Grady and Olsen families now? Oh, and produce the baby that will forever bind the two bloodlines?

Yeah, no one but the king knew there was supposed to be a *baby*.

That complicates everything.
Because of course it does.

Adjacent Members of the Family

Jonah Greene—Prince Torin's bodyguard and best friend
Colin Daly—Princess Fiona and Princess Saoirse's bodyguard and friend
Henry Dean—Prince Cian's bodyguard and best friend
Iris Lee—Prince Declan's bodyguard and best friend
Linnea Olsen (pronounced Li Nay uh)—woman arranged to marry Torin
Alfred Olsen—King Diarmuid's best friend, Linnea's grandfather (deceased)
Astrid Olsen—Linnea's sister
Alex Olsen—Linnea's brother
Miles Stafford—Astrid's PT and best friend (and bodyguard)

A Final Note About The Drunken Poker Game That Changed Everything

Twenty-something years ago, Alfred Olsen, Diarmuid's best friend, and the king got very drunk while playing poker one night. As they often did. This night, however, Diarmuid was out of money. You might ask how a king runs out of money. And that is a fair question. That no one has been able to answer and that Diarmuid won't address even to this day.

Because he had nothing left to bid, Diarmuid lost a grandson to Alfred.

Yes, a grandson.

Not even a specific one. Any one of the three would do. Though the one who will sit on the throne was preferred.

And what did Alfred intend to do with this grandson?

Marry him off to one of Alfred's granddaughters, of course.

He has two.

Linnea is the oldest. She's gorgeous, polished, classy, intelligent, and she loves Cara. She's everything a queen should be. Which makes sense since she's been raised to believe she will *be* queen since she was four years old.

Astrid is the younger sister. She's also gorgeous, but where Linnea is accommodating and patient and family-focused, Astrid is headstrong and independent and wants full control of her own life. She isn't interested in chaining herself to another person forever and the idea of being responsible for her family's entire legacy, not to mention the expectations of an entire country, is ridiculous to her.

The entire agreement between Diarmuid and Alfred was written out on the back of a playbill, and the words are smudged by spilled whiskey, but the family lawyer informed everyone it's still legal and enforceable since the men both signed it in front of witnesses. Of course, that lawyer is also a very good friend of Diarmuid's and owes him money from another poker game. The same is true for the 'witnesses'.

The most important fact, however, is that in Cara, there's no need for lawyers and judges. King Diarmuid is the law. So the "contract" is enforceable in the stupid, archaic way that anything having to do with royal families is enforceable. With much manipulation, a lot of money, and a pretty good dose of guilt.

But now that Torin has married Abigail (not an Olsen granddaughter) and Linnea has married Jonah (not a prince), the options have narrowed. It's clear that Cian and Astrid will be the ones united in holy matrimony.

At least, that's clear to Diarmuid.

Cian and Astrid are far from convinced.

Pronunciation Guide (those Irish names can be tricky)

Cian—pronounced Kee-an
Diarmuid—pronounced Deer-mid
Linnea—pronounced Li Nay uh
Oisin—pronounced Osh-een
Roisin—pronounced Row-sheen
Saoirse—pronounced Sear-sha
Tadhg—pronounced Tige
Torin–pronounced Tore-in

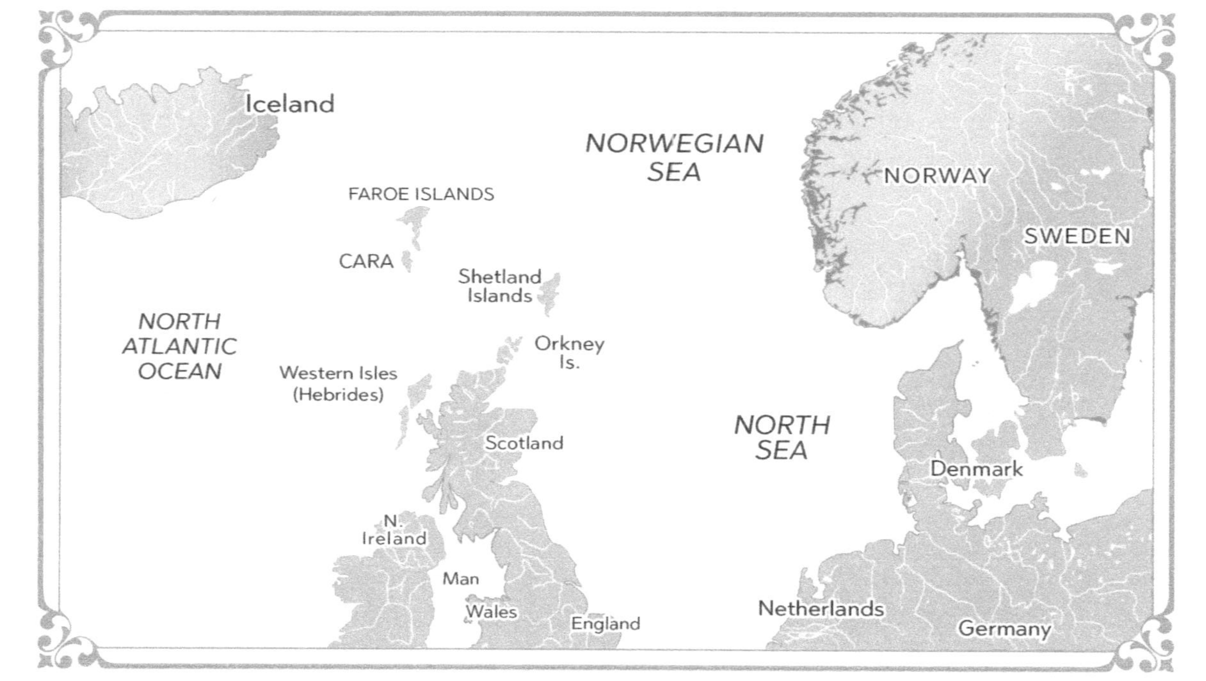

Iceland
NORWEGIAN SEA
NORWAY
SWEDEN
FAROE ISLANDS
CARA
Shetland Islands
NORTH ATLANTIC OCEAN
Western Isles (Hebrides)
Orkney Is.
NORTH SEA
Denmark
Scotland
N. Ireland
Man
Wales
England
Netherlands
Germany

"YOU HAD THE POWER
ALL ALONG, MY DEAR."

- Glinda, The Good Witch

The Wizard Of Oz
L. Frank Baum

CHAPTER 1
CIAN

"Everyone!" King Diarmuid's voice is commanding despite his eighty-two years and the precarious state of his heart after three heart attacks. "This is such a happy day!"

I grin. It really is. My brother, Torin, just got married to the love of his life. He and Abigail are clearly meant to be and will be an amazing King and Queen to our home country. Torin will officially take the throne from our grandfather within the year.

Everyone is happy. Everything is settled. And the wine they're serving with this late dinner for the family and close friends is the best I've had in years.

I smile and look around the table. Everyone is here except our eldest brother, Declan, but no one expected him today. But my sister, niece, parents, grandparents, and all of our closest friends are here, and the general mood is one of cheerful contentment.

"And I want to add to the merriment!" our grandfather

goes on. "Since everyone is together, this is the perfect time to tell you all what's next before you all jet off back to the US."

Many of those gathered in the room live in the US despite our ties to Cara. My brother who just became king, my sister, and I all abdicated twelve years ago and headed to the states. Torin rescinded his abdication and came home two years ago, but Fiona and I still live in Louisiana. Fiona is married now, and she's not going anywhere.

And I'm...not sure.

But that's been the case for most of my life.

As the youngest of the O'Grady royals, the spare to the spare to the spare, I have no responsibilities, there are no expectations of me, and I'm able to do whatever the hell I want.

So, I have.

It's pretty great.

"Diarmuid, I don't—" Linnea Olsen starts.

She's standing right next to Diarmuid and he now takes her hand, cradling it against his chest.

She's the eldest granddaughter of Diarmuid's late best friend Alfred. She's been a close advisor to my grandfather for years and was, in fact, arranged to marry Torin and become Cara's next queen, until he fell in love with Abigail.

"As you all know, I've always expected this day to include this lovely woman," Diarmuid says.

Everyone smiles and nods. It's no secret that Linnea and Torin are both fine with their 'engagement' being broken and that Linnea is thrilled that Torin and Abi are now married.

"We absolutely *adore* Abigail." My grandfather gives Abi a huge smile.

I look at my new sister-in-law. The shy, introverted

scientist, who balked at the idea of a life in the public eye as a royal, is blushing intensely even from this little bit of attention. She looks both embarrassed and confused.

"But," the king goes on, "what many of you don't know is that when Alfred and I entered into our agreement—"

I snort. A few others do as well. The 'agreement' he's referring to is the drunken poker game where he ran out of money—somehow as king?—and had to offer up something else of value to continue to play. He offered up a grandson, Alfred accepted, and...my grandfather lost. From that night on, one of Diarmuid's grandsons was promised in marriage to one of Alfred's granddaughters.

We all thought the whole story was a joke.

Until Torin returned to Cara, rescinded his abdication, and agreed to take his place as the next leader of the country...and got a fiancée as part of the benefits package.

My grandfather gives us all a frown, and everyone quiets again. "As I was saying," he continues. "Alfred and I wanted our families to be united. Alfred had only one granddaughter at the time." He smiles down at Linnea. "I had three grandsons. Contrary to popular belief, our agreement had nothing to do with the throne."

I frown and lean forward.

He's correct in saying that we all believed that Alfred made the agreement with the understanding that his granddaughter would be the future queen. Why else would he have done it?

But my grandfather continues, "It was simply the *assumption* that it would be a union of our first grandchildren. Then Declan left, and the agreement moved to my second grandson. But now that my second grandson is married to another, the arrangement will move to my third grandson."

I repeat his words silently.

The agreement was initially to marry Declan and Linnea. They are the first grandchildren in each family. Okay, if someone was going to take the arrangement seriously—which clearly Diarmuid and Alfred did, even if the rest of us did not—that makes sense.

But Declan left. My oldest brother abdicated and left for the US fifteen years ago. He hasn't returned to our tiny, remote island country in all that time. Not once. He's built several wildly successful businesses in the US and is now one of the richest men on the continent. Probably in the world. He hasn't once looked back at the throne. He barely keeps in touch with the family.

There was no question Declan was *not* going to be Cara's king. So when Torin returned to Cara, Linnea became *his* future queen.

But now that he's married, the arrangement will move to Diarmuid's *third* grandson?

Wait a fucking minute.

I'm not the third grandchild, but...

"Hey, *I'm* your third grandson," I say out loud.

My grandfather meets my gaze and nods. "Yes. *You* and Linnea will marry. We'll announce the engagement in three months."

Three months? *What?*

Linnea Olsen is amazing. She's intelligent, classy, kind, gorgeous. But...*I'm* going to *marry* her? Just because our grandfathers got drunk while playing poker twenty-some years ago?

"*I'm* going to marry Linnea?" I repeat. "Just like that? Are you kidding?" I quickly meet Linnea's gaze. "No offense."

I like her just fine. I can think of worse things I suppose, but I don't think Linnea and I have had a conversation one-on-one, just the two of us, in probably close to ten years. Yes, we knew each other growing up but she was a *brat*. She took the I'm-going-to-be-queen-someday thing seriously and acted like she was in charge of everything, even at a very young age.

Diarmuid nods his head. "Yes. The O'Gradys and Olsens *will* be united."

"That's cra—" I start.

"No."

Everyone looks at Linnea as one.

I feel relief rush through me.

Okay, Linnea is going to take care of this. Awesome. Diarmuid listens to her. This is good.

I smile and settle back into my chair.

"No," she repeats as she pulls her hand away from Diarmuid's.

My grandfather looks completely confused. "Linnea?"

She takes a deep breath and looks up at him. "I adore you," she says, sincerely. "You are *so* important to me." She turns to look at all of us in the room. "All of you are. The O'Grady family is so important to me. I'm so happy to be a part of it. And I hope I always can be, in some way, but…" She takes another deep breath. Then she lifts her chin, and her voice gets louder. "You all make me *crazy*. You have been messing with my life for…well, my whole life. Everything about *everything* has been about you all. What you want. Or don't want. One minute I'm engaged. Then I'm not. Then I am again, but to someone else. Now I am again to *another* one of you? No. Just *no*."

Thata girl, I think. But I keep quiet. My grandfather looks stunned.

But thank God, Linnea is handling this. I take zero offense that she doesn't want to marry me.

She looks at Diarmuid again. "I know what you and my grandfather wanted. I understand. And I've done everything you've ever asked of me until now. I've made Cara better. I've helped you. I've helped Torin. I've helped Abigail. And it's been my pleasure. It always will be. But… no. I'm not going to marry Cian. I'm not going to be an O'Grady. I'm in love with someone else and I'm going to marry *him*."

Oh, fuck yes. Even better. She's in love with someone else. No way will Diarmuid insist she marry me.

I let out a long breath and reach for my wine, taking a long gulp.

"I'm finally going to do what *I* want," Linnea says. "And…I want Jonah. I love him and want to marry *him*."

Oh. She's in love with my brother's bodyguard. That's nice. A little scandalous even.

I lean forward to look down the table at Jonah. I've known Jonah Greene for twelve years. He was hired as Torin's bodyguard at the same time Henry Dean was hired as mine. The men joined us within months of our abdications and move to the US. Colin Daly was assigned to my sister, Fiona, and her daughter, Saoirse, as well.

They all came on board to keep track of us and, I guess, keep us alive and out of trouble while we were "having our tantrum" as our grandfather initially referred to our abdications.

Henry, Jonah, and Colin have been with us for over a decade now, becoming more like family than bodyguards or employees. Especially since *we* weren't the one paying them or giving them any kind of direction.

Henry is like a brother to me, and I can't imagine what life would be like without him.

But Jonah fell for Torin's supposed-to-be fiancée, huh? That's juicy.

I glance at Henry.

He doesn't look shocked by any of this.

Which means he knew about Jonah and Linnea.

I roll my eyes. Of course he did. He always knows this shit way before I do. I'm certain he knows a bunch of stuff I have no clue about.

I'm cool with that. The less I know, the less I have to be worried about or responsible for.

He meets my gaze and lifts a brow.

That's his way of asking how I am.

I lift a shoulder. I just got engaged and dumped in the space of about three minutes, but I'm good.

In a very unusual display of emotion, Jonah practically jumps to his feet. "Yes. *Fuck* yes." He's around the table and stalking toward Linnea a second later.

I tip my head toward Jonah, Linnea, and Diarmuid where the king is clearly trying to wrap his head around what's going on and Linnea is confessing her love and Jonah has her face in his hands, professing his love as well, then kissing her.

Henry just nods.

Yep, he knew about it.

Can't believe he didn't tell me.

I glance around. Who else is sleeping with someone in this room that I don't know about?

"Our families will always be united in heart and spirit, and in the good works we do together," Linnea is saying to the king, pulling my attention back to their little drama.

"Oh," he says, patting her cheek. "Of course. But we can

still be united by marriage, *and*," he says, looking around at the group again, "by blood."

I do not like the sound of *that*. I frown. "What the hell does that mean?" I ask.

"A child, of course," Diarmuid says.

Of course? What am I missing? Are we talking heirs here? I mean I'm sure Torin and Abigail have been practicing. They've only been together for a few months and married for a few hours. Though my grandfather is not known for his patience.

"Fiona has a child," I say, pointing at my niece.

Saoirse grins at me.

Diarmuid's smile for his great-granddaughter is one none of the rest of us ever see. It's full of such genuine love and pride, it makes my eyes widen.

"Yes, she's an O'Grady. Potentially an heir to the throne. But not an Olsen," Diarmuid says.

So, he's *not* concerned about heirs to the throne?

"The agreement doesn't say anything about an O'Grady-Olsen child," my sister points out.

"We assumed that would naturally come of the marriage," Diarmuid says. "And more than one child would be lovely. But yes, at least one."

"So..." Henry finally speaks up. "That's all moot now, though. I don't think Jonah's going to let Linnea have Cian's baby."

"Oh my god, no!" Linnea exclaims.

"Damn right," Jonah growls.

"Don't be weird," I tell him.

Henry just shrugs.

"Of course not," Diarmuid says over the noise. "Obviously Astrid and Cian will marry and produce the heir."

I freeze with my glass of wine halfway to my mouth.

He's not worried about the throne.

He wants an heir to the family legacies. Both families.

Ours and...

Oh, shit.

All laughter immediately ceases and five seconds pass before Astrid and I speak at the same time.

"*What?*"

I look at Linnea's younger sister. She's staring at me.

Then we both look back to Diarmuid.

Suddenly everyone is on their feet, talking at once. Except for my mother and grandmother. And Astrid's mother, father, and grandmother.

Clearly, they already knew about this.

And are pleased by the idea.

I look at Henry.

Now he actually seems stunned.

Ha. Something he *didn't* know. And he didn't keep this from me. At least that's comforting.

Then I look back at the woman my grandfather wants me to marry.

She looks like she wants to throw up.

I sigh.

Just another crazy fucking day as an O'Grady royal.

CHAPTER 2

CIAN

So, can I marry a woman that I really like—a smart, bold, funny, sassy, gorgeous woman—and have a baby with her to make both our families, especially our grandfathers (even if hers is deceased) insanely happy?

Or do I keep holding out for the woman I'm madly in love with but who I haven't seen in a year and seven months because I can't fucking *find her* since she snuck out the morning after our weekend together, quit her job, and moved?

Okay, from what we've gathered, she quit her job and planned to move before she met me. It's not like she left the state *because* of me. Still, she's out there somewhere and I can't find her.

"How crazy would this be?" I ask Henry.

I've pulled him over to the windows in the dining room. Though we're still in the same room with both Astrid's and my families, the room is enormous—that's a palace thing, I guess—and we've got plenty of space for a private conversation.

"For you to marry Astrid?" Henry asks.

I feel the knot in my gut pull tighter. It's not as if I showed up to my brother's wedding with any clue my grandfather would pull out *another* arranged marriage and that I'd be a part of it.

But Astrid is...awesome.

I've known her all my life. We're definitely friends. I'd probably be an idiot to *not* marry her. Hell, it probably should have occurred to me that marrying her was a good idea even before now, honestly. Any normal, intelligent man would.

But my first reaction to my grandfather's announcement is *fuck no*.

Why?

Because of Scarlett.

Goddammit.

I don't even know her last name. I haven't seen her in *nineteen fucking months*.

However, I can also admit that at least a part of my resistance to marrying Astrid is simply because it's my grandfather's idea. His *command*. I've been working very hard, for over a decade, to be sure my grandfather thinks I'm too careless to be given any kind of meaningful command at all.

And it's been working. Perfectly. My grandfather has never given me any kind of responsibility. No one really has.

Apparently, marriage to his best friend's granddaughter doesn't count as a real responsibility though? That seems wrong.

"Say on a scale from one to a hundred?" I ask Henry.

"Probably in the seventies."

I lift a brow. "Not even in the nineties?"

Henry lifts a shoulder. "It occurs to me that perhaps we should have been prepared for this."

"Prepared for my grandfather to tell us on the night of my brother's wedding that *I* now have to marry *Astrid*?" I ask. Astrid and I are the youngest children in our families. And my brother's wedding was supposed to solve all this 'arranged marriage' stuff. "Why should we have prepared for *that*?"

Henry never bullshits me. "The agreement never said that the O'Grady grandson that married had to be the one that became king. Or even that it had to be the eldest grandson. It didn't stipulate which of you would be married to the Olsen girl at all. It simply states, 'an O'Grady grandson and Olsen granddaughter'." He pauses. "You and Astrid are the only ones left."

Right. My brother's marriage isn't to an Olsen. But Torin will be the next king of Cara and Abigail will be queen, and my grandfather is thrilled with that. With them. So we all assumed that made the agreement null and void.

I stare at Henry. "This is just now occurring to you?"

He nods. "We—I—really thought the goal was for Linnea to be queen."

I shove a hand through my hair. "Of course you did. We all did. *Linnea* did. She's been raised to be queen. The whole thing is over. The stupid agreement is settled."

"But evidently not," Henry says. "Seems a baby is actually the point."

I feel a jab in the gut. Yeah, that's news to us all.

The 'agreement' between my grandfather, King Diarmuid, and Alfred Olsen, has always been laughed off. They'd come up with it one night playing poker. Rip-roaring drunk. As the story goes—and mind you, the only people who have ever actually recounted this story are my grandfather and Alfred, so they could be making the entire thing up—my grandfather offered up a grandson in order to stay in the game. Alfred accepted the bet… and then, ironically, laid down a royal flush to my grandfather's measly pair of, perhaps even more ironically, kings.

I mean, what are the chances?

Maybe if they'd said Alfred had a full house and my grandfather had three of a kind. But the added 'flair' of the royal flush is a little much.

And if it's true, what the hell was my grandfather doing betting on a pair? Even if they were kings? That was stupid.

The whole thing seems fishy as hell to me whenever I think about it.

And my grandfather's delight—and stubborn insistence—over the idea of an O'Grady-Olsen wedding makes me absolutely willing to believe he bet a grandson on a losing hand on purpose.

Making my doubts even stronger, he and Alfred wrote up the agreement on the back of the playbill from the show they'd seen earlier in the evening. This "binding agreement" is whisky stained, smudged, and about seventeen words long. It was also witnessed by men who were just as drunk, not to mention subordinate to both my grandfather and Alfred. But everyone insists it's completely official.

'Everyone' being my grandfather, Alfred, and all of our parents. Meaning that legal or not, there is *a lot* of pressure, guilt, and manipulation within the family behind making this happen.

And hell, it might be 'legal' too. In Cara, anyway. My grandfather is the king. He is more or less the law.

And now, tonight, my grandfather told us all for the first time that they'd assumed a baby would be the ultimate outcome. He and Alfred wanted their families united by *blood*.

A child. A real, human *person* who would be a combination of two old, wealthy, influential families' DNA.

Jesus Christ.

I blow out a breath.

I'm the last man standing. The third and final available O'Grady grandson.

And Astrid is Alfred's only other granddaughter.

This is crazy.

But kings have this really annoying habit of thinking they can always get their way.

Because they can always get their way.

"Cian? Can I talk to you?"

I turn and find Astrid looking up at me with wide blue eyes. She looks absolutely panicked.

Which makes complete sense.

Miles Stafford, Astrid's best friend, is standing just behind her. He looks concerned as well.

"Yeah. Of course."

I've known Astrid my entire life. I have been living in the US for the past twelve years, but until I was seventeen, I lived in Cara. Our families have always been close. I've always liked Astrid.

Besides being smart, bold, and beautiful, she's also now famous. She's a gymnast. Was nearly an Olympian. If it wasn't for a devastating fall during the qualifying rounds, she would have likely brought a gold medal home to Cara.

Because of her, and her hockey star brother Alex, the world is discovering our tiny, remote country. Astrid and Alex have put Cara on the map, and they are truly heroes in our country.

Despite her injury, she's now an advocate for athletes

with disabilities, an inspirational speaker, a children's book author, and has a number of endorsements.

Yeah, I should probably just marry her.

If this had all come up two years ago—pre-Scarlett—I would have.

Astrid crosses her arms. "We can't do this," she says.

"No?" I ask.

"It's nuts," she insists. "We've always thought so even when it was Linnea and Torin who were supposed to get married."

I nod. "Did you have any idea this might happen? To us, I mean?"

"None," she says, shaking her head. "And I've never heard anyone talk about there needing to be a... ba—baby."

She stumbles over the last word.

I nod. "Me either."

"I really like you," she says, sincerely. "You're great." She gives a soft laugh. "You're a catch. And we'd have fun. I'm probably stupid for not wanting this."

I give her a grin. Astrid and I have a lot in common. She's got a great sense of humor, and she likes to go out, be amongst people, dance, and laugh, and party. Whenever we're both in Cara, we go down to the pub and hang out and have a great time.

And she's beautiful. Being close physically to this girl would not be a hardship.

But...not if there's an agenda.

And not if she's going to look like she's been sentenced to the gallows.

And not since I met Scarlett.

"It wouldn't be so bad," I say anyway.

Astrid blows out a breath and glances at Miles, then back to me. "I just can't...it's not you. It's me."

I chuckle. "You don't have to say that."

That gets a smile from her. "I mean it. I'm not interested in getting married. At all. To anyone. Ever."

She looks at Miles again. He's looking at her with a grim set to his mouth. I wonder if there's something going on between the two of them. I know I'm not the first one to wonder. They first got close after her injury and Miles became her physical therapist. They've been inseparable ever since. The media has certainly speculated on their relationship. But there's never been any proof, photographic or otherwise, that they're more than friends. And there would be no reason for them to keep that from the family if there was, so we all assume there's not.

Still, they're very close and he clearly knows things about her no one else does.

"Please tell me there's a way out of this," Astrid says to me.

Her grandfather passed away about two years ago. It's been hard on everyone. Alfred was one of a kind. And my grandfather has truly seemed lost without his best friend. We always knew that Alfred was the one person King Diarmuid would listen to when it came to policies and big decisions. Truly, the only off-the-wall thing Alfred ever did was this arranged marriage plan. In every other way, he seemed to keep my grandfather reasonable and open-minded.

Unfortunately, Alfred had suffered with dementia and there had been about five years before his death where he'd been fading, and his personality had changed.

My grandfather slowly lost his best friend and confidant, and we all saw the effects. My grandfather grew gruffer, and more stubborn.

I glance in the direction where our families are standing, gathered around the King.

I frown. I don't see my brother or his new wife at the moment. Or Linnea and Jonah. All of the people who most recently bucked the king's expectations. We could use some tips. But I watch everyone else.

Fiona is talking with our mother and grandmother. Very likely advocating for them to step in with the king. I'm sure she thinks this is crazy and doesn't agree with forcing Astrid and me together. Fiona has always taken care of me.

Hell, all of my siblings have in one way or another. I'm the baby. In every way. No one expects much from me and my three siblings have all given me everything from a home to jobs to advice. I'd left Cara because Torin and Fiona were leaving. Torin's ideas around abdication were grand and passionate and I was easily won over. Of course I was. My older brother is one of my idols. I'd happily settled in with Fiona and helped her with her mission of rescuing animals and running an endangered animal sanctuary and raising her beloved surprise baby.

I never had to worry about finding a place or purpose.

My siblings have given me both.

You could do this, step up and settle this arranged marriage thing once and for all. You could produce this all-important heir. You could finally be the one who did something big.

I ignore the voice in my head. I hate that voice. The one that nags me about being aimless and a little too carefree.

As I watch Fiona talking with my mother, I wonder briefly if Fiona could have married and produced an O'Grady-Olsen heir with Alex. Probably. Now that we know that a child is the ultimate goal rather than an Olsen sitting on the throne, it seems plausible that Diarmuid and Alfred would have accepted any combination. But Fiona is happily married. So she's not a possibility either.

That's what Astrid or I need to do.

The realization hits me right in the face.

Of course. It's obvious. All we have to do is be in love with and married to someone else.

That would put us out of contention just like Fiona, Torin, and Linnea are.

Or at least *one* of us needs to do that.

"Are you seeing anyone?" I ask Astrid.

"What?"

"Do you have a boyfriend?"

She shakes her head. "No."

"Anyone at all? Someone who's a really good friend who would step up and marry you out of convenience?" My gaze settles on Miles.

But Astrid is shaking her head. "No. I don't want to be married at all."

"You two couldn't just fake it for a while?"

"Me and Miles?" Astrid asks, looking shocked.

"Yeah. You're friends. People already speculate that you're a thing. Couldn't you claim that you're together? Maybe even get married to make it official for a while?"

She frowns. "Define 'a while'."

"I don't know." I sigh.

I hate to say until my grandfather dies. That just sounds so bad. Plus, he could live another twenty years.

"It's just an idea," I say. "Diarmuid accepted Abigail for Torin. He accepted Linnea and Jonah together. If one of us is in love and committed to someone else, he can't expect *us* to get married."

Astrid and Miles look at one another. Miles rolls his eyes.

"How about you and Henry get married?" Miles asks, looking at me again. "That would *really* put a stop to all of this."

I glance at Henry and give him a grin. "He's got a point."

"That would work except that they'd expect us to kiss each other in public and in front of them," Henry says, looking bored.

"They would," I agree, suddenly feeling lighter, because at least the four of us still have our senses of humor. "And we can't do that. You'd never be able to go back to women."

"Definitely my biggest concern," he says dryly.

And I laugh. Things are going to be okay.

Astrid and Miles are grinning too, but after a moment passes, Astrid sighs. "Are you serious?" she asks me and Henry. "I mean, you could be very progressive. Step out as a bi-sexual member of the royal family. That would be cool." She looks at Miles. "Or should we talk about it?"

"Well." Miles rubs a hand over the back of his neck. "I don't have a better idea."

Neither of them looks excited, which is interesting.

I look at Henry. Pretend to be involved with Henry in a romantic relationship? I mean...it wouldn't be a huge stretch. We already spend all of our time together, live together, like each other a lot, know each other very well. And I'm a royal-in-hiding in the US for the most part. A few people have figured out who my family is, but the number of people who see me on the street and know who I am is extremely tiny. Coming out as a couple with Henry wouldn't affect my life much.

"What do you think?" I ask him.

"I'd do it," he says. "But..." He blows out a breath. "Fuck," he mutters. Then he meets my eyes. "I found her, Cian."

I frown, trying to figure out what he's saying. "You..." Then my eyes widen. "*What*?"

"I found Scarlett."

I let that sink in.

"Scarlett?" I repeat. "*My* Scarlett?"

He nods.

Holy shit. He found Scarlett. The woman I haven't been able to stop thinking about since we spent the hottest, sweetest, best weekend of my life together. Before she snuck out Monday morning while I was sleeping and completely vanished.

I went back to where we met, where she was working that Friday night, but they told me that had been her last night. We went to her address after Henry dug it up, but the house was empty. Her landlord didn't have a new address for her. There was no forwarding information submitted to the post office.

I searched every place I could think of in New Orleans. Then every place I could think of in Louisiana.

Henry, who is plugged into a network of law enforcement and resources I don't even know or understand, has searched for her.

But it's like she never existed.

After six months, Henry staged an intervention. My friends tried to get me to admit that I was likely never going to see her again. But I couldn't fully let go.

I still haven't gotten to that point, but...we aren't actively searching anymore.

Or so I thought.

"You're *sure*?" I finally ask.

"Yes." He blows out a breath. "I found her sister first. But yes, I've...spoken to Scarlett. It's her. For sure."

I react without thinking. I grab the front of his shirt and push him up against the wall. "You've *spoken* to her?"

His eyes don't even widen. He probably expected this

reaction. Plus, he knows he can totally take me if this actu-ally gets physical.

"Yes."

"When?" I demand.

He hesitates. "Recently."

I tighten my fist on his shirt and press him more firmly into the wall. "When were you going to tell me?"

"When it was time," he says. "Maybe."

Fuck, I hate when he does that. "Stop it." I shove back from him and push my hand through my hair. "I hate when you get all vague and I-know-better-than-you," I tell him.

"I couldn't tell you right away," he says, smoothing a hand down the front of his dress shirt. "I had to be sure it was her. And then...there are reasons."

I can't fucking believe he found her and didn't tell me. That he's *seen her*, *talked* to her, and I'm just hearing about it.

"Let's go," I say. I turn back to Astrid. "I think I have a solution."

She's watching us with intrigue. "Scarlett?"

"I—" I look at Henry. "Let's put it this way. I'm going to get myself married. If it isn't to Scarlett, then Henry owes me. Big."

She presses her lips together, clearly trying to fight a smile. She nods. "Okay."

"I'll keep in touch. We'll figure this out. I promise."

She gives me a soft, genuinely affectionate smile. "Okay." She glances toward our families. "I'll cover for you."

"You will?"

"Of course. I'll tell them we've discussed things, but we need some time to really figure things out."

Right. My grandfather said the engagement would be

announced in three months. We've got a little time. But not fucking much.

I've been looking for Scarlett for nineteen months. Now I know where she is. Or Henry does at least. Three months is *plenty* of time to let her know exactly how I feel and what I want.

"Thanks, Astrid."

She nods. "You're saving me from marrying Miles. I owe you, too."

"Brat," Miles mutters.

She shoots him a smile, then looks back to me. "Where are you going?"

"I'm going to..." I look at Henry.

"Emerald, Ohio," Henry tells us.

I narrow my eyes. Emerald? Immediately I think *Emerald City*. Scarlett's mom, Judy, is obsessed with the Wizard of Oz. If I'd known there was a city named Emerald, I probably would have thought of looking there.

So we're going to Ohio. Okay, then. Makes sense why it was hard to find her. Ohio is a long way from the luxury hotel in New Orleans where I last saw her. Or the Pink Ladies strip club on Bourbon Street, where I first saw her.

But it's not too far away to keep me from going to her.

Nowhere is too far away.

CHAPTER 3

SCARLETT

"Oh my God! Mom! Did you hear the podcast?" Mariah comes sliding into the kitchen on stocking feet.

I place her breakfast burrito on the center island. I *really* want to say no. I really want to say, 'I barely think about that podcast until you or Ruby brings it up' and mean it.

But of course, I heard it. Because I've subscribed to the stupid thing, and I get notifications and that one pinged first thing this morning. And I'm clearly a masochist because I listen to every single episode. Usually twice.

I'm pathetic.

It's one thing to be hung up on a hot one-night stand—okay, it was three nights, and it was beyond hot, so I give myself a little grace there—but it's an entirely different thing to stalk the guy afterward. Especially after telling his best friend, in no uncertain terms, that I forbade him to even tell the guy where I am now living.

I can *not* see Cian O'Grady again.

I'd known that even before I left him sleeping, all gorgeous and rumpled and sexy in that hotel bed—the nicest hotel and best bed I've ever slept in. *Ever.*

I can't see him again because he's wrong for me. I'm wrong for him. We're wrong for each other. He's exactly the opposite of the type of guy I should ever get involved with. I'm not interested in any guy really, but especially not a guy like Cian.

And he doesn't want me.

I guess he thinks he does. According to Henry anyway.

Okay, and according to Cian and his, 'I know it's crazy but I'm falling in love with you, Scarlett,' that last night we were together.

I can't get that out of my head. I can still hear it as if he just said it last night.

But it was over a year ago. *Well* over a year ago. A year and a half now. Still, that deep, gravelly voice is crystal clear in my mind. And at night, when it's quiet and dark, I can close my eyes and conjure how his hands felt stroking my back, how his hard, hot chest felt against my cheek, and how those words wrapped around me.

Right before cold reality splashed over me as I remembered that he didn't know me. That he was falling in love with another woman all together.

Which was fine then and it's fine now. It was one weekend and *only* one weekend.

I believed that when I thought he was just a cute, young, sexy, rich guy who made me lose my mind for a weekend.

But now? I *definitely* believe it now. Now that I know he's a *prince* and has immeasurable wealth and power and influence.

Of *course*, when I do something spontaneous and throw

my inhibitions out and actually have a good time, I do it with a guy like that.

The universe hates me.

Actually…I'm pretty sure it's punishing me.

Still.

I force enthusiasm into my voice. "I did!" I give Mariah a smile. "Linnea and Jonah. Wow! I didn't see that coming *at all.*"

"Right?" Mariah asks, grinning at me. "They are *so* great together. I love it. Jonah is so hot."

He is. I don't comment on that though. She's fifteen and I know she's noticing how guys look and that's fine, but Jonah Greene is twice her age at least and is a bearded, broody, tattooed bodyguard. Not sure I want to know that's my daughter's type just yet.

I turn to refill my cup. "I really like what I know about Linnea. She seems pretty kickass. Good for her marrying someone unexpected like that."

Ugh. I know all about Linnea Olsen and I wish I didn't. Not because of *her.* She really does seem amazing. It's just one more sign that I know way too much about the royal family of Cara and their friends. And lovers.

I didn't even know that Cara existed until a few months ago. And there's no reason for me to know. I'm not a citizen of Cara. I'm not in politics in the US. I don't follow hockey or gymnastics, so I only know Astrid Olsen's name because of her post-injury advocacy work. There's no way I would have known her older sister's name was Linnea if it wasn't for Cian. I certainly wouldn't know who Linnea was in love with and who she'd married in a whirlwind wedding last night right on the heels of Prince Torin and Princess Abigail's wedding if it wasn't for Cian. I wouldn't even know who Prince Torin and Princess Abigail were.

Well, if it wasn't for *Henry* showing up and telling me all about Cian.

I wouldn't have known *Cian* was a fucking prince. I would have gone on living my life thinking I'd had a hot weekend fling with some amazing guy I'd met at my sister's club and would never see again.

But now I can see him whenever I want to… online. You have to search for them but there are lots of photos. And stories. There's a whole damned podcast that talks about Cian's family and they mention the youngest playboy prince as much as they possibly can.

He's understandably a favorite topic. He's fun and charming and adventurous and seemingly a bit of a troublemaker, which makes for amazing podcast material.

And terrible boyfriend material for a single mom from Ohio who needs to keep her head down and be humble in order to make the second chance in her hometown work.

Why can't Henry understand that?

He seemed to think that knowing Cian is a prince, that weekends like the one we had in the Presidential Suite at the Windsor Court hotel in New Orleans could be my everyday life, would be a selling point.

Nope. No way. Not at all.

Henry Dean, Cian's best friend, is on my shit list for a number of reasons.

First and foremost, for tracking me down.

Secondly for making my sister fall for him and then breaking her heart.

Thirdly for telling us who Cian really is and getting us all caught up in the royal history and gossip from his home country.

Ruby was the one that started all of this. She was very interested in the royal prince thing.

She's kind of on my shit list too, as a matter of fact.

"*Of course,* Linnea is kickass," Mariah says, plopping onto the stool across the island from me. "I think it's romantic that they couldn't wait. I bet they got all caught up in Torin and Abigail's wedding and just *had* to get married too."

Hmm. Two years ago, my cynical ass would have said no way do people get caught up like that. Love like that isn't real. People don't just look at each other and say *I can't live another day without you.*

In fact, *that* kind of emotion, in my experience, is the sure-fire way to send a guy running in the opposite direction.

But, then Cian O'Grady swept into my life...

Okay, I was the one that told him he could have anything he wanted from me for twenty-four hours. And when he asked for twenty-four more after that, I said yes. And when he asked for more after *that*, I said yes to that too.

But he was the one who pulled out his platinum credit card and gave me a fucking fantasy weekend straight out of the best romantic movie ever.

And that was even without the sex.

I might have been the one to ask if he wanted to go to a hotel, but *he* was the one who told me he was falling in love with me.

So hell, if Jonah Greene rocked Linnea Olsen's world even a fraction of the way Cian rocked mine, then said he loved her and asked her marry him, I don't blame the woman for saying yes.

If it works out, great.

If it doesn't... well, I still don't blame her for falling for it.

Chemistry can be very potent and idiot-inducing.

"But anyway," Mariah goes on. "That's not the one I'm talking about."

I sip from my cup. "What do you mean?"

"There was another episode published an hour ago!"

I frown. I'd missed that notification while I was getting ready for work. I glance at my phone, but resist reaching for it. I do *not* need to look. "Well, there's a lot going on. It's been a little chaotic over there." I feel my palm itching to grab my phone. What's going on? Cian was at the wedding. Do they mention him again in this new episode?

Ugh.

"Cian and Henry are missing!"

I freeze with my mug halfway to my mouth. I stare at Mariah. She's studying her phone.

"What?" I ask, trying not to sound too interested. Or worried.

I'm not *worried* exactly. I know Henry and there's no way anything bad happened.

But what does the podcast mean 'they're missing'?

I'd tried to resist. I'd told myself it was stupid to learn anything at all about the man I planned to never see again.

But it was very hard to ignore Henry telling me that Cian had been looking for me ever since our night together. That had made my heart beat a little harder, I'll admit.

I haven't forgotten him. I've replayed our weekend over and over again.

Of course I have.

I'm a single mom who does *not* date, does *not* have flings, doesn't even have sex, who is living back in my hometown where at least half of the people hate me, trying to prove that I've changed, trying to avoid my father, and trying to keep my dead step-father's garage in business.

There's not a lot of fun in my life right now. So does my

mind wander back to the weekend that felt like a fucking fantasy from start to finish? To the man who made me feel like a goddess from minute one? To the Windsor Court hotel, the luxurious bubble baths, the decadent food, the expensive dress he bought me, the laughter, the flirting, and the holy-shit-hot sex?

Um, yes.

Of course it does.

Often.

That weekend was like a dream come true.

And then I find out that I said 'what the hell', shed all of my careful ways, and I ended up taking my clothes off for a *prince*?

I mean…that can't be real, right? How does that happen?

But it's real. And in the past few months since Henry tracked us down, I've Googled the hell out of Cara and the royal family and learned the entire history, past and present.

Ruby and Mariah are just as obsessed.

Mariah is still studying her phone. She starts to read. "As we know they were at the wedding and then sources report they were at the late family-only dinner. But when everyone woke up this morning, they were gone, and no one knows where they went."

The three of us now listen religiously to the podcast *Wait 'Til I Tell Ye* and discuss each episode. The podcast is from Cara, and you definitely have to know it exists to find it. It's two women who talk about everything from the weather to beauty tips to local events like farmers' markets and art fairs. But they also love to cover the royal family. And lately they've had a lot of fodder.

It was like a royal reality show. It really is pretty

intriguing and kind of fun to follow. Beautiful, rich, powerful people are fun to watch from a distance. And in this case, they are all good people. Everything I can find points to that fact. They are generous, charitable, and are working on policies that will actually help people.

And yes, the podcast mentions Cian from time to time.

And even though every time I hear his name, my heart skips, I've learned some very important things. He's a playboy. He's the youngest of the royal grandchildren so he has no chance of taking the throne and, seemingly, has no real responsibilities of any kind. And everyone adores him. In the 'isn't he cute and fun' way. Not in any kind of 'we can totally depend on him' way.

He loves to party, he loves to travel, and he loves to have a good time.

Which is fine. That's his prerogative. It's none of my business.

Because we're nothing. We're each other's past. And we're barely that.

Mariah keeps going. "We also have it on good authority that they have *not* returned to Louisiana."

Cian and his siblings have been living in the US for the last several years. His brother Torin—the future king—just returned to Cara, but the others all live in US, including Cian and Henry who live in a tiny town in Louisiana where Cian's sister, Fiona, runs an animal sanctuary. There are giraffes and penguins on the bayou because of Fiona and friends.

Finally, Mariah looks up at me. "What do you think is going on?"

I take another sip of coffee, stalling. Mariah knows about me and Cian. She doesn't know all the provocative details, of course, but she knows we 'went out' the weekend before we moved to Ohio and now, thanks to Henry and Ruby, she knows that Cian thinks he's in love with me and wants to see me again.

Mariah is very much in favor of that.

As is Ruby.

I'm completely outnumbered.

"I have no idea," I finally say. "I don't know him that well. I don't know where else he'd go besides Louisiana."

Mariah sits up straighter, her eyes wide. "What if they're coming *here*?"

I shake my head. "They're not. You know that. You know I told Henry I don't want to see him and now Henry and Ruby have broken up. They're probably on their way to deep-sea dive or mountain climb somewhere."

That's more his style. He and Henry are always doing something fun and spontaneous.

Another reason we'd be terrible together. Spontaneity only gets me into trouble. I've proven that over and over.

I *cannot* see Cian. I have no desire to repeat...

Okay, that's a lie. I'd love to repeat our weekend.

But anything beyond that? No. Absolutely not. Had I met him a year before I did? Maybe. *Maybe.*

But now? A flashy, pseudo-famous, staggeringly wealthy boyfriend who is related to a king and a billionaire and who has some definite skeletons in his closet—beautiful women with broken hearts, parties with property damage, one- or two-night stints in jail, and God knows what else—is absolutely the last person I need in my life.

I'm laying low. I'm keeping my head down. I'm trying to prove I'm not the sanctimonious bitch I was when I lived here before.

I just want to live a good life and prove that people can

change, can see the error of their ways, and can make amends.

Cian O'Grady is not a bad person.

He's just not a lay-low-head-down-simple-life person.

Even in the fifty-five hours I spent with him I knew that, and now I've read plenty of proof.

Mariah slumps on her stool and picks up her burrito. "I know. Ruby's so sad. I hope she doesn't listen to this episode."

I nod. "Yeah, me too."

Henry Dean made my little sister fall hard and fast. He fell too. I believe that. But he realized he couldn't keep seeing her if he had to lie to Cian about it and despite her feelings for him, Ruby had my back and told him that if I didn't want Cian to know, then Henry couldn't say anything.

So they broke up.

Ruby insists that it was for the best and that she's fine.

She really isn't though.

She's sad. And I'm pretty sure she's cried. Ruby isn't the crying-over-a-guy type.

I feel like crap.

So I really hope she's quit the podcast.

Mariah's typing on her phone. I nudge her plate closer to her. "Hey, you need to eat and get to school."

"I know. Just a sec."

A moment later her phone pings with a message. She grins. "Henry says they're fine."

I straighten. "You texted Henry?"

She looks up. "Yeah."

"You...have his number?"

"Of course. He said to text or call any time if I need something."

I don't know how to feel about that. Henry Dean is clearly used to getting his way. He's charming but bossy. He definitely always thinks he's right. Though when he promised not to tell Cian where I am, I believed him. He has a lot of opinions, but he's also always been respectful and kind to both Mariah and me.

It just didn't occur to me that he might be an ongoing friend to Mariah after he and Ruby broke up a month ago.

"That's... nice." My daughter having a good friend who's a bodyguard can't be bad, right?

Her phone pings again. "He says he's with Cian. They're both good."

My heart trips. Just reading his name does that to me, so hearing it out loud and getting the news that he's fine—even though I didn't really think there was cause for concern (just curiosity and interest)—makes my heart do a double flip.

"Good," I say, hoping Mariah doesn't notice my voice sounds like I'm talking through a tight throat. "So now you can go to school and not worry."

She nods. "Yeah, exactly."

I study her for a moment. I think she was actually concerned.

Oh boy. Her being this interested in and caring about these men that Ruby and I do *not* want to see again is not good.

"Get going. And don't forget to run the dishwasher and put the casserole in the oven when you get home."

She slides off the stool. "I will, but then I'm going to Greta's to work on our project."

"Oh, that's right." I think quickly. "I won't be home from the shop 'til about seven. Ruby's bartending until five or so. Don't worry about the casserole. Can you just grab something before you head to Greta's?"

"Yeah," she answers, starting for the stairs. "I'll be fine."

She will. Ruby and I have raised Mariah to be very independent and to be a problem-solver. "Love you!" I call after her.

"Me too!" comes her answer from up the stairs.

When I hear her bathroom door shut, I grab for my phone and open my podcast app. *Wait 'Til I Tell Ye* is the first one on my list. I open it and scroll to the transcript for the latest show.

Because of course I do.

I really need to get over this.

Maybe tomorrow.

CHAPTER 4
CIAN

"You have some talking to do," I say to Henry.

As usual, Henry was able to get everything organized quickly, and we were packed and on the plane on our way back to the US within an hour.

I won't lie, I know that having a private plane is a luxury that I will probably never be able to get over.

I don't know who he told what and I don't care.

Now that I know that we know where Scarlett is, that is all I can focus on.

That and the fact that my best friend has known her location for a few months.

"I'm going to tell you the most important thing upfront," Henry says from where he is lounging in the buttery soft cream-colored leather seat across from me.

It's just the two of us, the flight attendant having left us alone and four and a half hours of the five-hour flight ahead of us.

I need the whole story before we get there.

Henry is now dressed in jeans and a casual, untucked button-down shirt with the sleeves rolled up. He has one ankle propped on his opposite knee and he looks far too nonchalant.

While my heart is pounding, and I feel restless and like my dark gray joggers and loose tee are too restrictive.

I lean forward, resting my forearms on my thighs. "I want to know all of it. I'm pissed, Henry."

He nods. "I know. And I'll tell you everything. But the most important thing is I didn't tell you right away because she didn't want to see you. Still doesn't."

I frown. "She said that?"

"A few times now. I've been trying to change her mind."

My frown deepens. "Why not?"

"In the beginning, it was because the only reason she spent that weekend with you was because she never expected to see you again. Considered you a young, hot, fun weekend-only fling."

I flex my hands. Of course, I know that's how it started. It was that for both of us. But it changed. Quickly.

For *both of us*, dammit.

I could fall in love with you, too.

I can still hear exactly how her voice sounded when she said that, sleepy, sated, her breath warm against my chest as I held her.

My entire body tightens and I feel an irrational surge of anger toward Henry. He's been standing between her and me for months. I flex my hand again.

Henry keeps talking. "The reason we couldn't find her for so long is because they literally left the state the Monday after you met her."

"They? They who?"

"Her and Ruby."

I scowl. "Her stage name was Ruby."

"Her *sister's* name is Ruby. And Scarlett was pretending to be Ruby when you met. They're identical twins."

I let that sink in. "Why was she pretending to be her sister?"

"Ruby is the dancer. Scarlett was filling in for her that night."

I shove a hand through my hair. I'd met Scarlett at a strip club. We'd been there because I'd tagged along when Henry had to accompany a guy he was working for as private security.

The idea that she'd been filling in for someone actually makes sense. I hadn't seen her actually strip. She'd seemed uncomfortable. She'd seemed like she didn't fit. I would have guessed it was her first time ever on a stage, to be honest. And something in me had prompted me to come to her rescue. I'd paid for private sessions for the rest of the night with her, whisked her off the stage, and taken her out for burgers.

Before taking her to the Windsor Court hotel and giving her an extravagant, sexy, amazing weekend. Thank you very fucking much.

Okay, I had seen her strip. Just not in the club.

"Okay," I say. "So she was filling in for her sister when we met. Then she and her sister, Ruby, moved out of state on Monday."

He pauses. "And Mariah. Scarlett's daughter."

I feel my brows pull tighter. "The daughter is Ruby's."

He shakes his head. "No. She's Scarlett's."

"Scarlett told me..." I blow out a breath. Henry knows better than I do. *Fuck.* "She's a mom?"

"Yeah. Mariah's fifteen. Dad's never been in the picture."

I process that. So...that's good. There's no ex hanging around. I mean, it's good from my perspective anyway. He's not the reason she doesn't want to see me.

My sister is a single mom to an almost-thirteen-year-old and Saoirse's dad has never been in the picture. That's all fine. Mostly. Except that all this time I've been under the impression that Scarlett is an amazing aunt who loves her niece as fiercely as I love mine. It was something I thought we had in common.

"Why didn't she tell me?" I ask.

"She was pretending to be Ruby that weekend," Henry says. He lifts a shoulder. "I can't tell you all the reasons *why*, Cian. That's her story to tell. But I can tell you what she told me. She was dancing in Ruby's place that Friday night when you met her. It was Ruby's last night of work." He blows out a breath and runs a hand through his hair. "It's confusing, I know. Ruby's the dancer. She had to show up that night or she wouldn't be able to collect her last paycheck. Scarlett filled in for her because Ruby hurt her ankle. Then Scarlett met you and...kept playing at being Ruby."

"But she gave me her real name," I say.

"Well...she was putting on a show the entire weekend."

Fuck.

Fuck.

"Keep going," I say tightly. "Tell me everything."

"The plan was for them to move the next day. Saturday," Henry says. "They had the U-Haul all packed up. They actually put that off for a couple of days because of you."

I let that sink in. Well...that's something. That fucking seems like someone who enjoyed herself.

"That explains why we couldn't find them. It explains

why she didn't think she'd see me again. But now that she knows she can, why doesn't she want to?" I ask.

Henry shifts, putting both feet on the floor and leaning forward. "They moved to Ohio to start a new life. They moved back to their hometown. Ohio is very far from Louisiana. She didn't want to have any ties. They were starting fresh."

Okay, I guess that makes sense. But *fuck*, I've held on to her for nineteen goddamned months and she was able to just walk away? Not even wonder about me? She's not even slightly curious now that she has a way of seeing me again? Talking to me once more?

"But you've been trying to talk her into seeing me again and she's not interested at all?" I ask.

Henry doesn't look happy about giving me this information and that doesn't surprise me. Henry is my bodyguard, but more than that he's my friend and really likes it when I'm happy. *He's* happiest when I'm content and having fun.

"I told her who you are. I thought that might help," Henry says.

"You told her? About Cara?" I ask. I'm surprised. We never tell anyone about Cara. I have literally been incognito for over a decade.

"They've been in their hometown for over a year. It's… not what they'd hoped it would be. I thought maybe the handsome charming prince who could sweep in and change her life angle would help," Henry says.

My chest tightens. I don't like hearing that things aren't good. "It didn't?"

"It made it worse."

I sit back in my seat. "Dammit. What are you talking about?"

"Scarlett isn't who you think she is," Henry says. "Scarlett was pretending to be Ruby. Ruby is the one who is outgoing, fun, spontaneous, sweet. Scarlett is…serious. A little…"

He trails off and my brows arch. "A little what?"

"Grumpy?" He says it as a question, as if offering it as an adjective in place of other, maybe not as nice, words.

He continues. "She's trying to live a simple life, keeping her head down in their hometown, trying to start over in a place that doesn't really want to give her a break. There's a lot of history. She's just got a lot going on. You would be a…complication."

I'm studying him as he explains all of this. It's a lot to process, but one thing is very clear every time he says Ruby's name. "Did something happen with you and Ruby?"

He nods. "Yes. But it's over. It won't work out between us." He sighs. "We broke up a month ago. I didn't think I'd see her again."

"And now we're on our way back there."

He doesn't look happy as he nods. "Yeah."

"How well have you gotten to know them?"

"Pretty well." He hesitates, then meets my gaze. "I've been there a few times."

I feel a stab of jealousy. He's gotten to know them. All of them. Scarlett as well as her sister and her daughter.

I want to know them. I'm trying to process the idea that I don't really even know Scarlett, but I already want to know the two people who are the most important to her. I know how important my siblings and my niece are to me, and I want to know that Scarlett's family is the same.

"You went to try to find Scarlett, but then you kept going back because of Ruby," I summarize.

He grimaces. "When I first found her, I thought she *was*

Scarlett. I found her at the bar where she's bartending now, and I assumed she was your girl. I felt terrible about being attracted to her and I tried to stay away. But I needed more information. So I talked to her and, after a couple of visits, finally just asked her about you. I found out Ruby wasn't Scarlett. And, yes, I fell for her."

"Why did you break up?"

"I had to choose between her and you."

I scowl. "What do you mean? Because of the distance? The job?"

He nods. "Yes. To be with you, I can't be with her. I can't do my job with you from Emerald, Ohio."

I nod. I guess that's true.

He goes on. "But besides that, Scarlett didn't want you to know where she was. I couldn't very well be madly in love *with her sister* and not tell my best friend. If I had to keep them a secret from you, it wasn't going to work."

My stomach twists. "She really didn't want to see me that badly?"

"I think she does, actually," Henry says.

The knot tightens. "What does that mean?"

"I think she does want to see you and that scares her because it would complicate her plans, and it's easier to avoid you completely. She doesn't want to live the life of a princess."

I bark out a laugh. "It doesn't have to be that," I say. "I haven't been living the life of a prince."

Henry gives me a smile that is affectionate and amused. "Haven't you? You have more money at your disposal than you know what to do with. You don't have a specific job and can spend your time and energy on whatever you want. You hang out with a bodyguard full-time. You have resources and influence and power that you can access at any time."

He looks around the plane. "You can hop on a private plane and show up on her doorstep with the snap of your fingers."

I blow out a breath.

Henry shifts so he's resting his elbows on his thighs. "There's something else you should know."

"Okay."

"Scarlett is convinced that you're actually in love with Ruby." He pauses, looking pained. "Everything she did and told you was what Ruby would have done and said. She claims she didn't tell you anything true about herself."

My stomach clenches. No. That's crazy. How could I be that intimate, spend that much time, feel that connection with somebody, and have it not be real?

"You're taking me to see her now though," I point out. "Why?"

"Because you need this closure. Because you can't really figure this thing out with Astrid as long as Scarlett is in the back of your mind."

I look at my best friend. He is *not* looking forward to this trip. "Of course we fell for identical twins. That's just like us."

He gives a short bark of laughter. But it does seem appropriate. Henry feels more like my brother than my actual brothers do a lot of the time. He definitely knows me better than my brothers do. That's intentional of course, but it makes Henry and me very close.

Henry shakes his head. "The Gale sisters are not going to be happy to see us."

I think about Henry's words. In three months, I need to have a plan to move on. I promised Astrid I would take care of this.

I settle back in my seat and look out the window, not

seeing the clouds. All I can see is Scarlett's face. Her thick, inky black hair, her bright green eyes, her sun-kissed skin, her full pink lips, the freckle beside her left ear, the tattoo on the inside of her left wrist with the date of her niece's birth—no, her *daughter's* birth.

I frown.

She said that date changed her life.

I loved that she was so dedicated to her family. That she was so close to her sister and niece. I felt that connection with her because Fiona and Saoirse mean that much to me.

But it was a lie.

Her *daughter* was born on January thirtieth. Not her niece. If she lied about something that important, she could have easily lied about her favorite sub sandwich toppings, her dream weekend, her favorite sexual position, and what she'd do with a million dollars.

All of those things were apparently *Ruby's* favorites.

Jesus. I scrub a hand over my face. I know a lot of fucking intimate details about my best friend's ex-girl-friend if that's the case.

And nothing about the woman I've believed I've been in love with for almost two years.

CHAPTER 5
CIAN

According to Henry, Big Dick's is not named for the obvious body parts nor is it named after a guy named Richard. Evidently the guy who owns the bar is actually just an asshole.

The story reminds me that Henry has been here a number of times and has information about Scarlett, her hometown, and her family that I don't. That he didn't share with me.

I feel the anger tighten my muscles again.

I've spent the last five hours stewing over everything and had decided to just go with the flow, let go of past beliefs and feelings and just start over.

Going with the flow lasted about five minutes.

Shocker.

I don't want to be pissed at Henry. I've never been angry at him for more than a couple of hours at a time in the past. Yes, that's definitely happened and it's almost always because he told me something I didn't want to hear, but that happens so rarely that Henry is possibly the person in my life I get along with the best.

Besides, my niece, Saoirse, and I are great friends. I was the third person to hold her after she was born, following my sister, of course, and Colin, their bodyguard, the man who would become Saoirse's surrogate father in pretty much every way.

Saoirse was surrounded by adults from day one—Fiona, Colin, me, Henry, Torin, and Jonah—but we had a special bond. I was the one who was always up to play. When the other adults had work or more adult things to worry about, I was always free for tea parties, playing pirates, pretending we were hunting monsters, and yes, even playing prince and princess. Saoirse has always gotten a kick out of her royal bloodline.

She's the only one in the family.

All of that makes me think about the fact that Scarlett is not the fun aunt who took her niece Mariah on spontaneous road trips, bought Mariah her first puppy—against her mother's wishes—did movie marathons with ice cream sodas, and who was the one to give Mariah the 'real' sex talk. Not the one about the physical technicalities, but the one about how a man should treat you, the bullshit red flags, the words to never believe, and what an orgasm is.

Scarlett is Mariah's mom. And apparently not fun.

I scowl. That can't be right. *We* watched movies and had orange soda ice cream sodas. We talked about the road trips we'd taken. And she definitely knows about orgasms and what she needs to get them.

And *I* know about her orgasms, how to get her there every time, how she feels and looks and sounds when she comes...

"You ready?" Henry asks as we stand inside the door and let our eyes adjust from the bright sunlight outside.

My first impression as I take in the interior is that...it's a bar. There is nothing unique or remarkable about it at all.

"You sure it was a good idea not to text her ahead of time?" I ask Henry.

"Trust me, it's better if she doesn't know I'm coming."

My usual upbeat friend sounds discouraged. "That bad?"

"I hurt her. She doesn't want to see me."

"What about when she *does* see you?"

"I have no fucking idea." Henry heads for the bar.

Damn. This is definitely a new side of Henry. This is going to be a very interesting trip.

There's a woman behind the bar with her back to us. She's slender, about five-six, with a nice curvy ass, long dark hair, and when she turns, I actually suck in a breath.

Fuck. She's gorgeous.

Because she looks just like Scarlett.

The sense of déjà vu is short-lived though.

Yes, this woman's shape, her eyes, and hair look like Scarlett. But it only takes me three seconds to realize that it's not her. I can't put my finger on a single specific thing but there's just something about this woman that makes her *feel* like a stranger even though she looks exactly like the woman I fucked for three nights straight.

Ruby freezes when she sees Henry.

Her mouth drops open, the towel she's holding hits the floor, and her eyes widen.

"Ruby." Henry's voice is gruff.

I cast him a quick glance. His face is etched with what I can only describe as longing.

Ruby blinks three times, then she rounds the bar. She

comes to stand directly in front of us. She looks back and forth between us. Then she pulls her arm back and slaps Henry. Hard.

His head snaps to the side. He sucks in a quick breath, then faces her again. Suddenly she bursts into tears and launches herself into his arms. He catches her with both hands under her ass as her legs circle his waist, and she buries her face against his neck.

He shoots me a look. "Give us a minute." Then he strides behind the bar and through a door.

Thirty minutes later, Ruby and Henry emerge from the back room.

It's clear Ruby has been crying, but it's also clear that she no longer has lipstick on and her hair is much more mussed than it was before. There's also definite whisker burn on her neck.

Ruby has her purse and says she got a replacement for the rest of her shift.

So, we follow her Jeep with our rental car into the town of Emerald, Ohio.

To my disappointment, it doesn't seem that the town has at all embraced the Wizard of Oz theme I was expecting. We pass the turn off to the main downtown area that completely missed the chance to pave Main Street with yellow bricks. Not a single building, least of all City Hall, is painted emerald green either. It's like they're actively trying *not* to bring up tornados and wizards and people coming here to figure out that there's no place like home.

Which would be a *fantastic* motto for a sweet little town.

We keep driving past a park, the high school, and then into a very typical residential neighborhood. The houses are older but well kept. Most are two stories with wide yards and well-established trees.

We pull up along the curb opposite the pale blue two story with white trim and shutters. It has a huge porch with a white porch swing and an immaculate front flower bed on either side of the porch steps. Ruby pulls into the driveway and then waits at the bottom of the steps for us.

She does not offer me a tour and it's clear Henry has been here before because he makes himself comfortable in the kitchen, pulling a soda for each of us from the fridge before settling on one of the tall stools at the breakfast bar.

Ruby starts making herself a sandwich. Henry watches every single move she makes. She seems to be trying very hard to ignore him.

Finally, she sighs, sets the knife she's using down. "Do you guys want something to eat?"

"We're okay."

"I could eat."

Henry and I both answer at once. I frown at him. We haven't eaten in hours. He rolls his eyes, but gets to his feet and rounds the counter going to where Ruby is standing. He nudges her out of the way and takes over making the sandwiches. She just stands watching him for a long moment, her lips pressed together. Then she turns and looks at me, crossing her arms.

"Scarlett doesn't want to see you."

"So I've heard."

"But here you are."

I nod. "Here I am."

"This might not go very well for you," Ruby tells me.

"I understand that. But I can't go the rest of my life without seeing her again."

Ruby doesn't respond to that. But fuck, she looks sad.

I don't know what's going on with her and Henry but, damn.

Just then the front door opens and my heart slams against my rib cage.

Scarlett is here.

My heart is clearly refusing to hear everyone telling me that she's not who I think she is and that she doesn't want to see me. I want to see her. I *need* to see her.

But the next moment we hear a voice call from the front of the house, "Mom?"

Ruby's eyes widen. "That's Mariah! She's not supposed to be home until later." She looks around quickly. "Hide." She points to a doorway.

Henry frowns. "The pantry?"

She nods quickly. "Hurry!"

"You're not going to tell her we're here?"

"Mom? Are you home?" Mariah calls again, the voice closer now.

Ruby calls back, "She's not home yet. I'm in here!" Softer, she says to Henry, "I'm going to tell her, but I need to prepare her."

"For?

"*Not* falling in love with you again," Ruby says with a frown, shoving him toward the pantry door.

"Ruby—" Henry starts.

She shoves him again. "And she's going to be shocked to see Cian. I don't know what to tell her about *that*."

"Just tell her—" Henry starts.

But Ruby plants her hands on her hips. "Get. In. The. Pantry. Henry."

He sighs but opens the narrow door next to the fridge and steps inside. I follow him with a grin.

Seriously, *everyone* falls for Henry's charm and confident I-know-best-don't-worry-about-it-just-let-me-take-care-of-everything attitude.

Except Iris, his boss, Scarlett apparently, and now Ruby.

Looks like he has his hands full.

Just what he needs.

"I like her," I whisper.

"Shut up."

"Sucks to not always get your way, huh?"

"How the hell would *you* know?"

I just chuckle.

We both zip it when we hear Ruby say, "I thought you were studying at Greta's."

A younger female voice that I assume belongs to Mariah says, "We were. But Mom is going to be getting an email from my principal. I thought I should come home and tell her about it before she reads it."

"Oh no," Ruby says with a little groan. "What happened?"

"It was completely Leah's fault," a new young woman's voice says.

I look at Henry. He mouths *Greta.*

"Mariah didn't do anything wrong. Leah needs to mind her own business," Greta says.

We hear scraping noises that sound like the wooden legs of the stools that sit at the breakfast bar sliding over the kitchen floor.

Ruby laughs softly. "Well, you're not exactly an unbiased witness."

"No," Greta agrees. "But seriously, we were just talking in study hall between the two of us."

"What were you talking about?"

"The podcast and how Henry and Cian are missing."

Henry and I exchange glances. Our departure from Cara has gotten more attention than we expected. How did the podcast find out? And who knew that two teenage girls in Ohio would be listening to the podcast from Cara anyway?

Well, I guess Henry knew.

Henry knows a lot. I'm still very annoyed by that.

"Mariah and Greta are huge fans of the podcast," Henry says softly. "Ruby too. I know Scarlett keeps up as well."

This makes my heart clench. They all pay attention? Because of us? That's...I don't know what that is.

It's...hopeful.

That's how my heart and head take it.

Scarlett is interested. She hasn't totally forgotten me.

She says she doesn't want to see me, but she still thinks about me. That has to mean something. Doesn't it?

But if she's nothing like the woman I've been thinking about, *what* does it mean?

Fuck. I need to see her.

"So what happened that caused the principal to get involved?" Ruby asks.

"Leah being Leah," Mariah says with disgust in her tone. "She said, *loudly*, that we're so ridiculous and do we not realize that no one believes us about all of this."

"All of what?" Ruby asks.

"That Mom knows and *dated* Cian O'Grady who is a *prince*. And that we all know his bodyguard."

There's a long pause.

I look at Henry, eyebrows up.

He winces, then looks at me.

"They talk about me?" I whisper.

"Um...yeah," Henry says. He rubs a hand over the back of his neck. "It's been a bit of a problem."

"No kidding," I say dryly.

Henry's been helping to keep my identity a secret for over a decade. But now these two teen girls are bragging about their connection to me and arguing with classmates about it?

"Her mom said there is no way Mom dated a prince and now doesn't want to see him. She said Mom is all about money and power, so this all has to be a lie," Mariah says.

I frown. I don't like this. I don't like that Scarlett is telling people she doesn't want to see me. Dammit. But I also hate the idea that I'm some kind of problem for her. And I really hate that someone is doubting her.

Okay, so supposedly I don't know the woman I spent the weekend with. These people do. She's from here. These people should know her and trust her.

But if she was into power and money, she would have wanted to see me once Henry told her who I am and that I want to see her.

And she's not fucking lying.

What is going on here with Scarlett and her hometown?

"So what did you do?" Ruby asks with what sounds to me, through a thin wooden door, like a touch of trepidation.

"Told her that she needed to mind her own business and stop eavesdropping."

"Okay, that's fair."

"Then she started preaching to me, the way she always does. About how lying is a sin and how I'm just trying to build myself up to seem more important and how I need to look within myself for my self-worth instead of making up stories about knowing important people."

I feel anger ignite in my gut. That sounds like bullshit. Who is this girl? She knows nothing about Mariah's mom's situation with me. She's lecturing Mariah about *her* self-worth? I don't know Mariah, but she's *not* lying. Scarlett definitely knows me. In the Biblical sense. I wonder if Leah would find that ironic.

There's a pause in the kitchen. "Can you believe that?" Mariah asks. "She thinks this *private* conversation I'm having with *not her* is my attempt to try to feel important? We were talking quietly. If I wanted everyone to hear it, I could have made that happen. But no, only Leah heard us and the only reason everyone else heard about it is because she opened her big mouth! And that I feel the need to make up stories because I don't feel good about myself? I'm *so* offended by that! I'm insulted that she thinks I care what she thinks about me!"

There you go, Mariah. I've never met this girl, but I want to fist-bump her right now.

"So then you just ignored her because you *don't* care and you just went on about your day, right?" Ruby asks, her tone full of hope.

"For the rest of study hall, yes."

"Good."

"But I do *not* appreciate being slandered like that," Mariah says.

Damn right, I think.

"Damn right," Greta says.

I smile. I like her too.

"I ignored her in English class too."

"Okay. Good."

"But then we had lunch."

"Oh." Ruby now sounds resigned. "What happened at lunch?"

"I thought about quoting Matthew seven to her about being a hypocrite," Mariah says.

I laugh softly and I look up to find Henry grinning.

"But then I decided to quote *Mean Girls* instead."

"You asked her why she's so obsessed with you, right?" Ruby asks.

Mariah laughs. "God, I love that movie."

Ruby sighs. Both Henry and I snort.

"Oh, I also spilled tomato juice on her virginal white blouse."

"Mariah!"

There is a door between us and I can't see her, but I swear I can hear that Ruby is trying to suppress a laugh though.

"She should really wear darker colors. I know she considers it a statement, but all of that white is a liability," Mariah adds.

"As if you wearing red all the time isn't some kind of statement?" Ruby asks.

"Of course it is. And I own it," Mariah says.

"Red all the time?" I ask Henry.

He nods with an affectionate smile. "Always at least a part of her outfit."

Mariah goes on. "Do you have any idea how many jokes I heard about Mom and the Scarlet Letter when we got here, *Ruby*?" Mariah asks. "And how many times I've heard about how their moms thought Grandma named you Ruby because of the Biblical meaning but then found out it was really the Wizard of freaking Oz? And how it's so *interesting* that the devil is always depicted wearing red? I'm just giving them what they want."

I knew about the Wizard of Oz, but the Scarlet Letter? Wow. This town is intense.

But I love the color red, and I already love Scarlett's daughter embracing all of this the way she is.

And I haven't even set eyes on her yet.

"Believe me, I've heard all the Scarlet Letter shit myself. I see their mothers still don't understand the full meaning of that novel," Ruby says. She sighs. "So what's the email say?"

I can almost picture Ruby rubbing her forehead.

"That the principal wants Mom to talk to me about my temper and my lying."

"Your lying?"

"She doesn't think it's true either, of course. She thinks I'm doing it to start fights."

"I mean...it *is* a crazy story," Ruby says. She raises her voice a bit. "Your mom didn't even believe it when Henry first told us."

I cast a look at my friend. He shrugs.

"But I'm *not* a liar!" Mariah exclaims. "And it's unfair that everyone is assuming I am! They can't prove that Mom *doesn't* know Cian. Plus, Mrs. Carter, the study hall teacher, is directing the school musical and has said that now she doesn't want me to be a part of it. She says I cause too much drama! Which is pretty ironic, right? She's the *drama teacher*."

"Wait, she's keeping you off the musical because of this?" Ruby asks.

I frown.

"Bitch," Henry mutters.

"Well, because Leah is one of the leads and she thinks I'll cause trouble with her. And because Leah's mom is Mrs. Carter's friend. It all goes together."

"I see." Ruby sounds contemplative now.

"It all sucks. Mom just needs to tell them it's true. That she knows Cian and that they did date for a little bit."

"Well, they didn't really *date for a little bit*," Ruby hedges.

"They don't need to know how long. She just needs to tell them she knows him. Or you need to let Henry go down and talk to them."

"He could get Cian on the phone!" Greta pipes up. "They could video call Cian and he could say that yes, he knows Scarlett."

Okay so...this could be interesting.

I look at Henry. He sighs. "Maybe Scarlett will be glad to see you after all?" he whispers.

Well, that would be nice.

Henry reaches for a bag of pretzels. I lift an eyebrow. He shrugs. So I reach for the Oreos on the shelf just over Henry's shoulder.

"I like your cologne," I tell him.

"It's yours," he says.

I nod. "Thought it smelled familiar."

He starts to unroll the top of the bag—the crinkle of the bag is *really* loud.

"I don't know," Ruby says, *loudly*, clearly trying to cover the noise.

I snicker and carefully peel open the Oreo package, removing three cookies and offering Henry one.

He sighs and replaces the pretzels on the shelf and takes the cookie.

Ruby keeps talking. "I mean, part of Leah's problem with you is that Hannah has problems with your mom."

"But Hannah shouldn't keep saying Mom is all about fame and fortune!"

I frown as I chew. What is this about? Why does this woman think Scarlett is all about that?

I'm even more interested in the woman I spent a weekend with all those months ago.

She'll probably hate to hear that.

"Uggggh!" Mariah groans. "Mom doesn't have *any* photos with Cian? Really? Who doesn't take selfies when they're out?"

Because we weren't out much, I think. *And taking photos of what we were doing wouldn't have been appropriate.*

"I don't think so," Ruby says. "But…I think maybe we can fix this. Maybe. Though your mom is going to hate it."

"What? Why?"

"Um…Henry?" Ruby's voice calls out.

"Henry? He's—"

Henry grins at me and grabs the bag of pretzels again.

Then he steps out into the kitchen. "Hey, kid."

"Oh my God!"

Mariah's exclamation is followed by squealing and Henry chuckling.

I don't know what I'm supposed to do here. Clearly, they're excited to see Henry. But they're having a reunion. They don't know me. And I don't know how Ruby wants to go about introducing me. But I feel like a jackass standing in the pantry.

"Why were you hiding? "Mariah asks Henry.

"Surprise."

"I'm so happy you're back! Have you guys made up? Are you back together?"

"No. He just showed up and surprised me too," Ruby jumps in.

"But you're in love!" Mariah protests. "You should be

together. She's been miserable without you," she says, I assume addressing Henry.

I smile. Mariah could be a great ally...or a frustrating opponent. I wonder which Ruby considers her at the moment.

"*Mariah*," Ruby says warningly. "Henry and I...have a lot of things to talk about."

"Well, can Henry come to school and tell everyone that Cian is real and that he really did date Mom? Because next time I might do something worse than spill tomato juice on Leah. I actually wanted to hit her."

"You're not going to hit her," Ruby says.

"Just don't hit her with witnesses," Henry says at the same time.

"Henry!" Ruby protests.

"You have to stand up to bullies," he says unapologetically.

"Exactly," Greta says.

"Can you teach me to throw a punch?" Mariah asks.

"Absolutely," Henry says.

"No," Ruby says over him.

"Why don't you just come to school and tell Leah and Mrs. Carter and our principal who you are and that Mariah is telling the truth," Greta says.

"Would she believe me? I'm just some guy," Henry says.

"You have your ID and your badge," Greta insists. "Plus everyone knows what you look like and your name."

"They do?"

"Sure. They all know about the podcast. Leah follows it too. And she's looked all of you up. Everyone has."

I wince. For some reason, this doesn't seem like a good thing. I can't say exactly why. Maybe it's just because I've spent the past decade trying to fly under the radar and I'm not used to people knowing who I am outside of Cara, and a tiny town in Louisiana. But I've always liked it that way. I can honestly say that everyone in my life likes me for who I am as a person, because they don't know about my title, my money, or my connections.

And dammit, that includes Scarlett. We had a great time. We had a real connection. She might've told me a few things that aren't entirely true, but she had a good time. *That* was true. She didn't fake the laughter, the contentment, or the orgasms.

And none of that had anything to do with me being a prince. It wasn't about my wealth or potential power.

And she doesn't know about the things that I've done with that money and those connections since we were together. But I was very much looking forward to telling her about that. I'm proud of it. And because it was her idea, I was looking forward to sharing it with her.

I tamp down all of those swirling thoughts and emotions and reach for the box of fruit flavored cereal at eye level.

One thing at a time. I need to see Scarlett again. I need to figure out what was real and what wasn't.

"The kids at school have checked out the podcast? Looked stuff up about us?" Henry asks Mariah and Greta.

"Of course," Mariah says. "It's not like I can get away with claiming to know someone like you without them looking into it. But the more they found out, the less they believed me."

"So what does the principal want?" Ruby asks.

"I'm not sure. We could get into Mom's account and read the email. But I'm guessing it has something to do with an apology to Leah. Probably publicly. And admitting I lied. And I would rather *die*. One, she butted into our conversation. Two, I'm telling the truth. I don't think I should have to apologize for a lie that isn't a lie."

"Are you sure that you don't have to apologize for pouring tomato juice on her?" Ruby asks.

"Yeah, Mom will make me do that," Mariah says, sounding dejected.

"Yeah, she will," Ruby agrees.

I frown. Leah sounds like a bully. I don't agree with an apology for standing up to her. But I haven't done a lot of apologizing in my life so I'm no expert.

"But," Ruby says. "I agree that you shouldn't have to take back what you've said about Cian and Henry and it's bullshit that they're trying to leave you out of the school musical because of this."

"Great," Mariah says. "Then I'll just have Henry come to school and back me up."

"Your mom will *hate* that. That is just more attention on her, on all of us, that she won't want. Especially from Hannah," Ruby says. "We need to figure out a way to placate Leah, without you having to apologize for some-thing you didn't do."

"Just telling her that Mariah is right and she's wrong will make her back off, right?" Henry asks. "Maybe I can just talk to Leah and her mom? Not make it public at school."

"That would be almost as bad," Ruby says. "No one hates Scarlett more than Hannah. She'll *hate* being wrong and will make Scarlett miserable. By making Mariah miser-able." Ruby sighs. "That's what this is really all about. Hannah found Scarlett's biggest vulnerability—Mariah. Now she's making sure Mariah is unhappy as a way of keeping Scarlett unhappy and in her place."

I scowl. What the hell is going on here? Why does

someone think Scarlett needs to be kept "in her place"? What does that mean? The woman I spent that weekend with was amazing. Everyone should think so.

She's not who you think she is, remember?

Yeah, I fucking remember. I shake more cereal out into my hand, toss it into my mouth, and crunch aggressively.

I'm going to figure out what *that* means too. Tonight.

But Scarlett would rather have people think her daughter is a liar than to claim having spent time with me? No.

I close the cereal box, returning it to the shelf, then step out from the pantry. "Well, we could just leave Scarlett out of it. I could show up and prove to everyone at school that *Mariah* knows me."

Mariah and Greta spin so fast on their stools they nearly topple to the floor. Then their gasps are so loud that I'm afraid they actually swallowed their tongues.

Henry looks vastly amused. Ruby looks torn between laughing and crying.

"This all seems really dramatic and easily fixed," I say.

"Oh my God," Mariah finally says. "You're Cian O'Grady. You're actually here."

It's so obvious this is Scarlett's daughter. She has the same silky dark hair, the same round face, the same nose. Even her eyes are the same shape as Scarlett's—and Ruby's, I guess—but her eyes are brown instead of her mom's green. Otherwise, she's a beautiful younger version of her mother and aunt.

"Yup." I decide to dive right in. "I'm here to see your mom." And now, I'm suddenly thinking that I'm here to save Mariah.

I've maybe been avoiding being a prince, but I think I could get into Knight in Shining Armor.

Mariah takes a step back and plunks down onto her stool, staring at me. "You really have been trying to find her. You came all this way just to see her?"

I smile. "Have you met your mom?"

Mariah's smile is bright in return. "She's awesome, right?"

"Very," I agree.

Mariah shakes her head. "But she made it sound like she was never going to see you again. I never expected to actually meet you." She looks at Greta. "Oh my God!"

"Well..." I hate hearing that Scarlett expected to never see me. To the point that she convinced her daughter it was never going to happen. "Your mom doesn't know I'm here. It's going to be a surprise."

"That makes sense," Mariah says. "That's probably the only way you'll get to see her. But she's going to hate that. She's not really into surprises."

Great. One more check mark in the bad idea column.

"This is *amazing*," Greta gushes.

I turn to the cute, skinny blonde. She is staring at me with less awe and wonder and more of a sly look. As if she's hatching a plan.

She grabs Mariah's hand, squeezing. "Leah is going to have to apologize to *you* for all the times she called you a liar. For all the terrible things she said about you and your mom. I can't *wait*!"

I don't know who Leah is, or who Hannah is, or who Mrs. Carter is...but I don't like any of them. If they're giving Scarlett and Mariah a hard time, they're on my shit list. I don't care if one of them is only fifteen or sixteen. I was definitely a pain in the ass when I was that age.

I'm further annoyed and even more restless to see Scarlett after we order burgers and fries via takeout from the diner downtown and settle in to eat around the kitchen island.

Ruby grabs the bacon barbecue burger with cheddar cheese and Sriracha pickles along with an order of seasoned curly fries. She leaves the teriyaki chicken sandwich with grilled pineapple wrapped up.

I frown as I take a huge bite of my basic double cheeseburger. I watch her eat for a moment, then swallow and ask, "Is that your favorite burger?"

She looks up at me, and nods. "I love barbecue sauce. On anything. I always get barbecue burgers. Why?"

"It's not Scarlett's favorite?"

Understanding dawns on Ruby's face. "She likes the teriyaki chicken."

"If she was going to order a burger with all of you, what kind would she get?"

"She doesn't usually get burgers," Mariah pipes up. "If she didn't have a good option, probably just a plain cheeseburger, though."

I take another bite of my burger and chew angrily.

Ruby watches me for a moment. "Did you eat burgers together?"

I nod.

"And she got *my* favorite?"

"Apparently."

Ruby and Henry exchange a look.

I set my burger down. "I know. I've heard you both. She was pretending to be Ruby. I don't really know her. I've got it."

Mariah wipes her mouth with a paper napkin. "I know she was pretending to be Ruby in a lot of ways, but she even ate the same stuff Ruby would eat? That's weird."

Ruby shrugs. "Maybe she thought it was her chance to

try some new things. You know her. She kind of sticks with her usual routine. It's comfortable and she knows what she likes. Maybe she thought that weekend was a good time to spread her wings and take some risks."

She meets my eyes as she says that last sentence.

My stomach is a knot of frustration and confusion. Why couldn't Scarlett just let me know *her*? How much do I really not know? And if she was just trying new things, taking some chances, but *liking it*, then do I perhaps actually know her pretty fucking well?

There's no way I can avoid thinking about all of the things we did. We didn't just eat burgers. Though yes, Scarlett seemed to enjoy the barbecue bacon cheeseburger. She did pick off the onions and pickles, but she ate the whole damn thing and licked the sauce off her fingers.

But that wasn't all she enjoyed. She told me exactly what she wanted. She was enthusiastic, eager, and vocal in bed and I fucking loved it. I didn't have to wonder what she wanted or how she was feeling.

There's no fucking way she faked any of her pleasure that weekend.

I watch her sister's face. Is that what Ruby is trying to tell me? That Scarlett was different with me, but that it *wasn't* all fake? That I had given her a chance to try new things in lots of ways?

I let it go for the moment, because the person I need to ask those questions of, the person who needs to give me the answers, is Scarlett.

And she's going to, by God.

The hiding from me is over.

CHAPTER 6
SCARLETT

I step through the back kitchen door and pause in the mudroom to kick off my work boots and strip out of my jeans and shirt. I toss them toward the hamper where all of my greasy, dirty work clothes go. Then I pad into the kitchen, barefoot, in only my panties and bra.

"Mariah!"

Greta's car is here so I know my daughter and her girlfriend are not studying at Greta's house. Which works out well. I need to know what the hell happened with Leah Lawton today.

I know that Leah is a thorn in Mariah's side.

I also know that it's my fault.

"I'm in here, Mom!" I hear Mariah answer from the living room.

"Want to tell me why Hannah Lawton is claiming I owe her sixty dollars for a new shirt for Leah?" I step into the living room. "And do I even want to check my email?"

I freeze two steps into the room.

Mariah and Greta are here, and while I don't make a habit of parading through the house before heading to the shower, me in my underwear is also not a brand-new sight for them.

For Henry Dean though? Yeah. It's new.

And since he's currently sitting in one of our recliners, he just got an eyeful.

And then there's the other guy. The one lounging in the other chair as if he has every right to be there and is perfectly at ease in my chair in my living room surrounded by my family.

Cian Fucking O'Grady is in my house.

His Royal Highness himself.

Looking the epitome of sexy, laid back, and devastating.

Devastating not just because of how handsome he is or because of how long it's been since I've seen him. Or even because this morning I was a little worried about him. It's truly because there is some kind of crazy chemistry between us. Again. Still. Evidently nothing about the weekend we spent together was a figment of my imagination.

I can still remember locking eyes with him from the stage and feeling this zap of awareness, this strange feeling of *I know you* and *I want you* that hit me out of the blue in a single moment.

It's as strong right now as it ever was.

Probably because I do know him.

At least I know things about him. Like that no matter what we were pretending to be that weekend, he truly is charming, attentive, possessive, and funny.

Devastating.

Despite it making it so much harder to be resolute

about not wanting him to find me, I've loved having that all confirmed via the podcast and online posts.

We had agreed not to give each other many details. Or so I thought. But it turns out, he wasn't just role-playing as Prince Charming.

"Hi, Mom," Mariah says into the thick silence. "I need to tell you about something that happened today."

Is it that a royal fucking prince showed up on our doorstep? Or is it about some stupid shirt and that little bitch Leah?

But before I can respond, Cian mutters, "What the hell?" Then he's suddenly on his feet and stalking toward me.

His big body blocks me from the rest of the room, and I realize that he's trying to hide my partial nudity from the other man in the room.

For some reason—probably because my brain is spinning with a myriad of emotions I can't fully process—I laugh.

He's right in front of me, frowning down at me. He's not touching me, but he might as well be. The heat from his body, and the intensity and sheer overwhelm of just having him here, seems to wrap around me and squeeze.

"Henry has seen every inch of Ruby, and we're identical twins," is the first thing I say. For some reason.

That does not amuse Cian. His brows slam together. He opens his mouth but says nothing. His gaze roams over my face. Then he closes his mouth, steps forward, wraps his arms around my waist, lifts me until my feet are dangling inches off the floor, and starts walking toward the kitchen.

It takes a second—or several—for my brain to catch up with what's happening. Then I wiggle. "Hey! Put me down!"

"In a minute," he says gruffly.

I look over his shoulder to see everyone in the room staring at us.

I narrow my eyes at Henry. "You're dead to me," I tell him.

He is the only reason Cian is here. He brought him here. After telling me—*promising* me—that he wouldn't.

I look at my sister. Ruby looks slightly worried, and the way she's curled up in the corner of the couch, away from Henry, makes me think that she's not fully happy they're here either.

Dammit.

It's my fault they broke up. It's my fault her heart's been broken for the past month.

I've broken her heart before. I spent years afterward trying to make it up to her. Ruby has always been there for me. And now, because of me—because of Cian—Henry is back to potentially make that heartbreak worse.

So I stop straining against Cian and let him carry me into the kitchen. This is done. Henry told Cian where I am and now they're here. Now I just have to deal with this. With *him*. And get rid of him as quickly as I can.

But as I let the feel of having Cian against me, the heat and firmness of his body sink into mine, his familiar scent, the feel of his arms around me, the actual impression of comfort which shouldn't surprise me, and actually makes tears prick at the back of my eyelids, I realize I don't know what to do.

But I'm not so sure that I can say goodbye to this man again.

He stops once we're in the kitchen and lets my body slide down his until my feet touch the tile floor.

He doesn't really let me go. He simply leans back. His

hands go from my waist to my face, cupping my cheeks as he searches my eyes.

"Hey, Glinda."

My heart flips and I feel my lips curl completely independent of my brain.

Glinda. The nickname he started using for me after I told him about my mother's obsession with the Wizard of Oz and how when she found out she was having twins, and only one could be Ruby, she floated the idea of using Glinda for me.

Thankfully, my grandmother talked her out of it and convinced her to just find another word for red to go with Ruby.

Cian had been delighted to learn about my mother Judy Gale who grew up in Kansas and became obsessed with Judy Garland and the character of Dorothy Gale. She has several editions of the book, including a rare second edition. She also has the movie in various formats, along with so many collectibles she has an entire room in her house dedicated to the story of the girl who'd been swept away to the Emerald City, met an entourage of weirdos, and learned a huge lesson about home. She'd even owned a Cairn Terrier named, of course, Toto, when she was a teen who lived long enough to be Ruby and my first dog.

Cian had immediately latched onto Glinda as a nickname. He had also called me his "little witch" and his "good witch", saying I'd enchanted him and put a spell on him.

Glinda had always come out with a note of affection that I had tucked into my heart. Hearing him use it now knocks several bricks out of the wall that I have tried to erect between me and this man.

"I can't believe you're here," I say, shaking my head.

His hands cup my face, and his thumbs move over my

cheeks. He gives me a small smile. "Really? You can't believe it?"

"It's been a long time. You should've moved on."

"I don't think that's how this works."

"One-night stands? Getting dumped?" But my voice lacks the snark I really should be using.

"We both know you didn't dump me."

"Then what was that sneaking out the next morning?"

"Running scared."

I suppose princes are born with a little extra ego. I cock an eyebrow. "Scared of what?"

"Falling in love in less than seventy-two hours could freak someone out."

I immediately start shaking my head, but he's holding me so I can't move much. See, this love thing is the whole problem. He told me he was falling and I...okay, I freaked out. "You're not in love with me."

His smile dies, but he continues to hold my gaze. "No, I'm in love with Ruby, right?"

Well, at least Henry explained that to him. "Yes." I hate telling him that. But I wouldn't change that weekend for anything. It was amazing, and if I had to do it again, I would. Exactly the way I had.

"I'm sorry I lied to you, but it was my chance to let go, to just be a little different than I usually am." I pause. "Or a lot different." I swallow. "I'm sorry I led you on."

He studies me for a long moment.

Then he leans in and kisses me.

I probably should've seen that coming. But as soon as his lips touch mine, I have no choice but to kiss him back.

The heat between us arcs, sudden and sharp. Like someone touched a match to fuse. One of his hands tunnels into my hair, I arch closer, our mouths open, and our tongues tangle.

His other hand slips to my ass, pulling me up against him fully. My hands find his shirt and I am suddenly gripping it at the shoulders, trying to pull him in closer.

Just as suddenly he rears back. He doesn't let me go though. He stares at me, taking in how fast I'm breathing, no doubt the flush to my cheeks and how my eyes have dilated.

Finally he says, "You didn't lie about that." His voice is rough.

I swallow hard and shake my head. "No."

There's no way I could have faked my physical response to him, and I won't try to pretend otherwise.

"We need to talk," he tells me.

His voice is firm, gruff, but I can tell that he's very serious. This is not the laid-back playboy I had the best sex, and best *time*, of my life with. This is a determined man who is frustrated and maybe even a little angry with me. I couldn't have imagined that before. He was fun, spontaneous, mischievous, naughty. But now, he seems...older. More mature. Harder even. But of course, there are sides to him that I didn't get to know in those two and a half days.

A shiver goes through me. It's probably a combination of trepidation and excitement. Getting to know other sides of Cian O'Grady could be very dangerous.

"Yeah, probably," I finally agree. I push away and step back. "I need to shower. I just got home from work. I need something to eat, too. But then we can talk."

His gaze scans over me and I suddenly remember I'm in only my bra and panties. My entire body heats as it remembers him—his touch, his mouth...other parts of him.

"It definitely wasn't all fake," he says.

I blush hotly. No man has ever known my body the way Cian did. Does. I certainly remember every minute of our weekend. Who knows how many women there have been in the past nineteen months, but there's been no one for me. He was the last man to see me naked. Hell, he was the last man to kiss me. And he's at least insinuating that he remembers things about that weekend too.

My body likes that.

My heart also likes it.

That is really, really bad.

"I'll be back down in a little bit," I choke out.

I spin on my heel and head for the stairs, not looking back, even as I feel his hot gaze on my back.

I get to the bathroom, shut the door, and lock it, then slump against it. I lift my hands to my face.

Honesty, transparency, being genuine and kind are all things I have been working on every day for the past fifteen years. Ironically, I let go of the honesty and being genuine and transparent for *one* weekend nineteen months ago and it turned out to be one of the best weekends of my life.

Now, the guy that I've told some of the biggest lies is back, demanding the truth.

I really do like the person I've become over the past fifteen years far better than the girl I was before.

But I also really liked the woman who spent that weekend with Cian O'Grady.

She wasn't *bad*. Exactly. She just wasn't the Scarlett Gale that I need to be to live in Emerald.

So, I need to get rid of Cian O'Grady. Once and for all.

Being a responsible human adult really sucks sometimes.

CHAPTER 7
CIAN

The screen door slaps and I hear footsteps pad across the wooden porch. My pulse quickens but I don't look back.

Henry looks at me from where he's sitting next to me on the top step. "Keep your cool," he tells me.

We came out here with glasses of iced tea after we heard the shower shut off upstairs. I figured Scarlett needed a little space when she came downstairs and ate some dinner and caught up with her family.

But she and I are going to talk.

Henry knows I'm barely holding things together.

Nothing about this is the way I imagined it.

I certainly did not expect there to be an exact replica of Scarlett. I didn't expect my best friend to have fallen for her sister. I didn't expect Scarlett to be a mom, rather than the cool aunt, and for her daughter to be a pretty great *teenager*.

But most of all I didn't expect Scarlett to not want to see me.

Henry stretches to his feet, giving up his spot next to me.

I don't know if they exchange a look or a smile, but they don't say anything to one another as Henry passes Scarlett on his way back into the house.

"Hey," she says softly.

I look up at her, dragging my gaze up her long, smooth legs on my way to meet her eyes. Fuck. She's so beautiful. She's barefoot, and is wearing denim shorts and a black tank top with spaghetti straps. Her long hair is wet and twisted up into a messy bun on top of her head. She smells fresh and sweet, and I tighten my hand around my glass to keep from reaching over and running my hand up her calf and tugging her closer.

If this was the woman I'd spent the weekend with, I wouldn't have hesitated. She would've welcomed my touch. But, as everyone keeps reminding me, this isn't her.

"So, I have to make some bars for a friend tonight. But I thought maybe we could talk while I do that?" she says.

"Sure." I get to my feet.

We're almost eye to eye with her on the porch and me on the first step down. We just stare at each other for a moment. Then she turns and heads back into the house.

I follow, trying to gather my thoughts. Where do I start?

Probably not with 'will you marry me?' but that's what's on my tongue.

She rounds the center island where three boxes of cereal, a bag of marshmallows, and a rectangular glass pan are already set out.

I take a seat on one of the stools at the breakfast bar. Maybe it will be good to have distance and big, solid objects between us. "What are you making?"

"Marshmallow cereal bars," she says. "Like Rice Krispy treats, but with three different types of cereal. Turns out kids don't care if you use generic brand cereal if it's coated in melted marshmallow and butter."

I smile. "Do kids care if you use generic brand cereal anyway?"

She shrugs. "Okay, the *moms* don't care. They can't even tell."

I don't say anything to that, but what moms are nitpicking what kind of cereal is used in sugary treats like this?

"Are these for Mariah?" I ask, watching her dump butter and marshmallows into a saucepan on the stove.

"Mariah makes her own stuff if she needs something," Scarlett says, stirring everything together. "These are for a friend's daughter. Harley, the little girl, has to bring treats to school tomorrow and her mom is working at her salon until nine tonight."

Ah. "Is she a single mom too?" Scarlett jumping in to help another mom makes complete sense to me. And makes me even more certain I *did* get to know her in New Orleans. At least important things about her.

I've realized I don't really care about what she likes on her burgers. I can find that out going forward. I know what I need to about this woman. I'm sure of it. I didn't fall in love with a lie.

"No," she answers. "But her husband works at the tire factory on the third shift so he's not at home tonight to do this. Harley didn't tell Amber she needed these treats until after school today. Amber called me in a panic."

"Is she paying you to do this?" It's none of my business and I wouldn't ask anyone else, but I'm planning to make an important point, and this goes along with it.

Scarlett looks over at me. "No. We trade for this kind of stuff."

"Trade what?"

"Amber cuts my hair for free. If a lot of these kinds of things pop up, she'll throw in extra services. It all works out."

I nod. This is exactly the kind of thing I would have expected. I'll bet she has a similar arrangement with other women in town too.

I'm impressed and gratified to know I'm right about her, even as annoyance pricks at me. She is going to keep insisting I don't know her. And she's wrong.

"So what was New Orleans?" I ask, jumping right in. "Besides you stealing my heart and keeping it for nineteen months?"

She freezes for a second, but then she shakes her head. "God. Dramatic much?"

I shrug. "Yeah. Often."

She laughs as if my answer takes her by surprise. "Do you also fall in love quickly and often?"

That one's easy. "No."

She looks at me.

I take in every detail of her face. She's so fucking beautiful. How can this not be the woman I spent that weekend with?

I decide to be honest. "Okay, I become smitten kind of easily. I've been infatuated a few times. And I was enamored once."

A flash of something crosses her face. Jealousy? That's just wishful thinking on my part, I'm sure.

She focuses on her stirring again. "I see. Well, New Orleans was fun. A fling. A crazy weekend."

"I've had a lot of fun. Flings. Crazy weekends," I say.

"But I've never felt like this, Scarlett." I keep my tone even, but I make sure she can hear the sincerity. "I've never not been able to get over someone. I've never been smitten or enamored or whatever for almost *two years*."

She swallows hard.

Finally, after several long seconds, she says, "I'm really sorry. I didn't mean for that to happen. I had no idea it would. You were... my last hurrah before moving back here where I knew everything would have to be...more...tame. Buttoned up. Strait-laced."

What the hell? "So you decided to live in your sister's shoes for a couple of days?"

She meets my gaze again. She nods. "Something like that. I've always been hyper-aware of my actions, my words, what people think of me. Ruby tells me I need to let go of other people's expectations and be less concerned with rules. When I met you, at first I told myself no way. You were absolutely not someone I would typically even talk to."

I frown. "Why not?"

"You were so...hot." She sighs. She keeps stirring. "You were clearly younger than me. Clearly comfortable being in a strip club. Once we talked, you were so confident and charming. I knew you had women throwing themselves at you all the time. And then you bought the rest of my private dances for the night, and I realized you had money and you were used to throwing it around." She shakes her head. "I never spend time with young, hot, rich, charming guys." She sighs again. "Then you just wanted to take me out. You bought me a burger." She laughs. "I was worried about embarrassing myself by coming too fast when we got to your hotel, and you just wanted to buy me a burger and talk."

Her mention of coming too fast sends lust coursing through my veins. "I did not *just* want to buy you a burger," I growl.

She had come fast. Not *too* fast, but very fast that first time. I'd loved every damned thing about that.

She doesn't comment on that. She keeps going though. "But then I remembered that we were leaving the next day. Not just leaving town but leaving the whole state. We were leaving our lives behind to come here. To start over in our hometown, where everyone knows us, where we have history. I knew if I was ever going to do something wild and crazy, that night was my last chance." She pauses for a breath. "So I said to hell with it, and seduced you."

My brows slam together. "You *seduced* me?"

She nods. "Yes. I thought you were interested in a one-night stand. That you were experienced with those. I had no idea you'd fall in love with me. If I had, I wouldn't have... done that."

"Seduced me."

"Yes."

Jesus. She thinks she had to talk me into that weekend? And that I fall in love so easily that she somehow messed up?

I shove a hand through my hair. I want to deny *all* of the conclusions she drew about me, but...I can't. I don't frequent strip clubs—didn't even then—but I'd been to a few before, and the nightlife and clubs were nothing new. The rest of what she said—the money, the women, the confidence—well, that was all spot on.

"You did not seduce me. I was a very willing participant and knew exactly where I wanted to end up from the first moment I saw you, Scarlett."

"But I asked you to take me to your hotel."

"Not because it hadn't occurred to me that's where I wanted you." I lean onto the countertop. "And I told you, I've never felt this way before. So stop with that."

She swallows. And doesn't agree. But she doesn't argue.

She removes the pan from the burner and carries it to the island. She starts stirring cereal into the marshmallow mixture.

"So Ruby's wild and crazy?" I ask.

She laughs lightly, but it doesn't sound amused. "Ruby is the fun one. Always has been." Scarlett looks up and meets my gaze directly. "I'm the good girl. The *very* good girl."

I realize that she's telling me this in an attempt to shut me down. Push me away. Turn me off.

It has the exact opposite effect.

"How so?"

She starts spooning the sticky cereal into the glass pan, pressing it down as she goes. "No partying. No night clubs. No staying out late. No drinking. No wild sex." She pauses. "Not really any sex at all. I'm very responsible. A rule follower. Above reproach." Her tone of voice changes slightly on those last two words. Almost as if she's mimicking someone else.

I grip my glass a little tighter. "I'm not sure you should've told me that," I tell her.

She looks up. One brow lifts. "Why not?"

"Because there's nothing hotter than a good girl who will be bad for only you."

Her cheeks get pink. She quickly turns away, setting the pan in the sink and running hot water into it.

I also don't need her to admit that there are several details of our weekend flipping through her mind like a very sexy movie. I know that's exactly what's going on.

When she shuts the water off, I say, "And you were a very good girl for me." My voice is gruff. "I think I told you that. More than once."

She thinks she seduced me? No way. She might have been the first to say the word 'hotel' but I was the one making her moan and gasp and scream all weekend.

Scarlett was a very good girl for me. Over and over.

She turns, but leans against the sink, as if she needs the support. She takes a deep breath and closes her eyes, shaking her head. "You have to stop that."

No fucking way. "See, I think there are actually a lot of honest things you told me that weekend, Glinda," I say. "I think you were *completely* honest when you told me how much you liked the way I ate your pussy. I think every time you begged me to fuck you harder and deeper, that was totally honest. I think that you were being entirely yourself when you asked if you could ride me."

She stares at me for a long moment, then groans, and covers her face with her hands. "Oh my God. Seriously. Stop it."

Under other circumstances, I might find this funny. But remembering that weekend and thinking about the fact that she is trying to convince us all that it was fake isn't fucking funny at all.

I stand and stalk around the counter, not stopping until I'm standing directly in front of her. I can smell the scent of her shampoo, count the freckles on her shoulder, study the tiny stud earrings in her ears.

I tug her hands away from her face. When she looks up at me, I'm hit with a rush of emotion.

There you are.

Unlike the moment I first saw Ruby, when I look into Scarlett's eyes, the familiarity hits me directly in the chest.

It's how I feel when I first step off the plane in Cara. It's how I feel when I smell my mother's perfume. It's how I feel when I hear my sister's laugh. It's how I feel when my niece comes running at me with a bright smile.

It's a feeling of home and contentment and belonging that sucks the air out of my lungs.

I take a deep breath. "You were pretty specific about the things you wanted me to do to you, Glinda. You got those all from your sister?"

Scarlett shakes her head. "Seriously, Cian. That weekend was a one-time thing. I am not usually like that."

Heat rockets through me. I couldn't have kept my eyes from dropping to her mouth for all the money in the world. I remember not only the things that gorgeous mouth did to me, but I remember every word it said.

"That makes it even better. It means those were *fantasies*. Fantasies that you shared with only *me*. Fantasies that you asked *me* to help make real. And fantasies are about the most personal, intimate things you can share with someone. Don't fucking tell me that you were anybody but yourself during those moments."

She's staring at me, her eyes wide. She's breathing faster and I'm guessing her heart is pounding.

Mine sure as fuck is.

"Okay," she finally says. "You're right. That was all me. That was me letting go. That was real. And I get why you have strong feelings about it. It was a very... fun weekend. But you're not in *love* with me. That was lust. It was physical. Chemical. And you can't tell me that you haven't had amazing sex before." She pauses. "Or since."

Okay, now I'm pissed.

Again.

I never get pissed and I've been wound up since I got on the damned plane in Cara.

I don't like being angry. Probably why I don't do it very often.

"First of all, no, I haven't had sex since," I say tightly.

She frowns. "You're telling me you haven't had good sex since we were together?"

"I'm telling you I haven't had *any* sex since we were together. Except with my hand if you count that, which I do not."

She opens her mouth to respond, but I lift my hand and press my finger over her lips, keeping her mouth shut.

"But here is why I'm mixed up and pissed off," I tell her. "I *loved* fucking you. But the reason I can't stop thinking about you is because of the program for single moms we brainstormed together. I fell in love with the woman who had *that* in her beautiful head and who got me excited and motivated to *do* something amazing with it."

Her big green eyes widen, but I don't move my hand away from her mouth. I'm not fucking done.

"I thought we both had a sister who is an amazing single mom. I thought we were both proud of how we'd been a part of their support systems. I fell in love with the program we dreamed up for moms who don't have family and friends like our sisters do.

"I fell in love with the way you got me excited about making a difference. With the way you gave me a purpose, a way to use my connections and money to do something important.

"I fell in love with how you made *me* feel important and passionate about something I could *do*. A way to finally contribute the way my siblings do. I told you how I feel like the sidekick to my brother and sister. How I've always wanted to find a way to measure up to the amazing things they do. I confessed some pretty fucking vulnerable stuff. And I thought you understood all of that."

I let my hand fall away from her face now.

"But you're Mariah's mom. Not her aunt. And that idea was all Ruby's, right?" I ask. I don't actually believe that, but I need to hear her tell me that. "*She* is the one who came up with the way to bring single moms together to support one another when they don't have family or friends to help."

I'm watching her face carefully, but I'm on a roll and I don't stop. "Did you get the idea to help your stylist friend from Ruby too? You help her with her daughter's school treats and projects and she does your hair in exchange? That seems like something Ruby would dream up.

"I suppose it's *Ruby* who loves elephants because of how the females create families and bonds that last all their lives."

I take a breath. "See, *that's* why I'm annoyed. The fact that the sex was *phenomenal* was because I *liked* you so fucking much. I felt like I really knew you. And vice versa. I've spent *nineteen months* missing that *connection*. Not just your amazing body, and hot mouth, and greedy pussy, and dirty imagination. All of that too, for fucking sure, but it was especially incredible because of your brain and how you made me *feel*." I step back. "But it was all really me feeling that connection with *Ruby*, right?"

I stand staring at Scarlett, watching her process all of that.

Is she going to keep lying to me? Is she going to let me keep thinking that? Is she okay with believing that I feel affection and respect for *her sister* based on the things Scarlett shared with me that weekend?

Things that I *know* are really about Scarlett.

All of that was *her*.

But she has to admit it. She has to let me in. She has to let me close.

She stares at me for several seconds.

The clock above the sink ticks at least ten times.

She swallows hard. Then again.

She starts to nod…

But then she stops and my heart squeezes.

She shakes her head. "No. Dammit, Cian."

"No *what*?" I press. She has to say it.

"That wasn't Ruby. I should let you think so, but…" She trails off.

"Which part wasn't Ruby?" I demand.

She tips her head back and closes her eyes. "All of it. The program for moms was my idea. I thought of it a couple of years ago when we lived in New Orleans and a couple of moms and I were exchanging favors. Like making bars and cutting hair, but on an even bigger scale. We always said that living together would make it all easier." She opens her eyes and our gazes lock. "When you and I brainstormed, that was me. And *I'm* the one who loves elephants." She takes a deep breath. "And I'm selfish enough to want you to like all of that about *me*, not Ruby."

Fucking finally. That's what I needed to hear.

"I do." I slide my hand into my front pocket, then take her hand and put the bracelet I've been carrying around for nineteen months in her palm. "I knew it was you. All along, Glinda. Every second."

She stares down at the silver bracelet with the elephant charm. Then her gaze flies back to mine. "*You've* had this? All this time? I thought I lost it."

"I would have happily returned it. If I could have found

you," I say dryly. The elephant is holding a gem in its trunk. "Mariah's birthstone, right?"

She nods.

I'd remembered the date from her tattoo, and I'd looked up the stone. It's a garnet. The deep red could also be described as scarlet.

I drag my finger over the tattoo on her inner wrist. "I loved the idea you were an aunt. That we'd both helped raise our nieces," I tell her. "But you being a mom is fucking amazing, Scarlett."

She takes a shaky breath. "Ruby *is* an amazing aunt. You two really are a lot alike."

I sigh. She's so fucking stubborn.

She takes a deep breath. Blows it out. "Okay," she finally says. "I'm...really sorry about...everything."

I frown.

I don't frown a lot either. All of this being annoyed is really starting to annoy me.

"Do *not* be sorry about anything we did or talked about that weekend."

She shakes her head. "No. Not that. I guess... the time since then. I'm sorry you..." But then she shakes her head again. "No. You know what? I'm *glad* all of that mattered to you. I'm glad you felt excited about something and that you felt important." She leans in. "You're a fucking *prince*, Cian. You've been hiding out for over a *decade*. What are you doing? You should feel important. You *are* important. You should be *doing* things. Making a difference. And I'm glad you felt a spark for that."

She's right. I should be making a damned difference. And I intend to do exactly that.

I reach up and cup the back of her neck, keeping her

face close. I study her eyes. "I felt a lot more than a spark, Scarlett."

I mean that in every way. For the project and passions we talked about, and for her.

She swallows hard. "I did too."

"Dammit, Glinda," I mutter. Then I kiss her.

I couldn't have kept my mouth off of hers for all the riches in the world.

There is nothing soft or tentative about the kiss. I immediately open my lips and stroke my tongue over her lips, demanding entrance.

She moans and submits.

I taste her fully, letting her know that I haven't forgotten a thing about our time together. I know how she likes to be kissed. I know that sliding my hands into her hair makes her whimper. I know that nipping at her bottom lip will make her arch closer.

I need more though. A firm surface behind her, so I can truly press into her. I need to be against her. I need more than her mouth.

Then she's walking me backward, and I feel one of the kitchen chairs at the back of my knees. She pushes me down into it and climbs into my lap, straddling my thighs. My hands move to grip her ass, pressing her against my aching cock as her hands slide into my hair.

We both groan at the contact. All of the contact.

It's been nearly two years for both of us, but it's as if our bodies have simply been waiting for one another. She circles her hips and I press up into her, relief and frustration flooding through me at the same time.

My fingers steal up under the hem of her shirt and I spread my palms over the bare skin of her back. I stroke up and down, absorbing the warm, silky feel of her.

She copies the action, dropping her hands from my hair to my waist and bunching my shirt up so she can get her hands underneath. She glides her hands up my ribs and around to my back, curling her fingers into the muscles, then stroking up and down.

The feel of her touch again after all this time sends a wave of lust through me.

I drag my mouth along her jaw to her ear. "Need you so bad."

She tips her head back so I can drag my stubbled jaw down her throat. My hands slide around to cover her breasts. She's wearing a bra, but I can feel the pebbled tips of her nipples, and I rub my thumbs over them, eliciting a shiver and moan.

"So much," I say against the front of her throat, kissing, then nipping lightly.

"Me too," she pants. Her fingers are digging into my shoulder blades again, holding me close.

Her breasts are small, but they fit perfectly against my palms. Her nipples are incredibly sensitive, and I remember every minute of teasing them with my hands and mouth.

I pluck a nipple. "Can I make you come? Right here like this?"

Her answer is a soft moan and her pressing down against my cock.

"Oh yes, I remember this greedy pussy very well," I say, kissing along her collarbone and moving one hand down to cup her through her shorts.

She grinds against my hand, almost instinctively.

"Cian," she practically pleads.

"Right here, my good little witch. Whatever you need."

Just then a door shuts somewhere in the house, and she jerks back.

I realize that she forgot where we were for a moment. I take pride in that. But now that she's remembered, we're done here.

For now.

She quickly pushes back then gets to her feet. She stands, staring down at me. She's breathing hard, her cheeks are pink, and she's clearly not sure what to do. I reach down and adjust the fly on my jeans that is pressing against my very angry-at-being-blocked cock.

Her eyes follow that movement. She squeezes her eyes shut and runs a hand through her hair.

"Scarlett," I say, keeping my tone calm. "It's okay."

She shakes her head, then opens her eyes and meets my gaze. "It's not. I can't do this."

"Fuck me in your kitchen with your family in the house? Or are we talking about something more?"

"Yes. More. Both."

"Okay, I get the not in the kitchen part. Why not the rest?"

"Because…"

Her eyes go to my still very evident erection, then come back to my face. She backs up until she's leaning against the kitchen counter, bracing her hands behind her. "I'm not the woman you think I am."

"So you keep saying. I'm getting very tired of this particular conversation, though."

She blows out a breath. "But it's true. So yes, parts of our weekend together were real. The sex was amazing. We talked about some real stuff. And I'm very glad that you felt important and got excited about doing something big. But, I am not fun or spontaneous or uninhibited or at all able or willing to be involved in a relationship with you."

"Why not?" I shrug. "You obviously *are* capable of being

uninhibited and having fun. Why can't you do that with me?"

"Because…" She gives a quick, humorless laugh. "I am actually a pretentious, uptight bitch."

I blink at her.

I repeat those words in my head.

Pretentious. Uptight. Bitch.

I frown. *What?*

"What?" I finally ask when nothing else comes to mind.

She moves to cross her arms. "At least I used to be. When I lived here. I spent six years of my life, junior high through high school, being a pretty terrible person. I acted like, actually believed, that I was better than everyone else. I was judgmental, stuck up, and bitchy." She lets out a heavy sigh. "So I'm here for a second chance. I'm back to try to show people that I've changed. To make amends. My goal is to lead a simple, humble life, and show them that I am capable of kindness and being genuine and that I know I'm not better than anyone else. But that means there is no way I can date a semi-famous, incredibly wealthy, powerful *prince*. That is the opposite of what I'm trying for here."

I let all of that roll around in my head for a moment. It's nearly impossible for me to imagine this woman, who is concerned with women and families having the support they need, who was self-deprecating and funny and sweet the entire time I knew her—okay for the entire fifty-two hours I knew her—is a bitch.

But she does keep telling me that I don't know the real her.

"So, you don't *actually* know me. Which means you can't *actually* be in love with me," she says when I don't speak.

This headstrong, gorgeous little witch. My palm itches

with the urge to spank her ass for being so obstinate. She actually thinks she can out-stubborn me? I've been resisting the King of Cara for twelve years. Please. I need to *show* her that I can be just as…

Wait a second. That's a great idea. "Okay," I say. "Prove it."

She frowns. "What?"

"Prove you're not the woman I think you are. Make me get over you. Help me get closure on this so that I can go back home and do what my family wants me to do."

"What does your family want you to do?"

"Get married."

CHAPTER 8
SCARLETT

G et married.

Of all the things I expected Cian to say, I can admit that those two words were not even in the top hundred.

I blink at him. "Your family wants you to get *married?*"

He nods. "Yes. My grandfather has it all arranged. We were just recently informed of it. Neither of us is into it. But my reason is you. If you're not actually who I think you are, then I don't actually have a great reason for not marrying her."

I am appalled by the stab of jealousy I feel in my gut.

I have no right to feel jealous. But I'm not entirely surprised either.

In another world, if I was another person, I would absolutely want Cian O'Grady for my own. And I would be jealous of any woman who got to have him.

Actually, even in this world, being who I am, I want him and am jealous of anyone who gets to have him.

It's just that I realize I can't.

"Do you love her?"

He scowls at me. "I've told you I don't fall in love. Except with you."

I'm also appalled at how my heart flips when he says that. It's ridiculous. He can't actually *love* me. But his continued insistence that I am somehow extraordinary and that he actually is in love with me never fails to cause a reaction.

"Do you *like* her?"

"I do. Very much. We're good friends. She's fantastic. I am certain we could actually be happily married."

"So why don't you want to marry her?"

He sighs heavily. "Because I think I'm in love with you," he says as if speaking to a young child who refuses to understand a basic concept.

"And you need me to help you get over that so you can go home and marry her," I summarize.

His eyes narrow. "Well, that's preferable to going home and marrying her and thinking about, and wanting, you every single day—and night—for the rest of my life."

Geez. How am I supposed to form good arguments when he says stuff like that? When I can barely remember how to breathe when he says stuff like that?

I swallow. "So what do you want? *Exactly*? How does this work in your mind?"

He stands from the chair and steps closer. That is bad. Because whenever Cian gets close to me, my heart rate kicks up and my body gets warmer.

"Nineteen days," he tells me.

"Nineteen days?"

"I've spent nineteen months thinking about you. Waiting for you. I've put my life on hold because of you. I haven't moved on. I haven't even considered another woman. Maybe if I had, I'd be involved with someone and this marriage thing wouldn't be an issue. But I haven't. I guess I can't ask you for nineteen months, but nineteen days seems fair."

"Nineteen days for what?" I ask, my heart pounding so hard I press my hand to my chest.

"Just let me get to know you. Be yourself and spend time with me. I figure nineteen days should be enough time for me to realize that you are not what I want. If you are all of these things you claim to be, then that should be enough time for me to get over you."

I guess that makes sense. "So we date with the purpose of convincing you we're *not* compatible?"

His expression is difficult to read. "Yes."

My stomach dips. I get to spend nineteen days with this man, but I have to try to help him get over me? I kind of hate this plan already. But I suppose I owe him?

He didn't seem to appreciate the idea that I seduced him back in New Orleans. Maybe that pricked his male ego. Whatever. The fact remains that he had essentially taken me out on a date. A nice, friendly, not-naked-all-weekend *date*.

I had been up on that stage standing by a *stripper pole*, scared, completely out of my depth, and he'd somehow seen that. He'd rescued me by asking for a private dance, which had gotten me off stage and away from all the other men. Then he'd paid enough money to the club to cover the rest of the night of private dances with me. Since I was spoken for, he convinced the club manager to let me leave early. And he'd taken me out for burgers and shakes.

Yes, there had been chemistry. Yes, he'd flirted. But I honestly believe, even now, that if I had not mentioned going back to his hotel, he would've just asked for my number.

I was playing a part that night and he fell hook, line, and sinker. That's on me. I was spontaneous and let my gut guide me instead of my head.

I know better than to do that, and this is one more instance where it's proven that my gut gets me into trouble.

So I owe him. We're in this…predicament…because I wasn't my usual careful, rational self that night.

There's only one problem.

"I still can't date you even for nineteen days," I tell him. "You're a hot, young, wealthy *prince*. That goes against everything I'm trying to prove here in town."

"No one needs to know any of that. I've been hiding out in the US for over a decade."

"But there are people here who could recognize you. They've looked you up because of things that Mariah and Greta have said."

He frowns. I have a point whether he likes it or not.

"That's the only problem?" he finally asks.

No. There's also the problem of me wanting him, wishing everything could be different, the temptation just to say fuck it and let this happen, the urge to be the woman I was with him nineteen months ago, but for good.

Instead of saying any of that, I nod. "Yes."

"I'll figure it out."

"You'll figure what out?"

"How to have you for the next nineteen days. "

My breath catches in my lungs. I cannot keep reacting this way. "The idea is to start *not* wanting me," I remind him.

"The idea is to spend time with you. The not wanting you is yet to be seen."

I let the warm tingles trip through me for a moment. Because they're actually quite nice.

But then I realize that yeah, hanging out in my hometown will easily convince him that I am nothing special.

But we can't hang out here. Leah Lawton will easily figure out who he is and the news will spread like wildfire. That will do me no favors when he moves on and I'm left here with even more to live down.

"This is never going to work," I tell him.

"There's something you should know," he says.

"What's that?"

"Things always work out for me."

I roll my eyes, but I have no trouble believing that.

I can't keep doing this. He's not going to give in and I can't stand here in the kitchen, alone, remembering how it felt to have him pressing that amazing hard, hot body up between my legs again.

I shiver. "I need to get some sleep," I tell him. "I have to be at the shop early in the morning."

He tucks his hands in his back pockets. "Okay."

"Where are you staying?" I ask, suddenly thinking about him turned loose on Emerald.

He lifts shoulder. "Not sure. Getting here was my only focus."

Cue another stupid heart flip.

"Probably a hotel," he adds.

I shake my head. "There's only one hotel here in town and you can't stay there. Someone might recognize you. Especially once you put your name in. You're a stranger. Everyone here pays attention to strangers."

"I'm open to suggestions."

"Henry usually stays here," I say. "And I know he and

Ruby will want to be together tonight." I sigh. "She's missed him so much."

"Even though I just found out about them last night, I can say he's missed her too. He hasn't been the same over the past month," Cian says.

That makes me happy at least. I really need Henry to love my sister as much as she loves him.

"But I don't know how they're doing," he says.

My heart drops. I'd hoped that the strange vibe between them when I'd come home had been just Ruby's initial hurt and anger over their breakup. Surely they were going to get past that. "Really?"

"She has been pretty icy since we got here."

"She was really hurt."

"Yeah."

We just stand there with unsaid words and a ton of emotions swirling around us.

"I guess you can stay on the couch," I offer even though I know it's a bad idea to keep him too close.

You could just put him in your bed. You shared a bed before.

But I immediately shut that voice in my head down. That is a terrible idea. The plan is to help him get over me in nineteen days. But there are absolutely no guarantees that *I* will be over *him*. I would like to mitigate the amount of heartbreak I'm in for, thank you very much.

"That will be great," he says.

Then I sigh. "No. You can have my bed."

His eyebrow quirks.

"I'll share with Mariah," I say quickly.

He smirks. "Don't vacate on my account."

"Oh, no," I say moving around the kitchen counter, covering the freshly made bars with plastic wrap. "It is purely for my sake."

"Well, you know where to find me," he says.

Yeah. It will be *very* hard to forget that.

I am acutely aware of him following me up the stairs. I don't know how I'm going to do this. How can I resist this man? Everything I've told him is true, of course. I can't date him and live the life I need to live here in Emerald.

But it's much easier to be determined about that when he's not in my personal space. Or within eyesight. Or within the same zip code.

When I get to the top of the stairs, I lead him to my bedroom. My entire body feels jumpy and overly sensitive. My shirt feels too tight, my shorts scratchy. As if my body is begging me to strip my clothes off. Cian O'Grady is standing outside of my bedroom. And I can't even kiss him. I certainly can't pull him through the doorway, push him down on the bed, straddle him, and...

I clear my throat. "Here's my room. I'll get fresh sheets. Just give me a minute."

His chuckle is low and deep. "I am looking forward to sleeping on sheets that smell like you, Scarlett. Please don't change them."

My cheeks get hot. I swallow hard. Fine. I don't want to change the sheets anyway. "Okay. There are fresh towels and linens in the closet just there." I point.

"Ruby and Henry are there." I point to Ruby's closed bedroom door. "And that's Mariah's room. Where I'll be. I'll be up early for work. Help yourself to whatever in the morning. And then... I guess I'll hear about your plans from Ruby."

"Are you trying to say good night to me or goodbye?"

I nod. "Yes."

He gives me a small smile. "Good *night,* Scarlett," he says.

I walk quickly to Mariah's room, knock lightly, and open the door without waiting for her to answer.

"Need to—"

Greta and Mariah are lying head to toe on Mariah's bed, both on their phones, music streaming from one of them.

They both look at me. "Hey. What's up?" Mariah asks.

"I was going to say I need to sleep in here with you," I say.

Greta frowns and sits up. "Oh. Sorry. We didn't think to ask. My mom says it's fine I stay over."

"Why aren't you in your room?" Mariah asks.

"Cian is sleeping in there."

Mariah tips her head. "So why aren't you sleeping in there? You've slept together before."

And I am blushing again. "Because it's not like that now. We're not going to have sex."

Greta is grinning at me. "I would love to know what happened between the two of you that has made him so gaga over you. I mean, he's been waiting for you for *nineteen* months. That is so romantic. And he's here looking for you after all this time? He wants you back." She sighs dreamily.

Mariah grins. "I, on the other hand, do *not* want to know what she did to make him so gaga."

Greta giggles and throws a pillow at Mariah. "I didn't mean it like that."

Mariah laughs. "Yes, you did."

I thunk my head back against the door. "Anyway," I say, raising my voice. "I'm not going to be doing anything with him now."

Both girls focus on me. "Why not?" Mariah asks.

"Yeah," Greta agrees. "He's here. He's crazy about you. And he's... him."

"Because I can't date someone like that. Everyone knows who he is. He's rich and jets around the world, rock climbing, and scuba diving. He lives a totally different life-style from ours. He knows famous, rich people." I'm working on *not* judging other people. But dammit. I'm here trying to prove to people that I'm happy doing a humble, basic service job and I can *not* date a guy who doesn't even really have a job yet has millions of dollars at his disposal.

"You know that I believe we should all be trying to contribute in a positive way," I tell the girls. There's never a bad time for a learning moment, I figure. "And I just want a regular life, nothing fancy or exciting. I don't need all of that. I don't need private planes and exotic vacations. I just want to help keep people's cars and trucks running so they can go to work and take their kids to school and make the most of their lives. That's how you contribute to a community."

And I'm hanging out with people like Amber, who does people's hair, and her husband Tony, who works at the factory, and my sister who...okay, she strips and bartends, but only because people in this town won't bring their kids to her for dance lessons. That's what she'd really like to do.

Not only do I want to prove my change of heart to my hometown, but I also definitely want to prove it to my daughter and her friend. I can be a good role model here. I can teach them this lesson. A simple life, doing a job that contributes to the community and helps others, living a life that you can be proud of, not judging others, not making waves, those are all things to be happy with. You don't need excitement or adventure. You can make up for mistakes. And you don't need big, grand love stories.

I have shared with both Mariah and Greta what I was like when I lived here as a kid. I've been brutally honest. I was not a nice person. I was the girl that the girls like them didn't like. I was a mean girl. The Leah—judgy, better than them, thought I had it all figured out.

I want my daughter and Greta, who has turned into a second daughter, to look at me now and want to be like me. Not like the girl I was then, but the woman I've become. Someone who can acknowledge her mistakes, can say she's sorry, and can change.

There's a knock on the door behind me and I suck in a surprised breath. I step away and open it. Cian is in the hallway.

"Everything okay?" I ask.

"Yeah. Just, your sister is in your bed. Didn't really think I should sleep in there."

I frown. "Ruby is in my bed?"

He nods. "She and Henry are not going to be sleeping together. Apparently."

I sigh. "Great." I glance back at the girls. "Anyway. We can talk about all this more later. You go ahead and stay," I tell Greta. At this point, it would raise questions with her parents if I sent her home, or if I sent Mariah with her. It's better if we just all bunk here together somehow. But only for tonight.

I step out into the hallway. Cian barely backs up to give me space.

I slide past him, very careful not to brush against his body. No matter how much I want to. I go to my bedroom and open the door.

My sister is propped up against my headboard, reading. She is definitely ready for bed. "What's going on?" I ask. "I figured you and Henry would be in your room."

She looks at me. "No way. I... can't." Her voice is shaky and I think she might be on the verge of tears.

Well, shit.

I turn around and look up at Cian, who is still out in the hallway. "I guess you and Henry are sharing Ruby's room."

He lifts one big shoulder. "I'm disappointed to not be wrapped up in your sheets tonight," he says. "But Henry and I will be fine. We've done this before. In worse circumstances."

I do not want to know.

But I do kind of want to know. There is definitely a part of me that wants to hear all of his stories. No, I can't date someone who is adventurous and exciting and who jets around the world, especially on a private plane. But hearing about it is tempting.

"Okay. Good *night*," I say.

The corner of his mouth curls and I know that he made a note that it was just a good night and not goodbye.

I step into my room and close the door between us. He can find the towels and whatever else he might need on his own. I need space.

I look at my sister. "Are you okay?"

She shakes her head no.

"I thought you'd be happy Henry's back," I say, crossing to the bed and climbing onto the mattress next to her.

Ruby and I have also shared a bed many times. Also, in worse circumstances.

"I mean, at first I was really happy to see him. I'm stupidly in love with him," she says. "But he's always going to leave, Scarlett. That's just our reality. He's not going to stay in Emerald, Ohio. Cian is his job. More, Cian is his *family*. There's never going to be a time when he can choose me over him. And I can't live a life where the man I'm in love with is here very part time. I don't think I should have to be second choice even if I understand why his first choice comes first."

This is something my sister and Henry actually have in common. Ruby has always been there for me. She has uprooted her life to go with me and Mariah more than once. She is amazingly loyal, and she would put me and my daughter ahead of anyone. Even herself.

"You know exactly where he's coming from," I say. "You're a lot alike."

She nods. "We are. Which is why he and I are not going to work out. I can't see him just here and there. I really don't think that I'm cut out for a long-distance relationship."

I would agree with that. Ruby is a very loving person. And while our inner circle is small, it's tight. She likes to be with the people she loves. She needs quality time. She loves cuddling, sharing meals, face-to-face conversations and laughter, making memories together. She can't go even two days without talking to our mother. And she can't be away from home for more than a week, even on a fabulous vacation.

"I'm really sorry." I reach out and squeeze her hand. "Why did we have to fall for those guys? Out of all the guys on the planet? Why the two that it will absolutely not work out with?"

She shakes her head. "I don't know. But—" she says pointing at my nose, "I don't want to hear about how it's probably some punishment. This is not the universe or God or karma or Dad somehow magically punishing you for past decisions or mistakes."

I don't say anything to that. That is exactly what I usually do. I assume that I deserve bad things to happen to me. I've been that way since I was about twelve. When our father started telling me that.

"Fine. You're right. It's just bad timing. Or bad luck. Or whatever."

Ruby nods her agreement. "It just sucks. Sometimes things just suck. But it's not because we deserve them to suck."

I turn and lie back on the pillow next to hers. I think about that.

Sometimes things just suck. But that doesn't mean we deserve them to suck.

That is actually a little comforting.

But it also seems really fucking unfair.

CHAPTER 9

CIAN

"Cian," Henry says, sitting forward in his chair. His tone is low and measured. This is his serious tone.

I'm really tired of things being so damned serious. I stick a French fry in my mouth. "Yeah?"

"I'm going to need you to not overreact or lose your shit. Just stay in your seat."

We're sitting in the café in downtown Emerald. As always, Henry is facing the room so he can see everyone coming and going and everything that's happening.

In the beginning I wondered why he always wanted my back to the room. What if someone was coming to stab or shoot or kidnap me? But he assured me that *he* needed to know if that was happening before I did and that he'd shoot them between the eyes before they got close enough to hurt me.

I have no idea if that's true. It's never been tested. I guess, thank God, though that would be exciting. I long ago decided that Henry wants to see the rooms so he can check out all the pretty girls and just keep an eye on the general action. He's an action guy. At least compared to me, he is.

I frown at him now, though. We're in *Ohio* and like five people on the planet know that. Or, more precisely, there are five people who know who I am who also know I'm in Ohio. Is there a knife coming my way? Other than a butter knife to spread more mayo on my burger? "What are you talking about?"

"This is not a good time for her to see you," Henry says.

Her. That one word rocks through me. That has to be Scarlett. Which means she's here. I turn and scan the room and immediately find her at the register paying for a sandwich.

I'm not shocked. This is the main eatery in the town where she lives and works.

But I am shocked by my reaction to seeing her. She was already gone this morning when we all woke up. Last night she basically told me she didn't think things were going to work out between us.

Yet my heart thumps hard and my entire body tenses.

I want to go to her. Right now. I want to pull her into my arms, kiss her, and *claim* her. In public.

But I get it. Henry and I spent this entire morning covering up who I am and why I'm here.

Fuck. It's already pissing me off.

She's wearing jeans, a dark green tank top that shows off her toned arms, and her hair is tied up under a dark green bandana. She's also got black work boots on.

She looks kickass and gorgeous.

I watch her turn toward the front door. Then stop, sigh, and turn back to the restaurant. She starts toward a table where three women are sitting.

"Do not go over there," Henry says.

"Who are they?"

"I don't know who they all are, but the blonde is Hannah Lawton. Leah's mom."

"*The* Leah? The one who's been a shit to Mariah?" I ask with a scowl.

"Yeah."

I sit, just watching, but I don't like it. This is a very strange protective instinct. I don't feel this toward many people. Mostly because the people I love don't need it from me. Not only are they surrounded by literal *paid* protection, but they're all strong personalities who don't take any shit. No one wants to be on the receiving end of my sister's ire. Or my niece's, even at age twelve. Oh, it gets her in trouble. Always has. But that hasn't done a thing to quell her instincts to stand up to bullies and people who are just plain wrong.

Right now, Scarlett is holding a roll of bills out to Hannah.

"You mean she shouldn't have lied?" Hannah asks, her voice raised now, clearly wanting to draw attention.

"No. I mean she shouldn't have spilled the juice on Leah's shirt," Scarlett says tightly.

"But she also lied," Hannah says. "Are you going to apologize for that?"

"Just take the money for the shirt." Scarlett looks exhausted.

"I'm really sick of Mariah making Leah uncomfortable and school so unpleasant for her," Hannah says. "School should be a safe space. They need to focus on learning."

"I agree," Scarlett says. "Let's talk to the girls about just ignoring one another entirely. They should just stay away from each other. They don't need to be friends or enemies. They can just be nothing."

Hannah sits straighter. The women with her are staying completely silent. As is the rest of the café. Everyone is listening, if not outright watching the interaction.

It has the feel of a new episode in an ongoing drama.

I look at Henry. He just shakes his head. I sigh. Do I want to go over there? Absolutely. Will it draw even more attention to Scarlett? Of course. But does it gnaw at my gut that she's standing there, *alone*, facing off with this woman trying to defend her daughter? It sure fucking does.

"Henry," I say quietly.

"No. You won't help right now," he says. "This isn't new."

"But—"

"Cian, just wait."

"But Leah *needs* to call out lying," Hannah says. "You know that. Or you *should* know that, anyway. She can't just look the other way when someone is doing something wrong and sinful."

I can see Scarlett's eye roll from four tables away.

"Seriously?" she asks. "Mariah's soul isn't Leah's responsibility. And not only are you judging *Mariah* unfairly, but you're putting a lot of pressure on Leah."

"Of course Mariah's soul is Leah's responsibility," Hannah exclaims loudly. "It's all of our responsibility." She looks at the two women sitting with her. They both nod. She even casts her glance around the diner. "*We* have to look out for her when she's stuck with the...influences she has. That's what being a *community* is all about." She gives Scarlett a sly smile. "Your father spoke directly to the youth group about it, in fact."

Scarlett's face gets pale and she straightens slowly. "Excuse me?"

Her tension, the shock on her face, makes me straighten as well.

"No, Cian," Henry says firmly.

"She's not okay."

"She's tough."

"She shouldn't have to be tough." Dammit. This is her hometown. She's talking about her daughter to a fellow mom. This should be her *community* but it's clear that what Hannah is talking about is not at all what I think of when I think of that word. And it's obviously not what Scarlett wants.

Hannah goes on. "Your father said that our kids can have a special influence for good on lost and confused kids."

"Mariah isn't lost or confused," Scarlett says. Her fists are now balled at her sides.

"Well of course *you* don't think so. But I think we're going to listen to our pastor."

"Did he use her name?" Scarlett demands.

Hannah smiles. "Of course. She's the prime example of someone that our kids can intervene with. It *pains* him to watch his own granddaughter reject the church and so blatantly lie, brag, and try to elevate herself with these false narratives."

I'm scowling now, my lunch entirely forgotten as my gut tightens.

"It *pains* him?" Scarlett's voice rises.

"What the fuck is going on?" I hiss to Henry.

"Scarlett and Ruby's father is the pastor of the big church here in town."

"*What?*"

"Their biological father. He didn't raise them. He was never married to their mom."

"He is *invested* in Mariah's future and well-being," Hannah says. "He'll do whatever it takes."

"What the hell does that mean?" Scarlett asks.

"For instance, the first one in the youth group to get Mariah to church gets a hundred dollars," Hannah says. She looks smug.

I really dislike this woman.

I glance around. The entire café is watching. They seem entertained. But not shocked by any of this. I need to know more about what's going on here.

I stand.

"*Cian*," Henry warns.

"I'm not just going to sit here."

"You will make it worse."

"Nah, I've got this."

I could absolutely be about to make this worse. I do that sometimes. But I'm not going to just sit by and let Scarlett do this alone.

"Well, I guess it's safe to say that there's no way Leah will ever be getting that money," Scarlett says with a fake, forced laugh. "Mariah would never go anywhere with your snotty, mean, *misled* daughter."

For the first time, Hannah's smile wavers.

"Keep your church bullshit away from my daughter," Scarlett tells her. "I don't want it and she doesn't need it."

"Oh, of course not," Hannah bites out. "Because you know everything and are perfect all on your own, right?"

Scarlett sucks in a quick breath, then presses her lips together and shakes her head. "That's not what I meant."

"Well, just because your *father* has given up on *you*, we still worry about our youth. Even Mariah."

She hasn't seen me yet, but I can see Scarlett's face and her eyes are glittering with tears.

Oh, fuck no.

I come up on her right side. "Scarlett! Hey! So glad to run into you." I step in front of her, between her and where Hannah is sitting. I take her elbow and steer her toward the counter.

I hear Henry addressing the table of women. "Afternoon, ladies," he says smoothly.

And *that's* why I don't worry about jumping into situations, no matter what they are. I have Henry.

"Sorry to steal her away," Henry said loudly enough for the whole diner to hear. "But she's fixing our car. We broke down here this morning and just got some news about the special part we need. It's a bit of an emergency. Here, let me buy your lunch."

I continue walking with Scarlett across the diner, until we get to the take-out counter and bakery case.

I turn her so her back is to the table and then lean in. "Breathe."

She stares up at me, confused, and it takes me a moment to remember my makeover.

She frowns. "*Cian?*"

"I'm actually going by Dean Brady." I give her a grin. "Kind of sounds like Cian O'Grady, right?"

Her frown deepens. "*What?*"

I've dyed my hair black, shaved, and I'm wearing glasses. I'm also wearing dress pants and a button-down dress shirt to cover my tattoos. It doesn't sound drastic, but all together, it's altered my appearance significantly. Especially for people who don't know me, have only seen me in photos, and are in no way expecting me to show up in their little town.

At least that's the plan.

Scarlett's voice drops. "What are you doing?"

"I'm undercover."

"You're kidding."

"Nope. You can't spend time with a prince who is regularly covered on a podcast that some people here have discovered, so I'm now a professor of world history and political science. My car broke down as we were coming through Emerald. You're fixing it. But it's a fancy something and you have to order a special part that will take a few days."

"You don't even know what kind of car you're pretend driving?" she asks, the tiniest hint of a smile teasing her lips.

I shake my head, fully smiling. "Henry made that part up. I didn't really catch it. The rest of this we've done before."

"You've been a professor of world history and political science named Dean Brady before?"

I nod. "Yep. Have the ID, the papers, all of it."

Her eyes widen. "Oh."

I shrug. "I've been doing the royal in hiding for a while."

"So who is Henry supposed to be?"

"Henry Duke. He says Henry is a common enough name he can keep using it."

"Is he also a professor?"

"I'm his boss, actually," Henry says, coming up beside us.

I also made him cut his hair—which he's pissed about—shave, and drop his British accent, which he says Ruby will be pissed about.

Then he sighed and said she's already avoiding him anyway so it didn't matter.

The two of them are really pretty pathetic.

"Head of the department at..." Henry frowns. "I need to

look up which college we're supposed to be with." He looks at Scarlett. "We haven't done this in about five years."

"Been professors who have car trouble?" Scarlett asks.

"We haven't had car trouble before. We've been traveling for book research. Traveling back from a conference." Henry glances at me. "Usually things that only require us to stay wherever we are for a night or so. We've never needed nineteen days before. We have to draw this one out."

She nods her understanding. "Well, you're both handsome, charming strangers. I don't think anyone is going to dig too deep. At least not as long as you're respectful to the right people. But to that end, you might want to go to church on Sunday."

I frown but Henry says lightly, "Sounds like I could make a hundred bucks if I tell Mariah I'm taking her out for donuts and take a detour."

Scarlett shakes her head. "God, that's fucked up, right?" She looks between us. "I mean, her *grandfather* is paying people to get her to church? Under the guise of what? Friendship? Maybe a cute boy pretends to be interested in her and tricks her into it?" She rubs her forehead. "That would be ironic. And hypocritical. But he'd do it that way."

She's almost talking to herself.

"Were those women mean to you in high school or something?" I ask.

She looks up at me, startled. Then she laughs. "Oh, God no. I was mean to *them*, Cian." She sighs. "I don't actually blame Hannah for totally hating me. I just wish she'd leave our girls out of it."

I have so many questions. I don't like *any* of this.

Henry suddenly moves in a little closer to Scarlett and stands taller. He clears his throat, then asks, "So you think it will be that long for the part?"

I realize a man has come up to the carry out counter and Henry has shifted into character.

"Isn't there anything you can do to speed it up?" Henry asks Scarlett.

Scarlett catches on immediately. "Yeah, sorry. We're a small operation. Not much I can do." Her eyes meet mine. "They said nineteen days to get it here."

Oh.

Oh. Fuck, yes.

CHAPTER 10
SCARLETT

Jen: So, we've been informed that Lady Linnea and Jonah Greene are off on their honeymoon. No one is telling us where they went, which is just fine. I guess. We get it. Linnea has sent us a few photos and it looks gorgeous. Anyone want to guess based on the photos we posted?

Lindsey: People have already guessed that they are back in North Carolina. Which makes sense. I don't think that Jonah's parents have probably met Linnea.

Jen: Oh, good point. Well, that's fun. We won't share anything more specific than that. They deserve their privacy on their honeymoon. But we hope they'll share details when they get back.

Lindsey: Well, not *all* of the details.

Jen: Speak for yourself. I wouldn't mind some shirtless photos of Jonah Greene sunbathing or something.

Lindsey: Okay, when you put it that way... Also, we've

had a lot of comments asking if we know anything more about Prince Cian and Henry. We have in fact gotten confirmation that they are completely fine and back in the US. Apparently it was just a big miscommunication about who was going where and when. We assume they're back in Louisiana, though our source didn't specify.

Jen: Well, where else would they be if they're in the US? If you told me they were skiing or white-water rafting or something I wouldn't have been surprised and would've assumed they were not in Louisiana, but if they're just hanging out and back to their usual life, it has to be Louisiana.

Lindsey: Exactly.

Mariah stops reading and looks up at us. "But you told people in the family where you really are, right?" She's directing this to Henry. We're all gathered around the kitchen table with two big pizzas spread out in the middle. Cian and Henry sprung for dinner tonight. I did insist the girls make a salad at least, but they never get pizza on a regular weeknight so they're treating this like some kind of special occasion.

Or maybe it's just Cian and Henry being here that makes it a special occasion. Though I don't want to admit it, that's how it feels to me.

The girls were amazed and delighted by Cian's and Henry's makeovers and the fact that they're going under-cover in our little town. Until it sank in that they can't let on that they know either of them.

Henry swallows a bite of pizza. "I told who needs to know. "

"But a lot of Cian's family is in Louisiana. They would know if he's not there," Mariah says.

Henry nods. "Like I said, I tell the people who need to know."

"Everyone just keeps everyone else's secrets?" Greta asks. "There's no worries about leaks or anything?"

"Everyone is very invested in keeping Cian safe. None of them would jeopardize that. Besides, I told them he's with me and that we're fine. And that we're in the US. Only a few people know exactly where we are. Everyone else is just content knowing that I'm with him."

Greta gets a goofy smile on her face. "That is so nice." She looks at me. "If we just disappeared one night, but then I called you and said don't worry, we are fine, Mariah is with me, would that make you totally feel fine?"

I arch my brows. "I wouldn't say totally fine, no. So don't get any ideas. But, knowing you are together would make me feel better than thinking she was somewhere alone."

Greta smiles and nods. "Plus when we're older, like Cian and Henry, it would be different."

I concede that point. "True. I hope you're both always the best of friends."

She loops an arm around Mariah's neck and gives her a little hug. "Of course we will be."

I look across the island at Cian and find him watching the girls with a smile. He apparently feels my gaze, though, because his eyes come to mine. I turn my attention back to my pizza. He and Henry are both so good with the girls and I'd be a huge liar if I said it didn't affect me.

Greta's dad is fully involved in her life and she has a younger brother, but she loves being at our house and there is a lot of estrogen around here. Mariah has never had a steady male in her life. She loved my stepdad, Brian—we all did—but she didn't know him very well since we lived away from Emerald. Far away. Sometimes I think we should have kept it that way.

"So you're staying for eighteen more days, and you're going to spend time with Scarlett," Greta says to Cian, pulling my attention back to our pizza party. "Our story is that you're a professor and your car broke down."

"Right," Cian confirms. "You're definitely part of the inner circle now."

Greta and Mariah share a grin. It's obvious how exciting they find that.

"What happens after the eighteen days?" Greta asks.

Cian's eyes lock on mine. "I get engaged."

Both girls gasp.

"*What*?" Mariah asks. Her eyes bounce between Cian and me

Cian sets down his piece of pizza and dusts his hands together. "That's the deal. I'm here because I'm supposed to get married in a couple of months. But I had to see your mom first. If we spend eighteen days together and end up being just friends, I go back to Cara and marry the woman my grandfather has picked."

Greta's eyes are enormous. "But what happens after eighteen days if you really like each other? What if you *don't* get over Scarlett?"

The corner of Cian's mouth curls up. He's looking at me again. "Then I think *Scarlett* should marry me."

The next gasp is even bigger and more dramatic than the first. I'm hoping they don't have food in their mouths or they might choke to death.

I look at him with wide eyes, but he's already grimacing. "Should I have not said that in front of your daughter?

You all kind of hang out as friends and for a second there I forgot..." He shrugs. "And it's what's on my mind."

"*Marrying Scarlett* is on your mind?" Greta asks.

He gives me a look that's *almost* but not quite apologetic. "Yeah," he admits.

I almost laugh. What am I supposed to do with him?

I look at Mariah, who is grinning like Cian just told her she can have four puppies, two ponies, and a new car for Christmas. "We talk about everything around here," I tell him. "Probably more than we should sometimes." I roll my eyes. "Like I *often* think about how my fifteen-year-old daughter and her best friend should probably *not* know about my weekend tryst with the undercover prince in New Orleans." I give the girls a pointed look.

They both just giggle.

"Yeah, she would have told me that you proposed anyway," Mariah tells Cian.

"He didn't *propose*," I say quickly.

"I *can*," he says. "If you'd like me to. There'd be a *big* ring." He gives Mariah a wink. "And a crown."

I shoot him a look that I know he knows means *knock it off*. He just grins.

Then he says to Mariah. "I just told your mom the situation with my grandfather and everything."

"That you need to get married. And that you really like *her*?" Mariah clarifies.

He nods. "Yeah."

Oh my God. Does he know what 'knock it off' means? I look at Henry. He just shakes his head. Which clearly means 'no, he doesn't'. Henry is a bit of a mind-reader, I think.

But I truly don't think that Cian O'Grady very often has thoughts, feelings, plans, or intentions that he isn't comfortable sharing out loud with whoever is around. Sure, he's used to keeping his true identity a secret, but his heart is on his sleeve. If I'd realized that in New Orleans, I would have also understood that I was being romanced by a real prince with real money and power way back then. Because it's becoming clear he didn't lie to me about a thing. That 'oh I intend to be your prince charming in every way and come to your rescue however you need me' was the full truth. Just like the 'I know it's crazy but I'm falling in love with you, Scarlett,' was how he truly believed he felt.

Those memories are doing me no favors. Especially when I'm able to conjure the exact timbre of his voice when he said it, and how his hands felt on my skin when he said it, and how good it freaking *felt* when he said it.

"Don't get all worked up," I tell Mariah and Greta. "Eighteen days is more than enough for Cian to realize that I am not princess material."

"But, *Mom*," Mariah says, leaning toward me. "You could *so* do that! I mean Abigail is the one that lives at the palace and has to do the official stuff."

She glances at Cian and he nods. I sigh.

"You wouldn't have to do that boring stuff or like wear dresses all the time or anything. But think of all the important people you'd meet!" Mariah gushes. "All the cool places you could go. And all the money you'd have! You could do so much charity work!" She leans further, her butt coming off her chair seat. "It would be *so, so cool!* Cian would be my stepdad!"

Greta is bouncing in her seat. "You would be a *princess!* Oh my God! Princess Mariah! That sounds *so great!*"

I can't even look at Cian. I give them both a frown. "Mariah, Greta, that's enough. This shouldn't be about Cian's money and title or you being a princess."

God, that is all so bizarre. What world am I in?

"No," Mariah says quickly. "I mean, yes, it would be awesome to be a princess and be able to *finally* prove to Leah that I wasn't lying about any of this. But—" She reaches out and grabs my arm. "I'm talking about the amazing things we could *do*. And the people we'd get to know! Look at Abigail! Her indoor farms are going to feed so many kids! And Princess Fiona saves endangered animals! And Linnea is working on green energy projects! And even Princess Saoirse has started doing some work as a spokesperson for a youth climate change group!"

I stare at my daughter. Then I look at Cian.

"Well, that's more because she knows a senator and he's big into climate change and wanted an enthusiastic young person who knows all about social media and doesn't have trouble talking in front of groups or on camera," Cian says. "Not so much because Saoirse is a princess."

Mariah looks at me with a "told you" look. "She knows a senator?" Mariah asks Cian.

"She does. One of her mom's friends is married to one of the senators from Louisiana. In fact, her bodyguard, Colin, also works for the senator."

Mariah looks at Greta and they both mouth *Oh. My. God* silently to one another.

I'm not surprised that she knows Cian's sister's name or even his niece's name, I suppose. I know them both because of the podcast and web searches I've done. But it sounds like Mariah knows things *about* them. And she's not just impressed with their relation to royalty. She's not talking about their clothes, or the private jets, or the palace in Cara that we got a look at through photos on the podcast's site. She's talking about the work they do.

I'm…proud of her. And I love her enthusiasm about the projects they're working on.

"I just—" I start.

"Oh!" Mariah cuts me off. "If Cian was my stepdad, *I* could do stuff like that!" Her eyes are round and she's nearly bouncing now. She turns to Cian, then back to Greta who is watching her as if Mariah has just announced that she is going to be on the next space mission. "Oh my *God*, I'm sure Linnea knows people who work for WHO!"

"Who?" Ruby asks.

"The World Health Organization," Mariah says. "I think I might want to be an infectious disease specialist and travel around the world helping with epidemics and stuff."

I look from my daughter to my sister. Ruby is watching Mariah with clear pride.

"You should totally do that," Ruby says. "You would be amazing at that."

"Or I might want to work on clean water initiatives," Mariah says. "Or building schools. Or I might stay here and run for President."

We all just grin at her.

Henry looks at Cian. "She and Saoirse are going to get along great."

Cian nods. "Not sure the world is ready, but we definitely need to get you two together."

Mariah looks thrilled.

I sigh. They're making plans. For the future. That involves Cian's family.

And I want to see these two girls together. Ugh.

"We'd be cousins, right?" Mariah asks. "If you and Mom get married."

Cian coughs and shifts on his chair. Oh, did someone

finally surprise *him*? He looks at me and gives me a slow smile.

"You would," he confirms. "And even if your mom and I didn't stay married, you would still be an O'Grady princess."

I frown. "What? How?"

Do not encourage him. But I tell myself that too late.

"Once a part of our family, always a part of our family," he says simply.

Henry nods.

"But that's not *legally* true," I feel the need to protest, for some reason.

"Oh, it will be," Cian says. "My grandfather and brother will love Mariah."

"What's that have to do with it?" I ask, leaning back in my chair and crossing my arms.

Henry chuckles and I look at him. He shrugs. "One of them will be the king. The king makes the laws in Cara. If they want her to keep her title, she will."

I roll my eyes. Royalty is so...weird.

But also, that's really nice.

"Really?" Mariah asks. "You think they'll love me?"

"Of course they will," Cian says.

"Definitely," Henry agrees.

Oh dammit. They're talking as if it's going to happen for sure. That she *will* meet these people. That they *will* love her. That Cian and I *will* be married.

"Like Brian with you and Ruby, Mom."

"Yeah, I know," I say past the tightness in my throat. Our stepfather, Brian, and our mother got married when we were eight and divorced when we were in high school, but he was still a part of our lives afterward. We saw him all the time, he came to all of our events, we went to his house for dinner once a week, and we knew we could call him anytime for any reason. And then he gave us this house and my business. Brian didn't stop being our stepfather just because he wasn't married to our mother.

Yeah. I definitely know.

"But…" Greta says, clearly working something through. "If Scarlett and Cian get married, and you become a princess, and everything… we can't tell anyone here."

"Why not?" Mariah demands. She shoots a look at Cian. "I swear I don't like you just because you're a prince, but I *would* want people to know."

He laughs. "I believe you."

Mariah turns back to Greta. "But why?"

"Because then they'll know we all lied to them about everything," Greta says. "That would be really bad."

Mariah slumps in her chair. "Ugh. We'd have to keep telling them he's a professor? And when we make trips to Cara, we have to make up someplace we're going for vacation? That sucks." She sits up. "What if the podcast talks about it though?"

"See?" I say. "This would be way too complicated."

No one even acknowledges me. Except Cian. Who just gives me a raised eyebrow.

"How are you going to keep telling people you're a professor?" Greta asks Cian. "You'll have to go to Columbus every day and pretend you're going to the college."

He laughs. "I don't know. I didn't think about that."

I roll my eyes. Imagine that.

"What are you *actually* going to do for work?" Greta says.

Cian shrugs. "I don't know."

"But how will you make money? You'll have to work somewhere that people in Emerald never go."

"I don't really need to make money," Cian says.

I roll my eyes *again*. Exactly and that is a big part of why we're *not* getting married.

"People will wonder," Greta says. "They wonder about *everything* in this town."

I look around the table, waiting for one of the grown-ups to suggest that we could move. It's all hypothetical anyway and not going to happen, but the idea of Mariah moving away would *kill* Greta. She'd think and worry about it every day for the next eighteen days.

Though she might just help me with my mission to turn Cian off of this whole idea...

"Linnea says she definitely knows people who work with W.H.O.," Henry says, holding his phone up.

Mariah's mouth falls open. "You just texted her? Just now?"

"Yeah."

"But... she's on her *honeymoon*!"

He laughs. "She wouldn't have answered if she couldn't."

"But it's like two in the morning in Cara!" Greta adds. Yes, she knows as much about Cian's family and home country as we do.

"She and Jonah are here in the states visiting his family," Henry says. "The podcast was right." He winks. "But don't tell anyone."

Mariah and Greta giggle. They are in heaven right now and I feel myself smiling just watching them. I'm going to have to talk to them about getting their expectations built up around me and Cian and everything, but I'll let them enjoy this for now.

My phone starts ringing, and I pull it from my pocket as Henry tells the girls about the time he met Jonah's parents.

Expecting to see my mother's name on my screen, I frown when it's a local number I don't recognize. But this happens all the time. I'm not the only mechanic in the area, but I am the only one right in Emerald.

"This is Scarlett," I say, standing up and stepping away from the table so I don't interrupt the conversation.

"Hi, Scarlett, it's Amanda Brown."

Amanda Brown is Mariah's principal. I try to keep my sigh inaudible. "Hi, Ms. Brown, what can I do for you?"

I'd responded to her email but, as with Hannah, I did not apologize for Mariah's words and I didn't make Mariah do so either.

"I'm actually hoping you have a phone number I need. I'm trying to get a hold of Dean Brady. They tell me you're fixing his car and I assume you have his number?"

I pause. Then I turn slowly back to face my kitchen table.

Where "Dean Brady" is laughing with my family over pizza.

"I do," I say. "I can give him the message to call you. I think that would be better than giving out his number without his consent."

Cian seems to sense my gaze on him and looks up. He gives me a smile that makes my stomach swoop. Why does he have to look so *good* in my kitchen with three of my favorite people in the world and my favorite pizza?

Yes, I like pineapple on my pizza *and* my chicken sandwiches.

"That would be great," Ms. Brown says. "Would you be able to do that right away? I need to speak to him about something that's a bit of an emergency."

I frown. How can the principal of my daughter's school

need to speak to Cian's fake persona about something that's an emergency?

"I'll text him right now. Maybe he'll be able to still call you tonight."

I'm going to make sure he calls her tonight. I have to know what this is about.

And if she's going to ask him out, to be her date to some 'last minute' function or something, I am going to...

I'm not sure. But I won't be happy.

Over the guy I don't want to date and cannot marry. Even though he did kind of ask me.

So there, Amanda.

"Thanks so much, Scarlett. I really appreciate it."

"You bet."

We disconnect and I walk to the table. "Amanda Brown, the high school principal, would like you to call her. She says it's a 'bit of an emergency'."

Cian straightens in his chair. "*Me?*"

"Well, Dean Brady."

Henry frowns. "What did you do? How could you have possibly gotten in trouble with the *principal* of the school here? How does she even know about you?"

"Because he introduced himself to the town at the *cafe*," Ruby says. "Nothing that happens there is ever a secret for more than five minutes. And you two are new to town. Of course people were paying attention."

It's amazing that no one recognizes Henry from past visits to Emerald, but honestly, every time he's been here, he's pretty much stayed here, with us.

Cian shakes his head. "No way am I in trouble. I've been with you every minute," he says to Henry.

"What's it about?" Henry asks me.

I shrug. "No idea." I totally sound normal and not at all too curious or, worse, jealous.

Everyone at the table is completely quiet, watching as Cian pulls his phone out. I hold my phone so he can see her number. He taps the numbers, then lifts his phone to his ear.

"Hi. Is this Amanda?"

His voice sounds flirty. Why does his voice sound flirty? I frown.

"Yes, this is Dean Brady. I understand you needed to get a hold of me?"

He pauses, listening. Then he looks surprised. Then he smiles. "I see. Well, that's very interesting."

It's *interesting* that she needs him to escort her to her niece's wedding this weekend? Amanda is easily ten years older than Cian. Hell, *I'm* six years older than him.

God, I'm six years older than this young, hot prince who thinks he's in love with me and thinks maybe we should just get married if he still likes me at the end of eighteen days.

"Yes, definitely," he says to Amanda.

Yes? He said *yes?*

"I'm glad you thought to ask me," he tells her. "I'll see you tomorrow."

He disconnects and I just stare at him.

I guess I thought the eighteen days we'd be spending together would be *monogamous* days. But, we didn't really specify that, did we? And I'm the one fighting the idea. Why am I upset about this?

"She wants me to substitute teach at the high school," he says, grinning.

That takes a little too long to sink in for me, so it's Henry that responds first.

"Substitute *teach*?"

"Yep. She heard about my history and poli-sci degrees, and it turns out that their history teacher is having some kind of hernia repair? They're expecting him to be out two to three weeks."

"Wow," Ruby says. "Just like that? They hear some guy is in town and they'll let him teach the kids for *three* weeks?"

"Well, I have a degree," Cian says, looking mildly offended. "And I assume they'll do a background check." He looks at Henry. "We have all of that in the system for Dean, right?"

"Yeah," Henry says. He glances at Ruby. "It's legit. Cian's fine. Perfectly safe to work around kids."

She laughs. "I'm not questioning that. I'm more curious about how he thinks he can teach history for three weeks."

"He can totally teach high school history for a few weeks," Henry says. "He's overqualified in fact."

"Well, I need to get a substitute teaching license and do employment paperwork, but I'm going in tomorrow to do all of that. Amanda said they'll help me with it and fast track it. They're in a tight spot here, so she's confident they can get it all approved before next Monday."

Ruby and I exchange a look.

"You're going to be able to fake it for *three weeks*?" I finally say. "I mean, one day, maybe. But you'll have to actually teach them something."

"That's Mr. Emerson," Greta says. "Me and Mariah have him."

I look at Cian. "You cannot *fake teach* my daughter, Cian."

He grins. "I'm going to teach them so much cool shit, I will be their favorite teacher *ever* and someone in that class will go on to major in world history just because of me."

"But—" Ruby starts.

"He actually has the degree," Henry says.

"What degree?" Ruby asks.

"The world history major. And the poli sci major. He's also got a few minors. And speaks French and Spanish along with English and Irish."

Ruby and I look at each other again, then look at Cian.

"You have a degree in world history?" I ask.

"Of course," he says. "Love history. Though to be fair, the classes were very easy. I knew so much of it before I even got to college here in the US. Cara's education system is vastly superior to the American system."

"Why did you get so many degrees?" Mariah asks.

He shrugs. "Kept waiting to find The One."

"The one what?"

"The spark. The *thing*. That thing that I was just born to do. So I tried a bunch of different things. And by the time I realized I wasn't going to find it in college, I'd collected enough hours for a few degrees."

I stare at him.

I had no idea he'd *actually* gone to college. I don't know why that surprises me. And I feel kind of bad that it does.

"So you're going to be my *teacher* and maybe my *stepdad* and you *are* a prince and I can't tell anyone that I even *know you*?" Mariah says.

But Cian and Henry are either used to young woman dramatics or they have just already figured Mariah and Greta out because they just nod, grinning, and say, "Yep."

She tips her head back. "This is so unfair!"

Mariah has no idea about unfair.

Unfair is having the man who gave me the *best* sex I'd

ever even imagined, who also listens and shares the connections with his family that I feel with mine, and who makes me feel brilliant and creative and inspiring sitting *right there*...and not trusting myself to reach out and take what he is offering.

But I've been spontaneous three times in my life. Three times I followed my gut and just went for it, selfishly letting my *feelings* lead me instead of my head.

And three times there were bad consequences. Not just for me, but for people I cared about, too.

So no, no matter how tempting Cian is, no matter how amazing he seems, I'm not going to let my feelings lead me here. It's all about my head and being rational and doing the common-sense thing.

Which is definitely *not* marrying the handsome prince with the great laugh who is completely pulling off the hot teacher vibe.

Definitely not.

Though if he keeps making my daughter and her best friend gasp and lean in and laugh as he shares facts and stories about world history in a naturally compelling and almost joyful style, I might have to tattoo DEFINITELY NOT on the back of one of my hands so I'll remember it.

CHAPTER 11
CIAN

"Hey, Greta, wait a second," I hear Scarlett say.

I need to get Scarlett alone so I'm hovering in the doorway between the living room and kitchen. I'm eavesdropping too, obviously, but this group is pretty open about sharing the things going on so I don't feel bad. Well, I don't feel *too* bad.

I'm just so fucking curious about *everything* having to do with Scarlett. I want to know it all.

"Yeah?"

"Do you know that someone is offering a hundred dollars to whoever gets Mariah to go to church youth group?"

"Yeah. Actually, it's to church or youth group or any church gathering at all," Greta says.

"Gotcha."

I can tell Scarlett is trying to sound calm.

"Do you know who's making the offer?"

"Yeah," Greta says. "Pastor Stevens."

"Yeah, that's what I heard too." Scarlett pauses. "Does Mariah know?"

Greta's voice is softer when she answers, "Yeah."

"And how does she feel about it?"

"Honestly?"

"Yes. Please."

"Okay, but don't be mad."

I feel myself frowning.

"Okay," Scarlett says slowly.

"At first, she thought, or hoped I guess, that it was her grandpa's way of getting her attention. Maybe getting a chance to spend time with her."

There's a long beat of silence before Scarlett asks, "Did she want that to be the reason?"

"I think so, kind of. But she's over that now."

"Over what exactly?"

"Over hoping he cares about her. She knows he doesn't. She figures it's either his way of messing with you, or his way of proving something to the other kids. Maybe that he really does have a lot of power or something? I guess he told them that it's a lesson in how difficult ministry can be sometimes. He's exposing them to people who the devil has worked really hard on."

I feel rage tighten my gut. Anyone who would say that the devil is working in a child is a piece of shit. But a man who would use his granddaughter that way? No matter what kind of family history is going on here, that is messed up.

Regardless of the feelings I might have about my grandfather and his manipulations, he would never say something like that. And if he did, he would be immediately denounced by the rest of the family, friends, probably our entire country.

Scarlett has been quiet for several seconds. Now she asks, "What made her realize that?"

"We saw him downtown one day. It was just us and him on the sidewalk. And he walked past her without even looking at her. It was like she didn't exist. She figured if he was actually interested in her, he would've taken that chance to try to talk to her himself. Ask her to come to church himself. Obviously whatever he's doing has to do with her having to interact with these other kids. She doesn't like that it's a whole big game to him. And she hates the way Leah and the other kids from church act. She said the idea that the way they behave and treat other people is the way to persuade her, or anyone, that they want to spend time with them in that church is ridiculous."

I agree, wholeheartedly, and wish I could see Scarlett's face right now.

"Exactly right," Scarlett finally answers. "They use manipulation and guilt and lies to get people to do what they want. Instead of just living good, happy, generous lives that might pull people closer. But," she sighs. "I fell for it. For a long time. So I'm not really someone who can judge others. I am so glad Mariah has you. And that she's smart enough to see through all of that."

"Well, she definitely has me," Greta says. "And you and Ruby are great role models for being strong and independent."

"Good. We don't always get it right, but I'm glad we're mostly doing okay."

They both laugh.

"But it sounds like she kind of wanted to know her grandpa? Or at least wanted him to want to know her?"

"What she said to me before is that she doesn't need a dad or grandfather. She just sometimes wishes that not everyone knew who hers are and all the drama around them. She just wishes that if she had to have one, that he was a good guy."

"Trust me," Scarlett says. "I get how complicated that can be."

"Thanks for letting me be here and involved in all of this drama," Greta says. I can hear the smile in her voice. "Mariah is the best friend I've ever had. I know it sucks here for you sometimes, but I'm so glad she's here. And I think I make things better for her."

"You *definitely* do," Scarlett says.

I love how close Scarlett and Ruby obviously are with Greta and how comfortable she clearly feels here. It reminds me of my own family and how Henry and the other bodyguards have become part of the family, not because of blood, but because of love. I also experience it tenfold in Louisiana with the Landrys. People who can make family out of anyone are special.

"I hope some of this works out for you," Greta says. "You deserve to have some fun and happiness here too."

I feel something twist in my chest. Does Scarlett not have fun and happiness here? I have the insane urge to step out and say, 'let me take care of that'. Fun and happiness I can do. The frustration and possessiveness are new to me, but fun? That's my specialty.

"Well, you know you're part of the family," Scarlett sighs. "I can't imagine you not knowing about all of this."

"I can't believe I have to tell you this," Greta says. "But you should definitely let the hot rich guy treat you like a princess for a little while even if you don't want to be one long term."

Yeah, I really like Greta.

Scarlett gives a laugh. "I think it's time for you to go home now."

Greta laughs. "Okay. But you know you'll see me tomorrow."

I hear the back door open and shut and make my move. I step into the kitchen. Scarlett does not seem surprised to see me.

"Hey," she greets as she finishes putting clean dishes into the cupboards.

I hand over the surprise I have for her.

It's a bag of saltwater taffy, her favorite candy when we were in New Orleans. The way she ate them, they were either already her favorites, and again, a truth she shared with me, or they were her sister's favorite, and Scarlett realized how good they were while pretending to be Ruby.

She takes them. "You remembered."

"I remember every single minute we spent together."

Her smile dies, and she swallows hard.

"Do you like these? For real?" I ask.

She nods and presses the package against her chest. "Yes. I love them."

Perfect. Day two and I've already found more things that were true than weren't.

"Come out on the patio with me," I say. I don't mean for it to sound like a command. I meant to request spending some time alone with her. But it definitely sounded a little demanding.

Still, she nods. "We need to spend time together, right? Only eighteen days to totally turn you off."

Yeah. Right. Can't forget that.

She turns to the refrigerator and pulls out two bottles of iced tea. She holds one up with a questioning look, and I nod. She tucks them under her arm, with the bag of taffy, and heads for the door that leads to the patio. I follow.

She sets the drinks and candy on the wrought iron table that sits between two chairs that are covered in thick outdoor cushions. She rounds the set of chairs and goes to the fire pit sitting a few feet in front of them. She grabs the box of matches, strikes one of the long wooden sticks against the side, and leans in to light the fire.

Once it's going, we both settle into the chairs and watch the flames for a few minutes.

I'm not even sure what to say first. There are so many thoughts, so many topics, so many questions. But then I start with the one that's really eating at me.

"Tell me about Pastor Stevens. This whole church thing. And you being the mean girl in high school."

Again, she doesn't seem surprised. She lifts her bottle of tea for a sip, then starts.

"My mom came to Emerald when she was twenty-one. She planned to just visit for a weekend or so, but the first night she was in town, she met a guy at the bar. They had a hot one-night stand. She left town two days later and didn't see him again, until she came back to town to tell him she was pregnant."

She leans over and grabs a piece of taffy, unwrapping it and putting it in her mouth. She chews for a moment. "He was not excited to see her," she continues. "He'd wanted just one night partly because he was starting a church here in town. And because he was engaged."

She swallows. "Obviously a one-night stand with a stranger that ends up with a baby out of wedlock isn't a great look for a young pastor. Or for a guy who's engaged to another woman. A woman who, by the way, had been saving herself for marriage."

My brows rise, but I say nothing. The story is good, I have to admit. Lots of drama already.

"So this young pastor, who is starting a church from the ground up, somehow manages to write my mother a two hundred and fifty thousand dollar check so she can go wherever she wants to. He tells her she can keep the baby. Or not. It was her choice. As long as she leaves town, never comes back, and does not name him on the birth certificate." She takes another sip of tea. "The thing about one-night stands," she says, sliding me a look. "Is that you usually don't really know the other person very well. He had no idea what kind of person my mom was. But he quickly found out. She took his money, bought a house here in town, gave birth to his twin baby girls, and raised them right here, where he'd see them often and everyone would know they were his."

Wow. I don't say anything because I have no idea what to say. I also know there's a lot more to this story. I reach for a piece of taffy, unwrap it, and pop it in my mouth. Before Scarlett came into my life, I had never had salt-water taffy. She'd declared that a travesty. Now it's one of my favorite things. But I know that's entirely about the memories it invokes rather than the candy itself.

"Let me guess," I say. "He denied you were his?"

"Oh no." Scarlett lets out a laugh that doesn't sound entirely forced. Almost as if she finds this legitimately funny. "He admitted we were his. Up in front of his whole congregation. Used us as proof that the devil is hard at work all the time and that even the best people can be tempted. But that they can rise up. They can walk away from temptation and go forward with a good life."

I turn to stare at her. "You're telling me that he walked

away from you and Ruby and your mom and used that as proof that he's a *good* guy? Used it in his *ministry*?"

She doesn't look at me, but she nods. "Yup. I'm not sure *everyone* bought that my mom was sent by the devil to test him because he was building a church and Satan wanted his downfall, but enough people did. His fiancée did. She married him anyway. And his church continued to grow." She shifts on her chair as if uncomfortable. "In fact, it worked so well, he continued to use us over the years. He would point to us as an example of his punishment. How even though he'd rejected Satan, he still had to face what he'd done every day and that kept him honest and close to God."

I can't believe this. What the *fuck*? Two little girls and the woman who'd done nothing but fall for his lines and bullshit were his *punishment from God*?

"He also always pointed my mom out as an example of why mothers should never want to be single. Why it's important to have fathers around. Why women need to be responsible and not promiscuous." She takes a sip of tea.

Again, I have no idea what to say, but this time it is because rage is clogging my throat.

"Then my mom met Brian, my stepdad. She never really let my dad get to her, but I do think she thought he would back off once she and Brian were married. Because according to his preaching, my mom was doing it right getting a man involved." Scarlett shakes her head.

She's still not looking at me. Clearly, she's seeing all of these people—her mom, her stepfather, her dad.

"But my dad actually criticized *Brian*. He said other men shouldn't step in and make things easier. Women who choose to have sex before they're married have to face the consequences and deserve the struggles of single parent-hood as their punishment."

I sit forward, my heart pounding as anger courses through me. "And there are people in this town who believe this? Who follow him?" My voice is tight.

She looks over at me. "Absolutely. "

"Why?" I demand. "Why would anyone believe any of that bullshit?"

"It makes them feel superior." Her voice is calm.

I feel like I could put my fist through a wall.

"It makes them feel accepted into a community that tells them they're better than people who make mistakes and have to struggle. The church is also full of the powerful people in this community. The past two mayors, the past two sheriffs, most of the city council, a lot of our county government officials, the state legislative representative for this area. Lots of people in power go to that church which gives it legitimacy. At least to some people."

I shove up from my chair, pacing to the end of the patio and back. "You do know how fucked up that is, right? Your mom was not wrong. She didn't deserve to be punished for anything." I stop right in front of her chair. "Neither do you. Neither does my sister. Neither do any of the women who are raising kids on their own."

She sighs. "Of course I know that, Cian. But you wanted the story. And it gets worse."

I stare down at her. "Worse?"

"Well, *I* became a single mom. And there were some pretty shitty times before that even."

I don't want to hear this. I have lived my very privileged life, male, wealthy, able to do whatever I wanted and rarely facing consequences. The ones I have faced have been softened by my family and Henry. Hearing about other people not having advantages always stabs me in the gut. It always makes me wish that I knew how to do something about it.

It was why Scarlett coming into my life with a fully formed plan that I could immediately implement seemed like such a gift. One that I had jumped on. One that I had fallen in love with.

Now I am wondering how much of my emotion for her is truly wrapped up in that idea she gave me. Maybe it's all just that. And great sex. Because the sex was really fucking great.

Eighteen days to really get to know her, to find out if what I feel is about *her*, or just about the plan that finally gave me a purpose, is a really good idea, I realize.

I return to my chair and drop into it. "Hit me," I tell her. "Tell me all the terrible things."

"So my mom raised us without my father. But we always knew who he was. And we definitely were shunned by the people in the church, and their kids at school. But there was half the town who didn't buy his bullshit, so we had friends. But then when I was twelve, after Brian had been in our lives for about four years, I decided that I would really like to know my real father. I don't really know why, exactly, but one day it just hit me. I was sitting in math class, and I suddenly decided that it was time I got to know him. I showed up on his doorstep that evening after dinner and told him that. And I asked if that was possible."

Scarlett sits back in her chair and tips her head up to look at the sky.

I brace myself. She told me the story was going to get worse. I already hate her father so much that I'm very afraid I may drive over to the man's house tonight after she tells me the rest of what happened.

"He said yes," she continues. "But I had to start coming to church. I had to become someone he was proud to call a daughter. And I agreed. I wanted to get to know him, I wanted his approval. I can't explain it other than to say I was a twelve-year-old girl. My mom was awesome, Brian was awesome. It was not a rebellion against them. And I probably will never totally forgive myself for rejecting them that way."

She turns her head to look at me. "But I started going to his church and youth group, doing everything he told me to do, buying into all the stuff that he told me. How to be a good follower, how to be someone he was proud of, how to live the right kind of life. And I bought into all of this stuff that he is apparently pressing on the other kids now. That we had to minister to the other kids at school, that we had to bring them to church, that if we could save them, we were saving ourselves."

She takes a deep breath, then blows it out. She's quiet for several seconds.

"The project that he gave me was Ruby. I was supposed to bring Ruby around to God and our father's church."

I can hear the emotion in her voice now. She's on the verge of tears, it's clear.

"Did it work?" I ask gently. I have a suspicion I know the answer already.

She gives a soft laugh. "No. In fact, it became a huge wedge between us and I ended up moving out of my mom's house and going to live with my dad. I spent my years from age twelve to nineteen judging everyone else, including my family, trying to get the other kids to come to church and live the way we thought they should live. And I was mean. To the other kids, especially the girls, and very judgmental."

"Does that include Hannah?" I guess.

"No, actually. Hannah was another church girl. She was actually the favorite girl until I came along. She always resented me. We had kind of a weird competition going on. But she didn't really start hating me until the summer after we graduated from high school. Because I stole the new, cute church guy before she had a chance at him."

I sit forward again, too restless to relax.

"Toward the end of our senior year, Eli came to town. He was finishing college, was going to be a pastor and wanted to study under my father as our church's youth pastor. He was cute, he started flirting with me, and I fell head over heels. It all seemed perfect. Eli was going to be my father's right-hand man at the church and I assumed that would mean that my father would approve of me even more. Eli and I would be together, get married, serve in the church right beside my father." She stops and swallows. "But we ended up getting pregnant."

The words hit me in the chest like a lead ball. Of course I should've guessed that's where this was going.

"I was honestly happy. I figured we would just get married sooner because of the baby. But I didn't think it would change anything. I think maybe Eli thought so too. But when we went to tell my father we wanted to get married, he was suspicious. We confessed about the pregnancy and…" She has to swallow again. "My father decided that we were the perfect sacrificial lambs."

I look at her, frowning hard. "What the fuck does that mean?"

"My father decided to tell his entire congregation, really the whole town, that we had slept together before being married and were now pregnant. That was our punishment. And he used us as an example to show his congregation that it didn't matter who stepped out of line, there would still be consequences. If he could reject Eli and me, he would reject anyone. It was his chance to make his followers even more committed, and let's face it, scared of him. So he fired Eli and made him leave town, and he kicked me out of the church and his house."

"Motherfucker." I stare at her. "I hate your father."

She gives me a small smile. "In retrospect, he did me a favor. At the time it didn't feel that way, though. Eli tucked his tail between his legs and ran. He didn't even talk to me again after that meeting with my father."

"What happened? You were on your own?"

"No." She looks at me, her eyes shining with tears in the firelight. "Ruby heard about it before I could do anything. She called me and said she was coming to get me. Ten minutes later she was at my dad's house, carrying my shit out to the car and forcing me into the front seat. Not that she really had to force me. Then she took me home. She and my mom took me back in without a second thought. Even though I didn't deserve it."

Her voice breaks then and I can see a tear slip down her cheek.

"Brian even came over. He and my mom had already divorced—of course my dad made a big deal out of that as did I, because I was a huge pain in the ass bitch. But Brian was there for me too. I stayed with them through the pregnancy until I had Mariah. Then Ruby and I moved out. We went to Chicago first. Then Kansas City. Then Nashville. Then New Orleans. We just kept moving a little farther and a little farther away."

I swallow hard. I don't even know what emotion I'm swallowing down at this point. There is rage, there's hatred, there is an intense urge to find her father and do *very* unChristian-like things to him. But there is also a nearly overwhelming urge to reach over and pull her into my lap.

So that's what I do.

CHAPTER 12

CIAN

To my shock and absolute pleasure, Scarlett lets me pull her into my lap. I lean against the back cushion, wrap my arms around her, and just hold her.

She pulls her feet up to rest on the seat of the chair and seems to curl up.

"Thank you," I murmur against her hair after a moment.

"For what?"

I run my hand up and down her back. "For letting me hold you like this."

She huffs out a soft laugh. "I should thank you."

"This is the first time I've felt like maybe I'm helping you by being here."

She leans in against me more fully. "If you need to feel that, let me tell you, you are. Having someone want to be around me, want to be this close to me, is nice. It's been a while. Besides Ruby and Mariah and Greta of course. It's pretty..."

I work on not tensing up underneath her. "It's pretty what?"

"Lonely."

Jesus. My heart clenches.

"Where's your mom?"

"She moved to Phoenix about ten years ago to be closer to some girlfriends. She was just...over this town." She sighs heavily. "I don't blame her. She and Brian stayed in touch though. They were still friends, so when he got sick, they talked about plans. She knew he planned to leave me and Ruby the house and business. Mom wanted him to just sell it all and give us the money. She's actually still a little annoyed with him for doing it this way. But he wanted us to have the chance to come back and have a second chance here if we wanted it. If we didn't, or we try it and it doesn't work, we can always sell. But the fact that he wanted to give us that chance made me want to try."

He gave them choices. That's great. But I think I'm on Judy's side here.

"Let me take you away from this," I say. I probably sound like I'm begging. But I will.

She gives a soft sigh. "I can't."

"I can take both you and Mariah away. Ruby too. Mariah would have a whole family to support her. A very cool cousin that she'd love. Grandparents she could be proud of. A grandmother who would love on her." I take a breath. "Let me give you the family and community you need."

She's quiet in my arms. When she finally speaks, she breaks my heart. "I want to make up for how I was before, Cian. I want them to forgive me."

I wait a few beats. I should let this go. We're just getting to know each other. But, in the end, I can't. "You can't make people forgive you. You can just be the person you want to be now. If they don't see it, or won't let the past go, that's on them."

She doesn't say anything.

"Do *you* forgive yourself?" I ask.

She's quiet and I think she's not going to answer me. Finally though, she says, "I'm not sure."

I tighten my arms around her. "That's all that matters. Just work on that."

She wiggles and I loosen my hold. I don't want her to get up, but I can't force her to stay on my lap.

But instead of pushing off my lap, she turns, straddling my thighs.

"I..." She stops, her gaze bouncing back and forth between my eyes. Then she mutters something that sounds like, "Fuck it," and leans in and kisses me.

Thank God. Fuck yes.

Those are the words that go through my mind. I need her mouth on me. I need her hands on me. I need to touch her, feel her, smell her, taste her. I struggle to keep control and let her lead this, but *damn* it takes everything I've got.

It feels like she's exploring. Her lips are soft, seeking. She pulls back, tips her head, then comes back at the kiss from a new angle.

She strokes my shoulders, my neck, down over my chest.

I want to growl, but I keep that inside too somehow.

Finally, she lifts her head. She stares at me for a few beats. "I've missed you," she finally says.

Fuck. That almost stops my heart. I'm not surprised by the sentiment, but I am surprised she admits it.

My hands are now resting on the outer curve of her ass.

I squeeze her. "I've been dying slowly without you." I can't *not* say that.

She gives a breathy groan. It sounds a little exasperated. And a little turned on. She starts to say something, then seems to think better of it, and instead leans in, pressing her mouth to mine again.

I let her lead the kiss for a few seconds. I don't know if she just wants a sweet connection and just getting reacquainted, or if she needs something more.

I want to consume her. I want to wrap myself around her and not let her go for days. Maybe weeks. I want to tell her I love her. I want to get down on one knee. I want to beg her to let me take care of her.

But I also know that I can't push her. I'm here to stay for the next couple of weeks, but how close she lets me get is up to her in large part. I will press every advantage. I am not too proud to admit that. I can be a gentleman when the occasion calls for it, but I'm not so sure that's the right approach with the woman in my lap. Scarlett needs to be pursued. She needs to be wanted. I sensed that even in New Orleans. She loved my words, hearing how much I wanted her, being praised. She responded every single time. But now that I know more about her past and her situation here, I realize it's even more important.

Which works out well, because I don't think I could leave her alone for anything. I fully intend to pursue her until she tells me to back the hell off. And means it.

She pulls back and studies me again, breathing a little faster now.

Her hand runs over my jaw. "I miss your beard. But you're really handsome like this too. You look younger though."

I lift a brow. "Is that a good or a bad thing?"

She presses her lips together. "I should probably say bad, but I don't think it is."

I bring her forward, making sure she feels my hard cock. "Because you think you're seducing me again?"

She nods.

"Scarlett."

I make sure her eyes are locked on mine.

"No one's manipulating anyone. No one's tricking anyone. I know exactly where I am, why I'm here, and what I want." I pause. "How about you? Are you here of your free will?"

She nods.

"And what do you need from me?" I ask gruffly.

If she pushes back, gets up, and goes inside, I will let her go. For now. But I'm going to try to make that a difficult decision.

She kept me waiting, wanting, searching for months. For the last two months, she's known where I have been and that I wanted her. For longer she's known who I am and where I am and she still kept herself away from me.

I should punish her for that. Make her needy and desperate.

I shouldn't let her know she has all the power here.

But she absolutely does.

"You," she finally says. "Having you here feels good. *You* make me feel good. I..." She trails off and swallows.

I just wait. My whole body feels tight, stretched thin, waiting for her to finish that sentence.

"I forgot how good you make me feel. Not just physically, but just in general. I actually pushed it away because I didn't want to remember. Because it made me miss you like hell. But now, I can't... resist it."

Jesus.

I can't do it. I can't keep anything from her. Especially myself.

"I will give you whatever you need. Anything you want," I tell her, my voice rough.

She pulls her bottom lip between her teeth, clearly battling with herself.

She must make some decision in that beautiful head of hers because she blows out a breath and leans in, kissing me again.

This one's different.

Her fingers curl into my scalp, she presses the middle seam of her shorts against my fly, moaning sweetly into my mouth.

As I grip her tighter and press her closer, she opens her mouth.

And that's it. The tiny bit of resolve I had crumbles. The fire ignites and we're both gone.

Our tongues stroke, our breathing quickens, and our hands roam.

I slide my hand up under her shirt, searching for bare skin.

I stroke up and down her back as her hands slip under my shirt, gripping my sides, kissing me deep, making delicious noises as she grinds against me.

I work my hand under the elastic sports bra she's wearing and slide around to the front, covering her bare breast in my hand, squeezing, my thumb teasing over her hard nipple.

She pulls her mouth away from mine. "Cian." She rests her forehead against mine.

"What do you need?" I ask. "You can ask me for anything."

"More," she says simply.

I pull my head back to look at her, still teasing her nipple.

"Do you need to come? It's been a long time. Do you need an orgasm, little witch? Has this magical pussy missed me?"

She sucks in a breath and when I think that possibly this is where she will push away, she nods.

I smile with satisfaction. "Fingers or cock?"

Her eyes widen slightly, but it's only because she's forgotten how I talk. She quickly remembers.

"Out here?" she asks.

She's not protesting. I know she's asking if I can assure her this is okay. The way she let me take the lead during sex in New Orleans was one of the biggest fucking turn-ons of my life. She was eager, vocal, happy to give me words, but also beautifully submissive. She loved having me take charge and lead the way.

"No one will come out here. It's just you and me," I tell her.

I know that Ruby and Henry will not venture out here. I also know that Henry will keep Mariah from coming out here. I'm certain my friend knows that even if I'm not getting Scarlett naked, we are talking about things Mariah doesn't need to hear.

Besides, Mariah's not stupid. I don't think she would be surprised, or appalled, if she found out what me and her mom were doing out here. She'd probably be thrilled, actually.

Still, it's not something any of them need to witness.

"Cock," Scarlett says softly.

If I wasn't already sitting, my knees would've given out.

I did not intend to fuck her when I came out here. But there's no way I'm passing it up.

Yes, maybe we should take this slower, but it's been nineteen fucking months. This is the woman I want more than I want anything else. If the sex was all that was really real between us—and I'm not at all convinced that's true—then I definitely want that. I want her to remember that. I want to imprint that on her in every way I can as soon as possible.

I run my hand up her back into her hair and then slowly twist her hair around my hand. I hold her still and bring her face in closer to mine. "I should make you beg for my cock. You're the reason we've both been without this for so long."

She sucks in a little breath. "I know," she says.

She does not apologize, however.

I file away the idea of making her really beg for later. I think she'd like it. She was *very* dirty for me in New Orleans.

For now I say, "How about a little please, Scarlett?"

She wets her lips, and her mouth focuses on mine. "Please."

"Please fill me up with your cock and make me come, Cian," I command.

"Please fill me up with your cock and make me come, Cian," she says obediently.

Oh, yes, she remembers how we were together.

She loved just letting go, letting me boss her around. I realize now that she has so much weight on her shoulders —being a mom, her work, her past—it probably felt good to just surrender to the pleasure.

Now that weight is all even heavier. This town, her reputation, her regrets and guilt, Mariah's issues at school...

I know what Scarlett needs.

I tug on her hair, tipping her head back and pressing my

mouth to her neck. I nip her throat then lick over the spot. "Has anyone ever made you come in this town?"

"No." She's already practically panting.

I wasn't sure what to expect with that question. This is, after all, where she grew up and went to high school, where she got pregnant with Mariah.

"Oh, that's right. You were such a good girl, weren't you?"

She tries to nod, but I'm holding her hair too tightly. "Yes," she says softly.

"Did you keep your legs together until Mariah's dad?" I ask against her throat, dragging my mouth up and down the smooth expanse. It's not as gratifying without my beard. I won't leave behind the whisker burns I would have otherwise. Still, I love the feel of her skin against my mouth.

I feel her swallow.

"Yes," she says.

"And I'll bet he had to take you out on sweet dates, buy you flowers, act like a real gentleman to get his hand into those pristine white panties, didn't he?"

She squirms on my lap. "Yes."

I slide my hand down, cupping her through her shorts, pressing the heel of my hand against her clit, rubbing. "Did he make you come?"

"No," she gasps.

I lift my head. I rub her more firmly and feel her pressing into my hand. No? He hadn't made her come? Oh, I fucking like that. And that probably makes me an asshole. "How many were between him and me?"

"Two," she says, her voice ragged. "And only one made me come." She sucks in a breath as I press harder. "And it was nothing like you."

I rub her faster. "Did you ride them, Scarlett? Has

anyone else bent you over and fucked you from behind after he spanked your perfect little ass? Did any of them eat this delicious pussy until you were screaming and then keep going until you were sobbing?"

Her fingers dig into my sides, and she tries to shake her head. "No. God, no. None of that. Not until you."

Fuck. I'm going to lose it right here without even getting her naked.

I nip her throat again a little harder. "Even if you're lying, you know exactly what to say to make me fuck you really well, don't you, my gorgeous witch?"

"You always fuck me really well. But I'm not lying."

I pull back and look at her. "You let me finger you in an elevator. You let me push you up against the door of a hotel, strip you down, and eat you right there. You *begged* for my cock."

"I know."

"Because that was the real you, wasn't it? That's what you *really* want and need. Being spanked, and bossed, and called a good girl and a dirty girl, and being spread out and absolutely worshipped from head to toe."

She stares at me. My hand is cupping her pussy. I can feel how hot and wet she is through the fabric of her shorts. She's breathing like she just ran four blocks. Every single memory of our weekend together is pinging back and forth between us.

Is she going to lie?

Finally, she whispers, "Yes."

I reward her with a squeeze between her legs. "Can you be quiet? I love making you scream, but we are on your back patio with people inside and neighbors who might have their windows open."

"I don't know," she says, honestly.

I nod. "Good answer." I let go of her hair and slip my hand from between her legs. I nudge her back. "Take your shorts off."

CHAPTER 13

SCARLETT

I scoot back off of Cian's lap and stand in front of him.

Adrenaline and lust are dumping into my system in equal portions and every single nerve ending in my body is firing.

I can't believe I'm doing this.

I'm outside on my back patio. My daughter and sister and Henry are inside.

I have neighbors on both sides of my back fence and Mrs. Arnold lives behind me.

But I don't care.

Of course, I don't think any of them can really see anything, even if they did happen to look out the right window just now. It's dark, there are trees, the patio is surrounded by bushes and potted plants on one side, and the neighbor's garage on the other. It's also late and I know Mrs. Arnold is in bed.

But even if they could see us, I don't care.

Cian makes me like this. He did this to me in New

Orleans too. I put off moving to Ohio for two full days because of him.

But...fuck it.

Things have kind of sucked here for the past, well, as long as we've been back and... honestly, for a long time when we lived here the first time too. I want a good memory here. I want *good* feelings. And this man? The one sitting in front of me watching me like I'm actually magical and amazing, the man who has been looking for me for nineteen months, the man who claims he hasn't been with anyone else since he was with me, *because* of me... yeah, he can make me not care about anything else and can *absolutely* make me feel good.

I hook my thumbs in the waistband of my shorts and push them and my panties down, stepping out of them. I'm not sure where they end up, because my eyes are glued to Cian and the way he grips the arms of the chair as I strip.

I think he memorized every inch of my body in New Orleans, but I still feel like I'm undressing for him for the first time.

All of that time with him in New Orleans ratchets up my excitement. He knows exactly what I want and need. I never realized sex could be like it was with Cian. I thought I was spending the night with a hot younger guy who would just be excited about getting laid and it would be a one and done. I'd *hoped* for an orgasm but hadn't really been betting on it.

But he was bossy and patient and all about me. He made me come three times before he fucked me the first time. He seemed to get enormous pleasure from my orgasms. He also loved telling me what to do.

I'd loved that too.

It was strangely a relief. I didn't have to perform. I

didn't have to have the right words. I didn't have to have any answers or worry about how things were for him.

He told me. Bluntly, graphically, over and over how things were for him. And what he wanted from me. And what he wanted to do to me, what he wanted me to do to him. Hell, what he wanted me to do to myself.

It was amazing. I could just shut my brain off and follow his lead and enjoy.

And oh, had I enjoyed. That had been heavenly.

And yes, it had resulted in me being more open and vulnerable with him than I was with anyone other than Ruby.

"Are you cold?" Cian asks.

The fire pit is about five feet behind me, the orange flames lighting the area in a soft glow but keeping us mostly in shadow.

"The very opposite of cold."

"Then I need to see all of you," he tells me.

I have never been naked in my backyard. I've never even been out here in a swimming suit. But I don't hesitate to peel off my t-shirt and then sports bra, tossing them to the chair beside Cian's.

"Come here."

I step forward.

He unzips his pants and lowers his jeans and boxers. I watch as he draws his hard cock out, stroking the length firmly.

I remember how well he filled me, how it felt to have him hammering into me, one of my legs thrown over his shoulder. I also remember how it felt to have him moving slowly and deeply as he looked into my eyes. I shiver. The sex had been intense, not just because of the size of his cock and how well he used it, but because of *him*. And yes, the connection between us, dammit.

"I've thought of you every damned night, Scarlett," he tells me, his voice rough.

He looks frustrated about that, maybe even a little angry.

I swallow. "Me too."

"Do you know how hard it is to resist the urge to throw you over my shoulder, get on my plane, fly to Cara, and tie you to my bed until you agree to marry me?" he asks.

My eyes widen. But not because of his words. I'm startled by how my heart flips and starts pounding.

I do *not* want that.

But it sure as hell is nice to have someone want me that much.

Yeah, yeah, the pathetic side of me that has been trying to be good but has had approval withheld since I was a little girl is a loud bitch sometimes.

"Is kidnapping legal in Cara?" I ask, trying to sound flippant and flirty.

"Everything is legal for the royal family."

I give him a half smile. "That doesn't sound right."

He shrugs. "Come here and make it up to me and maybe we won't need to worry about kidnapping and the legalities."

I note the 'maybe', but I don't need any further encouragement to get his hands back on me. I crawl onto his lap, straddling his thighs again. But this time I'm completely naked. When he slides his hand down to cup me this time there's nothing between his big, hot palm and my very wet center.

I suck in a quick breath as he slides his finger over my clit.

"So wet," he murmurs.

I nod.

"All for me." It's not a question.

I nod again.

He slides a finger into me and I moan, gripping his shoulders.

"Fuck, I've missed this," he says gruffly. "The dreams I've had about you and this perfect cunt." He adds a second finger and picks up the pace, fucking me faster.

He runs his other hand from my hip up my side to cup one breast. He rubs his thumb back and forth over it, teasing my nipple, making my pussy tighten around his fingers.

"Cian," I gasp.

Then he slides that hand to the back of my neck, pulling me forward until our foreheads touch.

He buries his fingers deep and says, "For the rest of these eighteen days, you're not going to deny us this. No matter what else we figure out, no matter how this thing ends up, you're going to let me worship you. You're going to let me give you what your body needs, at least. You're going to explore all of the things you want and need."

That hits me directly in the chest.

God, I want that.

I never let myself go like I did with Cian.

I know that he's realized I told him a lot of truths. The brainstorming we did about the program to support single moms was all me. The way I spoke about loving my family and how close I am to Ruby and Mariah was truly me. And the things I said and did and let him do in bed were definitely me.

Because he was safe. Because I didn't think I'd see him again.

But now...

I still feel safe with him.

Obviously, not seeing him again is not as easy as I antic-ipated—as it should have been and *would have been* with any other guy—but I still feel able to be fully myself.

I realize I've stopped moving. I'm even holding my breath.

"Don't hide from this," Cian says against my lips. "Don't pretend with this. You're safe with me. You can be and have whatever you want with me. As long as it's real."

Oh...fuck. This is...tempting as hell.

But it's temporary. Seventeen more days.

Then he'll go marry someone else.

My heart jolts hard in my chest at that.

But I have to be realistic here. I can't make a life with a guy like Cian.

Besides, he needs a princess. That is *not* me.

But he wants to have seventeen more days with me. He's insisting on it. Can I spend those days just having amazing sex? Can I have *two fucking weeks* of fun in this town? Why not? Do I deserve it? Maybe. Fucking, maybe.

Finally, I say, "Okay."

"That's my girl."

He brings me in and kisses me deeply, moving his fingers, fast and deep.

I grind down against his hand, kissing him back. But after a minute, I rip my mouth away. "Need you. Not just your fingers."

"Take what you need, sweet witch."

I reach between us and grasp his cock. "I still have the IUD," I tell him. "And I really haven't been with anyone else."

Of course we had the conversation about our health

and birth control when we were together. The first few times we used condoms, but by the end of our weekend together, we were going without.

He pulls back to meet my eyes. "I was serious too," he says. "There hasn't been anyone. Not even a drink with anyone else."

God, that's amazing. How is that possible? I don't understand it. But I do believe him.

He squeezes my neck. "Fuck me, Scarlett."

Yes, please. I'm doing this for seventeen more days, dammit. I spent *years* being proper and pious and have nothing to show for it. At least during these two-plus weeks, I'll have orgasms and be left with some additional memories to conjure when I pull out my vibrator in the years ahead.

I shift on Cian's lap, positioning him at my entrance, then sinking down over him.

We both groan as he slides deep. His fingers tighten on my hips. I grip his shoulder.

He's stretching and filling me, and I have to force myself to breathe. It's been a long time. Thank God I'm so wet.

He grips me tightly, pressing me all the way down on his cock. "My God," he rasps. "Jesus, Scarlett."

I just nod, not really able to speak. I'm not sure what I'd say. Other than, *I want to do this with you forever*, and *that* is not acceptable.

"I haven't forgotten a thing about you," he says, "But *damn*, you're so fucking tight."

"You feel so good," I say. "You fill me up and it's *so* good."

"You're so perfect." He kisses my throat. "I'm meant to fuck you forever, Scarlett. You own me."

Well... hell. What am I supposed to do with *that*?

I'd like to chalk it up to him being young and stars-in-his-eyes, but he's thirty, for fuck's sake. He's been around the world. He's been with far more partners than I have. When it comes to life experience, his has been cushier than mine, but it's also been more varied and vast than mine. I can't just pretend he's some hot, spoiled kid like I kept telling myself in New Orleans.

Oh, I think he's a little—or a lot—spoiled. But he's older and more accomplished than I'd realized.

Instead of saying anything at all, I just run my hands through his hair and move up and down on his cock, picking up the pace, and letting the delicious, hot sensations zing throughout my body.

Then he tips me so that I'm taking him even deeper and so that the angle ensures that my clit gets plenty of friction on each stroke.

It's been a long time and he's so damned good at this and...okay, I really like this guy...so it's not long before my orgasm starts to coil deep in my core.

"Oh my God, I'm so close," I gasp.

"Give it to me," he tells me, squeezing my ass. "Let me feel you."

I can't help the whimper that escapes when he presses against my lower back, grinding my clit against him. "Cian!"

He reaches up and covers my mouth. "Quiet, sweet witch," he says. "This orgasm is all for me. The neighbors don't get to hear how gorgeous you sound when you come."

That flips a switch inside me for some reason and I feel my orgasm begin to tighten, tighten, tighten, then let go.

"Yes!" I shout into Cian's hand.

I can fully let go since he's muffling the sound, and it

feels so good to just give into the pleasure and let it wash over me.

The orgasm rolls through me and I feel my pussy milking Cian's cock. He fucks me faster, clasping my hip, not uncovering my mouth.

"There you go, that's right, take it," he grits out, slamming up into me. Then his orgasm hits. "Fuck yes. *Fuck*, Scarlett. Jesus. Yes."

I keep moving over him, and he thrusts a few more times.

Our movements slow until finally, I slump against him, and he collapses back into the chair.

He wraps his arms around me, pressing my head into his shoulder. He runs his hands up and down my back.

And I just let him hold me again.

Ruby and Mariah are both huggers, but that's the extent of the physical touch I get, and this just feels too good to let go.

I did not expect this to happen when we came out here. But I regret nothing.

And I promise myself I won't tomorrow either.

It's sex. Between two consenting adults who've done it before.

I trust him. I like him. I've been upfront about what this can be and what it can't. And... I deserve this.

For now anyway.

We just sit for several minutes. Crickets and frogs are singing in the night. A car drives by on the road in front of the house. A dog barks somewhere a few blocks away.

Finally, I stir.

Cian puts his hand on the back of my head, keeping my cheek against his shoulder. "Before you say anything," he says. "Everything we talked about still goes. I'm here for eighteen more days—"

"Seventeen," I murmur.

He blows out a breath. "Right. Seventeen. And we're going to spend time together. We're going to get to know each other. And we're going to keep doing *this*. You're going to explore all of your fantasies. You get to be whoever you want with me, Scarlett. The real you. Maybe a you that you don't even know very well yet. But this is not the last time we're doing this."

Maybe a you that you don't even know very well yet.

That sucks the breath right out of my lungs.

That sounds so...nice.

I've been working on being a new me. A me that I like and that I'm proud of. I want to be someone Mariah can be proud of, and someone Ruby can feel is worth all of the time and energy and trouble. Someone Brian would have been proud of.

But she's not the me I am right now. And I'm fucking frustrated as hell by that.

I want to be accepted here in Emerald. I want to be a part of this community in a meaningful way. Someone who actually does *good*. Someone who actually takes the stuff I used to preach and practices it and is seen for that.

But damn, it feels like an uphill battle.

When I try to sit up this time, Cian lets me. I look at him for a long moment before I say, "How do you know that I'm still working on being the real me?"

He lifts a brow. "Because I'm extremely intelligent despite my laid-back playboy persona." He starts to give me one of his flirty grins. But he stops and lets the smile die. He shrugs, a more solemn look on his face now. "I like people. I pay attention. I *especially* like you and I paid a hell of a lot of attention to you. You let go with me because I knew nothing about you, and you thought you'd never see me again."

He's exactly right. Stunned, I nod.

"You need to be *that* Scarlett." He pauses again. "Right?"

I think about that Scarlett. There was a lot about that Scarlett I liked. A lot. And it wasn't just the orgasms.

I nod.

"You're going to have to learn not to underestimate me," he says.

I swallow. "Yeah, I'm figuring that out."

"Good."

We stare at each other for another long moment.

Then that dog barks again and I snap out of it.

Great. I'm probably falling in love with him while sitting naked on his lap right here on my back patio.

I climb to my feet and gather my clothes, pulling them back on, sans bra and panties. I'm just going upstairs to bed. Well, to shower, and then to bed. I can't sleep all sticky and messy and hot from him.

Though I kind of want to.

When I'm dressed, I take a breath. I have no idea what to say.

"I'll see you tomorrow," Cian says. He's still sitting, just watching me. Though he's zipped up. That's good. I guess. Less tempting at least.

But...he's not less tempting just because he's fully dressed. Not at all.

I'm in a lot of trouble here.

Why am I so bad at interpersonal relationships? I can handle anything having to do with engines, transmissions, really even most machines. Brian taught me all about cars, but I've figured out blenders, toasters, and even a lawnmower once. If something like that stops working, I can figure out the problem and fix it.

But people? I can figure out how to help them interact with each other, it seems, but *I* keep messing my own interactions up.

"Yeah." I can't help but smile, though. As if I could avoid him if I wanted to. And now that I've admitted that I don't want to, I'm in trouble. But I'll definitely be seeing him. "We have to see each other, right? Only seventeen days left."

He chuckles. "Should we get a big wall calendar and mark off the days as we go?"

I smile. "No worries. I've got it all right here." I tap my temple. Then I start for the back door.

"That sounds like you're eager to get it over with," Cian calls after me. "That's *wicked* witch stuff, Glinda."

I chuckle softly but as I make my way up the stairs and his words replay in my mind, my smile slowly fades and I'm frowning by the time I step into the bathroom.

I was definitely sweet and submissive and all in for all of that in New Orleans. And—I take a deep breath as heat hits me now, remembering then and just now on my patio —in the bedroom and other naked-together circumstances I think I still will be.

But Cian O'Grady needs to learn that I do indeed have a wicked side.

And not in the sexy spank-me-Your-Highness way.

CHAPTER 14

SCARLETT

I let myself into my bedroom quietly after my shower. I'm in only a towel and thankful I didn't run into anyone in the hallway. I pull on sleep shorts and a tank and try to slip between the sheets without jostling the mattress too much.

I close my eyes and try to think about *anything* but Cian and what just happened outside. Which is, of course, impossible.

God, why are things so hot between us? So *good*? Is it really because I let myself go when we were first together? Because I thought 'what the hell'? Or is it something more? Is it something about him? That's kind of depressing though, because I can't replicate that. Whereas *maybe*, possibly sometime down the road someday I could *hopefully* find another man I could feel comfortable letting down my guard with and letting go so that...

"What did you and Cian talk about for so long?"

I look toward Ruby's side of the bed. "I thought you were asleep. Sorry if I woke you."

She laughs softly and rolls toward me. "It's early for a bartender."

True. She's never in bed this early. "You okay?" I ask. "Have you talked to Henry?"

"I have not. And no, I'm not," she says. "But nothing's changed. There's nothing to talk about. I guess he did tell me that he and Cian are going to get rooms at the B and B while they're in town. I told him I thought that was a *very* good idea. He got huffy about the *very*."

I nod in the dark. It is. They can't stay here. Not only because it's risky for my heart, and there's the increased chance of Mariah getting way too attached, but because the town can't know that these two 'strangers' with a car in the shop are staying with us. That would be very odd and impossible to explain.

"So?" Ruby nudges my calf with her foot. "What did you talk about?"

"I told him about... my past. With Dad and everything."

She's quiet for a moment. This is a painful part of *our* past too. "Oh," she finally says.

"He asked about why things are so weird with Leah and Hannah and I thought it would help him to understand why I'm against being with someone with a lot of money and power."

Ruby blows out a breath. "Come on, Cian is *not* like Dad."

"His money makes me uncomfortable," I say. "I can't help it."

I look over at her. My eyes have adjusted to the faint light coming in through the window and I can make out most of her face. Of course, her face is like looking in a mirror.

"I'm worried he *could* be like dad," I tell her. "He's a *billionaire*, for fuck's sake. He has nearly endless resources. He could be doing so many amazing things. So much good. But he's...not. He's jetting around the world going on... vacation." I don't know how else to describe it.

The podcast talks about how he and Henry show up in various places for parties with celebrities, how they attend things like the World Cup and big international music festivals, how they skydive and deep-sea dive and mountain climb. Cian is not well-known in the US, somehow. But the podcast from Cara keeps track of him.

"He lives in a tiny town in Louisiana where he just..." I really don't know. "Hangs out, I guess." If he's doing much more than that, the podcast that makes it very much their business to know the business of the royal family—and somehow finds out some pretty amazing details—doesn't know it. "When we were together in New Orleans he described *himself* as the sidekick to Fiona and Torin." I take a breath and stare up at the ceiling. "And his family also *literally* rules over other people. They don't even get voted into their positions. They're just *there*. In charge, running the entire show."

"But they're *good* at it," Ruby says. "You've read about them. And Henry's told me about them. Cian's family is beloved. Their grandfather truly loves his people. Their country sounds like a damned nirvana. And his brother, the one that's going to be king—"

"Torin," I fill in.

"Right. He's the one who's been against a full monarchy and wants a more representative government. He's the reason he, their sister, and Cian all abdicated. I mean, they're aware of the whole 'ruling other people' thing being problematic."

"I know," I say softly. I've read the full history of Cara and the O'Grady family. I couldn't resist. Torin, Fiona, and Cian abdicated and came to the US in protest to their grandfather not agreeing to transition Cara's government to a democracy.

"And they didn't take the country over from someone else through war or anything. There was no colonization or anything like so many countries," Ruby goes on. "Their great-something grandfather was *given* the island because he saved the King of Denmark's life."

I also know this. It was Cian's great-great-great grandfather. He'd been an Irish sailor who had been on the ship with the King of Denmark on their way to the Faroe Islands when pirates attacked. Tadhg pulled King Frederick VII out of the ocean and to shore on the island that the King would give to Tadhg as a thank you and that Tadhg would name Cara, the Irish word for 'friend'.

Yeah, I could pass an exam or write an essay on Cian's family history and the history of his home country. So what? It's interesting. Especially considering most people didn't even know the tiny island south of the Faroe Islands even existed as its own country.

"Dad has money and power," I say. "He kind of rules over people. People follow him, but they do it because he makes them afraid. Of him, of other people, of the world, of eternal life spent in hell." I sigh. "And he's an unhappy dickhead who tries to keep people who don't agree with him in their place and punishes people who do things he doesn't like." I look at my sister. "Brian didn't have money or power. He didn't have any followers. He lived a simple, honest life, and he helped anyone who came to him. People listened to him because they *liked* and trusted him. And he was happy."

Ruby nods. "I know. I get it. I understand why you want to be like Brian and not like Dad. And I agree with you that, in general, we should eat the rich."

I chuckle.

"*But*," Ruby goes on. "I think there are exceptions. I think there *are* people who lead because they care about people, and I think good people with money can do *good* things. Cian's family is an example of that."

"So why isn't *Cian* doing good things?"

"Maybe he's still trying to figure out what to do."

That niggles at me. He was so excited about the project we'd dreamed up in New Orleans and he'd mentioned it to me again already.

"So you're Team Cian?" I ask grumpily. This had all seemed pretty clear cut to me—Cian and I couldn't be together for numerous very solid reasons, and I just needed to show him that so he'd leave me alone.

Now I'm questioning everything.

"Yes," Ruby says simply.

"Why?"

"Because I like him."

"You don't know him," I point out. "He's charming and easy to get along with. I'll admit that. But Dad is charming and easy to get along with too. As long as you're on his side. But Dad also has money, that he never uses for anyone else. He says that *him* being financially stable makes his followers feel secure. He claims the money means that he will always be there and will be able to fully focus on the church and his ministry. That, supposedly, makes his followers feel good."

I roll my eyes. Even fifteen years ago that had all

sounded strange to me, but it had seemed true. The people in my father's congregation didn't hesitate to give him money out of their own pockets and to constantly sell my father's books, programs, and classes to others.

"I suppose there's something to that," Ruby muses.

"What?" I look at her again, my brows pinching. "Seriously?"

"Well, we pay our politicians—from mayors all the way up to President—to serve in those positions to do the work we need them to do." She shrugs. "I suppose the king having money does make people feel more secure about him being able to do the work they need him to do for them?"

"Oh my God, that sounds so weird," I say. I take a breath. "Okay, but what about Cian then? He's not *doing* any work for the people. Why does he get to have all this money?"

"I..." Ruby trailed off. "I know that he helps Fiona with her animal park."

"Okay." I knew that too. "But the animal park is supported by tickets sales and grants and donations."

"Right. Mostly anyway." Ruby nudges me. "You should give him a job at the shop after the teaching gig."

Yeah, he's also got a teaching gig that he seems completely comfortable taking on.

"I don't even have enough business at the shop to keep *me* employed," I remind her. Brian had the building and all the equipment paid off and left me enough money to pay the bills for a few months in the beginning. That was the only way I'd kept the doors open. That and the fact that we had no rent or a mortgage to worry about because he'd also paid the house off and had money in a trust for the property taxes and any big maintenance issues like a roof or a new water heater if we ever needed them.

"Besides," I say. "How would we explain the professor suddenly becoming a mechanic?" We can't forget the cover story here. The cover story that will really only stand up for the next eighteen days. At *most*.

"Yeah, I guess that's true," Ruby agrees.

We're quiet for a moment. Then I blurt out, "We had sex."

Ruby gives a little squeak. "What? You mean since he's been *here*?"

"Yeah. Tonight. Just now. On the patio."

"*What*?" She laughs. "Good for you. That's...not what I expected to hear."

I cover my face. "I know. I shouldn't have done it."

"Why not?"

"Because I'm leading him on."

Ruby tugs one of my hands down. "What are you talking about? Did you tell him you love him or something to get his pants off?"

I give a soft huff of laughter. "No. I...God, I didn't have to really do anything." A hot shiver goes through me. "He was very willing to do whatever I asked."

Ruby sighs. "Fuck, that's nice. And sexy."

I nod. "It was. But it was totally me instigating it and I shouldn't have done that."

"Was it good?"

Good wasn't even close to the right descriptor. "Yes. It was...amazing." This is Ruby. Ruby knows everything about me. I can be honest with her. "I can be different with him. I can be more open and—" I swallow. "Dirtier. I have this side I didn't even know about until New Orleans, and he brings it out of me. Still."

Ruby gives a long sigh and then says, "God, I'm jealous."

"You and Henry aren't—"

She laughs before I even finish the question. "Oh, we *are*. Very much so. He's the best I've ever had. *God*, it's so good. That makes all of this being-together-but-not-being-together even harder. I'm jealous that you can just be with Cian whenever."

"But I can't," I insist. "He thinks he's in love with me. I'm trying to prove that this can't work out and send him away at the end of this ready to marry someone else."

My stomach tightens at that thought. But that is *not* fair, and I have to stop thinking of him being with someone else as a bad thing. That's how this has to end.

"Can I ask you something?" Ruby asks.

"Of course."

"Why does he think he's in love with you? I mean, I get that the sex was incredible. And *I* think *you* are incredible. But supposedly you didn't let him really get to know you. Still, you stayed with him for the entire weekend. And he's believed he's been in love for almost two years. And you haven't forgotten him either. So, what happened? There has to be something."

I roll to my back again and take a breath. "Okay, yeah there was more. We talked. A lot. I told him all about you and Mariah. He thought Mariah was yours and that I was the cool, fun aunt that helped raise her." I look over at her with a smile. "We bonded over having a single mom in the family and raising a little girl." I focus on the dark shape of my ceiling fan overhead again. "I told him about loving elephants because they form such loyal family units. We talked a lot about family, actually. It's really important to him too. He told me about how his siblings are all doing these amazing things and how he's always felt like he was just following along, because he never had better ideas than theirs. He was just so amazed by them." I frown remembering that.

He'd seemed truly in awe of his brothers and sister, but also a little frustrated. But the frustration had seemed self-directed.

"Then he asked me what I'd do if I had a million dollars. I think he was expecting me to say a trip to somewhere amazing or buying a house or something but… I told him the truth."

Ruby snuggles closer. "Ooh, what's the truth?"

"A home for single moms."

Ruby's quiet, so I go on.

"I want to buy a big house and make it a place that single moms can live together, with their kids, without rent. The only stipulation is that they help each other, like a family. They pool their resources to take care of the whole group. They cook together, for each other, for the group. They run errands and shop for and with each other. They all take care of the house. They schedule work shifts so that someone is home with the kids all the time, but they take turns. They take turns with school drop off. They can even work their schedules so someone can be at school programs or on field trips if they can't. And, just living together like that, as partners, they can also be there to support one another through things that no one else can really understand."

I'm quiet, letting that all sink in. Finally, I look over at Ruby. "I always had you. Cian's sister always had him and Henry, and Torin and Jonah, Torin's bodyguard. And her own bodyguard. The bodyguards became part of the family. So, Fiona had a ton of help. We were comparing notes about how much easier it is when you've got people, family, like that. But not everyone has that. It's *so* hard being a single mom and working or going to school. And really, sometimes, all they need is someone to lean on, someone who gets it. The best person would be someone who's in the same boat."

Ruby reaches out and takes my hand. She links our fingers. "That's amazing, Scarlett. That's a wonderful idea. I love it."

I smile. "Thanks. If I had a million dollars, I'd buy a bunch of houses. In lots of places."

"I love that," Ruby says. "Seriously. That's very cool." She pauses. "And Cian loved it?"

I nod. "*Loved* it. He said the houses should all have security and maintenance, maybe counseling if the women wanted it. He even said they could hire cooks, but I told him that shopping for groceries and making dinner could be a really nice bonding thing and that some people liked to do it. It's often just a burden if you don't have time. And if someone doesn't like to cook, then amongst the members of the community they figure out another way to pull their weight. Maybe they do all the dishes, or they do the laundry." I'm smiling as I remember our brainstorming. "We talked about it a lot. He really got into it."

"And that's part of why he fell in love with you," Ruby says.

I sigh. "I guess."

"It makes sense. It's something you have in common. It shows what a loving, creative, generous person you are."

"Thanks. But he doesn't really *know* me."

"But he was getting to know you. And he really liked what he did know."

"But I was pretending to be you."

Ruby laughs and squeezes my hand. "Bullshit."

"I was!"

"Besides my name... which you quickly told him was a stage name...and my burger order, what did you tell him that was me and not you?"

"That I was Mariah's aunt."

"That's nothing. Everything you told him about Mariah was true and your love for that girl is so obvious there's no way you could fake it if you tried." She squeezes me again. "Why did you give him your real name?"

I feel my cheeks get a little hot. "Because I didn't want him calling me Ruby during sex."

"Ah," she says with a grin.

"That doesn't mean anything!" I protest.

"It does too," she says. "It means when you were the most intimate you could be with him, you didn't want anything between you. And that—" she says, bopping me on the nose with her finger. "—tells me something even more important than if *he's* in love with *you*."

I frown. "What?"

"That *you* fell for him that weekend too."

Fuck.

"I told him my real name long before I fell for him," I say.

"Ah ha!"

Yeah, I didn't say I didn't fall for him. Because I can't lie to my sister.

"Whatever," I say. "I can't be in love with him *now*. I don't have time to jet off to Fiji even if I wanted to and I actually have no inclination whatsoever to...do whatever people do when they go to Fiji."

Ruby chuckles softly.

I frown though. It's true. I don't care about Fiji. "I've got shit to do *right here.* I'm going to prove that Dad is wrong about everything by living a simple, humble, *happy* life right here down the road from that gaudy, pompous palace he calls a church.

"I'll be serving the town, being a great mom and a good neighbor all *without* going to even one fucking weekend service. I'm going to be living all the principles he preaches but doesn't demonstrate right here in front of him and his whole congregation. I'm going to disprove everything he says about me and Mariah. And *you.*"

I look over at her. Our dad and his church have never bothered her as much as they have me, but then again, Ruby has never set foot on the church's campus. She honestly doesn't seem to care what he thinks or says at all.

I wish I could be like that.

"I'm going to show him that Mariah is *not* my punishment for a damned thing. That she's amazing and we're doing so great. That we're happy despite whatever he wished to happen to us. And I'm going to help anyone and everyone that church turns its back on."

I realize I'm squeezing Ruby's hand too tightly with my...exuberance...when she slowly peels my fingers back from hers. "Okay. Good. Got it. That all sounds amazing."

I take a breath.

She laughs and leans over to kiss my cheek. Then she says, "I guess I'm Team Cian because I love the way he looks at you and I want someone to stand beside you and say, "Fuck yes. That's my girl," when you say and do that stuff. And I think he's the one to do that."

God, I can imagine that so easily.

Why can I imagine that so easily?

"*You're* there cheering me on," I tell her.

"Sure," she agrees. "But I've always been there. I'm

programmed for this. Since the womb. I think it's good for you to know that people outside of me, Mom, Mariah, Brian, and Greta can believe in you and support you, Scarlett."

I feel tears stinging my eyes. Dammit. I don't need anyone else. We're fine. We've always been fine. Just us.

I blink quickly, glad the room is dark, so Ruby doesn't notice.

"I was hoping you'd tell me that it's fine if I just use him for sex for the next seventeen days," I finally say. And I'm serious.

She laughs. "Well…I mean, as long as you tell him that's all you want."

"Really?" Because I don't know that I'm going to be able to keep my clothes on around him for over two weeks.

"You tell Cian that all you want is sex and see what he says. If he agrees, then you're golden," she tells me.

"It doesn't make me a bad person to only want him for sex?"

"It doesn't make you a bad person," she assures me. "It just makes you a little stupid."

"Hey!"

"I'm just saying, if you can have *more* good things from him, it's maybe a little stupid to only want sex."

"I don't want to lead him on or hurt him."

"Okay. Well, then you just need to tell him that."

"I shouldn't just try to resist? Keep my clothes on? Avoid being alone with him?"

She laughs louder now. "No. Not that. If he's blowing your mind on our *patio*, then you need to get naked with him *often* over the next couple of weeks."

I actually feel relieved at her words. Which is ridiculous. Am I *relieved* to know I have permission to fuck Cian as much as I want to? Yes, that's exactly how I feel. Because I really want to, and I don't want to feel guilty about it.

"Thanks, Ruby."

She rolls over to face away from me. "Goodnight, lucky girl. I love you."

"I love you too," I murmur.

But it's another forty minutes before I fall asleep.

Because it's very hard to quiet the feelings tumbling through me at the thought of being free to get naked with Cian whenever I want to.

Almost as hard as it is to ignore the rush of emotions I get when I think about Cian believing in and supporting me.

CHAPTER 15
CIAN

"I could take out the basketball coach. He also teaches math. I could do that."

"Define *take out*," I tell Henry as I pour cream into my coffee.

He rolls his eyes. "Challenge him to a friendly one-on-one game and sweep his leg. Injure his knee just enough that he needs to be out for a while."

It's fortunate that I know Henry as well as I do and I don't take him completely seriously. But I take him about seventy percent seriously.

"You do not need to be at the school with me the entire time. It's Emerald, Ohio. No one here wants to kill me."

"I wanna kill you a little."

I snort. "That's because you're not getting laid, and you spend a lot of time with the only woman you want to get laid by."

He gives me a look that says *fuck you, I can't believe you just said that*, and *you're absolutely right* all at the same time.

Again, the beauty of knowing a man as long and as well as Henry and I know one another is that we don't have to actually *say* all of that.

"The fact that I am spending so much time in close proximity to Ruby is your fault. You're not helping your *don't kill me* case."

I take a seat at the table in Scarlett and Ruby's kitchen. "Just leave the basketball coach alone. Besides, they're not going to ask *you* to coach basketball and teach math even if he is out of commission. We've told the whole town you're the head of the history department at some college."

Henry sits back in his chair. Ruby is still in bed, or at least upstairs avoiding us. Scarlett, of course, already left for work. Mariah and Greta blew through the kitchen about ten minutes ago, grabbing food on their way to school.

I'm on my way up to the school too, but I've got another thirty minutes or so. I'm supposed to meet with the administration and then sit down with the teacher I will be covering for during his planning period.

"Fine. I'm going to be writing a book. That way I can hang out at various places around town, go for a run past the school, even stop in periodically."

I take a long draw of my coffee. Henry's plans are always well thought out, so I don't really need to ask, but I do anyway. "You're writing a book?"

He gives me a pissy look. "That's my cover story. That's what everyone will believe I'm doing while we're here. That gives me flexibility with where I am and my schedule. That way if you need me, I can get to you. Good thing this town is so fucking small," he ends on a mutter.

Ruby is absolutely getting to him. He's not ever quite as affable as I am, but he's generally laid back and has a great sense of humor. He goes with the flow, which is why he and

I fit together so well. But he's been a grumpy asshole ever since we got to Ohio. I'm glad I have to go to school.

"But you're *actually* going to just be bored and get more and more irritated, is that what I should prepare for?" I ask.

"The less I'm in this house with her, the better I'll be," he says scowling. "I slept better last night."

Henry had gone to check us into the bed and breakfast after I'd agreed to take the teaching job. He's always thinking ahead. So after Scarlett had come back inside from the patio, I'd headed over there.

As much as I would have loved to stay here in Scarlett's home, surrounded by her stuff, her family, her *life*, now that the whole town knows we're here, Henry and I have to act like travelers on our way through Emerald, laid over only temporarily.

"Oh yeah, clearly. You're so much sunnier this morning," I tell Henry.

"This teaching thing just makes me itchy. You don't do things for eight hours a day without me with you."

I tip my head. "I'm going to miss you, too."

"It's really more about trying to stay alive."

"You honestly think somebody's going to try to kill me here?"

"I am talking about me. When Iris finds out about this, she's going to want to kill me."

I chuckle. Iris Lee is the head of the royal bodyguards. All of the bodyguards, including Henry, report to her officially. But these guys have been doing these jobs for over a decade. And I'm sure Henry doesn't report every single move I make.

"She knows we're here in Ohio and why, right?"

Henry nods.

"Can we just not tell her about the teaching thing?"

He narrows his eyes. "Do you think that you can keep it from becoming some big thing?"

"Define *big thing*." I'd hate to make a promise I can't keep. I feel like most things worth doing are worth really *doing*.

Henry blows out a breath. "Exactly. It has to do with Scarlett and her kid. Of course it's going to be a big thing."

"The job doesn't have to do with Scarlett and her kid. It's just something they offered me while I was here, and it helps cover up that a rich and handsome charming prince is madly in love with Scarlett. No one but the family needs to know that. I guess." I'd rather shout it to the world, but I can respect her wishes to keep it quiet. I suppose. For now.

"So instead, the new guy, the handsome and charming *college professor* is going to be in love with Scarlett," Henry says. "Or are you going to pretend that's not the case? Are you and Scarlett going to sneak around?"

"The whole point of being here is to get to know her, spend time with her, get to know her on her own turf," I remind him. "I definitely don't want to sneak around. I want to take her out, date her. See if this can be something real." I shake my head. "Or rather, prove to her that it can be real."

"You've already decided that you know her well enough and that you want her to be the princess?" Henry asks. He doesn't seem surprised.

"She might think she lied to me about who she is, but she was completely real with me. I think real in a way she isn't usually, but in a way she *wants* to be."

Henry sighs but he doesn't argue. "Have you and Scarlett talked about that? Is she cool with publicly dating the new teacher?"

I frown. See? When Henry is grumpy and annoyed, he

makes me grumpy and annoyed. "We haven't talked about it specifically. But she's agreed that we are going to spend time together. What else would this be? I don't think she's going to be surprised when I say I want to go out in public with her."

I think I've been pretty clear even if I hadn't fucked her on her patio last night that I want her. That I want to give this every chance it has to turn into something real.

"Great, so I'm going to need to be over here at this house more often." Henry does not seem excited about that.

"There is definitely no one at this house that wants to kill me. Although I do think Ruby is blaming me, like you are, for her current frustration."

Henry glares at me. "We're not going to talk about Ruby. I'm also not coming over here every night for dinner. I can't just be around her and not..." He shoves a hand through his hair.

I sympathize. There's no way that I could be in that close proximity to Scarlett and not want to talk to her, tell her how I feel, touch her. "I'm sorry, man," I say. "Seriously. Maybe it will—"

"It will be fine," he cuts me off. "I'll just be bored off my ass for the next two weeks. Maybe I really will start a book."

"Seventeen days," I correct. "I have three days more than two weeks."

"Right," Henry says without humor. "Let's just both work on getting out of Emerald, Ohio, alive and well, okay?"

Alive and well.

I nod and finish off my coffee. And bite my tongue on the urge to say anything about how we might be alive when we leave Ohio, but well? I don't know about that one.

There's a very good chance that one or both of us leaves with a broken heart.

Everyone in the administration office at Emerald Public School is very nice. And very enthusiastic about me being here. Especially Amanda Brown, the principal. She tells me, "We're just so *grateful* to you for doing this," three times in ten minutes.

It seems Henry was right when he said that they would be so happy to have a qualified substitute that they wouldn't dig very deep into my background or story. And since I offered to donate my pay back into the fine arts fund —I don't feel right about taking money from the school— they are even less likely to care about anything other than me showing up and keeping the kids engaged for the class periods I'm assigned to.

The few teachers I'm introduced to in the teachers' lounge on my tour are also very nice. And eager to meet me.

Like Lily Singer, the cute, very young Spanish teacher. And Rachel Garrett, the science teacher, who looks familiar and I realize it's because she was at the table with Hannah Lawton in the diner the day Hannah and Scarlett had their confrontation.

I notice I'm not introduced to any of the male teachers. Or any married female teachers. What a coincidence.

I'm very happy to get to Bill Emerson's room.

Bill is a tall, husky man in his mid-fifties. He greets me with a wide smile and a firm handshake. He's apparently been at this school for twenty-four years and loves his job.

I like the guy. He admits to liking world history best but

is also an expert in US history. We chat easily about some current events in the United Kingdom and Egypt, and share our thoughts about Christian Waite, a US Senator who is apparently being groomed for a Presidential run. I refrain from telling him that my grandfather and brother both like Waite a lot and that he's been to Cara at least once to discuss a partnership in green energy efforts. But Bill likes him and that makes me like Bill even more.

It's clear that Bill knows his stuff and pays attention to world events and that he likes seeing I'm the same. He also seems like someone who really cares about the kids learning something and enjoying the material as much as possible.

"Well, I promise they'll be a little smarter when you return."

He chuckles. "I'm not worried about that, Professor. I expect that you can handle the lessons with no problem," Emerson says. "But if you have any problems with any of the kids, I'm just a phone call away. I might not be up for hiking or line dancing for a while, but I can get on the phone. Or even meet you for a meal or coffee. Mrs. Brown will have your back too," he says of the principal.

"What kind of issues might I have?"

"There're just some big personalities in the sophomore class," Bill says. "I assume at your level you haven't dealt with high school kids much."

I didn't deal with high school kids much even when I was a high school kid. I went to high school in Cara, but while my grandfather felt strongly about us attending the public schools, nothing could take away the fact that we were royalty. Henry wasn't a part of my life then, but there was extra security at the school, and eyes were on me all the time. I wouldn't have had any issues with anyone in my class. Or rather, none of them would've had any issues with me. They wouldn't have dared.

"Why don't you give me a rundown on the kids?" I ask.

Bill hands over a list of sixty names. "Yeah, I think that might be a good idea. Give you an idea for what you're getting into."

I scan the list and see both Mariah and Greta's names on it. I also note Leah Lawton's name.

After pointing out the "quiet but brilliant" girl, the boy with dyslexia, a couple of kids for whom English is their second language, a couple boys who simply struggle overall and compensate for it by being "little shits", Bill points to Mariah's name then Leah's. "You'll also want to watch these two."

I try not to look more interested in those names than any of the others. "Okay." I've been jotting down notes so I lean in to do so for these girls as well.

"They simply don't like each other. It's really as plain as that."

"Has anything happened between the girls in class?"

Bill sighs. "Leah tries to get under Mariah's skin. She goes to the big church here in town. Mariah's grandfather is the pastor, but her family doesn't go to church. Leah always seems to have something to say about that."

"In class?"

"Everywhere, it seems. Sometimes in class."

"Is discussion about religion encouraged?" I ask. "I assume it comes up from time to time since religion has played such an important role in so many huge historical events."

Bill nods. "Exactly. It does come up in here. And I try to encourage open conversation. Sometimes it just gets a little out of hand."

"I appreciate the heads up."

Bill studies me for a moment. "As an educator, and a student of history, I'm sure you can appreciate that I think these discussions can be healthy. I think it's good to discuss differences of opinion, and different beliefs. Societies are built—and torn down—based on a variety of ideas. Our beliefs about where we belong in the world, and what should guide and motivate us, are the basis for conflicts of all kinds, from small ones in the lunchroom at school to global ones that span continents."

I nod. "The things we believe in, and the things that motivate us to live our lives in certain ways, are the most intimate parts of us. They are the things that make people the most passionate."

Bill smiles. "Exactly. So, I don't shut the conversation down. Even when it gets contentious, I try to redirect them into expressing what they're feeling and thinking in more constructive ways. It doesn't always work. But let's face it, being a part of this world means you're going to run into people who think differently than you do and believe things that you don't. Listening to them, trying to understand them, and learning to express yourself in a way that *they* can understand, is really valuable. And if they can practice that at age sixteen, even if it's clunky and ineffective, I think something good can come from that."

I like Bill Emerson. "That's why school and teachers are so important," I tell him sincerely. I realize it sounds like I'm building myself up as well, but the truth is, I admire the hell out of what he does. "This is maybe the safest space these kids will have to learn these concepts and, as you said, practice for these conflicts. If they can have someone they like and trust and respect there as a referee, they can learn a lot from that."

Bill leans across the desk with his hand outstretched. "I think this is going to go very well. I really appreciate you coming in for these two weeks, Professor."

I feel a twinge in my chest at the title. It's a harmless lie. These kids will be fine. I *will* actually teach them something. No harm is being done here with this little white fib.

But what Bill does is important. I respect him. He's doing good work every day and dammit, I kind of wish I wasn't misleading him so that his respect for me felt legitimate.

CHAPTER 16
SCARLETT

As I step through the back door of my house, I pause but only kick off my boots rather than stripping down like I usually do. The delicious smell of dinner cooking hits me and my stomach growls. I hear voices in the kitchen, and I smile. I love coming home to this.

I don't hear Cian, but I know he's here. The car he and Henry are renting is out front. And he texted me. Three times today.

At eight a.m. I got *dreamt about you last night.*

Just after noon he sent *most worth it mosquito bite ever.* He included a photo of his muscular upper thigh where he did, indeed, have a mosquito bite. I find myself grinning stupidly at that. And wishing he'd included a wider shot.

About an hour ago he texted *can Henry and I come over for dinner? Want to show you something.*

I said of course. Not only did I agree to see him every day while he's here, but I've admitted to myself that I *want* to see him.

That complicates everything, of course, but I'm not actually stupid enough to think I can avoid being a little heartbroken when this is all over. Whether he realizes I'm not the girl he thinks I am and that I'm not princess material, or he just finally needs to leave Emerald to live his life, there will come a time when this will be over.

But he's here for now. And that seems like all the more reason to enjoy the hell out of the sixteen days and six hours I have left with him.

"Hey, Mom," Mariah greets me as I step into the kitchen from the mud room.

"Hey. How was your day?"

"Good." She shrugs.

I'm glad there's no drama to tell me about.

"It smells great in here," I give her and Greta both a grin.

They're studying at the breakfast bar. They have a plate of sliced vegetables between them with ranch dip. I grab a bottle of water from the fridge and then reach over and dunk a piece of cucumber into the dip. "Which casserole did you pick out?"

"It's not one of Diane's," Mariah tells me. "Cian made that."

I stop with the cucumber slice halfway to my mouth. A drip of ranch dressing hits the counter. "Cian cooked?"

"I'm offended that you sound so surprised."

I turn quickly at the sound of his voice. He's just coming into the kitchen from the dining room.

A wet drip hits my foot, and I look down to find ranch dressing dripping from my fingers. I shove the piece of cucumber into my mouth and then grab for the paper towels.

"You cook?" I ask him.

He comes to stand directly in front of me, looking down at me with a smile. It seems that he came into the kitchen just for me.

My stupid stomach swoops a little at that.

He lifts a hand to my head and pulls on the ponytail holder that has my hair gathered back. He slides it out of my hair, then runs a big hand through the strands.

I visibly shiver. His hands in my hair do obscene things to my body. Things I probably don't want my daughter witnessing.

But I can't seem to make myself step back.

"I do cook." He runs his hand up to the back of my head again and massages my scalp where the ponytail had been.

Holy shit, that feels good. I let out a long sigh and let my eyes slide shut.

"Though Henry and Jonah are both better than I am. They can make a whole host of things. But we all had to learn. We were all living together and when Saoirse got out of the baby food stage, Fiona told us we couldn't feed her frozen burritos or take out every night."

I open my eyes to look up at him. He keeps rubbing my head, smiling at the memory. He told me just last night that I needed to stop underestimating him, and it seems that is going to take me a little longer to learn.

"What is it?" I ask. I don't care, but I feel the need to say something.

This man with his big hand giving me a scalp massage while his low voice rolls over me, making my skin feel like he's massaging the rest of me, could serve me peanut butter on crackers and I'd thank him profusely.

"Pork chops and rice," he says. "Casseroles are my specialty. I love it when you can put everything in one pan.

Fewer dishes and you don't have to worry about getting a bunch of stuff all done at the same time."

That seems to fit Cian perfectly. He's competent, but also minimal fuss. I smile up at him. "I agree."

He pulls his fingers through my hair, then gathers my hair into a looser ponytail, looping the tie around it at the base of my neck. "Who's Diane?"

"Just a friend."

"Diane brings us two frozen casseroles every week," Mariah says.

I shoot Mariah a look. "That's right. She's awesome." That's all that Cian needs to know about Diane.

Mariah misses my look though because she's got her head bent over whatever she's working on. "But Mom doesn't take help very easily, so she insists on working on Diane's cars for free."

"It's only fair," I protest. "I don't have to worry about dinner twice a week because of her. That's huge."

"Yeah, except the car that you work on for her doesn't actually ever need any work," Mariah goes on.

"You're exaggerating," I tell her, but I look up at Cian. "*Anyway*." I say, trying to change the subject.

"What do you mean it doesn't need work?" Cian asks Mariah.

"Mom won't take the casseroles for free. Diane won't take money. So, Mom said she'd work on Diane's car for her in exchange. But Diane doesn't really drive that much. So she doesn't actually need an oil change every single month. She definitely doesn't need her tires rotated and her brake pads checked very often. But she still brings it in with *some* request, because that's the only way Mom will take the casseroles." Mariah laughs. She finally lifts her head and the look she gives me is fully affectionate. "And

Mom goes along with it. Obviously, she knows it doesn't need to have all of that stuff done but she lets Diane think she doesn't realize that. It's kind of a sweet little game they play."

I'm touched that Mariah thinks that, but I roll my eyes. "Okay, that's enough."

Cian tugs on my ponytail and he subtly tips my head so that I look back up at him. "Sweet witch," he murmurs.

Heat shivers through my body and I realize I need to step back before I kiss him in front of my daughter and her friend.

And maybe kissing him wouldn't be the end of the world. It's pretty clear we like each other. But it wouldn't be a kiss. It would be a *get me naked now* kiss. And that can't happen in my kitchen.

At least not until later.

"Thank you for cooking," I say, taking that step back, somehow.

He lets me go, but the look in his eyes clearly tells me that he was thinking about kissing me naked as well.

"Of course." He glances at the oven. The timer reads ten minutes. "Come see what I got today." He grasps my hand and starts tugging me toward the dining room.

"Is it something for school?" I ask his back. I know he went up to meet everyone today.

He shoots me a big grin over his shoulder. "Yep."

"So how did it—" I cut off as I step into the dining room.

Henry is sitting at the table, but it seems he's occupying the only empty space in the room.

The dining room table and all of the chairs are covered with plastic shopping bags. I can see that there are boxes of tissues and rolls of paper towels in one. Another holds boxes and boxes of markers. There are notebooks, bottles of glue, three-ring notebooks, folders, boxes of pencils.

It looks like an office supply store blew up in my dining room.

Henry looks up from his phone. "Hi."

"Hi," I greet, both brows arched.

"Professor Brady had a good day," he says dryly.

I look at Cian. He's grinning like a kid.

"Bill Emerson is a good guy," he says.

I nod. "He was a good teacher too."

"You had him for history?" Cian asks.

"Yeah."

Cian grins. "That's cool."

"Is it?"

He clears a chair by grabbing two shopping bags and moving them to the floor. One tips and a box of tampons falls to the floor. "That you and Mariah had the same teacher? Yeah. Kind of. Isn't it?"

I guess it is. Bill Emerson was always kind, and I did learn a lot from him. Though I'm embarrassed when I think back to how I behaved during the time I was in his class. I don't want to know what he remembers about me. I am happy that Mariah can show him that I raised an amazing kid, at least. There are two other teachers still teaching here that I also had when I was in school, and I feel the same way about them.

"What is all of this?" I ask, bending to retrieve the tampons.

Cian takes them, stuffing them back into the bag. "Stuff for the school."

I look around. "You need this many—" My gaze falls on a bag that has crayons in it. "Crayons, for your classroom?"

He sets the bag on the table. "Well, this is for multiple

classrooms. Including the elementary school. Did you know that teachers have to supply a lot of this stuff out of their own pockets?" He frowns. 'They ask parents for help too."

"I am aware of that, yes," I say with a grin.

He gestures at the cleared chair seat and I sit.

"Well, that's ridiculous," he says. "The school should be able to supply their classrooms. And I know it's a budgeting issue. But the *government* should be adequately funding schools." His frown deepens. "That definitely needs to be looked at."

I chuckle. "You know you're not the first person to think that, right?"

"Of course. But I do have some people I can talk to. And, regardless, I can certainly afford to buy supplies for the school." He scowls at the bag to my right. It's got construction paper and notecards in it. "I mean, how the fuck do they expect a school to function without *paper*? And tissues? Teachers are supposed to go to work, get paid a pittance, *and* buy tissues for their kids too?" He shakes his head. "That's unacceptable. We've already started the process for setting up a fund to take care of all of that."

My eyes widen. "A fund? That will pay for all the supplies for Emerald?"

"Yes."

"For this year?"

"Ongoing."

I stare at him. He lifts a brow.

I don't know what to say. I know he can afford it. I appreciate that he understands the need and wants to help. It was just a matter of making him aware of it, I suppose. "Too bad there aren't many billionaires that want to go into teaching," I say. "Or nursing. Or a bunch of other jobs. We could probably solve a lot of problems if they saw it up close."

"We could," he agrees. "Though I have some special privilege. I can dabble in all kinds of jobs. Most billionaires tend to stick with whatever made them rich."

His mouth has a strange twist to it as he says the words. Almost as if he's tasting something unpleasant.

"I suppose you have a point," I say about the other billionaires. There's not really anything else to say, so I just add, "Thank you, Cian. For doing that for Emerald."

He frowns. "It's not something I need to be thanked for. I'm simply supplying funds for something that needs to be funded. There must be a better way, and I've reached out to some people so I can understand the process better." He blows out a breath. "But for now I can buy some fucking markers and paper towels."

I want to kiss him so badly right now.

Smiling, flirty, charming Cian is hot. But outraged on behalf of teachers and kids Cian is nearly irresistible.

"And tampons?" I ask, looking at the bag on the floor.

He glances at it. "A bunch of high school teachers were saying how it's important to have period products available. They need to be easily available, and a lot of teachers keep a stash in their desks."

"Where were they saying this?" I can easily picture him already making friends in the teachers' lounge.

"Online. In some forums I've joined."

He's joined online forums for teachers. For a two-week subbing gig.

I'm not prepared to be this attracted to him.

"I texted Mariah and Greta to ask what kind to get, though." He meets my gaze and frowns. "Is that okay? Is that weird?"

If Henry wasn't here, I would throw Cian on my dining room table, strip him down, and ride him right there on top of the bags of school supplies for elementary school students.

I have to clear my throat before I say, "That's totally okay. In fact, that's amazing."

He looks relieved. "Good. It occurred to me after I got everything home that Emerson might already have stuff, but I suppose it's better to have too much than not enough."

Home. He referred to my house as home. That's...shit. Tempting. That's what that is.

"Oh, I also bought a new coffee machine, like a whole cappuccino-espresso thing, for the teachers' lounge." He frowns. "That was overkill right? I just know the girls in Autre *love* that fucking thing they have in the office at the animal park and the coffee pot in the lounge there looked really sad today. Teachers should *at least* have good coffee."

"You're going to make quite an impression on Emerald High School while you're here," I tell him.

His smile is bright. "If people don't remember you after you leave, what was the point of being there in the first place?"

Oh, boy. What a motto.

I don't think Cian O'Grady needs to worry about Emerald, Ohio, or the people of the town, remembering him when he leaves.

Which is more unfortunate for some of us than others.

CHAPTER 17

SCARLETT

Cian's casserole is not as good as Diane's are, but it's pretty damned good. Like *I could come home to this every night* good. The conversation around the table, and the way Henry and Cian both interact with Mariah and Greta, is also *very* good. Tempting. Dangerously so.

I could easily fall for all of this.

We laugh, we talk, Greta and Mariah fill Cian in on all of the kids in class, both in their grade and in the grades just above and below.

It's lively enough that we barely notice that Ruby and Henry are ignoring one another.

In fact, that isn't blatantly obvious until Henry excuses himself after dinner and heads back to the bed and breakfast, leaving the car for Cian because he 'needs some fucking fresh air and a walk' to which Ruby just rolls her eyes and goes upstairs to get ready for work.

Now Mariah and Greta are up in Mariah's room. They say they're prepping for a quiz tomorrow in English, but

I'm guessing there's going to be more gossiping and studying their social media pages than their textbook and notes. Still, both girls are great students with mostly As, so I don't worry.

And if I'm honest, and at risk of losing my Good Mom card, I'm happy everyone cleared out. Even if Ruby's a little pissed at Henry. Even if Henry's walking around in the dark. It's Emerald for fuck's sake. And he's a bodyguard. And even if Mariah and Greta miss a couple of questions on their quiz. Because Cian and I are now alone in the kitchen.

He's putting the last of the dinner dishes in the dishwasher while I store the leftovers in the fridge and it's so normal and he looks so comfortable rinsing dishes that I almost laugh. He's actual royalty, but he's standing in his socks at my kitchen sink with his sleeves pushed up to the elbows, glasses on, scrubbing a plate free of cheese, rice, and veggies from a casserole he made.

This is bonkers.

And I love it.

And it's the first time we've done this clean-up routine together and I already know I'm going to miss it when he's gone.

"Do you actually wear glasses some of the time?" I ask.

He puts the last plate into the dishwasher and closes the door. "No. These aren't even readers. Just glass lenses with no correction at all."

He's been wearing them all night and I really like the look.

Then again, I'm comfortable admitting the fact that I like every look Cian O'Grady has.

"Why do you still have them on?"

"Just getting used to them. Figure I'll keep them on at school." He dries his hand on a dish towel, then hangs it over the front of the oven. He pushes the glasses up his nose before bracing his hands on the counter behind him.

"It's funny that the Kent thing works," I say.

"The Clark Kent thing?"

"That you can just put a pair of glasses on and no one recognizes you."

He chuckles. "It's a little more than that." He rubs his hand over his clean-shaven jaw. "But people here have only seen me in photos. And some of those online are old. The most recent ones are from my brother's wedding and I am definitely in the background."

I agree that I would be surprised if anyone here actually recognizes him. But I think it's more because it would be out of context. It's amazing how hard it can be to put a name and face together when you see someone in an unexpected place.

"You feel ready for class on Monday?" I ask.

He shrugs. "I will be. Ready enough anyway."

"Ready enough?" I grin. "You know with teenagers, the main thing is to not show any weakness."

He matches my grin. "For sure. I've just learned that over-preparing for new adventures can be a waste of time. You have to go into new things with at least a little acceptance of the fact that you don't know exactly what's going to happen and you can handle it."

I think back to the times Ruby and I decided to move to a new city, find new jobs, find new places to live. It was terrifying every time and the only thing that made it better was preparing for every contingency.

"Maybe skydiving is different from moving your kid to a new city and finding a new apartment and job," I say. "But I've always found preparation to be very important."

He doesn't respond for a long moment. He just stands

studying me. Finally he says, "Having a child, someone who depends on you, probably makes a difference."

"And not having a bodyguard to make things safe and clean up problems."

"Right."

I can't read his expression. For just a second, I worry that I've hurt his feelings. But I replay my words, and I don't find anything untrue or especially snarky about them. They're all true.

But I decide not to be a bitch and point out that he'll have full classes of students depending on him to teach them something. I'm making a bigger deal out of this than I need to. And I'm projecting my suspicions that long-term commitments aren't really Cian's thing onto this situation that is very much not a long-term thing. Everyone understands that. The people who hired him, Cian himself, the kids. He's a *substitute* teacher. He doesn't need to commit. Not to the school. Not to me.

"I guess it's only three weeks," I say. "So that's also different."

He doesn't say anything to that. "So what are the chances that someone will walk in on us if I kiss you right now?" he asks.

I'm surprised by the shift of topic, and I guess the fact that he still *wants* to kiss me after I was clearly being judgy about his 'adventures' being less serious than mine.

He pushes away from the counter and comes toward me. "And what are the chances of it being a really bad idea if they did?"

I swallow. "I don't think the chances are very good. But it would be bad."

He looks surprised as he stops in front of me. "It would?

You don't think that Mariah and Ruby and Greta are expecting that we're kissing?"

"It's more the fact that I think the kissing will turn into *a lot* more. Things they won't appreciate having happen on the surfaces where they eat."

His gaze heats as his mouth tips up at the corner. "Are you saying you have no self-control around me?"

I nod. "That's exactly what I'm telling you."

"That's an excellent answer."

I step closer to him, his heat wrapping around me. I take a deep breath that's scented with his soap and cologne. "I need to tell you something before we kiss. And more."

"Anything."

"I think there's a good chance I will be using you for sex."

His right brow arches. "Is that right?"

"Yes. I still don't think anything can happen between us past the next sixteen days."

He sighs as if frustrated with my mental countdown.

"But I want to keep having sex. And I just want to be up front about that so you don't think it's a sign that I'm getting attached or that this is more serious. And to give you a chance to say no."

God, please don't say no.

He nods slowly, lifting a hand to my hair and pulling on the ponytail holder again. He drags the elastic loop down the length of my hair. When it's free, he slips it onto his wrist and then slides his hand up into my hair, dragging the strands between his fingers.

"You are a witch, you know that? I'm spellbound. You know very well I have no ability to say no to you."

I grasp his wrist. "You do. You can say no. You want more and it's not fair of me to lead you on."

"Hey, Glinda?"

"Yeah?" I ask softly.

"You go right ahead and take whatever you need from me. I'm here for you. Use me. Whatever you need." He slides his fingers through my hair again, then his hand comes up to cup my face.

"Cian—"

"Shh." He leans in and puts his lips against mine. "I'm okay. I'm in. You let me worry about all the other stuff."

"What stuff?" I whisper, my hands going to his sides and gripping his shirt.

"The falling in love stuff. The forever stuff."

Oh, shit. See that's the messy stuff. "Cian—"

"You've already cast your spell, Scarlett," he says, his warm breath coasting over my lips and making me want *more*.

Fuck.

Then he kisses me and any thoughts of pulling away and doing the right thing by *not* taking my clothes off for him again go out of my head.

I arch closer, and he doesn't hesitate to take over. He cups my face with both hands, aggressively claiming me, heating every inch of my body with just the strokes of his tongue against mine.

Well, I warned him. I told him I was using him, that all I want is sex. I *told* him. So if he thinks this means we're getting married or something, that's his own fault.

I hook my fingers into his belt loops and start pushing him toward the laundry room that's just off the kitchen. We *could* go up to my bedroom, but I share a wall with Mariah and Ruby is across the hall...and no, we couldn't go up to my bedroom. What the hell am I thinking?

About a bed. About a big horizontal surface. About a location for this where you won't get mosquito bites.

The patio last night had been sexy and hot, and I've been thinking about it off and on all day, heat flooding my body every time, but I don't want to do this on the patio again.

I push him into the laundry room, his ass hitting the dryer, the motion pulling our lips apart. I'm breathing fast as I swing the door shut behind us. "Will this work?" I ask, looking around. I eye the washer and dryer. They're both too high. The ironing board propped in the corner will no way hold even one of us. Dammit. I could bend over but...

"I'll make it work," he growls, reaching out and grabbing my wrist, pulling me to him. He kisses me deeply again, then turns me to face the dryer. "Hands on top," he orders.

I do it. God, I love when he bosses me.

If anyone had told me that before I'd been in New Orleans with him, I wouldn't have believed it. I would have said I'm a strong, independent woman who knows what she likes and needs. I'm sexually open and well-adjusted and I don't date men who I don't feel like I can talk to about what I want in bed.

Which is maybe why I've only had two partners other than Cian since Mariah's dad.

But Cian O'Grady, the seemingly young, cocky playboy had come along, taken charge, told me what I was going to do and how I was going to do it, and what he wanted from me and *oh my God*, it had been better than anything I could have come up with in my dirtiest daydreams.

"I have been thinking about this sweet pussy all fucking

day," he says against my neck. He might've gotten rid of the beard, but he has whiskers at this time of night and the roughness against my skin makes goosebumps dance down my spine.

I press back against him. "I've been thinking about last night too."

"What do you need?" he asks. "Right now, what do you need?"

"Just make me feel good. Like you always do."

"My fucking pleasure," he says.

While Henry set the table and Cian pulled the casserole from the oven, I'd quickly showered and dressed in loose gray cotton shorts and a T-shirt with a sports bra. Had I thought about the easy access of those items at the time?

Yes, yes, I had.

One of his hands steals up under my T-shirt, and pulls my bra up, exposing both breasts. The other slips down the front of my shorts.

"Have I properly praised you for your choice of evening attire around the house?" he asks.

"I dressed for comfort." My voice is breathy.

"Oh, my sweet liar, you dressed to get finger fucked against the dryer in your laundry room," he tells me.

One hand palms my breast, teasing my nipple, while the other cups me through my cotton panties.

He presses against my clit. "Spread your legs," he tells me. "Let me have this magical, perfect pussy that has me under this spell I never want broken."

I widen my stance, and he shifts to slide his hand into my panties, his middle finger rubbing over my clit. He circles three times then gives me a little pinch.

I gasp. "Cian!"

"Will you soak my hand, Scarlett? I want to make you

come hard and fast on my fingers. Please." The last word is deep and husky as he slides two thick fingers into me at once.

I can take it but it's a tight fit and I gasp again.

"That's my girl," he rasps against my ear. "You can take this. I stretched you out last night and you're such a good girl getting so wet for me. Let me make this sweet pussy purr." He kisses the side of my neck, then gives me a little nip. He thrusts in and out a few times. "But we both know what you really want. Play with your nipples, so I can have both of my hands free."

I shiver with lust. I know exactly what he's talking about.

He helped me discover some things about my body that I had never explored before. Or even thought about exploring. But with Cian I was safe. And he made it amazing.

"Oh my God," is all I can manage.

He reaches out and takes one of my hands from the top of the dryer, lifting it under my shirt to cup my breast. I squeeze my nipple, feeling my pussy ripple around his fingers. He slides his hand down my back and over my ass.

"You are incredible, Scarlett." He kisses my throat as he squeezes my ass. "God, the way you give yourself to me is like a drug."

I drag in a breath as he tucks his hand into the back of my shorts. Now he is cupping a bare ass cheek while he pumps his fingers in and out of my pussy.

"Need your legs wider," he says against my ear. "Bend over a little. Let me give you what you need."

I can't resist him. His rough voice in my ear, his fingers touching me exactly the way I need to be touched, the way he knows me, the way he's not getting any relief himself but still acts as if this is exactly what *he* needs.

I lean over, resting one forearm on the top of the dryer. His fingers thrust faster, his thumb rubs over my clit, and then with his other hand, he presses against my backside.

I gasp as lightning seems to burst inside me. "Cian!"

"That's right, my pretty dirty little witch. I remember all your secrets. How you like to be fucked deep in this perfect cunt but teased back here too."

He circles and thrusts and presses and I feel my orgasm coiling low and tight.

"I also remember how you like to have your hands tied to the bed, so you have to just lie there and take it."

The coil pulls tighter.

"And how you love to be spanked."

He thrusts faster. Presses deeper.

I inch even closer to the precipice.

"How you love to be eaten before I—"

I break apart. I cry out as my orgasm hits from deep inside and rolls out, swamping me in pleasure and heat.

"Cian!"

"That's it," he praises. He keeps his fingers moving, slowing but not withdrawing as the ripples continue. "That's it. Fuck, Scarlett. Yes, that's it."

I slump over the dryer, sucking in oxygen.

I feel him finally slip his fingers from my shorts. He drapes himself over me, kissing the back of my head, my neck, my shoulder.

After a minute or so, he reaches under my shirt and pulls my bra down, then pulls me to standing and turns me, gathering me in his arms. "Was that what you needed?"

I nod against his chest. "Yes. Though I want—"

He lifts my chin and kisses me. Then he says, "That's enough for tonight."

I pull back. "But what about—"

"We don't have time or space for more." He presses a kiss to my forehead. "But at least I have my own room now so I can get myself off when I get to the B&B."

I drop my gaze to the front of his shorts. "I could—"

He steps back, clearly reading my thoughts. "Not on this hard floor."

I look down at the linoleum under our feet. Oh. Yeah, that would be very uncomfortable on my knees. That's nice of him. "I could get a throw pillow from the couch."

He chuckles. "I'm okay."

I give him a 'really?' look.

He shrugs. "Okay-ish."

"Fine." I open the laundry room door, and he goes to the sink to wash his hands. I run a hand through my hair watching him.

God he's so...good.

And not just at the orgasm thing. He's just *good*. He's a good guy.

He comes back over to me and pulls me into his arms again, hugging me, and kissing the top of my head.

Then we load all the shopping bags into the rental car and I say goodnight.

"See you tomorrow, Glinda," he tells me softly, gathering my hair into a ponytail and slipping the tie from his wrist around it.

"Yep. Sixteen days left." But I think I say it more for *my* benefit than his.

He smacks my ass. "Wicked."

CHAPTER 18

CIAN

It's been three days since I fucked Scarlett.

But I've been to her house for dinner each night since then and I've given her orgasms in the laundry room both last night and the night before.

God, she's spectacular.

We've also talked, brainstormed some things for my ninth graders, made treat bags for her friend Amber's little girl's dance recital, and listened to the *Wait 'Til I Tell Ye* podcast with Mariah and Ruby.

Last night Ruby had to go to work early, Henry stayed back at the B&B, and Greta was at home, so it was only Mariah, Scarlett, and me. It felt really fucking good.

Probably too good.

Because Scarlett is still counting down the days until our get-to-know-you arrangement is over, and I'm already sure that I'm never getting over her.

But I still have fifteen days—well, fourteen days and a

few hours since it's now nearly five o'clock—to convince her to extend our time together to...well, forever.

I resist the urge to whistle as I head up the sidewalk toward Scarlett's garage from the bed and breakfast on the still-warm September Friday.

I cross the large, paved parking area to the big, wide-open doors where I can see just a glimpse of her arm and hip where she's bent over the blue Honda with its hood up.

The garage was her stepfather's and still boasts his name on the sign for *Brian's Garage*.

I prop my shoulder against the door and ask, "How did the prim and proper preacher's daughter learn to fix cars anyway?"

Scarlett peeks around the hood and gives me a surprised smile as she straightens.

"Brian said I could preach to him if I did it here and handed him tools while we talked."

She steps out from behind the car. Her hair is held back by a bandana. She's in black work boots and blue coveralls, though they are partially unbuttoned, showing a gray tank underneath.

There is nothing inherently sexy about what she's wearing at all. The coveralls are dirty and streaked with grease. Her boots are scuffed. She's got a smudge of something—again, probably dirt or grease—on her cheek. But fuck...I want to bend her over that car.

"You preached to Brian?"

She pulls a rag from her back pocket, wiping her hands. "It was one of my mandates from the church. I had to preach to the whole family. Brian was the only one who really listened."

"While he fixed cars?"

She smiles. "Yep. At first, I'd watch him work while I

talked. Then he'd hand me the tools, show me what to do, and then oversee my work while he told me his thoughts on whatever I was "teaching" him." She leans a hip against the car. "He knew a lot about the Bible and the church—widely and my dad's—and Christianity. He'd been going to church and religion classes since he was a kid. He was raised Catholic and as an adult was a regular at the protestant church Greta's family goes to over in Billsly."

"Did you argue?"

"A little. But mostly he'd just tell me a different perspective." She looks down at her hands, wiping the rag she's holding over her palm. "He'd also show up in my dad's church about once a month. That helped me out because my dad thought it was because I was 'getting through to him'. Brian told me it was because he wanted to support me and because he wanted to experience how my dad taught his congregation. Said it helped him understand me better." She looks up. "Brian never tried to talk me out of going to my dad's church. He understood that I wanted a connection there. But he wanted me to really understand what Dad was teaching me."

"And you picked up car repair along the way," I say, watching her. I'm fascinated by her. Maybe I didn't know the *real* her. I didn't know all the details, certainly. But every time I learn something new, I fall deeper.

She nods, not looking up. "Yeah. And when I needed a job, all I could think about was how Brian just patiently, day by day, little by little, taught me this thing that could actually support me." She smiles. "Okay, he taught me more than one thing. But this thing that I could make money at." She lifts her head. "So I went garage to garage, asking if they needed help until one said yes. Pete. He paid me almost nothing at first, but then I slowly won him over, proving I was more reliable and harder working than any of his other mechanics and he increased my wages and paid for me to go to the community college to take some formal classes to learn some additional skills and—" She shrugs. "Here I am."

I push off the wall and walk toward her. "Do you like this job?"

She looks around the garage. "No."

I'm surprised. "Really?"

"I don't hate it. I like feeling capable. I like being able to help people. But no. This is not a dream job. It's just something I can do that people need and that contributes to the town."

I stop just a foot in front of her. I'm glad this isn't her dream job. Because I have a better idea. But I also wish this woman was happy with *something* in her life. I know she loves her daughter and sister, but even there I sense a tension. She wants *them* to be happy and Mariah's issues at school and Ruby's issues with Henry upset Scarlett.

Things aren't how Scarlett would like them to be, and I cannot tamp down the urge to fix it all.

She looks up at me and tucks the rag back into her pocket. "So, what are you doing here?"

"I haven't seen you all day. Ruby and Mariah said you'd be almost done."

She glances at the car. "I still need to do a few things for Diane, but she doesn't need it back until..." She laughs. "She doesn't have a set time she needs it back."

I smile and close the space between us. "Why can't you just let Diane give you casseroles to help you out?"

Scarlett shrugs. "Because I don't really need those casseroles. I feel guilty taking them, I guess."

"Do they help you?"

"Sure. It's nice some nights to just throw something in the oven and not have to worry about ingredients and recipes and taking the time to put it together."

"And that gives you time to spend with Mariah, or to do something else like laundry, or to just relax, which is also valuable. So you shouldn't feel guilty."

"I just know there are other people who need help a lot more than Ruby and Mariah and I do."

I lift my hand and cup her face. "It's okay for people to take care of you, Scarlett. Just because they want to. Just because they care. It doesn't have to be a need thing."

She takes a breath. "I'm just not used to that."

I fucking hate that. Hate. It. This woman should be *cherished*. But on the other hand, it means I can come in and do it and there's no one I need to shove out of the way.

"Ruby's taken care of you, right?" I ask.

I know that's the biggest reason Henry and Ruby can't be together. Henry needs to be with me, and Ruby feels she needs to be with Scarlett.

"Yes. Definitely," Scarlett agrees.

I wonder if she realizes that she's pressing her cheek into my hand.

"But by being emotionally supportive and physically being there for me, she's also had to do without a lot of stuff. We've had crappy apartments, stressful finances, and schedules to juggle. One of the reasons Ruby started bartending and then dancing was because it was at night. I would drop Mariah off at daycare around eight, then work during the day. Ruby would come home after her shift, sleep for a few hours, then pick Mariah up from daycare in the late morning. I'd come home and take over and she'd go to work. It saved us a lot of daycare money by having Mariah there only for about three hours a day."

The more I hear about the ways these women, girls really in the early days, had managed, the more I respect them. And the more I want to take care of them all from here on.

"Ruby has to work tonight," I say.

Scarlett nods.

"And Mariah told me she's going to Greta's for the weekend."

Scarlett rolls her lips in and nods.

"That means you and I have Friday night all to ourselves." I run my thumb along her jaw.

"It does," she says. "And I was thinking…"

There's a little sparkle in her eyes now and I definitely want to hear this.

"What if we went to Columbus tonight and got a hotel room?" she asks. "We have the house to ourselves tonight. Ruby won't be home until around two thirty. But…" She wets her lips.

"But?" I prompt.

"We could go out to dinner. And we wouldn't have to worry about anyone in town seeing us together."

"Are we worried about that?" I ask with a frown.

She shrugs. "Kind of. You're a college professor just traveling through. It's probably better if the town doesn't find out we're sleeping together."

"I shaved my beard, dyed my hair, and am wearing glasses so we could spend time together and people wouldn't know who I really am," I remind her.

"But that was before everyone was going to get to know and love you as a teacher," she says.

I feel my chest squeeze. "You think they're going to love me as a teacher?"

She smiles. "Of course. You're fun and charismatic as

hell. You're so excited about all of it. I know that's going to show and the kids are going to love having you around."

Warmth spreads through my chest unexpectedly. I clear my throat. "Thanks."

"But that makes it more complicated than if you were just hanging around waiting for your car to get fixed," she adds.

"Why?"

She sighs. "If you were just Professor Brady, you could have played aloof. Mysterious. You could have laid low. But as a teacher, you're not going to be able to help showing your enthusiasm. You're going to be very engaging and enjoy the job, and they're going to like you, and want to get to know you, and will include you in things."

"You want me to be aloof in the classroom with the kids?" I will try. I'm not sure I can pull it off but if that's what Scarlett needs, I can try.

"No," she says quickly. She laughs lightly. "I don't think you could pull that off anyway, but no. I want you to enjoy it."

She seems sincere. "I guess that does put more of a spotlight on me, doesn't it?"

"Yes."

She seems amused that I'm just now truly realizing that. I probably should have said no when they asked me to take over this class.

"I thought these eighteen days would be just us," she says. "Now it involves the whole town."

She seems a little...jealous? A couple of days ago she was fighting the idea of spending this time getting to know each other. But now she seems annoyed that she has to share me. I don't smile at that, but I do like it.

"And you're upset about that?"

She frowns and steps back. My arm falls to my side. "No," she says after a moment. "Because you're so excited about it. It just means that when you're going to happy hour at the bar with the teachers and to football games and tailgates, I won't be with you. We'll have less time together and we'll have to be careful when we are together. I don't think they'll like me dating you."

"Why not?"

She shakes her head, her smile a little sad now. "The last time I dated the new guy in town that everyone loved, I tried to trap him with a pregnancy, and he got run out of town."

I frown. "Everyone loved Eli?"

She nods and hugs her arms over her midsection "Very much. He was a great youth pastor. When he left town, they blamed me for taking someone away from the kids and community that was doing good work and helping people." She shrugs. "I'm sure they'll feel the same way about you."

I step forward. "They can *not* feel like you don't deserve *anything* good."

"A lot of them do," she says.

And she does. I realize it as I study her eyes. She believes that they're right to feel this way about her and punish her.

"So *you* lay low and don't go to happy hour at the bar or to tailgates and football games. You just do your work and quietly help whoever comes along—like Amber and Diane —and that's it. You don't let them see you enjoying life or having fun."

"Ruby and I go out. Amber has even joined us a few times. And we'll do things with Mariah and Greta. Movies. A couple of football games."

There's a wistfulness in her eyes and I *hate* it. It's clear that she wishes she could do more.

"Because people have already determined Ruby is a lost cause?"

She nods. "Guess so."

"And Amber?"

"Amber is new to town and is an amazing stylist. That gives her some power. They want to stay on her good side. She doesn't go to any church at all and is nice to everyone and doesn't let people gossip in her salon. She is just a really good person who doesn't take sides. She goes out with other people too. I guess everyone gives her a pass because she's equally nice to everyone. They figure she doesn't know better about me."

I think that over. I'm new to town, will be an amazing teacher who they need—that gives me some power—and I won't go to any church at all. But I will take sides. I'll be on Scarlett's side every time. Fully. No matter what.

"I definitely want to spend this weekend with you. And if you're more comfortable somewhere else, that's fine," I finally say.

I had intended to whisk her out of town anyway, so this is all great. But I have a very strong urge now to parade her around this town and show everyone that she's amazing and special and *mine*.

Clearly that's jumping the gun. Not only would that clearly make her uncomfortable, but I need to fully establish the mine thing first.

That clears the worry from her eyes, and she grins. "I just thought it would be easier to stay naked the whole time. You never know when Ruby might be around or if Mariah and Greta might pop in. And that way I don't have to be quiet if we wake up at four a.m. and want to..."

Her cheeks are pink but I fucking *love* that she just said all of that.

I step close and lean in, cupping her face and dragging my thumb through the grease on her cheek. "So my little witch needs a proper all-night-long fucking where she can beg and scream?"

She sucks in a breath, but nods.

"Anything you want from me, Scarlett. I told you that."

"Great," she says on a breath out. "There's a hotel in Columbus that has—"

"Except that."

"What?" Her forehead wrinkles.

"Come on. I have a plan."

"A plan?"

"Yes." I take her hand and start toward her little office where I assume she has her keys and other things she needs to close up for the weekend.

"But...no hotel?" she asks.

"Who said that?"

CHAPTER 19

SCARLETT

This is definitely not the Hampton Inn with free Wi-Fi and complimentary breakfast.

I wonder for a second if Cian knows about free breakfast at motels. Or that people sometimes have to pay for wi-fi.

But then I step onto the hotel elevator and as the doors swish shut quietly and the soft instrumental music drifts to me and Cian pushes the button for the twenty-second floor, I realize that no, he probably doesn't.

And he's still a good guy. So that's okay.

But he stays in places like palaces. And the Windsor Court hotel. In the Presidential Suite. Even when he's entertaining a woman he picked up at a strip club just for the weekend.

I *loved* that suite. I'd had no idea hotels had rooms like that. The room has a baby grand piano in it for fuck's sake. Who needs a *piano* in their hotel room? It's also got two bedrooms, but Henry is still staying in a room on the floor below us. Because…well, the last time we were here we made use of *all* the rooms, just the two of us. Including both bathrooms. And both terraces. And yes, I was loud.

I feel my heart rate speed up and work on not laughing giddily.

I'd realized we were headed to New Orleans as soon as we pulled onto the exit for the airport. And I love that we're back in New Orleans where we met. We're having a do-over of that magical weekend. But this time we both know everything.

I didn't, however, realize how this would all affect me when we actually got here. I'm hit with excitement and, okay, lust. But also the strangest sense of nostalgia. I never thought I'd be back here. I definitely never thought I'd be back here with Cian.

God, our weekend together had truly been like a fantasy.

The sense of dropping back into a dream had hit me when we'd pulled into the front circle, and I'd seen the fountain and gorgeous trees and flowers surrounding the hotel entrance. The scent of the hotel lobby, the décor, the way Cian had rested his hand on my hip possessively as we checked in all thrust me back in time and I'd found myself swallowing against the emotions that made my throat feel suddenly tight.

I'd honestly wondered if I'd ever come back to New Orleans. I'd loved living in the city, but even though I hadn't consciously made the decision, I realized as we walked through the airport that I'd put "fun weekend get-aways and vacations" on my list of things I didn't get to do anymore.

Oh, people in Emerald go on vacation. Some girlfriend

groups maybe even do weekend girl trips. But I'd realized that *I* didn't think *I* was going to do them anymore.

People would judge. People would decide that I was spending my money frivolously if I took Mariah on a trip or being an irresponsible parent if I left her at home. If anyone knew I'd jetted off to New Orleans this weekend, they would assume I was spending my time down on Bourbon Street rather than wonder if I was at the numerous parks and museums and amazing restaurants.

And so what if I did? Bourbon Street was a lot of fun and enjoying the people watching and the drinks and the music didn't necessarily mean anyone was doing anything wrong. Anyone who visited New Orleans from out of town should spend at least an hour on Bourbon just for fun.

But no one in Emerald would listen to *me* explain that.

Which was really fucking depressing.

I'm lost in my thoughts when the elevator stops on the twenty-first floor and Henry gets off. He's been grumpy and quiet the entire trip. Not that the flight was all that long. But when I first met Henry and he and Ruby were together, he was laid back and funny and very likable. Now he's broody and bitchy.

But I can relate. It was how I felt often after I found out that Cian was looking for me and I told Henry that I didn't want to see him.

Okay, after I *lied* to Henry about not wanting to see Cian.

Henry tells Cian, "Call if you need me" and then turns right as the elevator slides shut. Cian and I don't say anything as we get off on the next floor.

I feel my heart pounding and I blow out a long breath as I wait for him to unlock the door to the suite.

I will never forget any detail of the room inside.

It was not only the most surprising and sexy weekend of my life, but it was by far the most luxurious.

He pushes the door open and nudges me through first.

I catch my breath.

It's exactly as I remember it and the sense of nostalgia hits me hard again.

The penthouse has a big main living room, with a fireplace, gigantic flat screen television, and built-in bookcases. The artwork is gorgeous and I'm sure expensive. The chairs and couches are richly upholstered, and the back of the couch is very comfortable when you're bent over it with a hot prince fucking you from behind.

Can you be *sentimental* about a place where every piece of furniture reminds you of sex? Sure feels that way.

I grin to myself as I look around.

The room's décor is light pastels and creams. There's a round dining table with six chairs near the windows and another smaller sitting area I can't see from here. There are also two bedrooms and two bathrooms. My favorite is the one with the tub that's deep and wide enough for two people to fit.

The butterflies are swooping so fast that I have to press a hand over my stomach and take several deep breaths as I stand just inside the door.

"You okay, Glinda?" Cian asks since I haven't moved a single step further into the room.

The combination of the nickname and his deep voice have a soothing effect.

I face him with a smile. "Yeah. Just remembering."

He sets our bags down and lets the door swing shut. I expect him to stalk toward me, push me up against the door, and pull my jeans and panties down before going to his knees and making me come with his mouth in under five minutes.

Just like last time.

Instead, he strokes a hand over his jaw. "Lots of good memories."

I nod. "Great memories."

His hand drops. "I want you so much," he tells me, his voice husky.

I take a step toward him.

He takes a step back and my eyes go wide.

"But once I get you naked, I don't intend to let you get dressed until sometime late tomorrow," he says. "And there's something I want to show you first."

This *is* a surprise. We haven't had sex since the night on the patio. I've been having orgasms. Really, really nice orgasms. But he hasn't even taken his pants off. And now he wants to wait?

"Something that requires me staying dressed?" I ask.

His gaze tracks over me from head to toe. I'm wearing jeans, simple flats, and a pretty blue blouse that matches his eyes and that I'm pretty sure is actually Ruby's.

Ruby did my packing. It seems this trip was Cian's plan for this weekend all along and my sister and daughter are in on it.

I'm also pretty sure they're thrilled.

"Cian?" I ask when he doesn't say anything.

"I'm trying to decide if I am strong enough to fuck you right now, then let you get dressed and actually leave this room."

I take another step forward. "Being dressed and leaving the room are overrated. I lived here for six years. There's not much in the city that I wanted to see that I didn't." I can't think of anything as a matter of fact. New Orleans is a fun city and Ruby, Mariah, and I saw all the famous tourist sites as well as lots of great local spots.

He takes another step back and runs into the small table sitting under a mirror in this little foyer area. He grips the edge of the table as if for strength. "Yeah, I'm not strong enough for that. And there *is* something here that you haven't seen before."

I narrow my eyes. "And it's that important?"

"It is. It's really the reason for the trip. Though having you in this room again is *definitely* bringing back some memories I'd like to relive."

I'm glad he's dealing with flashbacks too. "Okay. Then let's go. Quickly."

He smiles and shakes his head. "The way you want this too is so fucking sexy."

"Then prepare to be turned on for however long this takes," I tell him. "Because I really want this."

I try to tell myself that I'm just using him for sex, the way I told myself, and Ruby, and *him* previously. The sex with Cian is *so* good.

But I'm a damn liar. Every minute I spend with him, I like him more and I've found that I'm also really enjoying having him at home when I get there after work, hearing him talk and laugh with Ruby and Mariah, and the little smiles, touches, and special, flirty words he always has for me.

And as much as I like having him in my day-to-day life and comfortable with Mariah and Ruby, I'm very much looking forward to having him to myself this weekend.

Cian holds the door open for me again, and we head back down to the hotel lobby. He calls for an Uber, rather than asking Henry to go with us, which is interesting in a what's-going-on way.

It takes us twenty-five minutes to get to the older neighborhood where the car drops us off on a corner that seems unremarkable.

There's a florist in the building on this corner. Across the street is a deli. There's a convenience store a little further down. I can also see a market, a coffee shop, a dog groomer, and an urgent care office. But beyond the businesses are houses and apartment buildings.

"This way." Cian links his fingers with mine, starting down the sidewalk. We walk for two blocks before he stops. "Right here."

I look up at him, waiting for him to elaborate.

He grins down at me, then points. "There."

I follow his finger. He's pointing at the building complex across the street. It's a group of townhouses. There are three buildings arranged in a U-shape. Each building has four townhouses in it. They each have a porch, some with kids' bikes leaning against the railing, some with potted plants, one with a swing. There's a yard in the middle with play equipment. A tall wrought-iron gate closes off that yard from the sidewalk that runs along the front of the property.

"What am I looking at?"

"Scarlett Park."

I frown. "Okay."

"It's the community for single moms we brainstormed."

I look at up at him. And just stare as I process that. Then I look across the street again. I really study it this time. There are lights glowing from some of the windows. I take in the well-kept grass in the yard. I note that each building is a different color—one is sky blue, one is a butter yellow, and one is seafoam green—with white shutters and white porches with steps and railings. There are flower beds, baskets of flowers, and flowering bushes. So many flowers. So much color.

I feel choked up as I look back up at him. "Really?"

He tucks his hands into his pockets and nods. "I bought it about three months after our weekend. We renovated and remodeled. I hired a woman, Joann, who is a social worker, to manage it. She helps figure out what the women and kids need, helps explain to new residents how things work, and acts as the go-between with them and me. She lets me know what's needed and I make it happen. She's pretty great." He gives me a smile.

"Tell me more," I say, watching his face instead of studying the building now.

He seems thrilled that I asked. "There are two or three women in each townhouse, each has one to three kids. They get to decide how many people they want to live with. Joann manages who fits best together—the ages of the kids and the women's schedules and stuff like that They have weekly community meetings, and the guiding principle is that they all have to work together to make it function. Like a family would. The kids and their school schedules need to be covered. Their work schedules need to fit together. They deal with meals and shopping and household chores together in whatever way works best for everyone. Sometimes one woman cooks for a couple of houses if those women help her out with other things. That's all up to them. We cover the housing costs fully. They don't pay rent or utilities or any maintenance. But they take care of everything else. Unless Joann lets me know they need more."

"That's…" I don't know what to say really.

"We also have on-call maintenance twenty-four-seven and there's security that routinely drives by and a female officer does walk throughs. They can be reached directly and are only two minutes away in case there are ever any issues. Three of the women work shifts where they get home after midnight and a security guard meets them to walk them from their cars to their doors."

"That's amazing, Cian," I say softly. We'd talked about security when we'd brainstormed. He really had included everything.

"And we've only had two move out in the year and a half," he says quickly. "One moved to another city and one ended up falling in love and moving in with her boyfriend. Everyone loves living here."

I lift his hand, pressing it against my heart. "I'm sure they they do. Cian, it sounds perfect."

"It's what we came up with together," he says. "Exactly."

I nod. "I know."

I'm stunned. But as it sinks in, I realize I'm not shocked, actually. Remembering how excited he was about the plan when we came up with it and how easily he gives money when he discovers a need, this makes complete sense.

"I'd love to hear more about it," I say. "Do you know more about the families?"

He shrugs. "A little. But I haven't met them. That's Joann's thing."

I frown. "You haven't met them?"

"Nah. That seems strange. They don't need to know me."

"They'd probably like to."

"It's not about me," he says. "I provide the funding, but Joann knows a lot more about how to really run the place. And the women themselves know what they need."

That's true. But knowing Cian, he would love to know these families. He'd love to see how he was helping.

Then again, it's not about him. He's right, I suppose.

"Have you opened other communities like this?" I ask.

"Yes. There are six others."

Wow. I...don't know what to say to that.

"Do you want to get dinner? We can talk about it more. Now that I've got you back, we can talk about what else to do."

Now that I've got you back. Yeah, oh boy.

"Okay, yeah, let's get dinner." I really want to hear more. I realize my heart is beating fast and my mind is spinning with questions.

Are the other communities multiple buildings like this? We'd actually brainstormed buying big houses with multiple bedrooms. Has he done that anywhere? Where are the other ones? Is he going to do more?

"There's a great Italian place right down the block." He puts his hand on my lower back and we start down the sidewalk.

Antonio's smells *amazing* and it hits me that I'm starving when we step inside the cozy restaurant at the end of the block.

It's one of those places that is decorated in red and white and gold and dimly lit with sconces on the wall and fat round glass candle holders on the tables.

We're escorted to a booth along the far wall immediately by a grinning older man who greets us with an enthusiastic, "Benvenuti!"

After we have water, glasses of red wine, and a plate of bruschetta in front of us, Cian turns to me. "I want to offer you a job."

"A job?"

"Yes, as president of the foundation."

"What foundation?"

"The foundation I'm going to start."

He doesn't even have the foundation started. Okay. "You're starting a foundation?"

"Yes. One that will build even more communities like the one across the street. And other things." He leans in, pinning me with an earnest look. "We can come up with all kinds of programs, scholarships, school supply funds."

I smile.

"Whatever you want," he says. "We can fund all kinds of things."

"Me? What about *you*?" I ask. "What kinds of things do you want to do?"

"Anything. That's the thing I realized by putting that community together. I've got the money, and I can raise more. Talking to other rich guys is easy. Convincing them to give me money is easy. I've got connections. I can get resources together. I just need the ideas and plans to spend it on."

That must be a nice problem to have.

I study him as I think about what I already know about this man. He loves his sister and niece, he realizes that they lived a very privileged life though, despite her singleness. He was legitimately excited about building these homes for single moms when we talked about them when we were together.

"What would this job look like?" I ask.

"As president you would, of course, help with brainstorming projects. Recruiting people, getting the word out, managing the overall vision. You'd be the primary spokesperson to the media and donors—with my help—and other organizations. You'd head the Board of Directors and you'd help get the directors in place. Figure out what committees we'd need." He shrugs. "You'd do all of the big stuff. You'd be in charge. The boss."

"What would *you* do?" I ask, my heart pounding.

"CFO. I can get the money—use my own, fundraise, whatever. Figure out financing. I'd also help talk to the towns and officials that we need to win over, deal with permits and things like that as needed. We'll work together on every aspect."

"So I would need to travel? Do presentations and things?"

"Definitely."

"Oh." I sit back, shaking my head. "No, I can't do that."

"Why not?"

"I'm not... qualified."

He chuckles. "Of course you are. You'll know all about it. We'll come up with every idea together. It will be things you're passionate about. You'll just have to talk to people about it."

"I'm just a mechanic," I say. "I don't know anything about running a foundation."

"But you're a single mom. That's the biggest thing. Your story is why you're passionate about this."

"Your sister is a single mom. You helped raise your niece. You know what single moms need too."

I know that sounds like a weak protest. I should want to do this. But the idea of trying to talk people into things scares me. I did that for six years and I hate the person I was then.

"I'm a *guy*," he says. "A single guy with no kids of his own. Sure, I can share my story too, but who should be the face of this? A feisty, amazing woman who raised an amazing, brilliant daughter on her own. Okay," he says, holding up a hand when I start to protest. "With her sister. But that's the cool thing. You're a group of kickass women who want to help other women. Just like those elephants you love, you stick together and form unshakeable bonds and protect each other for life." He leans in and takes my hand. "I know you want to help other women that way. Let me help you do that. I have the money. Let me give it to you to spend."

I laugh lightly. Who wouldn't want to hear a billionaire tell them *here take my money*. Better yet, this one is saying *take my money and do something amazing to make other people's lives better with it.*

"I think an elephant should be a part of our logo, by the way," he tells me.

Dammit. It shouldn't be that easy, but I love that, and it does soften me even further.

"I can't travel. There's Mariah."

"Mariah is almost sixteen. And you have Ruby and Greta's family to be there for her. You can take their *help*, Scarlett. So you can do things for you. That's okay. And you don't have to travel for weeks at a time. Just a few days here and there."

He's going to have a really great counterargument to everything I say, but I still feel the need to push back.

"I can't—" I swallow. "I can't go around trying to convince people to do things *I* think they should do like that, Cian. I can't go into communities and tell them that they should go along with *our* plans and ideas."

He frowns. "That's not what this is. Whatever we do will be projects the communities want. We'll work with community leaders to provide things that they need." Then it seems understanding dawns on his face. He shakes his head. "We're not going to preach to anyone. We're not going to push this on anyone. We're not going to tell them they have to do anything or guilt them or coerce them. We're going to offer to help. We'll be there with resources for whatever they need."

My stomach twists, but I'm not shaking my head as earnestly as I was before. I spent all those years in high school trying to convince people to see things my way, to do things I wanted them to do, to put their time, money, *hearts* into something that mattered to me. And I never should have done that.

But, intellectually, I know this is different and I'm over-reacting. This isn't like going out and telling people they need my father's church or they'll be lost and doomed.

This is different. This is good.

But I'd believed what my father wanted and was preaching was good at the time.

I take a deep breath.

I'm definitely overreacting.

"Can I think about it?" I ask Cian.

He looks disappointed but nods and sits back. "Of course."

So, I lean in. "I want *you* to keep going with this. You've been hiding away in the US, not really doing anything that really lights you up. I love the look on your face when you talk about these communities and this foundation. You told me when we met that you feel like a sidekick to your siblings. I want *you* to have something you are passionate about."

He looks at me with such sincerity and tenderness that I suck in a breath. "I want you to stop hiding too. I want you to shine, Scarlett. I want the world to see you. But even more, I want *you* to see you."

My eyes sting and I blink rapidly.

"I wanted it before," he says, his voice gruff. "But now

that I've gotten to know you and your story, everything with Emerald and your dad...I want you to be proud of who you are, the way you've overcome and raised Mariah and how you've changed since you left Emerald. I want you to show him, and the world, but also *yourself* who you are now."

My heart is pounding and I feel like I'm going to cry. But I'm not sure if it's from happiness or sadness. Or just overwhelm.

This opportunity is...amazing.

I have no qualifications other than being a single mom.

That has defined me for the past sixteen years. It's shaped every choice I've made, everything I've done. It's made me proud and happier than I've ever imagined. It's also made me scared and more vulnerable than I've ever been.

It's the thing that changed my life. That took me down a road that absolutely made me who I am today.

And that person is who Cian O'Grady knows. It's who he sees. That's who he *wants*.

And he wants to give all of this...possibility to me, not just despite all of that but *because* of all of that.

The waiter arrives with our entrees and that helps us transition our conversation to talking about what other details Cian has about the women and kids that live at Scarlett Park—the name actually *really* hits me this time, and I'm touched while also feeling a little trepidation about how involved he truly made me. He really did take every single thing we talked about and implemented it.

We also talk about other cities where buildings or houses could be renovated, or new structures could be built.

Then we start brainstorming other projects. Or rather, I

sit and listen and ask questions about ideas Cian has apparently been thinking about for nearly two years. He's thought about getting involved in something to do with elder care, he has some ideas about criminal justice reform, as well as finding out what's needed in the area of service animals.

He has a wide range of interests. And doesn't know much very specific about any of them.

That's what he needs me for. To give shape and direction to all of these various ideas.

He's got a big heart. He *wants* to do good things. He recognizes his privilege. He just needs someone to help. Someone to be his partner.

Is that someone me?

I'm not sure.

But it really makes me like him. A lot.

CHAPTER 20

CIAN

Maybe I should have told Scarlett about the community for single moms before taking her there. I could have approached the idea of her leading a foundation that would do more work like that before we left Emerald, and she could've had time to process it. She did love the actual community itself. Seeing it in person, the actual embodiment of our ideas, touched her. I could tell she was impressed when she saw it and brainstorming more projects was just as fun as last time.

But I want her to be over-the-top enthusiastic. I want her to have work she *loves*. Work that shows off the incredible person she is and helps *her* see that she doesn't need to stay quiet and under the radar and wait for people to come to her. She can go out and touch people's lives even before they realize how much they need her.

I've seen my sister exhausted, angry, stressed about the work she does, but she's motivated and exhilarated by it at the same time because she believes in it. Fiona knows she's doing something meaningful.

In the short time I've known my sister-in-law Abigail I've seen the same. Abi doesn't fit into a lot of "normal" peer groups. She has social anxiety, but the work she does can make her downright chatty and charming when you get her going on a topic she's enthusiastic about, like the indoor farms she plans to build in cities across the US with my brother's money.

Astrid is the same. She's been through hell with her injury and rehab, and she's not the same sunny girl I grew up with, but when she talks about the advocacy work she does, there's a spark that nothing else gives her.

That's what I saw in Scarlett in New Orleans two years ago. It's what I see now when she's at home talking with Mariah, or when she's brainstorming with me.

But she doesn't talk about her work that way. She definitely doesn't talk about Emerald that way. She's in Emerald to prove points, and it sucks the life out of her.

I want her to be happy. I want to give her something that gives her the fire and drive, that taps into that part of her I've seen in all these other women in my life.

Fuck, I want that for myself. It's what I'm searching for.

I watch her cross to the bed in the suite and lean over to take her sandals off. It's September, which is still warm in Ohio, but it's downright hot in Louisiana which means Ruby packed Scarlett a sundress and sandals that she changed into on the plane.

She looks gorgeous and it is a testament to how into our conversation I was that I wasn't feeling her up under the table at the restaurant.

She turns and runs her hands through her hair which causes the hem of the dress to rise on her perfect thighs.

"You should know," she says, letting her arms, and hair, drop. "I'm proud of you, Cian. What you did with that community is incredible. I'm so glad you did it."

Hearing she's proud of me should not have the effect it has on me, but my chest warms and tightens.

I take a step toward her. "I'm glad. I thought of you every single day during the process."

"I wish I could've seen it coming together."

I come to stand right in front of her. "I do too. I kept worrying I was missing something. I kept wishing I could share the decisions. I kept wondering what you would think of certain things. I wished that you could meet Joann. And that she could know you."

"Have you told your sister about it?" she asks, looking up at me.

I shake my head. "Henry is the only one who knows about it."

Scarlett frowns. "Why? You should be proud of it."

I'm not sure why I haven't told anyone. Then I realize that's not entirely true. "Because I did it to share it with you. I guess when I couldn't, I just...kept it to myself. I wasn't sure it would mean that much to anyone else."

She looks sad and then frustration crosses her face. "They would think it was great. Your family is full of people who do things for others, who look for ways to improve lives. I know they'd want to know."

I feel a twist of frustration as well. "Maybe I'll mention it. Maybe when the foundation is established and there's more going on."

"Maybe you're putting too much pressure on it. Maybe you're thinking too big. No one's expecting you to solve world peace, or cure cancer."

I study her strand of hair with its blend of at least four

different browns from gold to caramel to deep rich coffee, instead of looking into her eyes. "Why not? People like me are supposed to be the ones doing that stuff."

Her hand comes up to circle my wrist. "Cian."

I look at her. Her big brown eyes are also a swirl of gold and a deeper chocolate brown.

"If you're waiting to do something *that* big, you're going to be sitting around letting small, wonderful things pass you by," she says softly, squeezing my wrist. "I'm not saying that if something big and wonderful comes up, you shouldn't grasp it and put your whole heart, and all of your resources behind it, but a whole bunch of wonderful little things can also add up." She lifts a hand to my face and smiles. "And sometimes those things that seem like small, wonderful things to a prince are pretty huge to regular people."

She lifts up on her tiptoes and presses her lips to mine.

I slide my hand to the back of her head and deepen the kiss immediately.

Maybe I can't help cure cancer, but I can be everything this woman needs me to be.

She has been real with me. Very fucking real. In this very room in this very hotel in this very city.

"For a woman trying to convince me not to be in love with her, you're doing a terrible job of it," I say against her mouth.

I feel the shiver that goes through her.

Her voice is breathless when she says, "I need you. The last two nights have been amazing, but I need more."

I know what she needs. She needs a place where she can feel safe and worshipped while being as open and free and sexual as she wants and needs to be.

I am *exactly* that place for her.

I brush my lips back and forth against hers. "You mean the last two nights when I've given you hard orgasms, but not let you have my cock?"

"Yes," she practically whimpers.

"The cock that you've always been so greedy for? The cock you took on your back patio where any of your neighbors could've seen you?"

This time she does whimper. "Cian."

I tug on her hair, tipping her head back so that I can nip and lick down her throat. "You're the one who has kept us apart for nineteen months, you wicked little witch." I suck on the base of her throat then drag my mouth up to her ear. "For six months you knew how to find me, but you stayed away. Even when Henry came to get you. You could have had all of me, any time you wanted me."

Her hands are fisted in the front of my shirt. "I know," she says raggedly.

"So you know what I want from you?" I ask, nipping her earlobe before lifting my head.

She looks a little dazed and her cheeks are flushed pink. She's fucking gorgeous like this.

"What?"

I run my thumb over her lower lip. "I want to hear you beg."

She sucks in a little breath, her pupils dilate, and her fingers tighten in my shirt. "Please. *Please*, Cian."

I give her a little smile. Then shake my head slowly. "On your knees, my pretty witch."

Her eyes flare with heat, then she nips the tip of my thumb. Lust whips through me, tightening my cock. Fuck.

"Now," I command, low and gruff.

She flattens her palms on my chest and then starts lowering herself to the floor.

The plush carpet here by the bed gives me zero hesitation about having her on her knees in front of me. I keep my hand in her hair, letting the silky strands slip over my palm until she's fully kneeling, with her hands resting on her thighs. Then I wrap the length around my fist.

"You've denied both of us for almost two years," I say.

She nods. "I know."

"This is your chance to ask me for forgiveness," I tell her.

She swallows and I see her wiggle her fingers. I know it's adrenaline. We established previously that she could easily say no to anything I asked of her. I was calling the shots, but she was always in control.

Pineapple was her safe word.

That comes back to me in this moment, and I almost laugh. Obviously, pineapples are a favorite of hers.

"What's your safe word?"

She looks up at me quickly, obviously also having forgotten we'd established one of those.

She doesn't have to think though. "Pineapple." She gives me a smile.

I nod. "Good." I unbutton and unzip my jeans. My cock is steel hard, already leaking at the top. She's had this effect on me from minute one.

She studies me, wetting her lips.

I take my cock in hand, stroking up and down my length, watching her face.

This is all just a game. I would gladly carry her to bed, lay her back, and worship her all night. I'm putting her on her knees because this is what she wants. I love that I know her. I love that I know she loves this dirty side of herself as much as I do.

Hands still on her thighs, she starts to lean in, but I grip her hair. "Greedy," I chide softly. "I haven't heard a single *I'm sorry* or *please* since your knees hit the carpet."

She looks up at me from beneath her lashes. "Please, Cian."

"Please what?" I stroke my cock in front of her face again.

"Please can I suck your cock?"

I blow out a breath. This gorgeous, amazingly strong, big-hearted, wounded woman is saying this to me, and I just want to tell her she's incredible and buy her flowers and run her a bubble bath and make love to her.

But she needs *this*.

I coach her. "Please can I use my mouth to make you feel good to make up for being a bad girl and keeping my pussy away from you for almost two years." I tug on her hair slightly. "Say that."

She repeats the words.

"Even though you made me feel better than anyone ever has," I say.

She obediently says the sentence back to me.

"Even though you filled my pussy up and fucked me so well I didn't take a step the next day without feeling you."

I see her fingers dig into her thighs as she makes a soft moaning sound before she says the words.

"I'm sorry that I made you fuck your own hand, replaying every second of being with me every night instead of sinking into my perfect pussy."

She whimpers softly, but again says the exact words.

Finally, I lean closer, dragging the head of my cock over her lips. "That was very wicked of you, Scarlett. And now that I have you here, alone, all to myself, I'm going to remind you of all the reasons you do *not* want to do that again."

She swallows hard. "Okay."

"You can suck my cock now."

Her tongue comes out, giving me a lick.

I hiss. "That's it," I urge.

I move my hand, and she wraps hers around the base. She strokes up and down as she takes more of me into her hot, slick mouth. Her tongue swirls around the top, then she slides me further in, sucking.

I grit my teeth. I taught her well last time. She remembers exactly what I like. And it has been a *long* nineteen months, and *fuck*, I've missed her hot, greedy mouth, her tongue, seeing her kneeling at my feet.

I want this to last. I want her to have this erotic moment. I want to remind her how fucking hot things are between us. But the chances of me lasting more than a couple of minutes are very slim.

"Take me deeper," I urge.

She moans and I see her reach between her legs.

I pull on her hair. Her eyes come up to mine. "Don't you dare touch yourself," I growl. "You are going to just have to suffer a little, sweet witch, and remember that it's your own fault."

She brings that hand up to cup my balls and begins to work me faster, moving her hand up and down my length, taking me deeper.

I think for a moment of pulling her off but I know she likes to swallow—that was a very nice discovery—and fuck, I need her to take it all. "Need you to swallow, Scarlett," I tell her.

She squeezes me and sucks harder and a moment later, I cup the back of her head as I come.

She takes all of me, happily, greedily. When she pulls

back, she's breathing hard. Her eyes are shiny with desire and her cheeks are pink.

I grasp her upper arms and pull her to her feet, sealing my mouth over hers. I pull back, resting my forehead on hers. "Jesus, you're incredible."

"I'm sorry I kept us apart," she says.

I chuckle. "Oh, no. You're not quite done being punished for that."

A shiver goes through her. "Oh...good."

I sweep her up into my arms and turn to the bed. I lay her back on the pillows, then step back, reaching over my head to grab my shirt and yank it over my head. I toss it to the side and bend to untie my shoes, kicking them to the side as I move to push my pants off.

She's watching me and as I straighten, she props up on her elbows. "What..." She trails off.

I follow her gaze to my left bicep. To my new tattoo. At least, new since we were last together.

She looks down at the bracelet she wears on her left wrist, where Mariah's birth date is tattooed, then back to my tattoo.

"You got my elephant as a tattoo?" she asks softly.

"I did." I leave my boxers on but kick my pants to the side. I kneel on the bed next to her, bracing my hands on either side of her hips.

She lies back but lifts a hand to trace a finger over the shape of the elephant holding a gem in its trunk. "Why?" she asks.

"Because I trusted I would return the bracelet to you eventually and wanted to keep that with me."

Her eyes lift to mine. "When did you get it?"

"On the year anniversary of us meeting."

"Cian..."

"Listen, Glinda, if you think you're going to get all mushy and distract me from all the very depraved things I have planned for you, you are *very* mistaken." I lean in and kiss her.

God, I want to be mushy. I want to tell her that I'm crazy about her. That I am *not* getting over her. In fact, I'm falling more in love with her every minute. But she doesn't really want that right now. And once I start all of that, I'm not going to be able to stop. So I need to keep this dirty and fun. There will be time for the rest of that later.

"Okay," she says, putting her hand against my cheek and giving me a mischievous smile.

"Now shut up and spread your legs and let me at this pussy," I say against her lips. "Because I've been *very* good and have been quick and quiet in the dark for *three* nights in Emerald, but now I want to be very, very bad and I want you wide open, lights nice and bright so I can see every single wet, pink inch, and I'm going to take my time and make you very loud."

She's breathing hard again and I'm not sure she could spell 'elephant' at the moment.

CHAPTER 21
CIAN

I skim my hands down her side and grasp the bottom of her dress, dragging it up, then urging her to sit so I can tug it over her head. I toss it to the floor and she reaches back for the clasp on her bra. She tosses it to the floor as my thumbs hook the top of her panties and pull them down her legs.

Then she's gloriously naked on top of the pristine white duvet.

My gaze tracks over every inch of her as she lays back against the pillow.

"Spread your legs," I tell her, pushing off the bed to round to the other side where I flip on the lamp on the bedside table.

The one next to her is already glowing, probably left on by housekeeping.

I wasn't kidding when I said I wanted full bright light so I could see everything.

"I have the image of you ingrained in my mind," I tell

her. "But nothing compares to the real thing." I climb up the bed from the bottom. "Fuck, you take my breath away, Scarlett."

"You too," she says softly, her eyes hot on my skin, coming back to the elephant tattoo on my left arm. "I missed you naked."

I've definitely been overdressed for our liaisons the last few nights, even on the patio.

I slide my hand up her right leg, squeezing her thigh. "I have so much to do to you, I don't know where to start."

Her left leg moves restlessly on the bed. "Anywhere. Please."

"I see you're getting better with the begging."

"I'll do anything."

Yes, she will. She's very good at following directions when she's naked on a bed with me.

I stretch out on my stomach between her legs and begin kissing up her inner thigh to the crease between her hip and pussy. "Remember you said that," I tell her. Then I use my thumbs to part her, my mouth watering at the sight of the pussy that ruined me for all other women.

I lean in and take a long lick.

She gasps my name, and I feel her hand land on top of my head, gripping my hair.

Her grip gets tighter as I continue to lick and suck. I circle her clit, sucking lightly, before stroking my tongue into her, groaning at her taste and scent.

After a few strokes with my tongue, I add a finger, then a second, as I focus my firm licks, and firmer sucks on the needy little nub of her clit.

I fuck and stretch her, rubbing over her G-spot with just enough pressure to make her pussy walls begin to tighten around my fingers.

"Cian!" she gasps.

"Louder," I command gruffly, fucking her a little faster.

"Cian!" she cries.

I feel her pussy begin to ripple and I pull my fingers and mouth away.

"No!" she protests. *That* is nice and loud.

I smirk at her as I lean in and kiss her inner thigh then give the spot a hard suck. "You want more of my mouth?"

"Yes. So much."

"You could've had that every night for the past—"

"Nineteen months," she interrupts, her tone exasperated.

I chuckle. "Exactly."

She grips my forearm. "Please, Cian. I'm sorry. Please, please make me come."

"All in good time." I rise up between her thighs. Damn, she's stunning. Laid out, breathing hard, skin flushed, dark hair spread out on my pillow, thighs open for me, on the edge of orgasm. All mine.

I cup my hand over her pussy. "This is mine, got it?"

She nods quickly. "Yes."

"I'm in charge of it. When it comes. How it comes."

She pulls her bottom lip between her teeth, clearly a little worried. Good, she should be. I give her pussy a little tap. She jumps and gasps. Not from pain, but from surprise.

I slide two fingers into her again, pumping deep.

She moans. "Yes."

"Just remember, my greedy little witch, just because I'm a gentleman doesn't mean I won't spank you."

Her eyes, which had fluttered shut, snap open and focus on me. Her pussy clenches around my fingers.

Yes, my good girl, my sometimes-bitchy preacher's daughter, likes to be spanked.

I reach up and cup one of her breasts, tugging on the nipple, then pinching harder as I continue to fuck her with my fingers.

She grabs my wrist and holds me against her breast, lifting her hips closer to my hand. "Oh God," she moans.

"Do you want me to let you come like this?" I ask her.

She quickly. "Yes, please."

I withdraw my fingers. "Cian!"

Now *that* is a shout.

I chuckle. "Patience. Trust."

She reaches for me, grabbing my wrist and trying to tug it back toward her pussy. "Come *on*."

"Oh, Glinda, that was the wrong thing to do."

But actually, it was very much the right thing to do. I pull my hand away and lean toward the bedside table where I stashed a few fun items. I withdraw a long pink silk tie. And a matching blindfold.

"You don't get to put my hands where *you* want them. I put my hands where *I* want them. And yours." I hold up the tie. "Hands up," I command.

She's breathing fast and again, pulls her lip between her bottom teeth. But she obediently lifts her arms over her head. She even grabs on to the swirling wrought iron pattern of the headboard.

I lean over her. "Good girl," I praise as I loop the silk tie around her wrists, tying them together, then thread the tie through the headboard. I leave a little slack so that her arms are not completely stretched out. But she's not getting out of these. Not without giving me a safe word.

"What do you say if you want to stop?" I ask.

"Pineapple."

I lean over and kiss her. "Very good." Then I reach for

the blindfold. I bring it to her face and slip the elastic band over her head.

A shiver goes through her body, and I sweep both hands down her sides to her hips.

"Where was I?" I slide two fingers back into her, pumping deep. I play with her opposite nipple, tugging harder than before, and am rewarded with a squeeze of her pussy around my fingers.

I add a third finger then circle over her clit with my thumb.

"Jesus, Scarlett," I say. "You have no idea how fucking gorgeous you are like this. Taking everything I'm giving you, wanting more, and all fucking *mine*."

I feel her pussy begin tightening around my fingers again and I know she's on the brink of an orgasm.

I pump three more times. But I don't give her that final satisfaction. Yet.

I pull my fingers from her body and she cries out. This time it's with true frustration "Cian, *please!*"

"Don't you trust me?" I ask her.

"Please let me come. Please don't punish me anymore."

"This is punishment?" I ask, tugging on her nipple and brushing lightly over her clit.

She gasps and arches closer. "Teasing me is."

"I don't know," I say, doing both again. "I would think *this* would be more like punishment."

I grasp both of her hips and turn her to her stomach. The tie twists along with the motion, allowing her arms and hands to turn without any pain. I pull her up onto her knees and give her ass a quick smack.

She gasps, then moans.

"Isn't spanking actually a punishment?" I ask my mouth against her ear as I run my hand over her ass. "Not playing with a pretty perfect pussy and making it all wet and tingly and needy. That makes you feel good. That's *nice*." I spank her again. "This is punishing, isn't it?"

She moans. "That makes me feel good too." She sucks in a breath. "Even though I don't know why."

I slip my hand between her legs, one finger sliding into her pussy. Her incredibly wet pussy.

"Maybe it's just having my hands on you in any way," I say gruffly against her neck.

She nods. "It is."

Fuck I love that.

"That's because deep down my little witch is actually wicked, isn't she? She loves to be dirty and naughty, and she knows she can do that with me."

She wiggles her ass and says in a choked voice, "Yes, God, yes."

I give her another quick smack then slide my finger into her pussy and give her three thrusts. "Well then, it's a good thing that *I* am a wizard when it comes to making you come."

I move in behind her, grasp her, hips, line up my aching cock, then thrust forward.

She cries out my name, her pussy gripping me immediately.

I grit my teeth and squeeze her hips, just pausing for a moment, afraid I might lose it if I move.

"Jesus. Christ. Scarlett." Single words at a time is all I can manage.

"Oh my God, Cian," she gasps.

Her pussy clenches around me and I give her a little spank. "Stop it."

She sucks in a breath. "Can't. Please move."

My hand rests on the warm pink handprint I've put on

her ass. I massage it. Then I start moving. She's stretched out in front of me, her hands grasping the wrought iron headboard, even though she's still tied to it. I thrust into her, and she takes every single stroke, babbling with simple responses like, "yes," "harder," "more," "oh God," and "Cian".

Despite the blow job, I'm on edge and I can feel my orgasm barreling at me.

"You can come now," I tell her. "Come on my cock, Scarlett."

She's been teetering on the edge anyway, and I know it is a combination of the force of my thrusts and the sharp command in my voice that makes her tighten around me and cry out as she comes hard.

I don't let up. I pound into her until my own orgasm slams into me with a force I swear I've never felt.

It goes on for several seconds and even after I'm spent, I continue gripping her hips, holding her ass back against me, breathing hard and waiting for her to show me a sign of life.

Finally, she drags in a long breath and lifts her head. "Oh my God, I really am sorry I've kept us from doing this."

That causes a laugh to burst from my chest. I slide a hand up her back, then I reach up and slide the blindfold off. "You should be." I give her ass one more little pat. "Don't let it happen again."

I let go of her hips and pull out, immediately reaching for the tie to release her from the headboard. I toss the tie to the floor and run my hands up and down her arms.

"You okay?" I ask as I pull her down next to me on the bed.

She snuggles in close. "Really good."

"You are amazing."

She lifts her head to look at me and gives me a sexy smile. "You did all the work. I just took it."

I reach down and find the warm spot on her ass. I squeeze it, then I massage it more gently. "You sure did take it. Like a very good girl. But my assumption about your witchcraft remains. I don't lose my mind like that with anyone but you."

She pushes up and gives me a serious look. "Good."

Is that possessiveness? Jealousy? I don't study her face any further because she leans in and gives me a deep, long kiss.

Then she slumps back down onto the pillow. "When I get a few bones back in my body, can we take a bath?"

We spent a long time in that bathtub last time. I'm all for it. "We're going to need some supplies. I'll call down to the desk."

The bath requires bubbles, chocolate-covered strawberries, and champagne.

Oh, and maybe something pineapple flavored. I didn't know about her favorite flavor last time, but now I'll do whatever I can to get her *exactly* what she wants.

Thankfully, I can easily supply all of those things.

But as I pull her closer and tuck her under my chin, I wish like hell I knew for certain that I could supply absolutely *everything* this woman could ever possibly need or want.

CHAPTER 22
SCARLETT

I roll over the next morning as Cian walks out of the bathroom with a towel around his waist. He hasn't shaved, but his hair is wet from the shower. He sees my open eyes and gives me a grin.

"Good morning," he rumbles.

"Morning."

"I ordered you some food. Henry and I are going to drive down to Autre. We shouldn't be gone for more than a couple of hours."

I sit up and run a hand through my hair. "Oh. I didn't realize you were heading down there."

He crosses to his suitcase. "I hadn't specifically planned on it but being this close, I'd feel strange if I don't stop in and say hi. Especially with Fiona and Saoirse." He shoots me a grin that almost looks sheepish. "I miss them."

My heart gives a little squeeze. I love that. He's close to his family. And I would feel the same way. I looked Autre up after hearing about it on the podcast. I could never be within twenty miles of my sister or daughter and not see them.

"Do you want me to get ready and go along?" I feel strange but I don't know if it's stranger to go along or stay back.

He pulls jeans and a tee from his bag and chuckles. "Are you going to agree to marry me?"

My eyes widen. "Um..."

"Until you are," he continues with a soft chuckle. "It's probably not a great idea to introduce you to everyone. When I get there, they're going to grill me about meeting up again with the girl I've been hung up on for two years. Not to mention my arranged marriage in Cara. If I bring you along, we're not getting out of there for seventy-two hours minimum. Not until they know everything about you and have completely won you over. And if you're not careful, we'll end up married by the local judge before they let us leave."

I swallow hard. "I thought your family wanted you to marry the other girl."

"Yeah well, the people down in Autre are mostly adopted family, and they are hopeless romantics. They love that I fell head over ass for you in one weekend and have been pining for you for so long. They're all Team Scarlett."

Lots of emotions are swirling, not the least of which is a warm fuzzy feeling that I probably shouldn't examine too closely.

"So I'm safer here," I say. "Got it."

He chuckles again and drops his towel to get dressed.

I stare.

He catches me and smirks. "There will be time for that when I get back."

"I have no idea what you're talking about," I say with feigned innocence.

"Ha ha," he says, pulling boxers and then jeans over the main subject of my interest. That still leaves a lot of skin and bulging muscles, though.

He rounds the bed and leans over to give me a kiss. "We'll be back in a little bit."

"I'll be here."

"Go to the spa if you want. Put it on the room."

Oh, I like the sound of that. I look toward the bathroom. "Or I might take a soak."

He straightens and shakes his head. "The bathtub is for both of us later."

I'm grinning stupidly as the door shuts behind him.

Damn, I really like that guy.

Room service arrives a few minutes later, and I am sipping a perfect cappuccino and munching on delightful strawberries when a thought occurs to me.

I suddenly have a wonderful idea of how to spend the next couple of hours.

And I end up grinning stupidly throughout my quick shower and my phone call to the concierge for help with my plan.

An hour later, I walk through the door of a tiny bar along Bayou Road in Autre, Louisiana. I never would've found it if it weren't for directions from the man at the gas station on the corner as I came into town.

There's no sign on the building, but this looks like how he described Ellie's bar.

I park my rental car on the edge of the gravel lot after spotting the car Henry drove us to the hotel in yesterday.

As I step through the door, the room is dark enough it takes my eyes a moment to adjust so it's the aroma that hits me first—beer, spices, bacon or sausage or both—then the sounds. There's laughter, conversation—including a loud, "Fuck no!", and clinking silverware against plates and cups. Once my eyes adjust, I take in a room full of mismatched tables and chairs of all sizes, a long bar along the one entire side of the room with stools of various heights and types.

But the mishmash of "types" doesn't apply only to the furniture. The people are a hodgepodge as well. There are all sizes, shapes, genders, and ages. And they all seem to be talking at once.

Which means the only person to notice me is the older woman behind the bar. She's short, has wrinkled tan skin, and wears her long gray hair in a braid down her back. She gives me a big grin. "Hey there."

Her smile makes me smile. "Hi."

She beckons me down the bar and points to an open stool.

Just then a loud laugh draws my attention, and I look at the back table. I see Cian right away.

He hasn't noticed me though, so I slip onto the bar stool. I can watch him from here. I'd love to spy for a few minutes and just watch him with his friends and family.

"What can I get you?" the bartender asks.

"Sweet tea and a menu?"

She hands over the menu, then starts filling a glass with ice.

I surreptitiously glance at the table to my left. Cian is sitting so that I'm to his left, rather than straight on so I can study the table without being noticed. I take note of the beautiful, dark-haired woman who I know is Fiona, Cian's sister. The girl to his right is his niece, Saoirse. For a second, I'm hit by a sense of what people must experience when they run across celebrities in public. I've only seen these people in photos, and I've read about them—or listened to stories about them—on the podcast so they seem a little larger than life to me.

I'm thinking of how cool Mariah would think this was, when Cian looks over. His mouth drops open, and his eyes widen as he straightens. Henry, who is sitting two chairs down, notices Cian's reaction and looks in my direction. His eyes widen, then he blows out a breath and pushes out of his chair and comes toward me.

I turn back toward the bar as the bartender sets my tea in front of me.

"Take your time with the menu. I'm Ellie. Just let me know when you're ready."

"I'm Scarlett. Thanks."

"Are you in town visiting someone?" she asks as Henry slides onto the stool next to me.

"No, um, just got hungry and asked where the best place to eat was."

"And that place was full so you ended up down here?" Henry asks.

"Just because you say it with that fancy accent doesn't make it funny," Ellie tells him, swatting at him with her towel.

Henry chuckles. "Love you, El."

"Look out for this one," she tells me, pointing at Henry. "Lots of ladies fall for that British thing. I get it. And the blue eyes aren't bad either. But he just got his heart broken, and he's gonna be flirty with you so you tell him he's pretty and charming and make him feel better."

I cover my grin with a sip of my tea as she moves off down the bar.

I look at Henry. "You've been here for an hour and they already know that you're heartbroken over Ruby?"

"Ellie is practically a mind reader," he says with a shrug. "Plus being sad gets me extra gumbo."

I look at him for a moment. "Sorry about the heartbreak thing, by the way."

He nods. "Funny thing is, if Ruby wasn't so dedicated to you and Mariah, we wouldn't have as much in common, and maybe I might not have fallen for her so hard."

I nod. "Ironic."

He turns and leans an elbow on the bar. "So, what are you doing here?"

"I figure he's undercover in my town to get to know me better, so I thought I could be undercover in his for a little bit and maybe pick up a few things about him."

Henry is giving me a look that seems almost impressed. "Okay. Well, the thing is, I'm going to have to sit here and pretend to flirt with you."

"Why is that?"

"Because you don't want everyone to know who you really are. And if anyone else flirts with you, Cian will come over and make it pretty obvious that you're taken. And if he does that... well, it's going to be pretty obvious that you're taken. And as soon as everyone knows that you're taken by him—"

"He said they would have us married before we left town."

Henry nods. "Something like that."

"Because they all love him?"

Henry's expression softens. "Something like that."

I look over his shoulder at the table. With the way Henry is sitting next to me, it's very convenient that I can pretend to be looking at him but actually watch Cian. I don't think that's an accident. "Or something exactly like that?" I ask.

"Scarlett," Henry says. "Everyone loves Cian. Everyone wants him to be happy. You might be the only person I know who's been able to resist giving Cian O'Grady what he wants. So, yes, if they catch on that you're *her*, they will want him to have you. Because that's what he wants."

I swallow and somehow refrain from admitting to Henry that I may not always hold the record for resisting giving Cian what he wants.

"Were Fiona and Saoirse really happy to see him?"

"Thrilled. Of course, they want to know all about you and our trip to Ohio."

"What are they going to think about you flirting with someone so soon after having your heart broken?"

"They're going to think I'm trying to get over it. And then when you leave without me, they'll feel bad for me and I'll maybe get an extra serving of bread pudding. I'll definitely get extra moonshine."

I laugh. "I hope you have a place to stay so you don't have to drive."

"Well, yeah, we live about four blocks away."

Right. Of course they have a place to stay. They *live* here when they're not in Ohio with me.

"Okay, so ask me your questions about Cian, his family, this town." Henry picks up his bottle of beer and takes a sip.

"Alright, who are all of these people?"

"Besides Fiona and Saoirse, Fiona's husband is the big guy with the longer hair at the end with the little girl on his lap. That's their youngest."

I couldn't miss him. He's the one with his hand on the back of Fiona's neck.

"The guy in the firefighter uniform is Michael, the fire chief. Cian does volunteer work with him."

I frown. "What? Cian is a *firefighter*?"

"Yeah. You didn't know?"

"No. That's what he does for work?"

"Volunteer."

Oh, sure, that makes it different.

"The other guys sitting around are mostly Landrys. Ellie's grandsons." He nods in the direction of the bartender. "Some of them own the swamp boat tour company, some of them work at the animal park. One's a cop. One does construction. They basically just take care of the town. Cian kind of works with all of them."

"Cian also works with the *cop*?"

"Okay, not the cop. But he does tours for the swamp boat tour company. He does some construction with Zeke. He's even worked for Knox, Fiona's husband. Knox is the city manager and he'll put Cian to work doing landscaping, painting, and whatever else he can come up with."

I turn even more fully on my stool and pin Henry with a serious look. "So Cian is a handyman? Does odd jobs all over town? Jack of all trades?"

Henry shrugs. "Yeah. I guess. He just likes to hang out with everyone and is happy to help out."

I shake my head. "And he's been building these communities and homes for single moms all over on the side."

Henry just nods.

"He said he hasn't told anyone else about the projects."

"Cian hasn't told anyone but me and he only told me because he had to travel to check them out and hire people to manage them and I had to go with him."

"Why do you think he doesn't want anyone to know?"

"I don't think that he's keeping it a secret necessarily. It just isn't something he feels the need to talk about."

"Why not?"

Henry puts his beer bottle down and rests his elbow on the bar, pinning me with a look. "Cian is extremely intelligent and is the youngest child of a family of very high achievers. He has a lot to live up to, but he's naturally curious and creative and sociable. He's used to being the supporter. The one who helps everyone else out. That's what he loves. Seeing where there's a need and pitching in however he can. Driving an airboat up and down the bayou, fighting fires, feeding tigers, braiding a little girl's hair, it doesn't matter. It's kind of all the same to him. He just wants to help."

I look at Cian again. He's watching me. When our eyes meet, I feel warmth swirl through me. He's such a good guy. *Everyone* should know that.

"So it's more that he just didn't think to tell anyone about the community project. He doesn't think it's a big deal? He's just helping those moms."

"More or less," Henry agrees. "He was excited to show *you* because he wanted you to know *your* idea was amazing."

"I was excited to see it, but it happened because *he* made it happen."

Henry nods. "It's also the first thing he's really built on his own, from the ground up. Everything else he does is filling in gaps on things other people already have going on. But because of you, he has something that's truly his. He's not used to that."

"So he doesn't know how to show it off?"

"Right." Henry pauses. "Seems you two have that in common."

I frown. "What do you mean?"

"I mean, you seem very happy staying quiet and that

you don't really want to do anything that would get people talking."

"Yeah, well, when people talk about me in Emerald it usually includes a 'remember when'? or 'can you believe her?'" I say dryly.

"And?" Henry asks. "Isn't the idea to show them that you've *changed*? How better to do that than to have them recall something from the past, while talking about something great you're doing now?"

I open my mouth, but then close it.

I guess...he has a point. Even if they did say, 'she's the one who got knocked up out of wedlock and kicked out of her father's church', but then talk about how I'm helping with a foundation that provides resources for single mothers, that really would show that I'm using my circumstances to grow and do something good.

"You and Cian talked about me and the foundation on your drive to Autre today?" I guess.

He smiles. "Of course. It's the biggest thing on Cian's mind right now."

"And you think I should consider his idea to make me president of the foundation and not just help behind the scenes?"

"Yes. I do."

"I would want to talk about him too. Everyone should know who he is and how he's involved. He deserves to shine."

"I agree," Henry says.

"You should tell him that. You're his best friend. You should encourage him. Or *you* should tell everyone what he's been doing."

"Nah." Henry lifts his beer. "You're way prettier to look

at and your voice gets this sweet little note to it when you say *Cian*."

I laugh and swat his arm. "It does not."

"Definitely does."

And I believe him, actually.

"Hi!"

Suddenly a petite brunette pops up between Henry and me.

Henry gives a little eye roll. "Fiona." He loops an arm around her neck. "It took you a lot longer to come over here than I expected."

This is Fiona O'Grady, Cian's sister, up close and personal.

I swallow.

Fiona grins at Henry but then looks at me. "I wanted to watch you talk to her for a little bit."

"Why's that?"

"To see how she acted toward you."

"How she acted toward me?" Henry repeats, glancing at me.

"Like she likes you as a friend, but like she doesn't want to sleep with you. Sorry." She sticks out her hand. "Hi, I'm Fiona. Henry's friend."

There is so much energy emanating from this woman that I'm still blinking and barely manage a, "Hi," as she takes my hand and shakes it. "Um, I'm Scarlett."

"You can't tell me she doesn't want to sleep with me while she's sitting right here," Henry tells Fiona, removing his arm, and pushing her away. "That's terrible wing-woman behavior."

"You asked what I thought."

"I didn't. I simply repeated 'how she acted toward me'. It wasn't a question."

"Oh. Sorry." Fiona doesn't seem sorry. "He's broken hearted," Fiona tells me. "Don't believe anything he says. I know the British accent really does it for some women, but he'll just be using you to get over her."

Right. Got it. Fiona is buying the ruse that Henry is over here flirting with me. And she's here to warn me off. Because he's heart broken. Over my sister.

Well, Fiona probably doesn't know that part. But this is...weird. And funny.

"Ellie said the same thing," I tell her. I give Henry a look. Wow, these women are *really* not wanting him to hook up. What's that about?

"Oh good. No offense, but we're hoping he can figure things out with her."

"The girl he's broken-hearted over?" I ask, definitely interested in that.

"Yes. I've known Henry a very long time and I've never seen him in love before."

"I'm not in love with her anymore," Henry protests.

Fiona ignores him. "There must be something really special about her. So we don't want him messing anything up before he has a chance to fix things. No offense," she says again.

I nod solemnly. "I understand. I actually agree with you," I tell her. "I think he needs to try to work it out with her, too." I meet Henry's gaze.

He narrows his eyes. "There's no way to work it out. We're not in love anymore."

We both ignore him this time.

"He told you about her?" Fiona asks me.

"I know everything," I say, not *exactly* lying. "It's clear they're a good match."

"How did *you* two meet?" Fiona asks.

"Henry and I stayed at the same hotel last night and Cian mentioned this is where they were coming for lunch today. So I did follow them, but you're right, I don't want to sleep with Henry." There, that was all truth. Technically.

"Oh, good then." Fiona seems pleased with all of that information.

Fiona's happy energy reminds me of Cian. Without thinking, I look up and find him, still sitting at the back table. But his eyes are still on me. He's watching my exchange with Henry and Fiona with a strange expression I can't quite describe, but he's not missing a single detail. I'm not sure he's even blinking.

"You should come to the animal park before you leave," Fiona says. "We're all heading over there now. It's got a whole fall theme going on with leaves and pumpkins and hay bales." She laughs. "We have a lot of hay bales anyway, but there are extras now for decoration. With scarecrows and all that fall stuff. It's adorable. Charlie loves this shit. Plus, we've got pumpkin spice lattes and cider and apple cider donuts and caramel apples. You'll love it."

It does sound fun and I'm actually kind of dying to see it. I want to take a swamp boat tour and walk down Main Street, and just soak this town in. This is where Cian has lived for the past few years. This is where so many people who are important to him are located. Not just his family, but lots of friends too.

I also want them to know who I am.

That thought hits me right between the eyes. And right in the heart.

It sucks my breath out of my lungs.

I don't want to just eavesdrop. I don't want to be undercover. I don't want people to think I'm here because Henry flirted with me at the hotel in New Orleans.

I want to be here with Cian.

I want to hold his hand. Have him introduce me to everyone. Have him show me around and tell me stories about the place and people.

I want Fiona to either smile and hug me because she's so happy that Cian found me or give me 'hurt him and I'll kill you' big sister vibes or…anything, really. I just want to be a part of all of this *with him.*

Dammit. This is the opposite of getting over him.

I smile at Fiona. "That sounds fun. I've heard of your animal park. Of course."

"Oh, love that," she tells me. "Tell the kid at the ticket booth "alpaca spit"."

I laugh. "What's that?"

"Code for a free admission. I'll see you over there." Then she turns and heads for the back table.

As if on cue, everyone sitting there starts getting up, talking, grabbing bags, and kids. They start filing out of the building, some through the front door, some through the back.

"You really want to go over to the park?" Henry asks.

"Well, yeah. They have giraffes and penguins."

He grins. "They certainly do."

"Is that okay?" I ask, suddenly not sure. "I mean, it's full of visitors, right? I can just blend in."

Cian ambles by and pauses for a second. "If you touch her, I'll put cayenne in your tea bags."

Then he keeps walking, following Saoirse out the door.

Henry chuckles and finishes off his drink. "Yeah, I don't think you're going to just blend in."

I look at him with wide eyes. "You're going to touch me?"

Henry shakes his head and stretches to his feet, tossing

a twenty on the bar. "No. But he's still not going to be able to stay away."

"You don't think so?" I slide off my stool too, trying to pretend like there aren't butterflies flitting about in my stomach.

"You, here? In one of his favorite places on earth? With his people? There is no way he's going to be able to pretend he barely knows you, not to mention being able to keep his hands to himself."

"Oh." I chew on the inside of my cheek. "Should I just leave?"

He laughs. "Hell no. This is going to be more fun than I've had in a week."

I start toward the door with Henry right behind me. "Oh, this is all about entertaining *you*?" I ask.

"Damn right." He pushes the door open for me, and I step out into the bright, hot Louisiana sun. "It's you and Cian's fault I've been stuck close to Ruby, seeing her, hearing her, smelling her, but not being able to have her. I deserve to see the two of you stammering and fumbling around for an hour or two."

"You know, if you hadn't spilled the news about finding me living in Ohio, you wouldn't have had to bring Cian to Emerald and you and Ruby could have just gotten over each other," I remind him.

Henry simply grunts at that.

I start across the parking lot. The road in front of the bar leads down to the Boys of the Bayou swamp boat tour company's docks and beyond that is the entrance to the Boys of the Bayou Gone Wild animal park.

I look up and notice Cian standing under a tree at the edge of the parking lot, clearly hanging back from the rest of the group that's walking down the road. He's got a baseball cap on now—a look I haven't seen on him before—and he looks like a regular guy. A very hot, regular guy. But my heart trips a little as I get close enough to see the way he's watching me. And the way his mouth tips up as I approach.

"Yeah, tell me again how upset you are that I brought him to you in Emerald," Henry says dryly.

Well, upset is probably an exaggeration.

"I'm really fucking glad you're here," Cian says when I stop in front of him. Henry continues on past us.

"Yeah?"

"And you gave my sister and Ellie your real name."

I nod. "I..." I swallow. "Just like with you, I didn't want them calling me someone else's name."

That makes heat and something that looks like affection—*very* strong affection—flicker through his eyes.

I take a breath. "But I didn't even think...did you tell them about me? My name I mean? When you were..."

"In love and looking for you for almost two years?" he fills in.

My stomach swoops. "Yeah."

"I told them about you. But I didn't give them your name. Scarlett won't give you away."

"Okay." That's probably good.

"But the way I won't be able to leave you alone today, probably will."

My heart flips. "I just really wanted to see the giraffes," I say, but my voice is stupidly breathless. And I can't hide my smile.

"Witch," he says softly, giving me a smile that makes my panties warmer.

Then he tucks his hands into his pockets, turns, and we start down the road. Side by side, not touching, yet I feel him—his whole presence—wrapping around me.

CHAPTER 23

CIAN

Watching Scarlett ask Saoirse one million questions about wombats, Saoirse's most beloved animal in the entire park, while Scarlett sits cross-legged on the ground, holding a red panda, is the final straw.

I am in love with this woman, and I need to figure out a way to make that work.

We've seen the entire animal park, snacked on all the special fall treats, and chatted with everyone. Henry, Saoirse, and Fiona have spent most of the day right with us and Saoirse is clearly enamored with Scarlett.

Saoirse and I also have the same taste in potato chips and action movies, so this doesn't surprise me in the least.

It's been an amazing day.

The park truly is decked out for fall even with the temperature being in the upper eighties. No one seems to care that it feels like summer. They are drinking hot apple cider as if there's a crisp autumn breeze ruffling the straw poking out of the scarecrows' sleeves and the petals of the potted mums that are everywhere I look.

Somehow they've even covered the ground with multi-colored leaves that they clearly imported from somewhere the foliage already changes in September. Possibly northern Canada. It wouldn't surprise me.

"The air smells like apple-cinnamon right?" Henry asks. "I'm not imagining that? Or having a stroke?"

"It does," I agree. I don't know how they pulled that off, but the marketing director, Charlotte Landry-Foster, can do anything and I wouldn't be surprised if she simply *willed* the aroma into being.

"You do know that you shouldn't look at your best friend's new girlfriend like that right?" Fiona asks from right next to me.

We're both watching Scarlett and Saoirse.

"She's not Henry's new girlfriend," I say. Henry and Scarlett filled me in on the cover story they gave Fiona.

"Okay, his weekend hook-up to try to get over the other girl."

I frown. "Not that either. They're just friends."

Fiona doesn't say anything and I look down to find her grinning up at me.

"What?" I ask.

"I know exactly who she is," Fiona says. "Your secret's safe with me. For now. Though I'm not sure why she's a secret."

Scarlett finally relinquishes the red panda back to the keeper and gets up, brushing her hands over her ass.

"I don't know what you mean," I say, watching her approach.

I'm not surprised that Fiona has noticed the way I look

at and talk to Scarlett. It's different than the way I've behaved around anyone in my entire life.

"Ha," Fiona says. "With the way you're looking at her? And the fact that she shows up here at the same time you do after you've been gone for a week?"

Scarlett stops in front of us. "Who are you looking at?"

"You," Fiona says.

Scarlett frowns. "Oh?"

"You're his Cinderella, right?"

Scarlett freezes. Then her eyes get wide. "W–what?"

I sigh. Dammit. My sister knows me *far* too well.

"You're the girl he's been looking for all this time. The one he went to Ohio to find," Fiona says. She looks *very* smug.

I narrow my eyes. "And if she's *not*, you just made this very awkward."

Fiona laughs and points at Scarlett. "I noticed her bracelet in the bar."

I look at the elephant bracelet that's wrapped around Scarlett's left wrist. I groan. That didn't even occur to me.

Scarlett quickly covers the bracelet with her right hand. "Oh, I...this..." She blows out a breath and looks at me, then back to Fiona. "You know about the bracelet?"

"He carried it around like a glass slipper for two years. And got a tattoo to match it," Fiona says with a laugh.

Scarlett moves to take it off, but Fiona stops her. "I've already seen it. So has anyone else who's going to notice. Like Ellie. But none of the other bodyguards are here and I don't think anyone else is paying close attention. They've all got their little ones running around distracting them."

I look around with a grin, watching friends chase toddlers, help little ones feed alpacas, and pet goats and rabbits. All of these people have become more than friends.

The way our bodyguards have become family over the years has always been very special to the O'Gradys, and it was amazing to come to Autre and find out that the Landry family functions the same way. Friends become family very quickly and seeing these friends all as mothers and fathers as they've all settled down one by one has been a lot of fun to watch.

Scarlett sighs and looks at my sister. "We didn't want to tell you who I was because we didn't want to get your hopes up."

"My hopes up about what?" Fiona asks.

"About us being together," Scarlett says.

"Well, my hopes are already up." Fiona looks at me. "I assume you're going to pull a Torin, and marry her before Grandfather makes you marry Astrid?"

I lift a shoulder. "That was the reason I went to Ohio to find her."

"So what's the problem?" Fiona asks.

"Scarlett thought it was a little fast. We're getting to know each other right now."

Scarlett steps closer and leans her shoulder against mine. I take that as a thank you as well as a sign of solidarity. I shift to wrap a hand around her waist. Now that the cat's out of the bag, there's no reason I can't touch her.

"Does Astrid know?" Fiona asks.

"Kind of," I admit.

"Great," Fiona smiles at me, then Scarlett. "Astrid will be fine."

Scarlett looks up at me with a frown. "Wait...Astrid?"

"The woman my grandfather wants me to marry," I say.

"Her name is Astrid? Like Astrid Olsen?"

"Yes. I mean...it *is* Astrid Olsen," I explain.

Scarlett's eyes go wide, and she steps away from me. "Your arranged engagement is with *Astrid Olsen*?"

"I wouldn't call it an engagement," I say.

Scarlett shakes her head. "But your grandfather wants you to marry *Astrid Olsen*?" she asks, her voice rising and her eyes getting rounder.

I step toward her and put my hands on her upper arms. I stroke up and down. "What's wrong? I told you about this."

"You didn't tell me it was *Astrid Olsen*."

"Why does that matter?" I ask. "And why do you keep saying her first and last name?"

"Because she's *Astrid Olsen*," Scarlett says. "Cian, why don't you want to marry her? She's amazing."

I hear Fiona snort, and I shoot her a frown. I turn back to Scarlett. "She *is* amazing. But I don't want to marry her because I want to marry *you*. Remember?"

"But she's…Astrid Olsen."

"Stop saying that."

"But she's beautiful!"

"And you're the most gorgeous woman I've ever seen. You are the only woman I want."

"And you *know* her. You've known her for a long time," Scarlett insists.

"I love everything I know about you, and I want to know more."

"But she's smart and brave and so inspiring!"

"Scarlett," I say firmly. "I want *you*."

"But she already has *so* many projects and causes! You could get involved and do so many good things—"

"Scarlett," I say through gritted teeth.

"You should really rethink th—"

I really want her to shut up about Astrid. So I do the only thing I can. I pull her in and kiss her.

CHAPTER 24
SCARLETT

I t seems that Cian kissing me sets off some kind of alarm because within a minute, we're surrounded by people.

Saoirse seems the most surprised. "Oh my gosh, Cian, what are you doing?"

I hear someone else ask, "Henry, you okay, man?" and Henry laugh.

At which point Cian finally lifts his head and looks into my eyes, still holding my face between his hands, "We're not done talking about this."

"That wasn't talking," I say softly.

"I communicated my feelings though, didn't I?"

Um, definitely.

I'm still freaked out about the idea that the woman he's supposed to marry is Astrid Olsen. But the more I think about it, the more that makes sense. If his grandfather is going to set him up to marry someone, it makes sense that it's someone close to the family. Astrid's family and Cian's family are very close. Her grandfather was Diarmuid's best friend.

I take a deep breath, then turn with Cian to face our little crowd.

"Everyone, this is Scarlett," he says.

They all just look at us. Everyone gathered around already knows my name.

"Scarlett and I met almost two years ago," he adds. "I've been looking for her."

His words seemed to take a few seconds to sink in, but once they do, everyone gasps, laughs, and steps forward to further surround us.

I don't remember all the names except that most of their last names are Landry. But there were two people in the crowd that I recognize easily. Charlotte and Amelia. Princess Abigail's sisters. I know who they are because of photos on the podcast website from the wedding.

The whole surreal is-this-really–happening feeling hits me again. But now everyone knows that Cian and I are together, so I decide to just go with it.

'Going with it' means I end up at the big back table of Ellie's bar.

Cian is sitting right next to me. I mean *right* next to me. His thigh is pressing against mine. He has his arm draped over the back of my chair and his chest is against my shoulder.

And I love it.

We haven't been able to be "public" together before and this feels so nice. Normal.

This time the place is packed with family, adopted family, and significant others. Honestly, the bar can barely hold any additional people when the entire Landry clan shows up.

It's loud, boisterous, and the feeling of being automatically included in a group who wants to feed me, and know everything about me, and are just happy to have me here is nearly overwhelming.

In a good way.

If someone had asked me how I'd feel about a situation like this and I would have imagined it, I probably would have assumed that I'd hate it.

But I don't. I really don't.

It's not like they're all laid back or that they clearly know boundaries or anything like that. They all talk at once. They give each other shit. And while there are a few quieter members of the group, as a whole they are loud.

And they laugh a lot.

They're also nosey as hell. But I find myself smiling and laughing and telling them far more than I would have expected.

They want to know *all* about me. And how Cian and I met. And why I haven't seen him in so long. And how I feel about seeing him again now.

So I tell them about Mariah and Ruby. I tell them about growing up in a small town in Ohio. I tell them my dad is a preacher but that we don't get along but that my stepdad was amazing and that yes, I get along great with my mom.

I tell them about how Cian and I met when I was pretending to be my sister, stripping in New Orleans. Cian fills in details as well. And they take it all in stride.

I tell them that I missed him and thought about him all the time and that I'm happy he came to find me and that I've enjoyed every minute of having him back in my life. And I look at him when I say that because I haven't told *him* that in so many words and I realize I should have.

I can't remember the last time I felt this way.

It's possible I have never felt this way.

The last time I was included in a big group was at church. My dad's church. And that group was hardly warm and boisterous. Everybody *seemed* to be welcoming, but the reason that we all got together was to hear instructions about how we were supposed to live our lives, how we were supposed to think, how we were supposed to interact with other people in the world.

At the time, it seemed we were a select, special group. That we were being let in on universal secrets. That somehow we had been specially chosen.

Now, knowing the truth—that was all about obedience and conforming—I realize there was a coldness and tension in the group.

There was always a sense that you could easily do something wrong or step out of line.

Something I found out personally when I fell in love and ended up pregnant.

Now, with the Landrys, who have literally known me for only a few hours, I feel none of that. I honestly felt like I could blurt out any flaw and they would laugh, nod, and share their own fuck-ups with me.

"How old is Mariah?" the woman sitting to my right asks. I can't remember if this is Juliet or Jordan. I'm pretty sure it's one of the J names though.

"Mariah's almost sixteen."

"She's amazing," Cian adds. "She's bright, funny, sarcastic. She would absolutely love hanging out down here." He looks to his left where Saoirse is sitting.

She's hardly let him out of her sight all day and I think that's incredibly sweet. Obviously, she's missed him.

"She knows all about you," Cian tells her. "She wants to meet you someday."

Saoirse sits up a little taller, her eyes wide. "How does she know about me?"

"She listens to *Wait 'Til I Tell Ye*. She's fascinated with the animal park and all of that. Plus, she found out that you were working with Bennett as a spokesperson for the climate change thing. She thinks you're cool. She wants to study some great stuff at college and travel around and do big work. I think you guys will be best friends."

My throat tightens and I have to blink quickly as Saoirse starts asking questions about Mariah and Cian gushes about her.

She's instantly interested in my daughter, and of course that's because of Cian's endorsement. But also, I think Cian's right. They would get along. And Mariah wouldn't have any of the bullshit here that hangs over her head in Emerald because of my past.

"What do you do, Scarlett?" another of the women at the table asks. I don't even try to come up with her name. There are just so many people here.

"I'm a mechanic, actually. My stepdad owned the garage in our town and taught me, then left it to me when he passed."

"Holy shit, that's amazing," the woman says.

I laugh. "Is it?"

"That you can fix cars and stuff? Absolutely." She looks down the table. "Sawyer, Scarlett's a mechanic." She turns back to me. "Sawyer's the one who keeps all of our engines running."

"Out of necessity," the big man says. "Somebody has to fix the boats and trucks to keep the business going." But he gives me a grin.

I shake my head. "I don't know anything about boats."

He lifts a shoulder. "It's not that different. I'm sure you'd pick it up."

I might actually. I'm actually pretty good with mechanical things.

But I realize that there's a bigger difference between what I do and what Sawyer does. It's not about the engines or vehicles themselves. It's about the why behind it. Sawyer probably loves his job because of *why* he does it. He's doing it for his family, for the business, because fixing those machines is part of something bigger that really matters to him.

I'm doing it because I need to make money and to prove a point to the town.

I like being able to help people out when they have car trouble and need a tow or need a flat changed. I know how scary being stranded can be. But ninety-nine percent of the tiny bit of business I get are oil changes and tire rotations and basic maintenance. Things a dozen other people in the area could do. And it doesn't make me feel excited or fulfilled.

It was different for Brian. Because he did it for true friends and neighbors. He was a part of the community, and his business was important. That's not my situation in Emerald.

That's a startling realization to have sitting in a bar in Louisiana. But it's true. I told myself going back to Emerald to run the shop was my way of showing the town I wanted to be a contributing member of the community but...that's not how it's working out.

"You should come down to the docks and take a tour tomorrow," the woman says. She looks at Cian. "Spend the night tonight. Have breakfast with us and then take her on the bayou tomorrow."

"I have a boat taken apart," Sawyer says. "I'd be happy to show it to you."

I have no intention of ever fixing a boat, but I have to admit it might be kind of interesting. More than anything though, I love this feeling of being included.

I look at Cian and he grins. "Want to see the swamp?"

I want to stay here longer. I want to hang out tonight. Eat more of this jambalaya that is hands-down the best I've ever had. Drink more sweet tea. Maybe something stronger. Get to know these people better. Hear more stories. Maybe get a selfie of me with Saoirse to send to Mariah. Maybe even video chat with Mariah *with* Saoirse. I'd be a damned hero to my daughter. Enjoy hanging out in public with Cian where he can touch me and kiss me and we can be a couple in front of other people. And hell yeah, I want to see him captaining a swamp boat.

"I do," I tell him.

His gaze drops to my mouth. "I like hearing those words from you."

I blush and open my mouth to reply, but one of the guys asks, "Hey, yeah, what do you think of this plan for Cian to marry Astrid?"

"Owen!" the pretty blonde next to him exclaims, then elbows him in the side.

"Ow!" he protests. "Dammit, Maddie, you know those ribs are sore."

"Your own fault," she says. "You knew better than to take the ATV out there and did it anyway."

"Wow," one of the brunettes says, throwing a biscuit at him.

He catches the biscuit and starts putting butter on it. "What? I wasn't the only one on the ATVs." He shoots a look down the table, but it's very difficult to know who else he's indicating was involved in the shenanigans.

"I mean bringing up Astrid in front of Scarlett," the biscuit-thrower says.

He takes a bite of the biscuit. "I'm just curious how *that's* all gonna work." He points the biscuit at her. "And I know you are too."

The brunette looks at the blonde. "Can't you control him?"

The blonde laughs. "Oh sure. If I could, we wouldn't have a fucking alligator coming up into our yard to be fucking *hand fed* every fucking morning, trust me."

"You should divorce him. None of us know why you put up with him," someone else says.

She grins up at Owen, who looks down at her with unabashed love. "Well, there are a few reasons that outweigh the crazy. *So far.*"

He leans down and says something in her ear. She blushes but laughs. "Yeah, that's on the list."

He straightens, grinning a *very* smug grin.

I can feel my own grin stretching bigger than I think I've smiled in a long time.

"See why I love it here?" Cian says near my ear.

I suddenly feel tears stinging my eyes. I simply nod. God, he could have *this* all the time, but he's hanging out in Emerald with me. Pretending to be someone else. Hiding out because I don't want anyone to know who he is.

Here, no one seems to care that he's a prince. He's just one of them.

"*Anyway,*" Owen says. "*You* should marry him, right?"

I feel my eyes widen as I realize he's looking directly at me.

Many heads around the table nod up and down. As if it's just that simple.

"I'm not really princess material," I tell them. My go-to line now.

Someone else snorts. "Trust me, *Abigail* is not princess material. If she can do it, anyone can."

Lots of affectionate laughter follows that statement.

And I smile. I know there was a lot of discussion about Abigail being shy, having social anxiety, preferring her plants to people, how she's more comfortable in muddy rubber boots and blue jeans than high heels and ball gowns.

But she wants to make people's lives better. She wants to, literally, get her hands dirty solving problems. She doesn't want to *talk* about it in public, maybe, but she's *doing* so many great things.

That's pretty princess-y to me.

"And hell, *Cian* isn't exactly prince material," someone else says.

I feel Cian chuckle next to me—feel it, versus hear it over all the other commotion in the room.

And I know he's said basically the same thing. That I wouldn't have to *be* a princess, exactly. And that he doesn't live at the palace—which is more obvious now—and I know that Torin and Abigail have the official titles and responsibilities.

But...something about the way everyone also nods along to that sentiment, that everyone seems to just agree that Cian is very *un*princely, suddenly rubs me the wrong way.

Because what is a prince really?

Someone who takes care of others, who serves others, who leads. But leading doesn't have to be with words. It can be by example.

Isn't that what I've wanted to do in Emerald? *Show* them that I've changed. *Show* them how to live a good, honorable life. *Show* them how to live by all the principles the church teaches rather than just preaching about it, guilting people into doing the right thing? *Show* people how to love, how to be generous, how to serve.

Mariah's words come back to me from the night in my kitchen not even a week ago.

I'm talking about the amazing things we could do. And the people we'd get to know! Look at Abigail! Her indoor farms are going to feed so many kids! And Princess Fiona saves endangered animals! And Linnea is working on green energy projects! And even Princess Saoirse has started doing some work as a spokesperson for a youth climate change group!

All of them are *doing* things that, by any measure I would apply, show they are true servants and real leaders.

I suddenly blurt out, "Cian is absolutely a prince. He's kind and generous and really wants to make other people's lives better. He's starting a charitable foundation. We're going to run it together."

Conversation stops and I feel Cian tense beside me.

I have no idea what they were talking about or what I interrupted. Maybe plans for Cian and Astrid's wedding.

Well, too bad.

"Cian's doing *what*?" Fiona asks.

I look at Cian. He's looking at me with an expression that clearly says *what the hell are you doing?*

I drop my hand to his thigh and squeeze, giving him a smile. Then I turn to Fiona.

"He's starting a foundation. He's been building communities for single moms all over the country. The first one is right here in New Orleans. The foundation is going to continue to support that project but we're going to expand into other things as well."

"Communities for single moms," Fiona repeats. She looks at her brother. "What is this?"

Cian's hand moves from the back of my chair to the back of my neck. He squeezes gently. I don't know if it's a gesture of happiness that I've agreed to do this with him, or a warning that I better not say anything more.

"It's a project I put together after I met Scarlett."

That's all he says. Fiona's brows lift. "What project?"

"Just a little thing Scarlett and I came up with."

She looks back and forth between us.

I finally laugh. He said he didn't want me being so quiet about things. I am *not* keeping my mouth shut about this. "It's *not* little. And it's amazing. I helped brainstorm the idea, but Cian made it all happen." I feel a lightness fill me as I launch into a description of Scarlett Park.

Everyone at the table stays quiet throughout my explanation.

"There are others like it. All over." I don't really know where they all are. "And we're going to establish more. And expand into other things."

"Like what?" Fiona asks. She seems completely fascinated.

I shrug. "Whatever we find people need."

I feel Cian's hand tighten on my neck. I look up at him. He's staring at me with clear happiness. And desire.

"Cian, I had no idea that you'd done that. Why didn't you tell us?" Fiona asks.

He shakes his head. "I don't know. It didn't come up." He looks down at me again. "I wasn't sure where it was all going to go. I needed to recruit the right person to be president. To help me lead it. Now that I have, we can really get things rolling."

I feel that light, warm feeling spread. We really have endless possibilities. That's how this feels, and it feels *so good*.

"That's really fucking cool," Owen tells him. "Good for you, man."

Cian tips his head. "Thanks." His eyes go to his sister. "I have a soft spot for single moms who need a little extra help."

Fiona looks choked up. "Oh...wow."

Cian's hand squeezes me again and I look up quickly to find that his eyes look a little shiny too.

Oh my God. This is so... great.

"Where is the place in New Orleans?" one of the guys at the end of the table asks.

Cian gives him the address but then says, "But it's not a tourist spot. I don't want a bunch of people over there or driving past. It's their home." He sounds very firm and a little protective.

"No, of course," the guy says. I think his name is Mitch. "But if you ever need any help with maintenance or repairs or anything, you know you can just ask, right?"

"Same here," one of twins with long hair and beards says. He's the one Cian does construction with sometimes, but I can't remember if he's Zeke or Zander. "I'm happy to help out."

Cian swallows hard and nods. "Thanks, guys."

"Where's your next one going to be?" one of the women asks.

"I'm not—" Cian starts.

"Columbus," I say. "Ohio."

Cian looks down at me. I just hold his gaze. Then he slowly nods as his smile spreads. "Yeah. Columbus. Near Emerald."

"That's just so..." Suddenly Fiona is up out of her chair and around the table and hugging Cian from behind.

He puts a hand over hers and squeezes her back.

"I'm proud of you, man," Knox, Fiona's husband, says.

Now Cian almost looks bashful.

Oh, God.

If sexy, charming Cian makes me say yes to things I shouldn't, and dirty talking, bossy Cian can get my panties off in less than ten seconds, and sweet, playful Cian has been slowly working his way into my heart, and quietly charitable Cian has made me rethink almost everything, then proud-choked-up-bashful Cian is going to make it impossible for me to resist him.

After Fiona releases him and everyone has finished with their effusive praise, Cian leans over and says in my ear, "You agreeing to lead my foundation is so fucking hot."

I lean into him. "You creating a foundation for me to lead is pretty fucking hot too. Now that it's sunk in."

"Though you telling my family about it..."

I tip my face up to meet his gaze. "Was very appropriate. They should know. *Everyone* should know, Cian. Not because you need the praise—though you deserve it—but because your name will bring in donors and volunteers and will give it a legitimacy that we need to get started."

"I suppose you think I should reward you for all of that?" he murmurs.

"Well... I'm not going to complain if you think I need to be *punished* instead." I lean even closer. "How thin are the walls in your house here?"

He gives me a grin. "Thick enough. Especially since I wouldn't mind the other people living there hearing you."

I blush hotly but tuck up against him more fully.

I like Autre. A lot.

I like the idea of my new job. A lot.

And I more than like His Royal Highness Prince Cian O'Grady.

CHAPTER 25

SCARLETT

S o...this is what it feels like to be in love.

I think it took me a minute to realize that's what's going on because it's been a long time and it's so different this time.

I was in love with Eli. I don't doubt that. But that was young love. That was first love. That was an inexperienced, starry-eyed girl falling for an older man who she saw as a future husband and the father of her children. A guy who she thought was exactly who she *should* fall in love with.

I fell in love fast. It was easy. It *felt* right and good.

Like this does.

But I'm more mature this time. I've been through some stuff. I know that love should feel good, but I also know that it has to be more than just feelings. It has to make sense. It has to stand up to tests and trials. And the only way to know that it will is with time.

But...I can admit that I *want* this to be real with Cian.

Cian O'Grady couldn't be more different from that soft-spoken, conservative preacher who'd had his life all planned out and his goals clearly defined.

And who'd run at the first sign of adversity.

This exuberant, sexy, charming younger man who thinks I can do things that I haven't even imagined for myself has made my life fun and happy and sexy. He is vastly different from my first love.

Cian doesn't let obstacles deter him. In fact, I'm not so sure he believes there truly *are* obstacles to the things he wants. He hasn't even let his own grandfather set the rules —not in where he's lived, or *how* he's lived, for the past twelve years, and not in who he should marry. I can't imagine Cian listening to *my* father try to impose *his* beliefs on Cian or his life. That makes me feel...safe.

Cian does what he wants to. That sounds very privileged, and it is, to be sure, but I also know his heart. What he wants to do is good. And when he says he wants to take care of me, I can't keep it from seeping in and making me believe it. Not just that he wants to, but that he will. He's brought a warmth to my life that I didn't even realize was so cold.

Eli ran away from me. Cian never stopped looking for me.

So, yes, I'm falling in love with him.

That's clear as day.

But I have to be smart. I have to be careful. I have to take my time. I'm a mom. I have to learn from my past experiences. Because it's happening so fast with Cian. And it has been easy.

Of course, some of what I'm feeling tonight might be due, at least in part, to the nearly non-stop laughing with the Landrys and their inner circle—which is *huge*—and the delicious food and drink. Particularly the moonshine that

Leo Landry makes right there in the backyard where everyone is sitting around in chairs and at picnic tables.

After Cian and I agreed to stay tonight, the party moved outside to the area behind the bar, where they threw together a crawfish boil when they found out I'd only been to one in all the time I'd lived in New Orleans.

Tables, dishes, and food seemingly appeared by magic. We ate and drank, talked, drank, told stories, drank, even danced...and drank some more.

I haven't had this much fun in forever.

Seriously, maybe ever.

Now I'm watching Cian cross from the other side of the firepit where he went to talk to Henry for a minute, back to me.

God, he's gorgeous. Absolutely gorgeous. His eyes, his smile, his shoulders, his ass.

He stops in front of the chair I'm curled up in, someone's hoodie draped over my lap. I tip my head back and smile up at him. "You're so hot."

He gives me a crooked grin. "Ditto."

"I'm having so much fun."

His smile softens with affection that steals my breath for a moment. He leans over, bracing his hands on the arms of the chair. "I love having you here."

"Kiss me," I say softly, the words going through my mind just spilling out.

He leans in. "Gladly. Any time. Any place."

He presses his lips to mine and I sigh against his mouth. It's a sweet kiss. Nothing hot or sexy. Just...affectionate.

Being the object of Cian's affection is addictive.

He pulls back only an inch to say, "I love being able to do that. In public. In front of people."

"Me too," I admit." I let out a long breath. "I could stay

here," I tell him. "Seriously. I really love your people. Mariah and Ruby would love them, too."

He pulls back a little further to look into my eyes. His expression is serious now. Possessive, if I had to pick a word to name it. "Be careful what you say to me. You know making you happy, making sure you can shine, is everything I want. You can *definitely* do that here."

I put my hand against the side of his face. "I do know that."

Emotions swirl in his eyes as he studies mine. Finally, he says huskily, "Okay, sweet witch, time for bed."

He pulls me to my feet and I happily step close and wrap my arms around his neck. He bends and sweeps me up into his arms, bridal style.

I rest my head on his shoulder. This feels really nice.

"I can probably walk."

"I like this better." He starts for the parking lot.

I feel my eyes sliding shut. But it's more out of contentment than fatigue. "Do you have a bathtub in your house here?"

"As a matter of fact, I do. A big one. All my own."

"Excellent news," I murmur. "And no matter how sleepy I seem between now and the time we get to that bathtub, I would really like to try it out."

He chuckles softly, and I love the way the sound rumbles through my body.

"Are you drunk?" he asks.

"Tipsy. Not too drunk."

He stops by the car and lets me slide down the front of his body. I stand looking up at him.

"I really like you," I tell him.

I think it's too soon to tell him I'm falling in love, but I can't not say anything at all.

If I said *love*, he'd drag me to the Justice of the Peace tomorrow. And there's a tiny part of me that would be fine with that. A tiny part of me feels the twist of adrenaline at the thought.

But I really am older, wiser, more mature now. I would have run off with Eli. I'd expected him to ask. After my dad shunned us, I'd had visions of him showing up at my house in the middle of the night, declaring his feelings, and whisking me away.

But Eli never came. He left town. Without me. Without even saying goodbye. Without a word about his unborn child or the future with him or her.

And now, sixteen years later, I can admit that was for the best.

But that pain changed me.

Being changed by pain is sometimes the way it has to happen. I know that and I know now that it's not my fault that I was hurt.

But being changed by hope, by goodness, and by love is a much better way to go.

Cian's expression is full of affection when he brushes my hair back from my face. "You make me actually feel like a king."

I smile. "You act like one, you know. Wanting to help people. Wanting everyone to be taken care of and to have a future and to feel good about their lives."

He shakes his head slightly as if he doesn't know what to do with me, then bends and kisses my forehead. "You are too drunk to take a bath by yourself though, right? I think it would be safer if I was in there with you."

I laugh softly. Actually, it's a giggle. A happy, I'm-falling-in-love giggle. "Oh, definitely safer if you're with me."

"Excellent answer."

He pulls the car door open and helps me in.

It only takes five minutes to get to the house that sits a few blocks from Ellie's, inside, and up to Cian's rooms.

Yes, rooms. Plural. Even though this is a seemingly normal two-story house in a small town in Louisiana, it's clearly been added onto and renovated. I suppose if there was a time when two princes and two princesses along with all of their bodyguards were living here, some of the accommodations had to be upgraded.

The upgrades include individual bedrooms and en suite bathrooms for everyone. I can't even imagine with the first floor, where the living room, offices, and kitchen are located.

For now, I'm impressed enough with Cian's bedroom.

It's bigger than Ruby, Mariah, and my rooms put together. The bed is enormous. It has to be bigger than a standard king. The duvet is a silvery gray, and the pillows are a mix of white and grays. The thick plush carpet is also a dove gray while the walls are white with a dark gray trim. He leads me to an overstuffed armchair near the windows. The view is of the wooded area behind the house. It's dark and the stars are twinkling above the tree line. He nudges me into the chair.

"Stay here. I'll get the bath going."

I immediately curl up into the cushy softness of the chair, pulling my knees up and wrapping my arms around my legs as I watch him cross the room to the door that obviously leads into the bathroom. I hear the sound of the water start in the tub and him moving around, opening and shutting cabinets.

He appears in the doorway a few minutes later. "I'm going down to Fiona's old room to see if there's any bubble bath."

I grin at him. "It's okay if there's not."

He comes toward me, leaning over, bracing his hands on the arms of the chair like he did at Ellie's. "Let me go look. Hayden stayed in that room when she lived here too. There has to be something."

I can't help but reach out to him, taking his face between my hands. I pull him in for a quick kiss. "Who's Hayden?"

"Colin's wife."

Colin was—still is sometimes? —Fiona and Saoirse's bodyguard. I know he now works sometimes for Bennett Baxter, one of Louisiana's senators and a member of the Landry family.

Cian gives me another kiss, then heads out the door.

I decide to save a little time and stand, stripping out of my clothes, then padding into the bathroom.

I stop in the doorway and take it in. It's gorgeous. It's almost as pretty as the bathroom at the hotel.

Dark gray tile covers the floor, the countertops are a lighter gray granite, and silver fixtures gleam in the soft light.

The tub is less a hot tub and more a Jacuzzi.

I grin as I approach it. Oh, this is definitely big enough for the two of us. Hell, we can invite guests.

I giggle. Not that I'm into that.

Sure enough there are water jets in various positions around the perimeter of the tub, and once we're inside, the water will easily come up to my shoulders.

I reach over to test the water temperature and find it absolutely perfect. I want to slip into it now.

I hear the bedroom door open and close again as Cian comes into the bathroom, triumphantly holding up a bottle of pearly white liquid.

He stops, taking me in. "I was going to undress you."

I tip my head. "Sorry to disappoint you."

His gaze travels over me from head to toe and I feel my body heating and tingling as if he's running his hands over me.

He comes forward, slowly. "There is absolutely nothing about you, inside or out, that is a disappointment, Glinda."

I take the bottle from his hand, unscrew the top and tip the liquid into the filling tub. Immediately bubbles start to foam up. I set it to the side, then reach for the bottom of his shirt.

"I can undress you though," I tell him. I slide my hands underneath the shirt, taking the fabric with me as I glide my palms over his abs, up to his chest.

He lifts his arms, and I get the shirt as far as I can before he has to tug it the rest of the way over his head because of the difference in our heights. He tosses it behind him. I smooth my hands over the bare skin exposed, tracing the tip of my finger over the lines of the tattoo of the elephant.

It still makes my heart beat faster that he got this tattoo.

He permanently inked a reminder of me on his body.

I lift my gaze to meet his as I slide the backs of my hands down his torso to the fly of his pants.

I unbutton and unzip him, watching his face.

He doesn't move to help me or stop me. My fingers skate over his hard cock and my pussy clenches with anticipation.

But I am overcome by the urge to take this slow.

Things are always so hot between us. I can't wait to get his hands and mouth on me. I want his words, his commands. I've accepted and gotten used to the idea that I can turn over my dirtiest desires to this man, and he will not only make all of my fantasies come true, but there is no judgment, and I am perfectly safe, not only with the things he will do to me, but I know he will keep my secrets.

But now, for maybe the first time, I don't want hard and fast and dirty.

I want to... love him.

I step closer, pushing his jeans and boxers down his legs. I press a kiss to the center of his chest. Then another. Then another. I kiss across his chest, letting my hands wander over his hips around his ass up his back, then around to his sides.

He groans, one of his hands going to my lower back, the other cupping the back of my head. "Scarlett," he says softly, his voice rough.

I move my mouth up to his throat, taking a deep breath, pulling in his scent. I kiss his neck, then his jaw. I tip my head back. "I need you."

He swallows, then nods. I can tell that he also senses the shift in emotion.

He kisses me, and it's deep, but it's also sweet, and slow.

When he lifts his head, he just looks into my eyes for a long moment. Then he steps back, leans over, and gets rid of his clothes. Then he reaches for the hair clip I didn't even notice on the edge of the tub. He reaches up, dragging his fingers through my hair, combing it out. Then he gathers it into a ponytail, twists it, then gathers it at the top of my head and clips it up out of the way.

Without a word, he takes my hand and helps me into the tub.

I sink into the warm, bubble filled water that smells like lavender and vanilla.

He steps over the side and joins me, taking a seat facing me.

We just look at each other.

I study his face, taking in every detail.

His beard has grown even further, and he's not wearing the glasses, and he looks more like the guy I met nineteen months ago.

But more, he looks like the man I've gotten to know over the past week. I can't believe it's only been a week, but I feel closer to him than almost anyone.

Ruby is probably the only person who knows me better than Cian right now.

And despite all of my past experiences with loving and trusting and believing in people and having that shattered, I realize he's gotten past all of that. He's managed to heal the cracks that Eli put in my heart and has glued back together the pieces my father completely chipped away.

Cian thinks he loves me.

And for the first time, after this weekend, and sitting here now, looking at him, I believe not just that he thinks it, but that I deserve it.

There are things that are lovable about me. Things that someone could be proud of about me. Things that someone could want to learn more about. Things that someone could want to experience every day with me.

I may not be exactly where I want to be in becoming the person I want to see in the mirror, but I feel a lot closer to her than I have in a very long time.

"I really like you," I tell him. Again.

"I know," he says.

And it doesn't sound egotistical. It doesn't sound funny. It makes me happy. I'm very glad that he knows that. It means I'm doing better at letting people get close and showing them how I feel.

"I'm glad you came to Emerald to find me," I tell him, moving closer to him.

"I know," he says again.

And again, I'm glad that's his answer. I want him to know that.

I float closer and I feel his hands reach out and circle my waist, pulling me in.

I straddle his lap and feel his cock nudge against me. "And I'm very glad you brought me here to New Orleans and Autre and introduced me to everyone. And told them who I really am."

Our lips are only a few inches away.

"I know," he says.

I'm so glad he knows all of that.

I lean in and put my mouth against his and say, "And now I would really like to make love to you."

I feel his hands tighten on my waist.

"Fuck yes," is his answer.

A little shiver goes through me, and I smile. One thing we haven't done is put me in the driver's seat when it comes to sex. He has absolutely taken over every time. And it has been everything I've wanted. I've needed it. Exploring what I like and want and need sexually has been amazing. Finding a man who is willing and able to figure out what I like, experiment with me, and has enjoyed it as much as I have has been amazing.

But it's also really nice to feel bold and confident about it now. And to know that there are times when he's very happy to follow my lead.

With my hands on his shoulders, I lift up, bringing one nipple to his mouth. "Suck on me."

He gives a little groan, leans in and happily flicks his tongue over my nipple, before pulling it into his mouth.

Lightning streaks from that spot straight to my core. My pussy clenches and I let my head tip back, relishing the sensations rushing through me.

I reach between us, finding his cock and stroking up and down, ready to position him so I can sink down on him, already plenty wet and ready for him.

But his hand snakes between us and he cups my pussy. "Easy," he tells me gruffly.

"I'm ready," I say breathlessly. "Need you."

"No need to rush," he says easing a finger into me.

Suddenly, I feel overwhelmed. Like I am on the verge of tears, or coming, or laughing, or all of the above. I know it is the combination of being here with him on the heels of realizing I am falling in love.

The emotions are intense and I understand that I'm going to have to make decisions about the future very soon.

And I just want him. All of him. I want to be connected and filled up and to somehow show him that I am new because of him.

I lock my gaze on his. "I was going to be in charge."

He moves his finger in and out. "You can have whatever you want from me. Always, Scarlett. I just want to be sure you're ready to take me. I want it to always feel good. No pain. Just pleasure."

The emotions surging are a combination of love and happiness, and also the need to show him how he's helped me. I want him to know that I am bolder because of him. And that I fully trust him. And suddenly I know what I want to do.

I push back, slipping off his lap, his finger sliding out of my body.

He frowns. "Scarlett—"

There's something we haven't done before. But I think we will both like it a lot.

I move back across the tub, not breaking eye contact.

"You're right. I need to be ready to take that huge, amazing cock. Deep and hard."

The heat in his eyes flares. "What are you—"

I lift myself up on the edge of the tub. It's plenty wide enough. The way the tub is set into the wall, it's up against the window. It's tinted so that if there was someone outside in those trees, they still couldn't really see in, but it gives the illusion that we're exposed. The ledge could easily hold dozens of candles, spa supplies, a wine bottle and glasses. So there's plenty of room for me to sit.

I prop one foot up on the ledge, letting the other dangle in the water.

My body wet and glistening in the soft light, my legs spread open, I slide my hand down my stomach to my pussy.

"Just want to be sure I'm ready."

His gaze is locked on my hand between my legs. His jaw is tight.

I glide my finger over my clit and suck in a little breath. This is hot not only because I'm touching myself, but because of the way he watches me. I really do feel like I've put a spell on him. I feel powerful.

"I think I need an orgasm before I ride you," I tell him. "You always fuck me so deep, I need to be nice and wet and hot to take you."

In the past, it has definitely been Cian who has done most of the talking. But I love the way he grips the edge of the tub, and the way his chest lifts and falls with his ragged breathing.

But he doesn't move. He's letting me do this. Take this control.

Oh, yes, having the power to affect this man is definitely addicting.

I circle over my clit, then slide my finger into my pussy. I usually use a vibrator, so I'm not as used to getting myself off with just my fingers, but I certainly know what feels good. And I can judge by Cian's face how it's going for him.

"Your fingers are thicker. I do like it better when you finger fuck me." I add a finger.

"Jesus, Scarlett," he grinds out.

"Are you okay?"

"Get that perfect pussy off so you can get over here and fuck me," he says, the words bitten off.

Oh, that helps. I feel my pussy clench around my fingers.

I move them in and out, but it is hard to reach the spots that he gets to. I drag my fingers out and up to my clit, circling and pressing.

"Spread your legs wider," he commands. "Spread your pussy so I can see."

I should probably remind him that he's not in charge, but I'd be lying if I said that wasn't working for me.

I move the leg in the water to the side and use my other hand to spread myself open.

His breath hisses out and I feel my muscles clench in reaction.

"Work that pretty clit," he says. "Make yourself come."

I work my clit faster. I press a little harder. I feel the orgasm starting to tighten.

"I want to hear my name when you come," he tells me.

I'm breathing fast, my gaze locked on his. I've never masturbated for another person. I've definitely pictured him while I've done it over the past year and a half, but having him actually watching me, clearly turned on, wanting this, is so much better.

His hand drops into the water, and I know that he's fisting his cock.

"Come on, Scarlett," he says. "Make that pussy hot and wet for me."

I circle faster and lift my other hand to my breast, squeezing and tugging on the nipple.

"No," he says sharply. "I want to see all that pink perfection. I want to see you wet. I want to see you dripping."

"Need—" I pant. "My nipples."

Then he's pushing across the tub, the water sloshing, to brace his hands on either side of my hips.

"Keep. Going." Then his mouth latches onto my nipple, sucking hard.

My orgasm crashes into me. "Cian!"

"Fuck." He mutters as his hands grasp my hips and he pulls me off the ledge.

I'm in his lap and he positions me over his cock. "Gorgeous little witch," he says gruffly as he pulls me down on his length.

He fills me up, stretching me as my orgasm is still rippling.

The sensation is incredible, and I swear my toes curl. "Cian!"

"You are so fucking perfect," he says, thrusting up into me.

I grip his shoulders, sliding up and down, riding him fast and hard.

My next orgasm is right on the heels of the first, and I come hard around him only a few minutes later.

His fingers dig into my hips deliciously. "Fuck, yes."

Then he stiffens, shouting my name, filling me up.

I wrap my arms around him, pressing my face to his throat, and breathe.

This is all so good.

He is so good.

And I really do think I could do this—*all* of this—with this man for the rest of my life.

CHAPTER 26

SCARLETT

It's two thirty p.m. on Monday, but I slump into my chair behind my desk at the garage and take a deep breath.

I'm exhausted.

I came in late even. I didn't have anything pressing to do and I'm still recovering from the weekend away.

But I can't help the huge smile, and the warmth in my chest that's been there, like a big, full bubble since Friday, seems to expand.

The weekend was a whirlwind.

I loved every minute of it.

After our bath Saturday night, I fell asleep in Cian's arms.

We slept late on Sunday, but we still had time for a huge breakfast at Ellie's before Cian took me on a swamp boat tour. I'd thought I was maybe going to get a private tour but there are just too many people that all like to hang out together. Our boat was full, and when I video called Mariah from deep in the bayou to tell her what I was up to, Saoirse joined the call, much to Mariah's delight.

The girls hit it off, exchanged numbers, and have already texted.

It was actually hard to say goodbye to everyone, but they all seemed to think it was only temporary and that we'd be seeing each other again.

I hope so.

I want to.

And I know I can make that happen. I just have to take a deep breath and dive into a full-blown relationship with Cian.

To distract myself from those overwhelming thoughts, I look around the office. Brian had thankfully kept his records and paperwork pretty organized, so going through things after I'd moved back hadn't taken too long. The office isn't huge. The real work in a garage happens out in the bays, after all. But the desk and chair, half a drawer in the file cabinet, and my laptop will at least get me started on putting together Cian's new foundation.

I open my laptop and pause with my fingers over the keys.

I don't even know what to type in.

How to run a foundation? Steps to setting up a foundation?

Is that even something I should just search the internet for?

We need a lawyer. Probably. Right?

You need Linnea Olsen.

I nod. "That's exactly who we need," I say out loud.

She would absolutely know how to start a foundation.

She could probably put it together in half a day.

Okay, maybe not that but...

Maybe.

I have zero idea.

So, instead, I start searching for logos that have elephants in them.

This isn't exactly what Brian had intended for me to do in this office when he'd left me this place, but I think he'd like the idea. I know he would like the single mom community idea. I know he'd like Cian. And I know he'd like me feeling like I was doing work that matters. Work that makes other people's lives a little easier, and better.

"Hello?" a voice calls from out in the first bay.

I push back from the desk and head out into the garage.

"Hey, Diane," I greet the older woman.

"I got your message that the car is done," she says with a smile.

I chuckle. As usual, the car didn't really need any work. I changed the oil first thing when I came in, checked all the fluids, the tire pressure, even intended to vacuum the floor mats. But since Diane had only put forty miles on the car since the last time I'd worked on it, there wasn't even one speck of gravel.

I dig her car keys out of my front pocket and hand them over. Then I have a thought.

I feel inspired from this weekend. After seeing the community Cian built, and hanging out with the Landrys, and witnessing how they all come together to make their family businesses work, but also seemingly take care of the entire town, I say, "Hey, Diane, can I run an idea past you?"

"Of course."

"Okay, you know I love our arrangement. But, you and I both know this car doesn't actually need this much attention."

Diane looks like she's about to argue so I hold up a hand. "Hang on, hear me out."

Diane pauses.

"Mariah is also getting old enough that she needs to learn to cook. And our schedules are crazy so we're not sitting down around the table quite as often."

"But that's the beauty of the frozen meals," Diane says. "They're just there whenever you need them. And the leftovers warm up well."

"They absolutely do. And they've been a huge help. But I just don't think we really need them as much anymore."

Diane looks a little sad. "Do you know why I've wanted to do this for you?" she asks.

"Because you're a wonderful woman and you knew that I needed some extra support?"

She smiles and says "Yes, I knew you needed support. But that's because when I was a working mom with young kids, my sister made frozen dinners for us." She swallows. "She died about three years ago. Cancer."

My heart squeezes and I reach out, putting my hand on her arm. "I'm so sorry. I didn't know that."

"I miss her. And now that my kids are out of the house, it occurred to me that this was a way I could kind of keep her memory alive. The things I make for you are all her recipes. Whenever we have them, I think of her. And when I make them for me and my husband, I figured I could just make extra and help someone else out the way she helped me."

I feel tears in my eyes and I have to blink rapidly. "Diane, I have a really wonderful idea that I think you're going to love."

"Really?"

"I trade services with a friend of mine, Amber Connors. Do you know her?"

"I know who she is." Diane furrows her brow. "She has really curly blond hair?"

"Yes. Always smiling. Really friendly," I say. "She owns a hair salon. She also does nails and facials. She has two kids in school, and she just found out she's pregnant."

Diane nods. "That's a handful."

"Very much so. She's got a great husband, but he works late shifts. I think she would be so incredibly grateful and it would help her so much to have someone like you help her with meals. And you need to get your haircut sometimes, right?"

Diane laughs and lifts her hand to her hair. "Of course." She looks down at her nails. "I don't really do manicures, but I've always wanted to try one."

"Oh, you definitely need to try a manicure," I tell her. "And a pedicure. Those are the best."

Diane smiles. "I bet Amber is really busy. And with three kids, they might need dinner more than just twice a week."

My grin grows. "I bet you're right." I already love this. It bothered me to let Diane cook for us even twice a week, but I am certain Amber is going to welcome this. And while she will happily do Diane's hair and nails, I don't think Diane will mind doing this cooking at all. In fact, it wouldn't surprise me if Amber ends up with some babysitting offers as well.

It does occur to me, however, that I hope Amber still needs help with treats for school and dance recitals once in a while because those are kind of fun for me.

Diane leaves and I place a quick call to Amber. I put her

on speaker while I explain the situation. She seems pleased and humbled.

"This is amazing," she tells me. "You know, we should form a group for this. There are so many people in town who could be exchanging services. I'm sure there are some older women who could use help with cleaning their gutters and mowing their lawns and they would love to pay in cookies or something."

I laugh. "And I'm sure there are a bunch of young guys with lawnmowers who would be absolutely thrilled to have homemade cookies."

"Brilliant." Amber sighs. "Seriously. I'm going to talk to some of my clients as they come in today. We should put this together. This sounds like the way my grandparents used to describe things. People just helped one another out. But if we need to formally organize it, so what? People are still going to get what they need, right?"

"Absolutely," I agree. While it would be great if this all just happened organically, I think there are a lot of people like me who feel funny accepting help without having something to give back in return.

"We should have a town meeting or something. Or maybe send out a mass email. Or put up signs?" Amber laughs. "I don't really know how to reach the whole town."

"You feel free to run with it," I say. "You know a lot more people. Especially younger families who could use help. I think the grapevine and word of mouth is probably best."

"But this was your idea. Besides, young families aren't the only ones who need help. We just need to come up with a way to connect everyone. Oh, a website!" Amber exclaims.

I still feel myself resisting being the one to do it. I think about Cian's foundation and the fact that I can work on that in Columbus and cities even further away. It doesn't have to involve Emerald or anyone here that I know.

I realize that's the bottom line. I don't want to be up in front of people in Emerald. I appreciated what Henry said on Saturday about people being able to truly see I've changed that way, but...I can just be happy knowing I've changed. That's enough. I don't need to be running my mouth around town.

"I think you should totally do that," I tell Amber. "Bounce it off some clients and see who they know that could build a simple website that could match people up."

"Okay, it's a great idea. I have to run, but thank you! I can't wait to talk with Diane."

We disconnect and I take a deep breath.

What was that? A tiny panic attack at the idea of getting involved in Emerald? Brian on the other hand, would've jumped at the chance to head down to the diner or the bar and start talking about the idea with people.

But Brian had friends. He felt like a true member of this town. It would have felt natural to him to be a part of something to bring the community together.

For me it would just be a part of this damned *mission* or whatever this is that I'm doing here, and I realize I don't want that.

I'd come here to just live my life. To raise my daughter. To run the business my beloved stepfather had left me. To...

I sigh. Who am I kidding?

I came here to prove a point. I wanted the people from my past to see me. The real me. The *now* me. I wanted them to notice the ways I've changed and be... I'm not sure what word I'm looking for. Impressed? Maybe not that. But affected. Moved. I wanted it to make an *impression*. I wanted it to make them think of me differently.

I see now that there's no way that was really going to happen because I'm not letting them know me. I'm not doing anything that would *make* an impression. I'm keeping to myself, trying to keep off their radar. Do I wish living a quiet, simple life could be enough? Maybe.

But then I look at Cian doing all those little things like captaining swamp boat tours and helping Zeke—I'd figured out which twin was which by the end of Sunday—do construction jobs around town and I realize that those jobs mean a lot to the Landrys because they are *theirs*, the way this shop was Brian's. It's what makes them truly happy, because it's taking care of their people. Their family, their friends, their town, their bayou, and their animals.

My people—Ruby and Mariah, and yes, Cian—don't need this garage and they don't need a community program that connects people who can exchange services.

We need more than that. We need to think wider. We need to find things that make us truly passionate.

So, I open my laptop.

I have a foundation to run.

Or a foundation to create so that I can then run it.

I hear a knock on the door frame and look up.

A very handsome prince is leaning into my office. I immediately grin. "What are you doing here? Aren't you supposed to be enlightening young minds?"

He chuckles and steps into the office. "Do you even know what time it is?"

I look down at the clock on the corner of my screen. It's after four. After school.

"Oh my gosh," I say, looking up with a laugh. "So how was the first day?"

He comes in and settles his hip on the corner of my desk. "Awesome."

His face has lit up. He also looks damned good in those glasses. He shaved today and I miss his weekend scruff. But I like the khakis and dark blue button down rolled up to the elbows and open at the neck. He's wearing brown dress shoes that are a little scuffed and he's totally pulling off the casual, but still sophisticated hot professor vibe. I'm very into it all.

I grin. "It was good?"

"Totally nailed it."

I lean back in my chair and prop one of my boots on my opposite knee. "Why am I not surprised? Is there anything you're not good at?"

"The kids were great, got through today's lessons with no issues. I think it's going to be fun. And," he says. "I have a ton of the football players in my classes."

I laugh. "It's not a very big school. And a lot of the boys play football."

His grin gets even bigger. "They've already told me about the big tailgate party and the game on Friday. I can't wait."

"Do you like football? Do you play football in Cara?"

"Mostly hockey and what's called soccer here. But I do like American football. Haven't played it myself. But it's a big deal in Florida and Louisiana, as you know. I learned so I could blend in but ended up really liking it."

That makes sense. "It's a big deal here too."

"Oh, I've been informed." He laughs. "So, we'll go to the big tailgate party, then hang at the game, then they said a bunch of teachers head down to the bar afterwards. Sounds fun, right?"

I frown and shake my head. "Count me out. But you go have fun. Ruby will probably go. And Mariah."

"You don't like football?"

"I like football a lot," I say. "I don't really like big community social events in Emerald."

He settles more fully onto my desk and braces his hands on either side of his hips. "I see. I don't have to go."

My eyes widen. "No. Don't be ridiculous. You should go. Like you said, a lot of the players are in your class. You probably have a bunch of cheerleaders too. And kids who are in the band. The whole community gets involved in these things."

"Except for you."

"Okay. Except for me. And maybe six or seven other people." And that's not even much of an exaggeration. I'm not kidding when I say football is a big deal in Ohio too.

"I am here in Emerald because of you, Scarlett," he says, his voice a little gruff. "I want to spend time with you."

"I know. But one football game, a few hours long, won't hurt."

He hesitates and I can tell he really wants to go to the game. I'm not jealous. I just wish, for the millionth time, that I was living in my hometown as a normal alum of the high school and could go and enjoy things like this.

"Go. I'll be fine. I'll see you after," I tell him.

"Why does Ruby go if you don't?"

I shrug. "When I got involved with the church, I burned a lot of bridges with childhood friends. The church kids were my friends. But when I was thrown out of the church, I lost all of them. So I don't have a friend group here in Emerald anymore. But Ruby stayed in touch with a few of her friends from high school when we left town."

If anyone asked me if I have a little niggle of envy over the fact that my sister feels more comfortable and fits in here even after all these years, I would deny it. And I would be lying.

But it's my own fault I don't have friends here. Ruby kept her relationships going. There were several people who were happy when she moved back. And I told her what I am telling Cian now. I am fine on my own and she deserves to go out and have fun once in a while. She doesn't have to stay home with me just because I was a stuck-up bitch in high school. I'm glad those friends don't hold that against her.

"I'll come over after the game," he says.

"Sure. That's great. Just go and have fun. You'll know where to find me."

"I really liked this past weekend," he says. "When we didn't have to sneak around. When I could touch you and kiss you in public. Where everyone not only knew we were together, but they were thrilled for us."

My chest feels tight. "Yeah, me too."

And I mean it so much that it's scary.

"Can I show you something?" he asks, pulling his phone out.

"Of course." I sit forward in my chair.

He opens a screen and holds it out to show me. It's a text message. The top of the screen says TORIN.

Fiona told me what you're up to. Sounds amazing. Let me know if you need anything.

I look up at him. He's smiling. "Fiona told Torin about the moms' community?"

He nods. "And the foundation." He taps on his phone screen and holds it out again.

This message is from Abigail.

Torin told me your news but Charlie had already filled me in! Amazing!

I look up and his smile is bright.

He taps again and then turns the phone.

LINNEA is at the top of the screen now.

I can't wait to hear more! I'm at your disposal to help in any way I can! Jonah too.

"I was just thinking that she could be a fantastic resource!" I say.

He grins. "Definitely. We'll talk to her soon."

He pulls up another message.

ASTRID: *Wow. Knew you were more than a pretty face. Way to go!*

I look up at him, my brows up. "Really? You're showing me texts from your *fiancée?*"

He narrows his eyes playfully. "Watch it, little witch. I will spank you right here."

Of course, my body responds to that instantly. But I say, "*You're* the one getting texts from hot, single girls."

He leans over and tips my chin up. "I'm getting texts from family and *friends.*"

I smile up at him. "I know. And I'm really happy for you. *This* is what should be happening. I'm so glad they all know."

He sits back and turns the phone again.

DECLAN: *Nice work. Let me know what I can do to get involved.*

My eyes are wide when I look up. "Wow. That's…" Suddenly I'm choked up. *This* is what I wanted for him. At least in part. I want people to know what he's doing, and I want him to be praised for it. Especially from the people he most admires. I sniff and say, "With Declan's help, you won't have to fundraise at all."

Cian chuckles and I can see how much this all means to him. "But I still will. All those other rich fuckers need to give their money away."

I laugh.

He sobers slightly and taps once more, turning the phone.

KING D.

I look up at him. "Your grandfather?"

He nods, and now he seems a little emotional.

I read the message: *Well done. I'm proud of you.*

Now tears definitely fill my eyes. I put my hand on his knee and squeeze. He covers my hand with his.

And it hits me that Cian's family is truly seeing the man he is. Maybe for the first time. They're proud of *him*.

They've probably also seen him as a 'sidekick'. I know they love him. That was more than clear this weekend. I'm positive Fiona knows how much he did for her and Saoirse. But, as Henry said, he's been the guy who's always been there, helping everyone else out, filling in the gaps, but not taking anything on by himself.

Now he's making a difference, doing something big on his own, and they're *seeing* him. They're seeing that growth and change. They're impressed. And they're supportive. *They* want to help *him*, now.

These are the things I've wanted from Emerald. Or so I thought. But it has to mean so much more coming from his family and friends. The people he looks up to.

But that wasn't why he did it. Cian did something good for other people, not to prove anything, not to shut anyone up, not to impress anyone or to get accolades. He didn't even tell his family about the communities he built. He created those communities simply because he wanted to and because he could. He liked the idea and thought it was something that would help people. His motivation was pure.

And I realize that's why I haven't been inspired to actually do anything in Emerald beyond the garage. I haven't had the right motivation. Being here is all about proving people from my past wrong.

But why do I care what Emerald thinks?

I don't admire my father. I don't want to be like Hannah. I don't want to return to the church.

So, why do I care if they approve of me?

I stand and move between his knees. His hands come instantly to my hips and I wrap my arms around his neck.

And I just hug him.

And he hugs me back.

"You are an amazing person, Cian O'Grady," I tell him, leaning back after a minute. Surprise flickers in his gaze, but it's almost immediately replaced by the affection I'm getting very used to seeing there. "Thank you for coming after me."

"I will always come after you, Scarlett."

I sigh happily. "God, I want you right now."

He squeezes my hips. "Want to go to the B&B? Mariah is probably home by now."

"Yes," I say quickly. Surely there's a way for me to sneak in and out of there.

"Or," he says, moving his mouth to my neck. "We could stay here. I've had fantasies of bending you over a car or fucking you on a hood."

Tingles shoot through my body. "Have you now?"

"Only every single time I see you in these boots. Or these coveralls. Or in this garage. Or with a streak of grease on your face."

I step out of his arms and cross to the door, where I turn the sign to CLOSED and lock it. Then I head into the bay, hitting the button to close the big garage door on my way past.

"You coming?" I ask him over my shoulder.

He's right on my heels.

I lead him toward the ridiculously expensive Rolls Royce parked in the second bay.

"Is this the car Henry got?" he asks.

"Yep, this is the car I'm supposedly fixing for Professor Dean Brady," I say, unzipping my coveralls.

"Oh, this is going to be fun." His hands go to my waist, and he lifts me onto the hood.

"I've never had sex on such a nice car," I say, my fingers on his shirt buttons.

He stops sliding my coveralls down. "But you *have* had sex *on* a car before?"

"One of the guys I dated in New Orleans was a mechanic at the same shop as me and we—"

He covers my mouth with his hand. But his eyes are sparkling. "Witch," he says affectionately. "Have you ever been turned over the hood of a car and *spanked*?"

I shake my head quickly and I know *my* eyes are sparkling with excitement now too.

CHAPTER 27
CIAN

"I'm glad your first day went well," Ruby says from the other end of the island where she's chopping vegetables for the salad.

"Thanks," I tell her. "Now that Scarlett has met the Landry boys she can probably tell you that it's no surprise why I get along with teenagers just fine."

Ruby and Scarlett both laugh.

"The Landrys are all so great," Scarlett tells her sister. "We had the best time." She bends to take the casserole pan out of the oven. "You would like them so much."

Ruby grins at me behind Scarlett's back. "Yes, you've mentioned that."

Yes, she has. In different ways. About five times while we've been making dinner.

I love it.

I'm so fucking happy that she's happy. I knew that's what I wanted, but until now, seeing it and hearing it happening, I'm not sure I realized how it would affect me.

Things feel like they're on the right track. This is working. We have eleven and a half days left of our nineteen days and things are going great.

"Well, this is a shit show!"

We all turn toward the back door where Mariah just came in.

Or maybe not.

"What's a shit show?" Scarlett asks, frowning and crossing the floor to Mariah.

"Having him as a teacher," Mariah says, pointing at me.

Yeah...*not*.

I haven't seen her since fifth period. Her history class.

After stopping by the garage, Scarlett and I had come home—yes, I'm aware that I'm thinking of Scarlett's house as home—and taken the last of Diane's casseroles out of the freezer and put it in the oven for dinner.

Ruby was here and we've been filling her in on the weekend's activities, including telling her about Scarlett Park and the foundation.

Ruby's very interested and impressed and I have to admit that having her approval feels almost as good as having my own siblings and grandfather congratulating me. I've spent so much time admiring the people in my life and the things they do that I hadn't realized how incredible it would feel to have that admiration in return.

I've been flying high since Friday when Scarlett and I landed in New Orleans.

Everything about the weekend was perfect and I am one hundred percent madly in love with her.

Even my first day at school had gone amazingly well.

Or so I thought.

"What happened?" Scarlett asks Mariah. "You knew last

week that was going to happen. You and Greta both thought it sounded fun."

Mariah tosses her backpack on one of the kitchen chairs.

"It's weird! I had to call him by a different name. And then, when Leah brought up the podcast, I did have to flat out *lie*."

Mariah presses her lips together, and I think for a moment she might cry.

"I *hate* that," she says. "Before when she accused me of lying, she was wrong. I was telling the whole truth. But today, I *did* have to lie. She was right calling me a liar. Because I couldn't tell her that Cian was right down the hall in the history room. Then I had to walk into class and I could barely look at him. I was afraid I was going to call him the wrong name or stand up on my chair and yell *that's him! I know more than even the podcast does!*"

"I have no idea what you're talking about," Scarlett says, glancing at me. "Leah brought Cian up again today just randomly? Why?"

Mariah stares at her. "Because of today's podcast. Because of you guys!"

Cold trickles down my spine. This doesn't sound good. I scowl and stomp to the counter where my phone is charging. "What did they say?"

I don't know who feeds the podcast all of the information about the royal family. We've all wondered at different times. It seems that it must be a mix of people. But I don't know anyone who would have known we were in Autre this weekend who would've told the podcast already.

I start tapping and scrolling trying to find the most recent episode.

Scarlett and Ruby are doing the same.

I suppose we didn't specifically tell anyone that Scarlett needed to be a secret. Because why would they think that? I was clearly over-the-moon in love with her. Why would they think for a second I wanted to keep that under wraps?

Because I don't.

Fuck.

Lindsey: If you haven't seen the latest photos that Lady Linnea posted from their honeymoon trip, be sure to go to her social media pages.

Jen: Definitely. She and Jonah are so hot and so sweet together. And how we all missed that there was something between the two of them, I will never know.

Lindsey: Well, it seems that maybe the royal family and their close friends are better at keeping secrets than we thought.

Jen: <laughs> You have a point. We have some juicy news to share, listeners. You know how Prince Cian and his bodyguard Henry jumped on a plane and supposedly disappeared after the wedding?

Lindsey: And then everyone said never mind, there's no story here, just a miscommunication. They're back safe in the US. No worries. Move on with your lives.

Jen: Well, they *did* head back to the US and they *are* safe, but there was a reason for that sudden pre-dawn flight.

Lindsey: Can I say, I love that there's always more to the story with this family? It certainly makes our show popular.

Jen: That. Plus, it's just fun. And romantic. It makes my little romance-loving heart swoon.

Lindsey: I'm rolling my eyes for everyone who can't see

me. I mean, of course it has to have something to do with romance, right?

Jen: <laughs> Some of us love love!

Lindsey: These people are a little over the top though.

Jen: Well... yes. And Cian is no exception.

Lindsey: That's for sure. Tell everyone what's up.

Jen: Turns out that Cian jetted back to the US for a *woman*.

Lindsey: <groans>

Jen: <laughs> But wait...it gets *better*. He's been *looking for* this woman. They met almost two years ago! And suddenly he found out where she is and just had to go see her.

Lindsey: What? What do you mean he just suddenly found out where she was? They didn't exchange numbers or anything?

Jen: Those details are a little fuzzy. I guess she moved right after they met. Anyway! He found her and immediately had to go see her. And that's where he's been. He hasn't been back in Louisiana. He's been hanging out with his new love. They call her his Cinderella. <happy sigh>

Lindsey: Well, that *is* interesting. I guess that explains why we haven't seen Prince Cian with any girlfriends for a while. But you're telling me that our favorite playboy prince has been hung up on a woman for almost *two years*? Hey news flash, Prince Cian...you could have *any woman* you want! What are you doing?

Jen: No! I mean, yes, he could. Obviously. But this is so great! Pining for her. Obsessed with her. Fell in love in a weekend and then lost track of her. Isn't that *amazing*?

Lindsey: Do they have a royal therapist on staff?

Jen: <laughing> Stop. I'm sure they do and I'm sure he or she would simply say this is *love*! You should try it!

Lindsey: <laughing> Uh, I'm good. So, who is this woman? Where is she?

Jen: We don't have all of those details. Our source is kind of a tease.

Lindsey: Well, I guess we'll have to keep digging. We will definitely keep you updated! Just wait 'til we tell ye!

I look up and meet Scarlett's gaze. Her eyes are wide and she has her hand covering her mouth.

Ruby jumps in. "They didn't really say anything about *you*. No one knows who you are. They didn't say where you are. This is...nothing."

"This is all true, though," Scarlett says. She looks at me.

"I don't know who shared this," I assure her. "I will see if someone can find out."

She shakes her head. "What good will that do? It's already out there. It's not like you can punish them or get them to take this down. People have already seen and heard it."

I walk over to her and take her upper arms in my hands. I stroke my hands up and down her arms and lean in until she's looking directly in my eyes. "This isn't a big deal. No one knows your name or where you are. Besides, even if they did, what's the big deal?"

"The big deal is, that you're *here*," Mariah answers, clearly frustrated.

We turn to face her.

"And you're lying to the entire town about who you are. And if they find out, that means all of *us* are lying to this whole town. My friends, Greta's parents, my teachers!" Mariah throws her arms wide. "Leah confronted me today in the lunchroom. She said obviously you are not in love with my mom because you're off with some other woman." She stands staring at us for a moment. "*You* are supposedly Dean Brady. A professor who is teaching us history. And my mom is here. Single as always. But the podcast says that Prince Cian is somewhere with the woman he's in love with. The woman he fell in love with two years ago and has been looking for. So to Leah, and everyone else, that is obviously not my mom which makes me a liar when I say that you two dated."

Right.

All of that makes sense now. And Mariah is correct, if this ever comes out, we *have* lied to the entire town.

"So, I am completely right. I haven't lied about any of it. Until now." Again, Mariah presses her lips together. "You all have turned me into what my nemesis has said I am all along."

She turns and stomps out of the room, up the stairs, and a few seconds later we hear her bedroom door slam.

"Well...this *is* kind of a shit show," Ruby says.

Scarlett blows out a breath. "Mariah is almost always right."

We eat dinner, discussing the women's community and getting the foundation started, avoiding the real subject which is: we kind of fucked up.

My spontaneous move to hide my identity and stay in town has gotten complicated and it's involved Mariah.

Scarlett had said she didn't want the town to know she was dating a prince. So, I'd reacted. I'd taken that factor out of the equation. I'd focused on *us* and why we were so good together. I'd tried to make it simpler.

I hadn't realized that could actually muddle things. I especially hadn't realized it would affect Mariah.

Because we figure she blames us the most, Scarlett and I

stay in the kitchen to clean up while Ruby takes a plate up to Mariah.

She comes back down empty-handed which we assume means Mariah will at least eat.

"You should just leave her alone for tonight," Ruby says. "You can't really put this toothpaste back in the tube, you know? But," she adds. "You two probably need to figure out what you're going to do going forward. Mariah has a point. If the town ever figures out who you really are, they're going to realize we all lied to them. That could really be problematic for Mariah and me with our friends. Not to mention your hope of ever getting back on the good side of anyone," she says, looking at Scarlett. Then she heads out the door for work.

Scarlett sets down the dish she's holding and looks up at me. "What are we going to do?"

"About Mariah? Or the town?" I ask. I don't actually have an answer for either of those.

"Mariah is on our side. She'll be okay. Though I'm glad lying bothers her so much," Scarlett says. "But I guess, if this turns into something long-term—"

I step right in front of her and look down at her, meeting her gaze. "This *is* something long-term."

"Then we're in trouble. You've been a royal in hiding for twelve years. But you've been using your real name. You've still been Cian O'Grady. Just no one here really knew who Cian O'Grady was. If you stay here, do we come clean? And, just live with the fact that the whole town thinks we're liars? Or do you continue to live with a fake name? Which then compromises what we want to do with the foundation. I want your name on that. I think you do too. And that's how you fundraise. That's how you'll get the word out. It's something you should be proud of."

"You definitely want to stay here?" I ask her. I love that she's talking about the future, but yes, we now have a problem. "Or would you let me take you somewhere else? Somewhere that you don't have to worry about what these people think? Where you don't have a history? Where you can start fresh?" I lift my hand and run it through her hair. "We could go back to New Orleans. And you liked Autre."

"I do like Autre," she says with a smile. "But the thing is, they don't need us. They've got all the people they could possibly need pitching in and helping out and keeping things running. We should be somewhere that needs *us*."

"There's probably a hundred places like that. Thousands."

She nods. "Yeah. I guess we should think about that. Ruby would probably be okay leaving. She does have friends here, but she's left before. But I do hate that she always has to leave because of me. Mariah is different. She has friends here and especially Greta. That would be hard. But I hate to drag her into all of this."

"We don't have to solve this tonight. For now, no one knows who the woman is that Cian O'Grady is chasing. None of this has exposed either of us. Let's just...think about it."

I wish I could tell her we have time to figure this all out. I wish we did have time. That would make all of this so much easier.

But even though Scarlett hasn't brought up the fact that we only have eleven days left, I'm aware of it.

And even if we extended that deadline, my grandfather still has one for me.

And I'm not sure I can solve all of Scarlett Gale's problems in two and a half months.

CHAPTER 28
CIAN

Jen: Oh my God, Lindsey, we've been getting some very interesting news that we haven't had before about the royal family.

Lindsey: I know. It makes me want to go back and think about everything that happened with Torin and Abigail also.

Jen: I know. But it's especially interesting in light of the information we have about Cian going to look for this mystery woman in the United States.

Lindsey: We need to fill everyone in. According to our sources, apparently the king is *pressuring* the grandkids to get married. The source isn't saying exactly why. It has to do with some long-standing agreement that they would all be married by a certain time or something. Our source either doesn't know the specifics or isn't sharing. But either way the grandkids are feeling some pressure.

Jen: All I really hear is that we might be having some more royal weddings coming up. Bring it on!

Cian: what's your favorite dinner? Home cooked. Not burgers or pizza.

Mariah: chicken Parmesan bake.

do you know how to make it?

yeah

can you teach me tonight? We're out of casseroles.

what happened to Diane?

Cian: I heard your mom talking to her and then on the phone with Amber. She set Diane up to help Amber instead.

<heart eyes emoji> of course she did.

Mariah sent me the list of ingredients for the chicken parmesan bake. It's cubed chicken breasts, sautéed with garlic and butter, penne pasta, heavy cream, and a ton of Parmesan cheese.

It sounds perfect. It actually doesn't require much time in the oven. Just enough to melt and brown the cheese on top. Still, it will be delicious and will smell great when Scarlett gets home from work.

More, it will hopefully cheer Mariah up and give us a chance to talk.

Today at school was another shit show.

This time I got to witness it.

Leah had approached Mariah in the lunchroom. Yes, I had lunch duty on my second day.

There was a new podcast this morning and Mariah, Scarlett, Ruby, Henry, and I had already checked it out. We weren't going to get caught unaware again.

This time, Lindsey and Jen talked about the fact that my grandfather wants all of us married.

Thankfully, it didn't mention that he was arranging our marriages. There also wasn't discussion about the poker game or Alfred. They made it sound as if my grandfather really just wanted us all married and happy.

There was no hint that Abigail and Torin were married for reasons anything other than true love. They didn't say a thing about Linnea being the assumed queen since she was four years old, or the fact that she had been engaged to Declan, then Torin, then kind-of me for about two minutes. There also wasn't a single mention of Astrid.

Still, Leah had felt the need to bring up to Mariah that it seems Cian... *I*—yes, this is all very weird—am spending time with this mystery woman with the assumption that she will soon be a princess.

While all of that was true, Leah is also under the assumption—rightly so, to be fair—that this woman is not Scarlett.

Again, proof in her mind that Mariah has been lying about my previous relationship with Scarlett.

They actually got into a shouting match across the lunchroom.

Mariah had insisted that Cian—*I*—proposed to Scarlett. Leah had tossed back that clearly he has moved on if that ever was the case. Mariah insisted I—Cian—is in love with Scarlett. Leah refused to accept that for obvious reasons. Mariah told Leah that she has no idea what she's talking about, and Leah laughed.

Mariah had stomped out of the lunchroom without eating her lunch.

I had found myself literally fighting to keep from crossing the room and doing whatever I could to cut Leah Lawton down to size.

Of course there were two problems with that. One, that would mean exposing myself, and I couldn't do that without talking to Scarlett about a plan for what would happen when everyone found out the truth.

Two, and probably more importantly, a grown man didn't do that to a teenage girl.

Mariah steps into the kitchen as I've finished dicing the chicken.

"This is as far as I've gotten," I tell her.

She swings her backpack off her shoulder and onto one of the kitchen chairs. She looks over everything I have laid out on the counter. "That's a pretty good start," she tells me.

Okay, we're speaking. That's a good first step. I wouldn't blame her if she was angry with me. All of this is really my fault. I'm not sorry that I came to Emerald and I'm not sorry for respecting Scarlett's boundaries when she said she didn't want anyone to know I am here for her. But my spontaneous decision to go undercover has created a much bigger issue that I definitely did not think through.

Mariah goes to the sink and washes her hands. She reaches for a towel and is drying them when she says, "My mom thinks that you should just live your life and be a good example of what you want people to think of you. But you shouldn't have to tell people who you are and what you believe in. People should just know by how you act and the things you do." She hangs the towel up and turns. "Mom says that words can be weapons and that we should be careful with them. That we should judge people by what they do, not what they say." Mariah braces her hands on the edge of the sink and leans back. She studies the floor instead of looking at me.

I stay quiet, grateful that she's opening up and honestly, not totally sure what to say anyway. But I put down the utensils and turn to face her, giving her my full attention.

"I think about that with my grandfather," she goes on. "He tells the kids at church that he wants me to come to youth group and to services, he says he wants me to be closer to God, but he doesn't *do* anything to get me there himself." She scuffs the floor with the toe of her shoe. "I used to think that sending the kids after me was him doing something but...it's not. That's easy. He can send them and then blame them when it doesn't work." She takes a breath. "My mom used to talk to Brian about stuff. But anytime she wanted to talk about God or the church, Brian made her *do* stuff at the same time."

"Yeah, she told me," I say. "She said that's how she learned to fix cars."

Mariah nods her head. "Yeah, but other stuff too. He told her he listened better if he was doing something while he was talking. So sometimes it was fixing someone's screen door or taking them groceries. Things like that. He'd always make her go along. And if she wasn't giving him a "lesson", he'd sometimes call and tell her he wanted to talk about something." Mariah smiles. "She told me that in the end, those actions always made a bigger impression on her than my grandpa's words on Sundays. She would hear him preaching from the pulpit about taking care of our neighbors or welcoming strangers, and she'd think about Brian."

I wait a couple of beats. "Did you know Brian very well?"

She lifts her shoulders. "Kind of. We spent holidays here sometimes. But I know most of the things about him from her stories." Her smile gets a little sad. "She doesn't really have stories about my grandpa. Which tells you a lot right?"

I nod. "Right."

"What about your grandpa?" she asks, pushing away from the sink and crossing to the counter. She grabs the pot and takes it to the stove where she starts the butter heating.

"What do you want to know?"

"Well, he's a king. Literally runs a country. He probably *does* a lot of stuff. But he also talks a lot. Which do you think is more important?"

I carry the jar of minced garlic over to her, and she adds it to the butter, stirring them together. I turn back to the counter and start chopping the onion. "That's a good question," I finally say. "I guess there's a lot of both with my grandfather. The *doing* directly impacts people's lives. But I know people also look to him to explain things, to reassure them, to inspire them. I guess at different times, they're both important. If the words are sincere. And I think you're right that words and actions need to match up."

I bring the onions to her. "I can tell you about my brother, the one who's going to be king. He talked a lot about how he didn't believe in a monarchy and thought we should be a representative government, but then he also did something about it. He abdicated and left home. I went with him. And not so much because of his words, but because of the action. Because I figured if he believed in it that much, it must really matter."

Mariah dumps the onions into the sizzling butter and garlic.

"There is a time for words though," she says. "Even though with Leah, I know I shouldn't, sometimes I just want to yell. I just want to say *I'm right. You don't know everything.*"

We add the chicken to the pot as well and she continues to stir.

"I agree," I say. "My sister is a good example of that. She *does* a lot. She shows up, rescues animals, actually puts her hands into work. She'll go without sleep, she'll drive hundreds of miles, she'll do whatever it takes. So those actions matter. And if she tries to talk to the people who are illegally smuggling animals or abusing them, it doesn't make a lot of difference. People like that don't care.

"But there are times when she *has to* speak out. To law enforcement, to people she needs to donate to her cause, to potential volunteers when she needs extra hands, and definitely to lawmakers. She's had to appear in front of state and federal government committees to try to get laws in place or strengthened. She'd really love to take them all with her on the rescues so they can see it up close and personal, but she has to rely on her words with them."

We're both quiet as the meat continues to brown. Mariah adds the cream and then the cheese. Finally, we add the pasta and cover it to let the pasta cook.

She takes a breath. "Yeah, I guess with Leah I just need to figure out what to do and what to say. And when."

"Mariah." I wait till she looks up at me. "Sometimes, with some people, it's not *you* who has to do the doing or the saying. Sometimes you need other people to do it for you. And that's okay. I promise you, there will be a time when Leah will know that you were right. About all of it, all along."

I have to give this to her. Mariah is an amazing person. And she's lying because Scarlett and I put her in this position. That's not fair. We have to make this right for her.

I've never felt this protective of anyone other than probably Saoirse. But it's different even with her. She has always had *a lot* of people looking out for her. There have always been endless resources to take care of her. I've never really worried that much about her.

Mariah has had two fierce women looking out for her, but she deserves to have more. She deserves to have an entire team at her back. An entire community surrounding her.

"What's going to happen if they find out who you really are?" she asks.

"We'll deal with it. We'll face it," I tell her. "We'll tell the truth, say we're sorry for lying, but we had good reasons. And," I add. "It won't change the truth. You *are* right. Your mom is the woman I love, the woman I've searched for. And I did propose to her."

Mariah sighs. "God, I can't wait to see Leah's face when she has to call me Princess Mariah." She laughs. "I know I shouldn't care about that but...that will be really fun."

I smile, but don't say anything to that as she removes the pot from the heat, pours the mixture into a casserole dish, tops it with more cheese and then slides it under the broiler.

But the *truth* is, I can't wait for that either and I think a tiara is going to look really great on this girl's head.

CHAPTER 29

CIAN

"Mr. Brady!"

I'm on my way to the parking lot after school on Wednesday when I hear Amanda Brown call my name. Well...my name for this week anyway.

I've come to hate it. I like the kids in my classes. I like feeling that I'm actually teaching them something. And hearing them thank 'Mr. Brady' rubs me wrong.

It makes even more sense to me now why Scarlett wanted me and everyone in Autre calling her by *her* name.

I turn, the bag on my shoulder swinging and bumping my hip. I'd sent Henry to secondhand stores in Columbus to find something well-used so it wouldn't be obvious I was carrying a brand-new book bag like a kindergartner on the first day of school. The weathered leather messenger bag is perfect. A college professor would definitely carry something like this, and I intend to keep using it.

"Hey, Amanda."

"Dean," she says with a smile.

The name also reminds me that we're lying to all these people, and I honestly don't know what's going to happen when it all comes out.

Because it has to.

Unless Scarlett lets me take her away from here.

"What's up?"

"I wanted to check in. How are things going?"

"Just fine." It's true. I could teach this section of history to teenagers even without Bill's lesson plans.

"I'm so glad to hear that. You've really come through to help us out in this pinch."

"No problem. I've enjoyed it."

I start walking toward the door again. I am hoping to catch Mariah on her walk home and offer her a ride. I have four new casserole recipes on my phone. My buddy Spencer is somewhat of a casserole aficionado and does all of the cooking for him and his fiancé. He was happy to send me some of his favorites. Tonight, I'm making a chicken fajita casserole. I'm hoping Mariah might want to help, or at least keep me company in the kitchen.

"You'll let me know if there are any issues in class?" Amanda asks.

I turn back. "What kind of issues?"

"I've just been touching base with all of the teachers who have Leah Lawton and Mariah Gale in their classes together. There's been a lot of tension between the girls this week. More than usual, it seems."

Yes, that has not escaped my attention. "I haven't noticed any issues in class," I say carefully. I've been watching. Mariah and Leah seem to ignore each other while they're in class. Their first argument this week had occurred in study hall and the second at lunch. I haven't heard about anything today. Maybe everything's blown over.

Then again, maybe the podcast didn't post anything today. At least not about me. I'm sure they did post. But they have to run out of gossip about me. No one knows I'm in Ohio with Scarlett.

I feel my chest tighten. That's actually not true. Everyone in Autre knows. It kills me to think that someone there is feeding the podcast family secrets. Then again, none of this should be a secret.

I'm in love and I want the world to know.

"Good to hear. Please keep an eye on them and let me know."

"What exactly is the problem?" I ask, wondering about Amanda's interpretation of the issue between Leah and Mariah. How does the town see the rift between Hannah and Scarlett for that matter?

"Leah Lawton is a bit of a bully," Amanda says honestly. "And there's tension that goes back to the girls' mothers. Mariah handles herself for the most part. But I've had to sit down with them before. Leah is not contrite, however."

"What is your policy on bullying?" I ask. I assume, and hope, that there is zero tolerance.

"I've made it very clear to Leah that school is not the time for her to talk about church. However, she is defiant. She claims that she is supposed to talk about church whenever she has a chance to teach someone and if that results in negative consequences for her, she is willing to take them."

I widen my eyes. "That's conviction."

Amanda nods and sighs. "It can make things difficult. But we stay firm and consistent. Leah has served a number of detentions. She has also had to miss school activities.

Unfortunately, that has made her something of a martyr with her peers and the church."

Damn. This is a little bigger than I expected.

"Thanks for the heads up. I'll definitely keep my eye on it." My hand is on the door when I turn back again. "How does Mariah handle it?"

"She tries to stay quiet and ignore it. When it does get to the point she can't, she will speak out. She's also served detentions and such. Again, we have to be fair about our school policies."

I arch a brow. "What policies keep a kid from standing up for themselves?"

"When it gets physical. That's only happened once," Amanda adds. "There was some shoving. And she threw tomato juice on Amanda last week. But Mariah more often uses some...colorful language. We also have rules about that. But she is also willing to accept the consequences for her actions." Amanda shakes her head with a small smile. "Very headstrong young women. I have no doubt they're both going to be great leaders in whatever field they choose. I hope they both choose wisely. And for the greater good."

I think about that. I hate the idea that Mariah has to deal with Leah always being in her face, telling her she's wrong, trying to publicly shame her. But I like the idea that Mariah is strong and sure of herself. That's certainly a credit to both Scarlett and Ruby.

"Wouldn't it be easier to assign them to separate classes and try to keep them apart?" I ask.

Amanda smiles. "It would. We've done that when we can. But as confident women with strong beliefs, they are going to run into people in the real world who are going to push back against them. I think they can be good for each other in a way. They can practice confrontation and dealing with not only how to handle conflict but also work through their feelings about it. With adult supervision and guidance of course. That's part of what we do here. We don't just give kids homework and keep them busy all day. We're trying to help prepare future citizens of the world."

I think about that. All of our experiences shape us. I can admit that my experiences may seem broader than what Scarlett has had. I've traveled the world, met people from walks of life she's never run into. But my world is a bubble. Everyone inside it has some level of power and influence. And most of them like me. I don't get a lot of pushback.

In fact, no one has really pushed back against me until Scarlett.

On the other hand, Scarlett has had struggles I've never experienced. And she's had a lot of pushback. Judgment. Conflict. Confrontation. It's shaped her and made her a lot tougher than I am.

It's also made her confident in what she believes in. I've never really had anyone question my choices. I've followed Fiona and Torin and trusted that choice was the right one. If something wasn't easy, we had the money and people around us to fix it.

Scarlett has had to truly consider her beliefs and what she's willing to work and fight for since she was twelve. In the beginning, she believed in her father. And because of that, she also had to learn to handle hurt and rejection. More things I've never *actually* dealt with.

She knows what she believes and what she's willing to stand up for.

She's so fucking amazing.

And Mariah is right there with her.

Yes, I want to whisk them away. I want to protect them,

make everything easy, give them everything they could ever want.

But the fact that they haven't had it easy, and have had to struggle, has made them into the two people I've fallen in love with. Two people who inspire me and who I know can teach me a lot.

"Thanks for filling me in, Amanda."

"Of course. I think you're doing a great job here."

I give her a sincere smile. Damn, that does feel good. I've only got another week and a half and in the overall scheme of these kids' academic careers it's nothing, but it still feels good to be doing well at it. I'm really already addicted to being told "good job".

I push through the side door and step out into the parking lot. I dig my keys out of my pocket as I stride toward the rental car. But I stop when I hear voices around the side of the building.

I immediately recognize Mariah's voice. Then Leah's. It's almost as if I conjured them.

"Just leave me alone. I'm so fucking sick of this."

"We're just trying to help," Leah says to Mariah. "It's clear now that you actually believe what you're telling us. And that's so sad. Let us help you."

"I do not want to talk about this with you."

I hear the sound of feet shuffling on the parking lot surface and frown. I move closer to the wall of the building.

"Just admit you were lying," a boy's voice says.

I scowl. So it's not just Leah and Mariah. My jaw tightens.

"I wasn't lying. And I'm done repeating myself to you," Mariah says firmly.

"What's the big deal?" another girl says.

Three on one? This is not good.

"Are you doing this to get the money from my grand-pa?" Mariah asks. "How about *I* pay you a hundred dollars to leave me alone?"

"Eternal life is priceless," the girl says in a sweet voice.

I roll my eyes.

I hear the boy mutter, "But a hundred bucks would be nice too."

"Your mom is dating Mr. Brady now, right?" the girl says. "Just admit that."

"Yeah, so?" Mariah asks.

The kids know about me and Scarlett? Well…that's okay, I guess.

"So, your mom and Mr. Brady were both gone this weekend. We know they were together," Leah says. "We also know from the podcast that Prince Cian was in Louisiana. With the woman he's seeing. He's introducing her to the family. This is really serious. Just admit that your mom was never with the prince. That's all we want."

"Yeah. Admit it and we'll forgive you," the boy says. "But you have to admit it on camera, or come to our youth group meeting and admit it to the whole group in person."

"What makes you think I care about you *forgiving* me?" Mariah asks. "This might shock you, Hunter, but I don't care what you think of me at all."

"Admit you lied, admit that your mom is sleeping with a guy she's not married to, then come to church with us and everything will be fine," Leah says.

"The chances of me doing any of those things is less than zero," Mariah says.

"I don't think you're gonna like what's going to happen if you don't," the boy says.

That is so fucking enough.

I step around the corner. "What is going on?"

The knot in my stomach tightens when I see that Mariah is backed up against the side of the school and there are five kids in a semi-circle around her, Leah at the center.

They all take a step back and I see the relief in Mariah's eyes when she looks at me.

I have to force myself to stay where I'm standing and not stalk over, shove all those kids back, and pull her into my arms.

"Leah?" I ask. "What's going on?"

She lifts her chin. "Nothing, Mr. Brady. We're just talking to Mariah about a personal matter."

"What would that be?" I ask, taking a few steps closer.

"Some things that aren't about *school*," Leah tells me. "It's after school and we're outside so we don't have to tell you. We're fine."

"It doesn't matter where you are or what time it is," I tell her. "This looks to me like five people are intimidating one person, and that's not fine with me. You all need to go home."

"We can *talk* to her," Leah says, her tone snotty. "We weren't hurting her." She looks at Mariah. "Were we, Mariah? You're not *hurt,* are you?"

"You're hurting my *head* with your constant babbling," Mariah tells her, sounding more tired than angry as she leans against the wall behind her.

"Leah," I say, proud that I actually sound calm. "I've had you in class for three days, and I know you're extremely intelligent."

She arches a brow, knowing there's more to come.

"So I know that you know that you can't *force* someone to listen to you. You can't make someone care about something. You can't control what someone believes. You can talk to them. You can give them evidence. You can preach sermons. You can talk, cajole, even yell. But all you can do is tell people what *you* think." I take a breath. "And, if you have good reasons for what you think, if you're passionate and if what you're saying is compelling, then people will want to know more, and they'll come to you."

I glance at Mariah. "But nobody knows Mariah better than Mariah. She gets to choose what she thinks. If she says something wrong, that's on her. That's not your concern. If she insists that she's right, that's also on her." Mariah is watching me and I can tell she's okay.

I can't put my finger exactly on what it is, but there is an air about her. A confidence. Something that goes deep. And I know that comes from her mom, her aunt, Greta, and I hope maybe me and Henry. All the people she's met, all the people she will meet, who will believe in her.

"You've said your piece," I tell Leah. "Now go home. And," I add as an afterthought. "Maybe look up the definition, and consequences, of harassment. And slander while you're at it. Because you might need to know those in the future."

Amanda is right about Leah. If this girl turns her confidence and sense of righteousness to something good, she could make a huge difference in the world. Wouldn't hurt for her to know there are boundaries that she can't cross in her attempt to get her point across in the meantime.

"Fine. But we all know what you really are," Leah says to Mariah.

I open my mouth, but before I say anything, Mariah laughs. She actually laughs and it doesn't sound forced or fake.

"Of all of the things you *don't* know, and there are many," Mariah tells Leah. "What I *am*, is one of the biggest. You don't really know anything about me." She pushes off the wall and takes a step forward. "And I think I'd actually really like to keep it that way."

Leah looks a little taken aback. Obviously she's very used to people caring what she thinks.

Amanda was correct when she said these two are good for each other. Leah can help strengthen Mariah's convictions, and Mariah can be that little bit of pushback that Leah doesn't get anywhere else.

Leah and I might have more in common than I'd like to think. She's surrounded by people who've made her life very easy, kept her in a bubble, where they've told her who she is from a young age, where she hasn't really had a reason to question that or break out.

Yet.

A beautiful woman with the last name Gale inspired me to think that I could do something more. Maybe the same will happen for Leah.

"Whatever, loser," Leah says to Mariah before turning and stomping off toward her car.

Of course, her self-actualization might take a little longer.

Mariah blows out a breath, her shoulders slumping as the kids disperse. "Thanks."

"You didn't need me," I tell her. "You would've handled her."

"Yeah. I handle her all the time. But it's kind of exhausting. Sometimes it's really nice to have someone else come along and do it for me."

That hits me right in the chest.

"I really like that. I don't mind being there for you whenever you need it."

"It's like what you're doing for Mom," she says.

"What do you mean?"

"Mom doesn't really need you either. She fights her battles and deals with stuff, but I can tell she really likes having you around. She's a lot happier. She smiles a lot more. She's more relaxed. And I know it's because you're here. One more person on her team, having her back. She deserves that."

And now she didn't just hit me in the chest, she reached in and wrapped her hand around my heart and is squeezing.

"I just really…"

Mariah smiles. "I know."

I'm not sure what Mariah thinks she knows but… She's probably right. I'm learning she's right about a lot of things.

"So the podcast talked about us again, huh?"

"Yes, and these people are so stupid," she says with an eyeroll. "You and Mom were gone for the weekend. The podcast reports that Cian and his mystery women were in Autre for the weekend. But nobody is adding this up? I'm surrounded by idiots."

I chuckle. "People see what they want to see. Leah does not want you to be right. Plus having a prince just walking around, teaching history at the high school, is a little far-fetched."

"And yet here you are." She turns and starts toward the parking lot. "Can you give me a ride to Mom's shop? I need to tell her about this."

"Of course. Then will you come help me make dinner for tonight?"

"I'll sit at the island and watch and supervise. But I have history homework to do."

I chuckle. She does. They have a test in my class on Friday.

CHAPTER 30

SCARLETT

"I wanted to slap her. I did. I'm not proud of it, but I really did for a second."

Cian yanks his shirt off and tosses it by the bed.

I fight a smile as he paces to the window.

"I know I shouldn't say this—as an adult, a kid shouldn't be able to get to me like this, but I swear to God, Scarlett, Leah Lawton is such a little bitch."

"I know she seems that way. It's not totally her fault," I tell him.

He was his usual fun, happy self during dinner and clean-up but the minute Mariah left to study for her history test at Greta's, he told me *his* side of the confrontation between Mariah and Leah after school.

He is *not* happy and seeing him so protective of my daughter has my heart—and my ovaries—all twisted up.

"I wish she would leave Mariah alone about church and youth group, but I can't help but feel a little sorry for Leah," I say. "She's just trying to please her parents and her church leaders. She is trying to be who she thinks she's supposed to be. She's trying to get their approval and their love."

"It *is* her fault," Cian argues. He shoves a hand through his hair. "Every time she opens her mouth about this, she's making a choice. I know she's sixteen. I know she has a lot of people in her head influencing her. But this is as good a time as any to learn to mind her own business."

I shake my head. "The church thinks everyone's lives are their business."

I'm in bed. In only a T-shirt and panties. Fresh out of the shower. He's in his sweatpants, and no shirt. We have the house to ourselves. Ruby's at work and Mariah is at Greta's until eleven.

But even my panties-only attire *in bed* isn't distracting him from today's situation with Mariah and Leah.

Mariah told me everything. From the podcast to what Leah said to what *Cian* said.

I'd already heard the podcast. I'd listened twice, fast forwarding the second time through the parts about Abigail's upcoming online gardening club meeting, Linnea and Jonah's return to the island next week, and a new recipe that Lindsey had tried.

But I'd wanted to re-listen to the part about how Cian had introduced the woman he's in love with to his family and how they all loved her.

Cian moves up the side of the bed. He sits down on the mattress next to me. "I *hated* seeing Mariah vulnerable like that. But she was tough. She was...sure of herself. That was amazing."

I smile.

"Then she told me that she's okay standing up for herself but that it's really nice to have other people do it sometimes." He shakes his head. "That really got to me."

It gets to me too. I know she can handle herself, but should she have to? Really? All of this is because of me.

"How does ridiculing people and publicly pointing out their flaws—or their perceived flaws—win them over?" he asks. "How can that church actually think that's an effective method of bringing people in?"

I drop my eyes to the duvet. "It doesn't win people over. But it makes people afraid. No one wants to be the odd man out. No one wants to be painted as bad or wrong. So they fall into line."

Cian is quiet for a long moment, then he reaches over and tips my chin up. "Tell me."

Obviously, he can tell there's a story here. But it's not one I want him to know. It's not one I'm proud of. "I know exactly what happened with Mariah and Leah. Even before Mariah told me. Because it's what Hannah and I used to do."

Cian's expression is a combination of frustration and sympathy. "Fuck, Scarlett."

I nod. "It's terrible. It makes the person being pointed at feel awful and, supposedly, want to be embraced into the group. It makes the group feel superior and bonded because they're already "in". But it's awful. And I hate that it happened to Mariah. And honestly, I hate that it's happening to Leah, too. Because she's being turned into a mean, manipulative person. And there is a very good chance that someday she is going to feel terrible about this. It's possible that she's going to carry guilt over this for years. If she doesn't, then she's going to be stuck with a group of people that never truly care about her or vice versa, but are together because they're stuck." I sigh. "I hate the way Leah treats Mariah, but I feel bad for Leah too. I know Leah, because I *was* Leah."

He looks at me for a long moment. "You kill me a little bit every time you tell me about the church and your dad."

I take a deep breath. "I'm sorry."

"Don't be sorry. I want to know every part of you." He leans in, bracing his hand on the mattress on the other side of my hip, caging me in. "Do you forgive yourself for all of that? Do you believe that you are a good person? That you've grown past all of that and that you don't need to beat yourself up about it anymore?"

Slowly, I nod my head. "Yes. Most days. Sometimes it still nags at me. But I think that I am a more empathetic person and that I can see past people's meanness and mistakes more easily because of all of that. And maybe that's a good thing."

He cups my face. "It is a good thing. Because I want to rush in and hurt anyone who hurts the people I love. But Mariah needs to learn to try to see deeper into other people sometimes. She's learning a lot of strength from you."

"I want her to fight for herself. I want her to stand up. I don't want her to accept cruelty and intimidation."

"I know. We have to teach her all of that. How to be forgiving, how to be compassionate, while still standing up for herself."

All of his words reach into my chest and wrap around my heart. I feel it beating hard and a voice in my head tells me not to ask the question on the tip of my tongue.

Still, I do. "*We* have to teach her all of that?"

The look he gives me clearly says *really*? "In case I haven't made it clear, I love your daughter. I think she's amazing and I've had nothing to do with that, but I would really like to be around to watch her turn into the incredible woman she's going to be. You and Ruby have been an amazing support system for her, and I'd love to see all the things she can accomplish with all of my people around her too."

I swallow hard. It's difficult to force anything, air or words, past the tightness in my throat. "I'm not sure you have any idea how sexy it is that you feel protective of and amazed by my daughter."

"I'm not sure you have any idea how sexy it is that you are a single mom who lets her daughter see that she's not perfect, but that she knows how to apologize and how to try again and to love so much even with a broken heart."

My breath feels like it's stuck in my lungs.

Of course, this whole thing with Cian and me affects and involves Mariah. I've never *not* realized that. But we joked about her being a princess. We talked lightly about her meeting Saoirse and Abigail and Fiona. But now I *truly* realize what this would mean for her.

Cian would be her Brian.

I wouldn't be who I am without Brian. A lot of the good inside of me wouldn't exist without Brian being a part of my life. After the hurt and rejection and confusion I'd felt with my father and Eli, I still understood love and acceptance and forgiveness because of Brian.

I feel tears fill my eyes.

That doesn't seem to make Cian even blink. "I want to be out loud about you," he says. "About us. About Mariah. And I don't mean as Dean Brady. I mean *me*. I hate the hiding and lying." He blows out a breath. "And I hate that we're making Mariah quiet and making her hide the truth. She wants to be out loud about her family, the *good* things, the happy things."

"Okay," I say softly.

His eyes light up and his brows arch. "Okay?"

"After next week. A few more days. You finish teaching or it will be awkward but then...okay."

"Fuck," he says, but it sounds almost reverent. "Yes."

Then he kisses me with a passion and a sweetness I haven't felt from him before. And I definitely can't speak. But I don't have any words anyway, so I just wrap my arms around his neck, pull him down on the bed, and hope that as I make love to him, he understands that my heart isn't so broken anymore.

CHAPTER 31

CIAN

I watch as the kids file into class on Thursday.

Leah ignores me as she walks past though I say, "Good morning. Good job on the quiz yesterday."

She just keeps walking.

Still, it's true. The quiz was practice for the big test tomorrow and she aced it. She's not only strong willed, but she's incredibly bright. I can only hope that she starts thinking for herself a little.

Mariah and I exchange a smile and nothing more as she comes through the door.

It still makes my day just a little better.

I think it just makes sense to like my future step-daughter and to know she likes me in return.

Right on Mariah's heels is Henry.

Mariah turns to see who I'm frowning at and Henry nearly plows her over.

"Oh! Um, hi, Hen..." She clearly forgets his pseudonym in her surprise at seeing him.

"Miss Gale," he says. Then he looks at me. "I need to speak with you. Immediately."

He looks serious. That combined with the fact that he's here at school is cause for alarm. Henry hasn't come up to the building once this entire week while I've been here. There are no security threats and the two times that he's needed to ask me something, he simply texted, and I've gotten back to him during my break. I've been having dinner with Scarlett and Mariah each night, but I get back to the B&B in time for him and I to chat. Last night was the only night Scarlet and I have had sex since coming back from New Orleans.

We haven't wanted to sneak around anymore. Now that we've been able to experience being together fully again, the laundry room and patio aren't enough. But as soon as I finish this teaching gig, we're coming out. And we'll deal with the consequences. Somehow.

"Everyone take your seats," I tell the class. "I'll just be a moment." I step into the hallway and Henry pulls the door to the classroom shut. "What's going on?"

"It's Diarmuid."

I freeze. My entire body gets cold. "What?" I ask. "What happened?"

"The king had a heart attack early this morning."

I stare at him.

I try to make the words make sense.

A heart attack? The king? My grandfather?

A *heart attack*?

Fuck. *Fuck*. No.

I run a hand over my face. "How bad?"

"Bad. He's in serious condition. We need to go."

My head is swimming a little, but I feel myself nod. Henry puts his hand on my shoulder and squeezes.

"Cian. We need to go *now*."

It's a very long trip to Cara. Hours. If it's serious we might not make it…

I look up at my best friend. "Yes. Okay."

"The Autre group is chartering a plane out of New Orleans. We're going to do the same in Columbus. We don't have time to wait for the plane from Cara to come."

That would double the flight time. That makes sense. "Okay," I say again. I glance at the door to my classroom. "I need to—"

"I already told Mrs. Brown," Henry said.

The sound of shoes on the linoleum reaches me and I look around Henry to see Amanda coming for us. "I'll cover your classes today," she says. "We'll get a sub for the rest. Go."

I don't know what to do.

My grandfather had a heart attack. His fourth. It's serious. It will take us nearly eight hours to get there. He could die before then. I might never see him again.

I suddenly feel sick.

Henry squeezes my shoulder again. "Come on. Let's go."

I suck in a breath. "I need my bag." My phone is in there. It's probably blowing up with messages from my siblings. Fuck.

Amanda opens the door and the sound of twenty high school sophomores all talking at once hits me.

They quiet when they see the principal.

"Get it," Henry says shortly.

I step into the room. My gaze immediately finds Mariah. She looks scared. I grab my bag from behind the desk and make a decision. It's probably a bad one, but I can't just leave. "Miss Gale?" I say. "Can I see you in the hallway, please?"

Her eyes get wide, but she immediately stands. "Y-yes."

There is a murmuring of conversation and I'm sure there are all kinds of rumors now spreading in room two-oh-eight.

I can't worry about that now.

We step into the hallway. Henry frowns at Mariah but I turn to her. "I have to go to Cara. My grandfather had a heart attack."

"Oh my God," she says quietly. "Is he okay?"

"We... don't know." I swallow hard. "I'm sorry. I... I just didn't want to leave without saying goodbye."

Her face is etched with concern. She nods. "Thank you."

It's *killing* me not to hug her. I can't believe I have to say goodbye to her like this. I can't tell her when I'll be back. I can't tell her that I love her. I can't say we'll talk soon. I don't know if that's true and I'm just her teacher here. And I don't know when I'll be back.

"Okay, so..."

"Are you going to tell Mom?" she asks.

"Of course."

"Cian," Henry says. "We don't have much time."

"I have to see Scarlett," I snap.

His jaw tightens but he doesn't say anything more. For now, anyway.

I focus on Mariah again. "Kick ass on the test. Make me look like a good teacher, okay?"

I see her eyes fill with tears. It's clear she's thinking about hugging me too. But she only nods. "Yeah. I will. You *are* a good teacher." She drops her voice to a whisper. "And a good friend. I'll miss you."

Fuck. "Ditto," I tell her. "Now get back to class."

She does. I blow out a breath. Then start down the hall. We get in the rental car Henry has waiting at the curb.

"We're going to the garage. I don't want to hear any shit about it," I say.

Henry doesn't say anything at all, just turns the car in that direction.

We drive for about three minutes before I ask, "Should I ask her to go with me?"

"She can't do that." He doesn't seem surprised I asked.

"Why not?"

He looks over. "We don't have time to deal with all of this."

That makes my chest hurt. I might lose my grandfather. And I don't have time to make sure the woman I love is okay and understands why I'm leaving and that I don't want to, but I have to.

"Are you taking her as a friend?" he goes on. "Your girlfriend? Your fiancee? How are you going to introduce her to your grandfather, who just had a serious heart attack and who wants you to marry Astrid?"

I nod. He's right. This isn't the time to introduce Scarlett to my grandfather. Definitely not. It's not fair to either of them.

"What do I say to her?"

"Tell her that your grandfather just had a heart attack, and you need to get on a fucking plane *now* so you can start the hours-long flight to get to him," Henry says, clearly beyond irritated.

I get it. I'm sure Iris is on his ass. Torin may be too. His entire objective is to get me home as soon as possible.

"Fine."

"Don't complicate this right now. For anyone," he adds.

"Got it." He means for *him*, but also for my family and for Scarlett.

I do understand. But I don't have to like it. Leaving like

this feels like I'm leaving in the middle of a movie where I really want to know how the story ends, or the middle of a conversation that has a lot still unsaid.

Henry pulls right up by the door to the shop and Scarlett is already walking out of her office when I stride through the bay.

"Mariah texted," she tells me. "I'm so sorry."

She wraps her arms around my waist, and I gratefully hug her tightly. I pull in a deep breath, taking in the scent of her hair. I absorb the feel of her against me.

I would really love to have her on this flight with me, holding my hand. Walking into the palace with me where I have no idea what might be ahead.

"Is he okay?" she asks against my chest.

"I don't know. I'm on my way to the airport. We're leaving right away. I just stopped by to..."

Fuck, I can't even say the word 'goodbye'.

She pulls back. "I know," she says. "You have to go."

"I'm sorry this is all such a rush." I know without asking that Henry has all of my stuff already packed up and in the car.

She frowns. "It's not your fault, Cian. I understand."

"I just..."

But I don't know what to say. I don't want to go. But I *do* want to go. I need to get there. I have to be there. I need to see him again. I need to be there with my family. My grandmother. Torin. I'm sure he's going to step up sooner than planned even if my grandfather pulls through.

Scarlett's hand against my face pulls me back to the moment. I focus on her beautiful face. "Cian, I'm okay. I'm not upset that you have to leave. This is your *family*. Of *course*, you have to go. I'm fine. We'll be fine."

I nod. She will. Of course. She's been more than fine

without me for thirty-six years. She and Mariah and Ruby are amazing. They don't really need me at all. I'm being ridiculous.

These are *not* the thoughts I want to take with me thousands of miles from here.

"Go," she says softly. "You know where to find me now." She gives me a little smile.

Fuck. I love her so much. But there's not time to get into that either. I want to spend hours telling her how I feel, talking about the future, making plans.

Dammit.

Instead, I cup her face in my hands and kiss her, trying to pour everything I'm feeling into that.

She grips my shirt, kissing me back, and I tell myself I feel all of it coming from her too.

I let her go only when I sense that I've pushed Henry's patience to the very edge.

I hold her gaze for a long moment, but neither of us says anything.

Then I turn and somehow walk out of her garage and get back in the car.

We're halfway to Columbus when my phone pings with a text.

I look down.

It's from Mariah.

Leah figured it out. She knows who you really are.

Oh...fuck.

How? I type back. Not that it really matters.

Mariah: *The podcast. They're talking about your grandfather.*

That damned podcast.

But, of course, they're talking about the king's heart attack.

I rub my forehead. *Are you okay?*

Mariah: *I'm in the principal's office.*

I scowl at my phone.

She sends a second text. *I'm kind of in trouble, actually.*

"We have to go back," I tell Henry.

"Excuse me?"

"It's Mariah. She's in trouble."

Henry curses under his breath, looks in the rearview mirror and executes a U-turn without asking me a single question.

He accompanies me back into the school fifteen minutes later. I stride into Amanda's office without knocking.

"What happened?"

"Mr. Brady," Amanda greets me coolly. "Or is it Your Highness?"

"Cian is fine," I tell her.

I look at the other two people in the office. Mariah is watching me, Leah is *staring* at me.

"I shouldn't be surprised you figured it out. You're one of my brightest students," I tell her. Then I really take the two girls in. "Is that *ice*?" I ask.

Leah is holding a lumpy plastic bag against her lip. She pulls it away to say, "She hit me." Her lip is swollen and has clearly been bleeding.

"I hit your *phone* and it hit you in the mouth." Mariah huffs out a frustrated breath. She's holding a bag of ice against her eye.

"And what the hell happened to *you*?" I demand.

"Her phone hit me in the eye."

"What is going on, and how can we speed up whatever it is?" Henry asks.

Leah gingerly feels over her bottom lip with her tongue, winces, and replaces the ice pack.

Mariah just slumps further into her chair. "Leah hasn't told anyone else," Mariah says. "I overreacted. She turned her phone toward me in class and mouthed, "is this Professor Brady?" I freaked out and tried to cover her phone up before anyone else could see it."

Leah looks surprised. "Well, of course I wouldn't tell. He could go to jail."

I frown. "Me?"

She looks up. "Yeah. You've been *teaching* a bunch of *kids* while lying about your identity. That's illegal, I'm sure."

"You *really* need to stop talking about things you aren't one-hundred percent sure of," I tell her. "And you have to stop exaggerating. I actually have all the degrees I claimed to have. I filled out all the necessary paperwork. My background check is clean. I'm just using a pseudonym for safety reasons. Like authors use pen names or actors use stage names. No harm, no foul."

Amanda jumps in. "Mr. Henry Dean, Mr. Brady's assistant—"

"Mr. O'Grady, actually," I say.

"Right." She looks at Leah again. "Mr. Dean explained the need for privacy and provided everything we needed to ensure Mr. Br...O'Grady was legitimate. Everything was perfectly legal."

I nod. "And what I told you about a family emergency is true. And I need to leave." I turn back to Mariah. "I wanted to be sure you're okay."

"I am." She gestures to Leah with her ice pack. "Just tell her that you *did* meet my mom two years ago, you dated her for a weekend, you're in love with her, and you've proposed."

I look at Leah. "That's all true. Mariah's been right about everything."

"But the podcast said the prince was searching for a woman…"

"That was Scarlett."

Leah frowns. "But they said that you spent last weekend in Louisiana with her."

"I did."

Mariah looks at her. "You thought you were so smart today, but you totally missed that."

"Well today was easy," Leah says. "The king has a heart attack and suddenly Mr. Brady is rushing out of class for a family emergency? I thought that was a weird coincidence but then when he called *you* out into the hall…"

I sigh and avoid looking at Henry who I know is giving me I-told-you-so eyes.

"*That* was weird," Leah says. "And you seemed upset when you came back in. So I looked at the article about the king again. Then noticed a photo and… I suddenly realized Mr. Brady looks *a lot* like the prince." Leah looks at Mariah. Slowly she shakes her head. "Wow. So this whole time, all of that *was* your mom."

"I fucking *told* you that," Mariah mutters.

"Miss Gale," Amanda admonishes.

"Sorry," Mariah says. But then she sits up straighter in her chair. "But I *did*. I didn't lie *once*. But Leah's been going around accusing me for days. Most of the time we just kind of avoid each other and maybe glare across the room, but this week I've had to deal with her, *hearing her* and *talking to her* every single damned day."

"She did," Leah admits.

I'm surprised to see her looking a little discomfited.

"My mom just said that your mom lied a lot in high

school and always wanted to be the center of attention and that you were doing the same thing." She gives Mariah an abashed look. "But you don't try to be the center of attention. And I would know that better than my mom does."

I look at Amanda and see that she looks as surprised as I feel.

Mariah is still frowning, but she crosses her arms and responds with a quieter, though still grumpy, tone, "Don't talk about my mom. You don't know her."

"But she's right."

We all turn to find Scarlett standing in the doorway. Her gaze holds mine for a moment, but then she looks back at her daughter. "I did lie in high school. I did do a lot to get attention, and I was pretty terrible to anyone who wouldn't listen to me."

Mariah slumps back in her chair. "*Mom.*"

"It's time we all tell the truth and own up to what we've been doing," she says.

"Fine! Cian has been lying about his identity so that he can get to know Scarlett without this town turning it into a bloody disaster!" Henry finally erupts. He grabs me by the upper arm. "He has to go *now*." He marches me toward the door. "Mariah, Scarlett, we'll be in touch," Henry tells them. Then he looks at Leah. "Miss Lawton—"

She straightens.

"I'm the head of Prince Cian's security detail. He tells me you're very bright. I'm going to assume that I don't need to explain in any depth how important it is that you keep details that you learn about the prince and the royal family to yourself until given permission otherwise."

Leah's eyes are wide as she nods. "Of course."

"Hey!" Mariah protests. "No! I want her to have to tell

everyone that I was right and that a prince really did propose to my mom!"

"All in due time," Henry tells her. "But look on the bright side. Now you have someone in addition to Greta you can gossip with about everything."

Mariah and Leah are looking at each other with circumspection as Henry tries to drag me out the door.

But I suddenly realize that everyone in this room knows who I am and how fucking amazing that is.

Because it means that I can kiss Scarlett in front of them in this public space and it doesn't matter.

I wrench my arm from Henry's grasp and reach for her, grasping her wrist, pulling her up against me with a little, "ooof", and then dipping her back and sealing my mouth over hers.

"Yes!" Mariah cheers.

"Mr. Brady! I mean O'Grady! I mean Your Highness..." Amanda tries.

"It's no use," Henry tells her.

"Oh, wow," Leah says.

I finally let Scarlett go and take in her stunned look and then the little smile that curls her lips as I bring her upright.

"Okay, that was pretty great," I hear Leah say to Mariah as I finally let Henry shove me through the doorway and down the main hall of Emerald High School.

CHAPTER 32
SCARLETT

I watch Cian and Henry through the window of Amanda
Brown's office until they disappear around the corner. I
turn back then and take a deep breath. "Okay," I say to the
room. "Now what?"

I'd gotten the call from Amanda's secretary, telling me
that Mariah and Leah had been brought into the office after
a fight in class.

It looks to me like everything has been handled.

Amanda sighs. "I think the girls have reached an understanding." She looks at both of them and they nod. "I feel
like they're best served by going back to class and finishing
their day." She looks at me. "Unless you feel that all of this...
personal stuff is going to be a distraction for Mariah."

I shrug and look at my daughter. "Well? What do you
think?"

She shakes her head. "I'm fine. There will be a lot more
talk about me if I leave now. I can handle staying." She

looks at me. "Will you text me if anything bad happens with the king?"

I feel a pang in my chest. God, Cian's grandfather had a heart attack. I hate that. I hate that his family is going through this. I hate that Cian and Fiona and Saoirse are so far away from him. "Do you think that's a good idea?" I ask Mariah.

"I just want to know. I want everything to be okay."

"There is nothing we can do. Focus on school and we'll check on everything when you get home."

"I'll say a prayer for him," Leah says.

I hate that my initial reaction is to say no thanks. But she's a sixteen-year-old girl who truly believes that her church is guiding her correctly. This is coming from a good place. "Thanks," I tell her. "We appreciate that."

"Okay, girls," Amanda says. "Back to class."

I step out into the hallway with them and they take a left while I take a right. I round the corner and nearly run over Hannah Lawton.

Well, of course. I had wondered why she hadn't been called to the office for this altercation.

"What happened?" she asks in her usual snippy tone, pulling the strap of her purse up onto her shoulder.

"More or less just a misunderstanding. They're both fine. On their way back to class."

"You know, you should be more concerned—"

I put my hand up. "I'm going to stop you right there. I'm not interested in what you think about my life, my daughter, how I'm parenting her, or even what toppings I put on my pizza, Hannah. I really don't care what you think about *anything,* to be honest."

I start to step around her when she says, "I don't want Mariah anywhere near Leah."

I turn back. "Then tell Leah to leave Mariah alone. She's the one starting most of this."

Hannah scoffs. "There's no way. If Mariah is telling you that, she's lying. But what else would I expect, growing up in that house with you and Ruby?"

I do not want to do this. I am feeling a number of emotions, including worry about Cian's grandfather, worry about Cian and the rest of his family, and I'm already missing him. I'm also feeling restless. Having him leave so suddenly when things are very up in the air between us, feels strange. Wrong. There's no other choice, of course. He had to go to Cara. But I am feeling discombobulated. The last thing I want to deal with is Hannah.

"Hannah, I really don't care what you think of me, but you will not speak about my daughter or my sister in a disparaging way. I'll admit that you know some things about me that are not good, things I'm not proud of. They're from my past, and I've changed, but if you don't see that, I can't control that. However, you do *not* know my daughter or my sister well enough to say a word about them."

She props a hand on her hip. "I don't need to know them. I hear all about them. I hear about Mariah from Leah and her friends. And everyone's been hearing about Ruby over the last few days."

Do not ask. Do not ask. Do not ask.

"Hearing what about Ruby?"

"The lies she's been spreading about the city council and the church. "

I shake my head. "Ruby doesn't care about the city council or the church. Whatever you're hearing isn't true."

Hannah gives me a smug, bitchy smile. One I've given too many people, too many times.

"Really?" Hannah asks. "Ruby hasn't told you about the gossip she's been spreading?"

I really don't know what this is about. Ruby can handle herself. She has friends in town. I'm sure someone overheard her talking about something and took it out of context. I do not have to get involved.

"Hannah," I say, meeting her gaze. "I just want to tell you, and I mean this with all my heart, I hope you have the day you deserve."

Then I turn and walk away.

When I hit the sidewalk outside, it only takes me two seconds to decide where I'm going. I'm not going to get anything done at the garage. I don't have any cars to work on anyway and I'm far too distracted to work on any foundation business. I head home, knowing that I'm going to pull up *Wait 'Til I Tell Ye* and see what I can find out about the king.

I let myself in through the back door and find Ruby at the kitchen table. She's painting her toenails while listening to the podcast.

She looks up. "Oh my God. Is Cian okay?"

I toss my purse on the table. "He's on his way to Cara."

Ruby drops the foot she had propped on the chair seat to the floor. "Babe. I'm so sorry."

I shake my head. "Don't be. He had to go. Of course."

"Yeah. And you couldn't go with him. That would've been crazy."

Yeah, of course it would've been. "In the midst of a potential family drama isn't really the right time to meet everyone, you know?"

"For sure. But you saw him?"

"Yeah. He came by to say goodbye. And then I saw him again at the school." I frown as I realize what that really means. He was on his way out of town after he said goodbye to me. I pull the chair out and sit down. "He actually turned around and came back because Mariah had a problem at school."

Ruby recaps her nail polish. "What do you mean?"

"Mariah and Leah got into it and Mariah must've texted him or called. He turned around and came back." I look at my sister as all of this occurs to me. "He came clean. He admitted to Amanda Brown and Leah Lawton who he really is. That Mariah was right all along."

Ruby's eyes go wide. "No shit?"

"Then Henry basically threatened Leah not to say anything. "

Ruby huffs out a breath. "Of course he did. "

"And strangely, when I left, I almost felt like Mariah and Leah had sort of a truce friendship thing going."

"Friendship? That's probably pushing it."

"Yeah. But sometimes when you have a secret with someone, it's a bonding experience."

"Do you want her bonding with that girl?"

I lift a shoulder. "Not really. But maybe I want *Leah* bonding with *Mariah*." Mariah could be a good influence on Leah, actually. "Hey, speaking of drama, I ran into Hannah on my way out of the school. She says that you're spreading some kind of gossipy rumor around about the city council?"

Ruby gets up from the table and goes to the fridge, pulling out the iced tea pitcher. "It's not a rumor. It's the God's honest truth."

"What's going on?"

She takes down two glasses and fills them. "I was talking about your program, the moms' thing that you and Cian are doing, at work. One of the girls told me that they have this thing over in Melton. The city helps with housing assistance for single moms. They help pay rent and house payments and stuff."

I take the glass of tea from her. "Really?" I'm definitely interested in that.

She reclaims her seat. "Yeah. It's part of a grant from the state. The city covers a third of the program and the state covers the rest. Single moms can apply for up to three years at a time."

"Wow. That's unexpected. Melton is so small. I'd thought briefly about building one of our communities here, but Emerald is almost too small, don't you think?"

"There are single moms in small towns," Ruby says with a shrug. "You could just buy a house or two."

"True."

"In fact, guess what else I found out?"

"What?" I grin at how excited Ruby looks.

"Melton has this cool community program where some of the older women make frozen dinners to supply to these single moms. Guess where they got the idea?"

I feel a little prickle on the back of my neck. "Where?"

"Diane. She goes to church over there. She told them about what she does with you and the exchange of services. Her little group of friends at church decided they should get together and do that for the single moms in town."

I stare at Ruby. Diane got a whole community program going because of what she and I were doing? "That's..."

"Amazing," Ruby fills in. She takes a drink of her tea. "So anyway, Melton has this whole cool thing going. They help with housing payments, they have a meal program, so the single moms are being supported by the town and the church. So I'm bitching about how nothing is happening here like that in Emerald and why doesn't *our* city council or the freaking church here do something like that and somebody tells me that Kathie Myers applied for the same grant for Emerald last year."

"Kathy Myers? She was on the city council, right?"

"Yes, left the council early. For "personal reasons"," Ruby says, putting air quotes around "personal reasons".

I lean in. "Okay, come on. Tell me everything. Obviously there's more to the story."

"There is. Emerald got the grant. But the mayor turned it down. The mayor who goes to church at our daddy's church. Our daddy who doesn't want single moms getting support. Our daddy who believes in punishing single moms."

I stare at her as all that sinks in. "You're telling me that Emerald could've had the money to help single moms right here, but our dad, the *man of God,* talked the mayor into declining it."

"Yep," Ruby says. She scowls, "So, damn right I've been telling people about it at the bar, down at the café, when I get my nails done, anywhere I go. I even had fliers printed up." She takes another drink of her tea. "So, Hannah is right that I am spreading news about the city and the church. But it's not gossipy lies. "

I am suddenly filled with rage.

It flows through me like a shot of tequila, starting in my chest but quickly spreading through my body, igniting all of my nerve endings.

All this time, I have been living here in this town, keeping quiet, trying to stay out of the way, trying to live a simple life so that people will see that I've changed, that I've become "a good person", so that I will get forgiven for past sins. All this time I've felt like the best thing for everyone would be to just stay out of the way and not rock the boat. Not call attention to myself or the rift between me and the church. Avoid my father and just live my life separately, live well, let people draw their own conclusions about the two of us.

"They are never going to let me be happy here, are they?" I ask Ruby.

She sets her glass down. "Who are we talking about?"

"Hannah. Dad. The church. All of those people that I was with before."

"Well," she says carefully. "No. They're not gonna go out of their way to make you happy. But, Scarlett," she says, leaning in to rest her arms on the table. "No one *lets* you be happy. Only you can do that. You can also keep yourself from being happy."

She's completely right.

And what makes me happy is helping other people. Knowing that there can be a ripple effect like there was with Diane. Knowing that talking about people and what they need and brainstorming how to meet those needs, can turn into amazing things. Sometimes small, amazing things like a meal program. And sometimes huge, amazing things like an entire charitable foundation.

But neither of those things came about because I stayed quiet. Neither of those things happened because I was staying out of the way.

They're never going to *let* me be happy here.

So, I'm going to *make* myself happy.

Right. Fucking. Here.

"I think I need some coffee," I say, getting to my feet.

Ruby looks startled by the change of topic. "Okay."

"Walk with me down to the coffee shop."

She nods. "Okay."

That's Ruby. She'll always be by my side, no questions asked.

She starts to walk past me, I assume to get her shoes, and I reach out and grab her arm. I pull her in and wrap my arms around her, giving her a huge hug.

She only hesitates for a moment before she hugs me back. "What is this for?"

"For making so many things possible for so long," I tell her. "All that time I spent in church, listening to Dad and trying to do what he wanted me to do, and you've been out here living a good life all along. Taking care of others, loving unconditionally, forgiving me over and over."

She squeezes me tight and then pulls away. "You're my sister. There was never another option."

"Not for you there wasn't," I say. "Because you are one of the very best people I know."

She laughs and squeezes me again, then goes to get her shoes. She really doesn't know how incredible she is.

We're headed down the sidewalk toward downtown when she asks, "Why are we really going to the coffee shop?"

"Do you know what happens at the coffee shop on Thursday afternoons?" I ask her.

"Delicious biscotti and decadent lattes?"

"That, and men's Bible study." I let that sink in. "Because you can't have Bible study at the church. You have to have it out in public where everyone can see you doing it."

"And let me guess," she says. "Our dad and the mayor both attend the Bible study."

"They sure do." In fact, our father leads it. Because of course he does.

CHAPTER 33
SCARLETT

When we push through the door to the coffee shop, a merry little tinkle sounds overhead. The smell of coffee and sugary baked goods greets us.

I immediately see the huge group of men smack in the middle of the coffee shop. They pulled four tables together and are taking up most of the space. Heaven forbid anyone else trying to get any work or studying done while they're here.

"I'll take a white chocolate mocha," I tell Ruby. "I'll be right back."

I head for the center of the coffee shop as well.

"Excuse me," I say, raising my voice above the conversation happening at the large table and the instrumental music playing overhead.

Everyone in the shop stops talking and turns to look at me.

I haven't actually been in front of a group of people from Emerald in about sixteen years. But I sure did spend a lot of time before Emerald audiences back in the day. My dad loved to put me up in front, preaching and teaching, happy to show the good people of his congregation that his daughter was taking after him.

"I just wanted to take a moment to make a quick announcement and clear up some misinformation that's been going around."

"Scarlett, you're interrupting our meeting."

I turn and look at my father, meeting his eyes for the first time in sixteen years.

The impact of it takes my breath away for a moment.

The last time I looked directly into his face was when he told me to leave his church and never come back.

At the time, I never would've believed how I'd feel in this moment. But now, I can honestly say that him kicking me out of his church was the nicest thing he's ever done for me.

"No worries, Pastor," I say. My voice is a little wobbly, but I manage the words anyway. "This won't take long."

I turn and look at the rest of the room. "I understand that there's a rumor going around that our good Mayor has declined some grant money that would've provided for struggling single mothers here in Emerald. I'm here to tell you that that is true."

There's some murmuring around the room and out of the corner of my eye, I see said mayor. He's been serving this town far too long. We really need term limits here.

"But I'm also here to tell you that we are going to correct that oversight."

"Who's *we*?" someone calls.

I smile. "Me and my family." I quickly point at my father. "Well, not *all* of my family."

There are more murmurings around the room.

I raise my voice. "If the town and the church don't feel that it's their mission to take care of *all* of the citizens of this town, then that is something we'll all have to discuss when it comes election time. And, I guess, for some of you to consider on Sunday mornings. Or whenever your church committees meet. But Emerald will not be a town where citizens are left to struggle and where we cast judgements on who deserves help and who doesn't.

"Starting next week, the Ruby's Way Foundation will be providing funds here in Emerald for any family who is struggling financially. There will be housing assistance, meal assistance, transportation, and medical assistance. There will be a simple application process, a twenty-four-hour hotline, and we will have people ready and willing to help however they can.

"I would very much love it if you would help spread the word. It's really about taking care of one another. I know that you all want your friends, family, and neighbors to have the best lives that they can, but you'd also love for them to have those lives here, in this town *you* love. Let's make that happen. With Ruby's Way, there is another option for them if they don't feel welcomed by the other groups here in Emerald."

My father is now on his feet. "How dare you!"

I look at him with confusion. "How dare I what? Help take care of this town where I was born and raised? The town that was so important in shaping who I am? Now that I am grown, successful, and understand what it truly means to be a loving neighbor and a kind human, it only makes sense that I would come back here and help make this town better."

"We are doing just fine. We don't need your... foundation." He says 'foundation' the way I imagine he says 'dog shit'.

"Well, that's great, if you don't need it, then you won't access it. But other people might. That's really the way all of the groups and services in town should be, don't you think? Available to whoever needs them but without any pressure on anyone to take part in something they don't actually want."

"You and your sister are just trying to make me look bad," my father says. "That's petty and juvenile."

"It's interesting to me that *us* offering charitable services in our hometown somehow makes *you* look bad," I say. "Maybe that's something you should spend a little time thinking and praying about."

Ruby joins me and hands me a paper cup that smells absolutely delicious.

"God bless us, every one!" she says, raising her cup in a little toast to the entire coffee shop.

"The audacity," I hear my father mutter as he sinks back into his chair.

I grin at him—a bright, sincere grin. "I think audacity is genetic. On our *mother's* side."

Then we turn and leave, and I have to admit that the tinkling bell overhead sounds even happier on our way out.

We walk about a block before either of us says anything.

Then Ruby says, "Holy shit—pun intended—you were fantastic."

I laugh. "I just told the truth. I honestly wasn't trying to make him look bad." I sip from my cup. "Okay, that's not entirely true. No more lying. I'm glad it made him look bad. But, I do want to offer the services."

"Ruby's Way?" she asks.

I stop and turn to her. "I haven't been able to come up

with a name for the foundation. And I figure if our foundation does things Ruby's way, we're going to be doing a really good job."

Her eyes fill with tears and suddenly she's crying.

"Ruby, stop." I reach out and give her a side hug.

"No way." She wipes a tear from her cheek. "That's amazing. You just made my entire year."

"I won't tell a certain British bodyguard that you said that."

She rolls her eyes and sniffs and we start walking again. "That British bodyguard is a non-issue. I'm done with him."

"Yeah, okay." I don't believe her for a second and I don't think *she* believes her either.

We walk another block and she asks, "How long do you think Cian will be gone?"

"I don't know. I guess if it's not long, that means the king is doing well. Or things took a really bad turn quickly."

Ruby makes a sad noise. "If the king passes, does that change this whole marriage thing for Cian?"

I frown. "I haven't even thought about that. I have no idea." I lift my cup and drink as I think that over. "I'd really hope Cian is able to talk to his grandfather. I would love for him to tell his grandfather more about this foundation. I'm glad his sister told everyone, but I want *him* to feel like sharing that stuff with them. To know they want to hear it." I think about how Cian looked when he was showing me the texts from his family. "I know Cian knows they all love him and are proud of him, but I want him to *hear* them say that." I feel a heavy weight pressing on my chest as soon as I share that thought out loud. "Ruby," I say, stopping.

She stops too and faces me. "Yeah?"

"I didn't tell Cian that I love him before he left."

Ruby looks appalled. "What? Why not?"

"I just haven't said it yet. I thought…we had time."

"But…" She shakes her head. "You *do* love him, right?"

"I do." I nod. Vigorously. "I really do. So much. I'm sure of it. And… fuck!" I'm suddenly so mad at myself. "Why didn't I say it? I want him to know how much he's loved and how proud everyone is of him. I want him to *hear* those words and feel appreciated, but then *I* don't say it?" I grab my sister's arm. "What's wrong with me?"

"Nothing," Ruby says quickly. "Nothing's wrong. Him needing to leave happened really fast and there was a lot going on. It doesn't mean anything that you didn't say it."

But then she frowns and presses her lips together.

My eyes get wide. "What?" I demand.

"Nothing!"

"Ruby," I say warningly. "Tell me what you're thinking."

"I was just…" She swallows. "I was just thinking about how Cian really liked how proud his family was of him. How he felt like he was doing something important like they all do."

"Right," I agree. But my stomach is knotting.

"And now, their grandfather might be dying," she says.

"Right," I say again, slowly.

She takes a breath, then ask in a rush, "Do you think that Cian would marry Astrid?"

My stomach roils. I gasp. Then I shake my head. But then…I stop shaking my head. I stare at my sister.

"I mean, it's what his grandfather wants," Ruby says. "It's really important to the king. What if it's like a deathbed wish?"

My heart is now pounding so loud, her voice sounds muted.

"Astrid is really close to the family," Ruby goes on.

"She'll probably be there. What if, in the midst of all the emotion and everything, they think they can make Diarmuid happy in the end and get married before he dies."

I'm squeezing Ruby's arm harder now. "But…" I start. Then I honestly can't think of anything else to say. I'm the dumbass who didn't tell him I love him. And his *grandfather* is dying.

"So…you haven't told Cian that you love him. And now you have sent him home where his grandfather is dying and his final wish might be for Cian to marry an amazing, beautiful, very successful and—"

"Ruby," I interrupt. "Can we skip over the part about how his fiancée is fucking incredible?"

"Right. Sorry. It's just that she's *Astrid Olsen*."

I finally let out a long breath. And nod. "I know, right?"

"Okay," Ruby says, shaking us both. "You need to call him and tell him that you love him."

She's probably right. But instead I say, "I think I need an airplane."

"Oh," she says. "*Oh.*" Then she nods. "Okay."

"How do I get to Cara? If I fly from Columbus, I could go to Chicago? New York?"

Ruby pulls her phone out of her back pocket. "Are you seriously telling me that you think you're going to fly commercial? That will take forever!"

"Well, I don't have a private plane. My maybe, sort of, boyfriend who is also Astrid Olsen's fiancée does. But it's kind of in use!" I think my voice is suddenly much higher pitched than usual.

Ruby holds up a finger, telling me to wait and puts her phone to her ear.

A second later, she says, "Yes, it's me." She pauses, listening to the other person. "No, I'm okay." She frowns. "I know I told you I was never going to call you again, but Scarlett needs a favor. She needs an airplane to bring her to Cara." Ruby pauses, listening, then she says, "Fine." Another pause. "Yes, *fine*." She sighs. "Okay."

She disconnects and meets my eyes. "Henry's going to take care of it. You need to go home and pack. Actually, we all do. Henry insists that Mariah and I come too."

"You called Henry?"

"He's the only one I know who can get a private plane on short notice and who's number I have in my phone."

"Even though you said you were done with him and told him you weren't going to call him ever again?"

She gives me a little smile. "I'll do anything for you, Scarlett."

I pull her into a hug. "And you're going to come with me."

"Well, Henry said that was a condition of him sending the plane."

I grin as I'm hugging her, so she can't see it.

I don't think the British bodyguard is quite done with my sister no matter what she might think.

CHAPTER 34

CIAN

We've been in Cara for nearly two hours by the time everyone has arrived, settled in their rooms, and had a chance to see my grandmother. The king is sleeping, and the doctor asks us not to go in to see him. At the moment he is stable, however.

We're now all finally gathered in the most comfortable sitting room where there is enough space for all of us. It is a less formal room where the family never entertains, yet the high, arched ceilings, ornate trim, polished floor with the expensive rug, and the antique furnishings still scream *Royal Palace!*

Additional couches and chairs have been brought in by staff, a long table is laid out with food and drink, and everyone is trying their best to relax and just chat.

But we were all just here together a little less than two weeks ago for a truly joyous occasion and the difference between that and this is stark.

I'm trying to eat, though I don't feel hungry, and I'm

watching Torin across the room. My brother looks haggard. I'm sure the last several hours have been a lot for him. He will be the new king much sooner than he expected and that's hitting him on top of the emotions around possibly losing our grandfather.

Of course, we all hope Torin's coronation will occur because Diarmuid steps down to take better care of his health rather than because Cara *must* have a new king, but none of us can shake that real possibility. I'm sure Torin is no exception.

I watch as Abi comes to his side and Torin wraps his arm around her, almost seeming relieved. His expression relaxes and he leans into her. She says something softly for his ears only, and he even manages a smile before pressing a kiss to her temple.

My heart aches watching them. I am so damned happy my brother has her. And it makes me miss Scarlett with an intensity that surprises me.

"Hey."

I look to my right and give Astrid a smile. I knew she and her family would be here. Linnea and Jonah arrived about an hour before we did. Astrid and her brother, Alex, were already here as well.

"Hey, how are you?" I ask.

We both stand looking at the room full of family.

"Um...okay," she says. "How about you? I'm so sorry about Diarmuid."

I nod. Astrid and her family are close enough to mine that I'm sure this feels almost like her own grandfather had a heart attack. That's how we all felt when Alfred got sick at the end and when he passed. "Me too. I...don't know why, but I didn't expect this."

She smiles sadly. "Me either. I think it's because he's

larger-than-life. I know he's had three other heart attacks, but they were like nothing happened. He was up and around practically the next day. I can't imagine anything short of a bolt of lightning from Heaven itself could actually take him down."

I laugh softly. "I think that's exactly it."

Astrid turns to face me. "So, have you had a chance to think about anything else? Like maybe you've come up with a plan?" she asks. "I'm worried about the king, of course. But I'll be honest. I'm freaking out."

I shake my head. "A plan?" But a trickle of trepidation snakes down my spine. "For what?"

"They haven't talked to you?"

"Who?"

"Your grandmother. Or mine."

"I've talked to both of them," I say. "But only about my trip to get here and my grandfather's health."

"Great," she says. "So they're hoping to not give us enough warning."

"Warning for wh—"

Just then, my grandmother moves to the center of the room. She holds up her hands and the room quiets. "Everyone, it's been such a long day," she says. "I'm so very happy to have you all here. Thank you so much for rushing to be with us. There is one thing I want to make you aware of tonight so that you can prepare for tomorrow."

I tense. Is there something going on with my grandfather that we need to prepare for? Has he taken a bad turn?

"While Diarmuid continues to improve, we feel it is very important to ensure that he has joy and hope all around. We want to give him everything to live for. To fight for." She turns to Astrid and me. "We will hold the wedding tomorrow morning."

I just stand there for a long moment. I stare at my grandmother. Then I hear Astrid mutter, "Told you we need a plan."

I glance down at her. She tosses back the rest of the drink in the glass she's holding. She doesn't seem shocked. Apparently, this is what they talked to her about earlier.

I look back to my grandmother. "My wedding to Astrid?"

"Of course, dear," my grandmother says. "It will be smaller than anticipated, but still lovely. The important thing is that it will make your grandfather happy."

I am, of course, all for making my grandfather happy right now.

But I'm in love with another woman. I can't marry Astrid.

"There is a problem—" I start.

My grandmother gives me a look that instantly reminds me that she is Queen.

"I expect that the 'problem' will be taken care of by tomorrow morning at ten a.m. when the ceremony begins."

"That's not enough time," I protest. We need to at least stall until we can think of something better. "Astrid needs a dress. We'll need to announce it so people can get here."

My grandmother waves her hand. "Don't be silly. This is an emergency. Astrid has several lovely dresses and looks like a vision in anything."

Well, hell, how can I argue with that? Say it's *not* true? Sure, that's the princely thing to do.

I glance at Astrid. She just rolls her eyes.

"And," my grandmother continues as she gestures around the room, indicating all of our family members. "The most important people are already here."

Of course she's right. Dammit.

"But shouldn't we be focusing on Grandfather?" I take a step toward her, my tone sounding as desperate as I feel. "How will it look for us to be planning a wedding, a party and frivolity, while he's struggling?"

My grandmother frowns at me and I'm very glad Cara doesn't behead people who annoy the monarchs.

Though, there's a very quick and easy process to rewrite the rules around here.

"*This* will *help* him," she says firmly. She points a finger at me. "You *will* be standing before your grandfather, the *king*, tomorrow morning at ten a.m. Sharp."

"Fuck," I mutter as she turns and sweeps from the room.

"We *definitely* needed a plan," Astrid says.

"I'm not doing this," I tell Henry as I shrug into my suit jacket at nine fifty a.m. the next morning. "Do you have the plane ready?"

We're not doing the full wedding dress and tux thing. The ceremony will be family only in my grandfather's quarters.

"I do not," Henry says. "The pilots all tell me they are under strict orders from the queen to not transport anyone anywhere without her permission."

Of course they are.

"A hide out somewhere on the island then?"

"Not that either," he says.

He waits until I turn, then says. "Marry her, make Diarmuid happy today. Torin will take the throne, then grant your annulment."

"What the fuck am I supposed to tell Scarlett?"

"That she should've accepted your proposal when you first asked?"

I glare at him. "Is that supposed to be funny?"

"Was she going to marry you?" he asks. "You left in a rush, it was a few days before your big talk was scheduled, but do you think she was going to say yes?" He steps forward. "Because that's what this was all about. You wanted to find her before you made any commitment to Astrid. You found her."

"And we fell in love," I tell him

"She said that?"

"No. Not the words. Not yet." I feel my chest tighten. I didn't want to rush her, so I didn't say the words either. Not directly. Not specifically. But I *should* have. Dammit. And I really fucking want to hear those words from her. "But it was happening," I tell Henry. I believe that. I trust that Scarlett loves me. And I know Henry can see the sincerity in my eyes.

He blows out a breath. Then nods. "Then call this off. Tell Astrid you can't do this. Tell your grandmother. Tell your grandfather."

I need to. I do. I need to show my family who I am. I need to let them know the real me. "*Fuck,*" I groan. "This could *kill him*, Henry."

They told us this morning that my grandfather slept through the night and his vital signs are stable. The doctor thinks that he should be wide awake and able to participate in the wedding ceremony. But he has the king resting, with no visitors allowed, until then. Even if I was willing to risk his heart giving out with my news, I couldn't get in there to tell him before the ceremony with our entire family around anyway.

"Do you want to *marry* Scarlett?" Henry asks.

"Yes. She's it. She's the one I want to spend my life with. It can't be anyone else."

Henry gives me a single nod. "Okay, then."

"What does that mean? Okay then?"

"It means that my entire job is to keep you safe and happy. And I'm pretty fucking good at it. I don't expect that to stop today." He returns and stalks out of my room.

I have no idea what that means.

So I put my tie on and go downstairs.

Everyone is gathered in the sitting room outside of my grandfather's bedroom. In any normal household, that room would not be big enough to hold a wedding. But this is a palace, and he's a king.

He's propped up in one of the armchairs.

I stop inside the door as soon as my eyes fall on him.

He's pale. And he looks so small.

My grandfather is actually a big man. Tall, broad, and more, he has a presence that fills an entire room. He has a deep, commanding voice. And he is very used to having all of the attention on him.

I've always perceived him to be a giant.

Seeing him sitting, surrounded by pillows and wrapped in a blanket, his skin pale and his face drawn, I have to swallow hard before I continue into the room.

I cross to his chair and bow. "Grandfather."

He smiles. "Cian, my boy."

I lean over and press a kiss against his cheek. It's very cool. "It's good to see you."

"It's good to be seen. Especially on this day. Thank you."

My chest tightens and my heart squeezes. Fuck. He really wants this.

He wants his family united with Alfred's. That is actually not hard for me to understand. Alfred was like a brother to him. Like Henry is to me. I understand, especially now that Alfred is gone, Diarmuid's desire to keep Alfred alive and with him in whatever way he can.

I glance behind me and see Astrid standing near the windows.

She looks beautiful. Of course she does.

She's wonderful. We could do this. We could make both of our families incredibly happy, grant my grandfather's final wish, have a good life together.

But I just can't.

As long as Scarlett Gale is in this world, I cannot even pretend to give my heart to someone else.

"Grandfather, there's something I need to say to you," I tell him, turning back.

"What is it?" he asks, looking concerned.

"I am so sorry. But it's time that I tell you, all of you, my family, the people I love and trust the most, who I really am."

My grandfather nods. "Of course. We love you and we're so proud of you."

I feel my heart kick hard at those words. God, I love them. I want to make these people proud. "Grandfather, I want to *be* Cian O'Grady to the world. Torin, Fiona, and Declan's brother. Diarmuid and Roisin's grandson. I want everyone to know who we are. We have all been too quiet—in the US and on this tiny unknown island—for too long. And I want to be a part of making the O'Grady name known and esteemed."

He gives me a heartfelt smile. "I know you do. You are doing that, Cian. There are so many great things ahead."

My heart feels like it expands in my chest.

"And Astrid will do so much as a part of that. As an O'Grady," the king adds.

Yes. She would. "I agree," I tell him. "But I love someone else. I want someone else to be my partner in all of the things ahead of me. Someone who makes me a better man, who makes me believe I can do more, who supports and loves me and wants to see me do great things."

Diarmuid frowns. "I see. And who is this?"

Suddenly, I feel a hand on my shoulder, pulling me back. I turn and find Henry standing there.

"Your Majesty," he says with a bow. "Forgive me."

"Wha—" Diarmuid starts.

But then Henry pulls me in and presses his mouth to mine.

Multiple gasps are heard all around.

I hear my grandfather say, "I see."

Then my grandmother's voice says, "I always suspected."

I'm almost too distracted by Henry *still* kissing me to hear the next voice from beside him that says, "Oh for fuck's sake".

Henry is pulled away a second later and that same voice says, "This is really not necessary."

Henry swipes his thumb over his lips, scowling at the man who interrupted. "Dammit, you don't understand."

"I understand perfectly. And how is *you* marrying him, or whatever this is, solving anything?"

I blink at the man, then say, "*Declan*?"

As usual, my brother is in a dark, expensive, custom-tailored suit that looks like he was born in it. I have never seen him fidget with a cuff link or mess with his tie as if it's too tight. He seems as at ease in suits as I am in sweatpants. Declan is taller than me by about two inches. He's got darker eyes than the rest of us. Torin, Fiona, and I all have blue whereas Declan's are a deep brown. But he has the same thick, dark hair and is also sporting a short-cropped beard. He has also got his usual broody expression on that Fiona calls his resting asshole face.

"It was stopping *this* wedding," Henry says. "That was the main objective."

"You could have just kidnapped him. Knocked him out and tied him up in a closet," my oldest brother tells Henry.

"I was going to *marry* him. *That* would keep him from being available to marry Astrid," Henry insists.

"That's ridiculous," Declan says. "We would still have the same situation."

I blink at my brother. I haven't seen him in five years. He hasn't been back to Cara in seventeen. When he left home, abdicating the throne, he fucking *meant it*.

But he's here now. Standing right in front of all of us.

Standing in front of our grandfather.

"Well, *Cian* wouldn't be a part of the situation," Henry says.

"Declan," my grandfather's weak, hoarse voice makes us all turn.

"Your Majesty."

To my shock, my brother bows to my grandfather. "I'm glad you're alright."

The king gives him a single nod. "You... came."

My grandfather seems as stunned as the rest of us. And King Diarmuid is almost never stunned.

"Of course. I wanted to check on you. And—" Declan looks around the room. "I have a problem to solve."

His gaze stops on Astrid.

My eyes widen and I look at Henry. He seems just as out of the loop as I feel.

I look at everyone else. All of my siblings and their significant others are here. My mother and grandmother are seated on one of the settees. The only person in the room who doesn't seem completely shocked to see Declan is Iris Lee, his assistant and bodyguard, who is standing just inside the door. She obviously came with him. And she looks...resigned.

Declan starts across the room toward Astrid.

What the hell? I follow him.

Everyone in the room has, of course, been watching Declan, the prodigal son, so they all move closer to him and Astrid as well.

Except, I notice, for my grandmother. She goes to my grandfather and takes a seat in the chair next to him. She takes his hand and leans in, blocking his view of Declan and Astrid by the windows.

I frown and turn back to my brother and my sort-of fiancée.

Astrid looks surprised when Declan stops right in front of her.

"Cian won't be marrying you today," Declan tells her.

Astrid smiles brightly. "Okay." She picks up the skirt of her dress and starts for the door.

"Astrid."

She stops and looks back at Declan. "What?"

"You and I will marry."

CHAPTER 35

CIAN

Astrid drops her dress. She stares at Declan. She looks at the rest of us, then back up at him. Then she starts laughing. "Um. No," she says. "But gee, thanks for asking." She picks up her skirt again and turns, but she hesitates when she sees the rest of us just standing there, staring.

Not laughing. Not moving. Not speaking.

She frowns.

Her sister, Linnea, steps forward. "Declan, this seems like an overreaction."

"No," he says simply. "It doesn't. It's the only option."

"But you can't just spring this on Astrid like this," Linnea protests. Jonah moves in behind her, quietly supportive.

"Astrid is incredibly bright," Declan says. "I'm sure this isn't a shock to her. She understands the situation and that she and I are the only O'Grady and Olsen left that can make this match."

"Actually, I haven't thought about you at all," Astrid tells him.

He doesn't even look at her because now I step forward. "You can't force her, Declan."

"I don't need to. She'll do the right thing."

I look at Astrid. She's looking at Declan. But she doesn't look shocked or worried.

She looks...almost amused?

Declan is a formidable person. The only person in this room who even comes close is my grandfather and that's when he's in good health. Declan is very used to getting his way. Bossing other people around. Being the most powerful man in the room.

He would have made a great king.

He's also about ten years Astrid's senior and when he scowls, he seems even older. He takes a step closer to her. "Tell them all that you understand this," he says to her. "Alfred and Diarmuid want the families united. You and I are the only ones left. There's no other option. So we *will* marry."

She actually laughs at that. "Well, the entire agreement between Diarmuid and Alfred never *made sense* at all and surely *you* know that. You can't really think I'm going to agree to marry you just because everyone else got out of it? Because I just happen to still be single when you waltzed in and decided you were going to 'solve the problem'?" she asks, her fingers making air quotes.

"I think you're going to marry me because it is what your grandfather wanted. No one else in this goddamn family will do things the way they're supposed to." Declan casts a glare around the room, collectively for all of us, before focusing on her again. "None of this is going according to plan. So I'm going to take care of it myself. I will pay you whatever you want. I will give you whatever you want. You can have absolutely anything. As long as you walk down that aisle and say I do."

"So that's all you need? My name on a marriage license?" she asks.

"Yes. And a baby."

No one in the room is moving a muscle. But I know, at least for me, this has moved from being scared Declan might try to kill me if I did, to I'm not going anywhere and missing a second of this.

Astrid narrows her eyes. "For how long?"

"I expect our child to live a nice long life."

She blows out a frustrated breath. "I mean the marriage. Till death do us part?"

"Whatever you want. As long as we are legally married when the baby is born, so there are no... complications or questions."

She seems to be considering that.

This is *so* interesting.

"Well, there are a couple of things you might need to know first," Astrid tells him.

But Declan, it seems, is done talking it over. "Astrid, I don't care if you hate me, if you're a lesbian, if you're dying. I am rich enough, powerful enough, and stubborn enough to make any of those problems not matter in the least. All you need to do is walk down that *fucking* aisle."

Oh wow, a *fucking* in front of not just one grandmother, but two.

He's definitely not used to hanging out in the palace.

I glance over my shoulder. My grandmother seems to not have heard a thing. She's leaning in, talking to my grandfather. I'm hoping that's keeping him from hearing anything as well.

Astrid plants her hands on her hips. "You really think that you will always get your way, don't you?"

"Yes." Then he says, "if it makes this easier, your grandfather would have been thrilled with our union."

Astrid shakes her head. "How do you know that?"

"He told me."

Her mouth drops open. She looks at Linnea. Then Torin. Then back to Declan. "He *told* you that he wanted *you and me* to get married?"

"No. He told me that he wanted our families united, *no matter what*. I took that to mean *no matter what*. He thought it would be Torin and Linnea, of course." He shoots an exasperated glance in my brother and Linnea's direction. "He would have been fine with it being you and Cian."

She looks at me and I shrug. I'm not sure what I'm supposed to say here.

"But I was his favorite," Declan goes on, sliding his hands into his pockets. "And he worried about you the most. So having me taking care of you would have pleased him, I'm certain."

Astrid's eyes get even wider.

No one else makes a single sound.

"He...*worried*...about *me*...the *most*?" Astrid finally splutters.

"Yes," Declan says.

"And *you* were his favorite?" she asks.

"Yes."

Wow. I don't know how I feel about that. I'm *way* more fun than Declan, and Torin and Fiona are both friendlier. But, in Declan's defense, he spent a lot more time with Alfred than any of us did.

"And you would be *taking care* of me?"

"Of course."

"Declan O'Grady, I would rather—"

Astrid's sentence is cut off by Miles putting his hand over her mouth and dragging her over to the side, away from Declan.

I follow.

"You're making this so much worse," Miles tells her.

"*I* am not making this *anything*," she tells him. "He's ridiculous! I'm not going to just *marry* him!"

"But…" Miles casts me a look that says *help*. "He's right."

"You've *got* to be kidding," Astrid tells him.

"I'm not," Miles says. "Your grandfather wanted this. That matters to Declan. A lot."

She narrows her eyes. "You're telling me *that*—" She jabs her finger in Declan's direction. "Is Declan being soft and caring and nostalgic and…what? Loyal to my grandfather?"

Miles sighs. "Yes."

She snaps her mouth shut. She frowns. She studies Miles face. "How do you know that?"

"I talk to Iris a lot," he says without missing a beat.

"Did you know that my grandfather *worried* about me?"

Miles looks very unhappy about this conversation, but he nods. "Yes."

She steps closer to him, needing to tip her head back to keep her eyes on his.

"He also knew that you were going to do great things, Astrid," Miles says. "Your grandfather was incredibly proud of you. He saw…magic in you. That's what he said. He was *so* pissed when you got hurt. He wanted you to have every opportunity."

Astrid's frown seems to go from angry to confused. She

swallows hard and blinks rapidly. "He'd want me to have a *baby* with Declan? *That* kind of opportunity?"

I watch Miles's face. He looks pained. "I didn't know about the baby. But I do think Alfred would feel very good about you being with Declan. Yes."

"*Is* Declan his favorite?"

Miles nods. "Yes."

She looks thoughtful.

"Astrid," I finally say. "We can figure something else out."

She looks at me. "What?"

"I won't make you marry him. We'll...get you out of here. Figure something else out." I look at Miles. "Miles could marry you."

He looks *very* uncomfortable at that. "Declan won't let that happen."

Astrid looks at him in disbelief. "He doesn't get to decide what I do."

Miles nods. "Okay. Fine. I'll get you out of here. If that's what you really want."

She looks at him for several seconds. Then looks at me. Then looks past me.

I glance over my shoulder to find Declan literally glowering at Astrid. When I look back at her, I'm certain she's watching Declan as well.

"I'm fine. You don't have to save me," she finally says.

"You're going to marry Declan?" I ask.

"I think...I'm going to teach him a lesson," she says.

"Astrid—" Miles starts.

"No, I'm fine." She smiles up at Miles. "Trust me, Declan O'Grady will want to annul this marriage sooner rather than later."

Miles rolls his eyes. "You're going to single-handedly teach Declan that he doesn't always know best?"

Her smile gets even bigger. "I'm going to marry an O'Grady and make Diarmuid and Alfred happy."

Miles lets out a breath.

"*And* I'm going to teach Declan that he isn't as smart as he thinks he is."

"Astrid," Miles groans.

"Doesn't that seem like a great way to make the world a better place?" she asks, suddenly a little perky as she picks up the bottom of her long dress again.

"I think it seems like a great way for me to end up with daily migraines," Miles says.

Astrid reaches up and pats his cheek. "Good. You deserve that for not giving me even a hint this might happen." Then she brushes past him and heads for Declan.

She stops in front of him.

He lifts a brow.

"I'll do it," Astrid says simply.

Declan just gives her a nod and turns toward the king.

Linnea steps forward. "Astrid—"

Astrid looks at her sister. "I'm okay."

Alex is right there too. He's scowling. "Astrid, seriously."

"I'm good, I promise," she says. She looks up at Declan. "Oh, but I want the hockey team."

My brother owns the Portland Greys. The team Alex plays for.

Declan doesn't even blink. "Fine."

"And my own room."

The muscle in his jaw jumps, but he says, "You'll have your own wing."

She gives him a sweet, completely fake smile. "I don't think you have any idea what you're getting into here, Mr. O'Grady."

"I'm a risk taker by nature, Ms. Olsen."

She just stares at him for a long moment. Then she looks at her grandmother.

I look over too.

The older woman is watching, without saying a word. But I can see the hope in her expression even from here.

And when Astrid says, "Okay," to Declan, her grandmother exhales in relief and smiles.

No one's smile is as big as Diarmuid's though.

Astrid and Declan walk toward the king, stopping in front of his chair.

"Astrid," he says, his voice weak and wobbly. "My beautiful girl. Thank you."

I watch Astrid's shoulders lose some of their rigidity and she nods. "I'm ready."

"My beloved family and friends—" Diarmuid starts.

"Wait!" a voice calls from the back of the room.

A feminine voice.

We all turn and my heart stops.

"Oh my God! Please stop! I'm so sorry, but you can't…"

Scarlett is rushing across the room and down the aisle.

She's wearing jeans and a flannel shirt over a gray T-shirt. Her dark hair is falling out of a ponytail. And she's got her black boots on.

She's the most gorgeous thing I've ever seen.

I meet her halfway up the aisle and catch her in my arms. "What are you doing here?"

She grips my arms, panting, trying to catch her breath. "Oh God, Cian." She breathes in and out. "Please don't get married. Not to someone else anyway."

She looks past me.

"Oh *God!*" Her eyes come back to mine, filled with panic. "Did you already? Did you do it? Am I too late?"

I pull her in and crush her to my chest.

She's here. *Here.* She flew here, she came after me.

To stop my wedding.

I cup the back of her head and just hold her as I start laughing.

Ruby and Mariah burst into the room just then.

"Scarlett!" Ruby sees her in my arms and rushes forward. "Shit, she got away from us," she tells me. She looks around, her gaze hanging on Henry for a second, before continuing around the room. "Oh, no, are we too late?"

Mariah has stopped at the back of the room. She seems frozen in place. But her eyes are huge and she's taking in every detail.

"No, you're not too late. It's not happening." I pull back and look down at Scarlett. "You're the only one I want."

"But," she says, peeking past me again. "It's *Astrid Olsen.*"

I growl. "Witch…"

"I mean right *there*," she says. "At the end of the aisle. In a really pretty dress. Looking very much like a *bride.*"

I turn with her in my arms. "Yes, it is. And she's about to marry my brother."

Astrid lifts a hand. "Hi."

"Hi," Scarlett says timidly.

Astrid looks up at Declan. "We'd better get going before I find whatever part of my mind I've lost to agree to this."

"Declan, do you take Astrid to be your wife?" Diarmuid asks.

"Oh my God, that's the king," Scarlett whispers against my chest.

I kiss the top of her head. "Yes," I whisper back. "I'll introduce you after the wedding."

"I do," Declan says.

"Astrid, do you take Declan to be your husband?"

"I guess I do," she mutters.

"I declare you wed. Go forth with my blessing." Diarmuid waves his hand.

"That's it?" Scarlett asks, tipping her head back to look up at me.

"Not usually. But he's the king so he can do it however he wants to. This is all formality. The license is what makes it official anyway."

She nods, then looks back at Astrid and Declan. "They're not going to kiss?"

Astrid has already gone over to where her mother, grandmother, sister, and brother are gathered. Declan is talking to Iris and Torin.

"I don't think so."

"So that's…"

"Not at all what our wedding will be like," I tell her.

She looks up at me quickly. "Our wedding?"

"Yes. Our wedding. I love you, Scarlett. And I intend to marry you. When it's time," I add. I cup her face and stroke my thumb over her jaw. "I promise I'm not going to rush you. There's no pressure now. We have all the time we need. I won't let anyone else pressure you either. In anything. You can be whoever you want to be, and you can show that to the world however you want to."

She swallows. "I love you, Cian. So much. And I'm done hiding. I'm done being quiet about *anything* I love and believe in. I want the world to know me, to know who I am and what I believe in and what, and who, I love."

"Well, that works out really well," I tell her, my heart feeling like it's going to explode. "Because now that you've shown up in Cara *at the palace,* there's about a ninety-five percent chance that you're going to be a main topic of conversation on a pretty popular podcast."

CHAPTER 36

SCARLETT

Oh my God, I made it in time.

Cian didn't marry Astrid. I finally told him I love him. We can be together.

Okay, I didn't *actually* break up his wedding at the last second, so my podcast episode won't be as dramatic as it could have been, but this is still really great.

Cian cups my face with both hands, his smile and his eyes full of love and wonder.

"What are you thinking?" I ask.

"You chased me down this time."

My heart melts a little at that. "It was my turn."

His smile grows. "I fucking like that."

I grasp his wrists. "I *love* you," I tell him, needing to say it again. "I've known it for a while but I was afraid to say it. But, Cian, it's the thing that's made me braver than I've ever been. I'm so sorry I didn't tell you before you left."

His eyes darken. "I love you so damned much." He takes

a deep breath. "But this could possibly be one of the worst times to tell me that you love me too."

"What? Why?"

"Because we are surrounded by some of the most dramatic people you're ever going to meet. And they're all going to want to meet and talk to you. Which means I'm not going to get you alone for hours." He leans closer. "And I want to hear you *screaming* I love you."

How can he do that? Say just a few words and make heat wash through me like I just took a shot of whiskey? When I'm standing in the middle of a room full of people?

I cast a glance around. His whole family is here—even his brother Declan who never comes home to Cara according to everything I've read—and everyone is talking, but I can see them all glancing in our direction. "Surely they would let me go change clothes and freshen up before I meet everyone for the first time?"

"You're a genius." He kisses me quickly, then takes my hand and starts up the aisle toward Mariah.

It's also toward the door and his grandmother seems to notice. She raises her voice. "Brunch will be starting in ten minutes."

"We'll be back. The girls need a few minutes. It's been a long trip."

I look over at his grandmother as Cian stops in front of my daughter.

The queen looks annoyed but resigned. This maybe isn't the *best* first impression to make on the royal family but I'm serious about changing clothes and at least brushing my hair. And I need a minute to breathe after charging in here to break up a wedding. That was a true test for my new *hey world look at me!* attitude. Now I really would like even five minutes alone with my prince.

"Hey," Cian says to Mariah.

"Hey." My daughter is clearly overwhelmed by everything.

He reads her easily. "You'll get used to it." Just that simple phrase, insinuating that there's a future here finally makes her smile.

Then he reaches out and tugs her into a hug. She hugs him back and my throat tightens and my eyes well with tears.

"I'm going to have Saoirse show you around. I think you should share a room," Cian says.

Mariah pulls back. "Really? That would be nice."

She knows Saoirse from texting and obviously his niece knows all the ropes around here.

Cian nods. "Saoirse," he calls.

His niece comes running over as if she was just waiting for the invitation. "Hi, Mariah," she greets enthusiastically. "I'm so excited you're here. Finally, someone my age to hang out with!"

"Hey," Cian protests. "I'm basically your age. Mentally anyway."

"I think you're actually younger than me mentally," Saoirse tells him, nudging him with a grin. "But Mariah *really* is my age. Roughly. Plus she's a girl."

"That's sexist," Cian tells her.

"Maybe a little," she agrees. "I shouldn't assume your terrible taste in books and you not loving Benedict Bridgerton enough is because you're a guy. Henry is awesome to talk books with and Jonah agrees that Benedict is the best Bridgerton."

"Now *that's* just hurtful," Cian says, putting a hand over his heart.

Mariah gives Cian a funny look.

He leans in. "Benedict for you too?"

"*Obviously*," Mariah tells him.

He sighs. "How am I wrong to think Eloise is the best Bridgerton?"

Mariah and Saoirse share a look and an eye roll.

He looks at me for help. I shrug. "I like Michael Stirling best."

"He's not a Bridgerton," they all say together.

I laugh. "Okay, then Anthony."

They sigh and Cian asks Saoirse, "Will you show Mariah around? Get her settled in your room? Introduce her to everyone?"

She has already taken Mariah's hand and started for the door. "I'll take her upstairs now and she can unpack."

Cian watches them go with a look of such pride and affection I feel my ovaries tingle. *Ladies, you need to settle down.*

He looks down at me and for a second I wonder if I said that out loud.

"We can take Ruby up with us," he tells me. "There's a room a couple of doors down from mine."

I look over to where my sister is standing a few feet away.

"I've got her," Henry says, moving in close, obviously never too far away.

Ruby's gaze snaps up to his. "Absolutely not."

"I can show you to a fucking room," Henry says, his voice low and tense.

Ruby shakes her head. "No."

"I'll show you," Linnea says smoothly, coming to stand with us. "Hi, Ruby, I'm Linnea."

Ruby's eyes get a little rounder. "I know."

"It's very nice to meet you." Linnea gives Henry a look.

"We'll take care of Ruby and Mariah." She looks at Cian. "You make sure Scarlett gets settled." She lowers her voice. "I would suggest you be back down within an hour, or your grandmother may come looking for you. Or your big brother."

"I will not come looking."

I look up to see that Torin O'Grady and Abigail—*Prince* Torin and *Princess* Abigail—have joined us.

"I meant Declan," Linnea says. "The sooner all of this is over, the sooner he'll be able to head back to Portland." Her voice gets a little softer. "With my sister." She shakes her head as if she can't believe that.

"He needs to stay until Grandfather is stable," Torin says. "I'll speak to him." Then Torin smiles at me. "It's nice to meet you, Scarlett."

I swallow. "Hi, Your Majesty. Your Highness?" I have no idea if I'm supposed to bow or curtsy or...

Torin chuckles. "Just Torin." He extends a hand. "Especially for family."

Now I'm starting to feel a little dizzy. I take his hand and absorb his warm smile. Cian's hand on my waist gives me a squeeze of encouragement.

"It's very nice to meet you," I tell Torin.

"Oh, believe me, the pleasure's mine. For the longest time we thought Cian was making you up."

I look up at Cian. "No. I am very real."

The look in Cian's eyes is very hot. And very full of love.

"Hi, I'm Abigail. But you can call me Abi," the princess extends her hand as well.

"I know who you are too," I say, taking her hand. "I follow the podcast."

Abigail laughs lightly and her cheeks turn pink. "Oh. Well, they do get *most* of it right."

More people start moving in our direction and Cian clears his throat. "We're going to head upstairs for a little bit." He nudges me toward the door. "See you later," he says to the group at large.

He takes me down a few long hallways, decorated with amazing art pieces, huge portraits of people I assume are his ancestors and family members, and up three enormous cream-colored marble staircases.

"I am definitely going to get lost here."

He shakes his head. "Impossible. I'm not letting you out of my sight."

I grin. The stress and anxiety of getting here on time are finally fading. The overwhelm from everything that was happening in the room when I rushed in is starting to be replaced by the realization that everything is fine.

Better than fine.

In the place of all of those emotions is a warmth and happiness that is filling me and making my heart soften and expand.

I'm with Cian. In Cara. We're in love. And I am ready to tell the world.

As soon as the bedroom door shuts behind us and Cian turns the lock, he stalks across the carpet, cups my face again, and kisses me. Hungrily.

He starts stripping me, tugging the shirt I'm wearing over my tee down my arms, dropping it on the floor, gathering the t-shirt up and taking his mouth from mine only long enough to pull it over my head.

"I named the foundation," I tell him as his fingers find the clasp on my bra, disposing of it quickly. "Ruby's Way."

"Love that." He takes both breasts in hand, cupping, kneading, and tweaking my nipples.

His mouth returns to my jaw, kissing down my neck as I

tip my head back as I say, "And we're going to fund a program in Emerald to help with housing costs and a meal program for single moms."

He squeezes both nipples, causing bolts of heat to shoot to my clit. He kisses up to my ear. "Awesome." His hands slide down my sides to the button on my jeans and he unbuttons and unzips, pushing them over my hips.

"I also stood up to my dad. In the middle of the coffee shop. In front of a bunch of his cronies."

Now Cian lifts his head. "That's amazing. I'm so fucking proud of you."

I nod. "It felt so good."

"You're incredible."

I grip his forearms, stopping him for a moment. "But that means we need to stay in Emerald. For a while. At least until Mariah graduates. I want to make a difference *there*. Other places too, but there for sure. I want to show people what loving your neighbor and caring about their lives *really* looks like. Not telling them how to live, not judging their decisions, but supporting how they choose to live and just helping them do that the best way they can. And," I swallow. "Admitting that we all need help sometimes so that they can know how good it feels to help others too. I want to give people an alternate community if and when they realize that my dad's church isn't what they want. But I want to be obvious about it. Loud about it. Joyous about it. So no one misses it."

"*Incredible*," he repeats. His voice is gruff. He's looking at me with a true admiration I've never seen before.

"You'll stay there with me?"

"It would be the honor of my life to do all of that with you, Scarlett."

Yeah, not just my ovaries tingle at that.

"Really?"

He rests his forehead on mine. "You've had this power all along my beautiful, amazing witch."

I smile even though tears are stinging my eyes. "That's a Wizard of Oz quote. Kind of."

He nods. "It is. And it's so damned appropriate." He kisses my forehead then leans back, looking into my eyes. "You don't need me for any of this. You can do all of this all by yourself. But if you are going to invite me to come along and witness you work your magic and make the world a better place? Yes. With my whole fucking heart and soul."

My entire body feels like it melts and I lean into him. "I love you."

"I'm so, *so* glad."

"You are incredible too," I tell him. "I think *we're* pretty magical together."

He looks so touched by that, I put my hand against his cheek and kiss him softly.

When he pulls back, he studies me for a moment. Then he kneels, strips my clothes the rest of the way off of me, stands again, and picks me up.

My legs automatically wrap around his waist, and he carries me into his bathroom.

He sets me down as he leans in to turn on the shower.

Oh, a shower after the long flight and everything sounds great. But then I turn and...

"Oh my *God*."

He looks over. Then laughs. "Later. No time for that now."

"But...Cian..."

The bathtub in this room is absolutely magnificent.

It's practically a small swimming pool. There are three steps leading up to it. The massive window behind it looks out over the rocky cliff that falls off to the ocean. There are jets all the way around the tub, built in seats, and *three* different depths.

I could stay in that thing for days.

Suddenly I'm swept up into Cian's arms.

A naked Cian's arms.

He steps into the shower with me.

When he sets me on my feet inside the glass encased stall with the multiple shower heads and built-in bench, he says, "My shower is very nice too."

"But that *tub*," I say reverently, still looking at it through the glass.

"Let me show you," he says as he starts soaping my body.

And yeah, okay, twenty minutes later, I admit—loudly, with him pounding into me, and at his insistence—that I like his shower *very much* too.

CHAPTER 37

SCARLETT

"I know it might be in my head, but this terrycloth is actually thicker and softer than any other in the world, right?" I say to Ruby as I rub the lapel of my bathrobe against my cheek.

She laughs. "Well, it's a *royal* bathrobe. It's supposed to be superior. But I don't think this is terrycloth."

"Then what is it?"

"Angel yarn?"

She has one too, but she's actually gotten out of hers since it's nearly eleven a.m. She's even left her room.

I haven't done either thing.

She's sitting across from me at the little breakfast table in the sitting area outside of Cian's bedroom having a very late brunch with me.

Late because Cian and I slept in after being up all night making love. Also, because I finally got in his bathtub this morning. And most definitely didn't want to get out. It was only in part because of the tub, amazing multiple jets, and unbelievable view. It was also because of the hot prince that got in the tub with me. And the lilac vanilla bath salts that Princess Abigail makes herself. But mostly the prince.

I give a happy sigh as I gather the plush robe around me and sink deeper into the armchair.

"Those happy-in-love-well-fucked sighs are very annoying," Ruby tells me, popping a piece of the *best* pineapple I've ever had into her mouth.

I grin. "Sorry." I'm certain I don't look a bit sorry.

She laughs. "Do princes have friends that are princes? Like princes from other countries? Surely they do, right?"

I don't actually know. And I can't ask for her because Henry would kill me. Or be really mad at me for the rest of my life. And yes, I think Henry is going to be around for the rest of my life. "Not sure. But they have hot, noble, charming bodyguards."

She narrows her eyes. "Shut up."

I push the plate of pastries closer to her. "They also have *really* talented in-house bakers."

She reaches for one of the little turnovers.

"This is all real, isn't it?" I look around the room.

The high arched ceiling, the elaborate crown moldings, the built-in stone fireplace, the breathtaking view outside of these windows as well is all fairytale stuff. And it's finally all sinking in. I'm in love with an actual fucking prince. And I'm over the moon about it.

"It's really real," Ruby says. She gives me a big grin. "But you will have to take your robe off for your princess dresses eventually."

I've never really been a dress girl. In high school during my make-dad-happy phase, I wore conservative clothing, including modest dresses and skirts. I hated them. But the church was big on girls looking feminine. I've always been more comfortable in pants and jeans. And I love my coveralls.

"I've been assured by Mariah and Cian both that I don't have to make official appearances. I mean, I can be talked into a dress here and there, but long flowing gowns with trains and lots of lace and satin, are not really my style." I stick my foot out and wiggle my toes. "Not too many sequined gowns go with grease-stained work boots."

She laughs. "Maybe we can get you some sparkly *clean* work boots."

Just then my bedroom door flies open and Mariah comes bounding in. I swear I have never seen my daughter walk with as much bouncy energy as she does around the palace.

"Saoirse and Abigail just asked if I can go to the ranch with them today. They've got horses! And all these pretty trails and stuff! Is that okay? We might spend the night there!"

"Uh...sure." I would honestly let her go anywhere for anything with any of the people in Cian's family, but I only vaguely register her words because I am staring at what she's wearing.

She's got a tiara on her head.

That is not a dress-up-and-play-pretend piece. That is a real actual tiara. And even one of the glittering green jewels probably costs more than everything I own.

And there are *a lot* of glittering green jewels on that thing.

She also looks really beautiful in it.

"What are you wearing?" I ask, trying to act casual and not like all the royal stuff has now *truly* sunk in.

Her hand flies to the tiara and she grins brightly. "It's Saoirse's."

Now that I take her in fully, I note that her long, dark hair has been curled and put up in an elaborate twist that shows off her long, slender neck. She's also wearing a gorgeous off the shoulder blouse that is not hers, and a floor length skirt.

She does not have a single splash of red on. Her signature color. The color she wears in some form at all times.

"And what is all of this?" I ask, waving my hand up and down.

"Saoirse, Fiona, Abigail, and Linnea have been talking to me about princess stuff." Mariah laughs lightly. "Not as much Abigail. She's still learning too, and she doesn't have many skirts or dresses and she says she always forgets she has her tiara on and it ends up slipping or falling off." She grins and twirls. "But I've been practicing for when I have one to wear. Of course, mine will be blue like Cian's."

I'm choked up. I can't help it. We've always been a house full of women, and Ruby in particular has had a lot of fun playing dress-up with Mariah, fixing her hair, and doing things like painting her nails. I know Mariah has always felt secure, loved, and supported. But now, overnight, she has a whole new group of cousins and aunts, and they've all embraced her so easily. She's practically glowing from all the attention and excitement.

Cian and everything about the Cara royals made Mariah the target of ridicule from Leah and her group for weeks. Now he's made her an actual princess and any of those girls would trade places with her in a heartbeat.

I know she doesn't *need* all of this to be happy and well-adjusted. But it still feels like sweet justice all the same.

"You're choosing blue like Cian's?" I ask her. The way Mariah and Cian have bonded never fails to move me.

"Well, no," she says, finally flopping into one of the

chairs at the table. "Each of the O'Grady grandchildren has a different color. Fiona and Saoirse wear green jewels. Their tiaras and crowns are green. Torin's color is purple. So his and Abigail's crowns and tiaras have purple stones. Technically that should have been Declan's since he's the first born and should have been king, but it went to Torin when he became Crown Prince. Now Declan's is the red jewels. It would be cool if Cian's jewels were the red ones since he's with *Scarlett*," she says with a grin. "But his are blue. So your tiara and mine will actually be blue." She touches the tiara again. "Saoirse is just letting me wear it to get used to it."

I stare at her. There are actually certain colors assigned to each of the siblings. And they're already talking about how Mariah and I will also have tiaras with the same color as Cian's.

My stomach swoops at the idea of being identified as 'belonging' with Cian that way. Even though I do not think I'm the tiara type.

"Your wedding ring will also have blue stones," Mariah tells me, somehow sitting sideways in the chair with her leg draped over the arm, despite the skirt she's wearing, and still keeping the tiara on her head. Maybe she's a natural.

Then her words sink in.

My wedding ring will have blue stones.

My *wedding* ring.

My stomach swoops again.

I may not be the tiara type, but I am very much the type to wear a wedding ring that identifies me as Cian's wife.

I smile and feel myself tearing up *again*. What is going on? I don't *cry*. But watching my daughter carry herself with confidence and joy and watching her in the past fourteen hours be surrounded and absorbed into this group of people, I realize *she* is the tiara type. She is a princess in attitude and potential. She is going to be able to do amazing things and this family can give her the support and resources to change the world.

"You look amazing in that tiara," I tell her, my voice choked-up-mom thick.

She gives me a knowing smile and eye roll but says, "Thanks."

I catch Ruby watching me and give her a smile.

"Blue is really one of your best colors," she tells me softly.

Yeah, I'm definitely going to cry. I have to swallow hard. "Thanks."

"Oh," Mariah says, sitting up straight in the chair. "I forgot to tell you. Linnea and Henry have talked to Mrs. Brown."

"Your principal, Mrs. Brown?"

"Yeah. They've arranged it so that I can do remote learning for the rest of the semester. They've assured her that I will be able to take all of the exams from my classes and pass them. They will make sure that I am doing all of my work and learning all of the material while we're gone and said I'd even do an extra report on indoor farming that includes an interview with Abigail and a history paper interviewing King Diarmuid."

I frown. "While we're gone the rest of the *semester*?"

She nods. "They want us to stay here for a while."

"I guess I figured we would for a few days, but..."

There's a knock on my door.

"Come in," Mariah calls.

Linnea peeks in. "Do you have a minute?" she asks.

The robe I'm wearing is huge so I am completely

covered. I also have no desire to get out of it any sooner than I need to, so I wave her in. "Sure."

Linnea comes in, followed by Jonah, Torin, and Abigail.

I sit up straighter. Okay. Well, I would have gotten dressed if I'd known I'd have this many guests, including the *prince* and *princess*.

Ruby gives me a grin.

I am really not used to having this many people around all the time and she knows it.

They all drop onto various sitting surfaces. I'm not sure how to host a meeting like this in my boyfriend's bedroom.

"Anyone want coffee?" I asked.

"We're fine," Linnea says, clearly comfortable answering for the whole group.

"Where's Cian?" Jonah asks, looking around.

"I'm here." Cian strides through the door.

My heart gives a funny little staccato beat when I see him, even though he just left me about an hour ago.

He makes a beeline for me. "Jesus, I didn't think you were going to accost her." He scoops me up, turns, and sits, settling me on his lap, and clasping my robe shut across my breasts, even though there's so much material there's no way anyone can see anything.

He uses that grip on my robe to pull me up so he can kiss me quickly. "Hi."

"Hi," I say with a little laugh.

"Here you all are," Henry says, also coming into the room.

Is this what it feels like to have a bunch of siblings, I wonder. Because this familiarity, and the way they all seem to always want to be together, feels a lot like how Ruby and I are. No one seems to blink at the fact that I am still in a robe, or that they're all gathered, essentially in Cian's bedroom.

I notice that Henry immediately looks at Ruby when he comes into the room and that my sister stoically keeps from looking at him.

Henry takes a seat at the table right next to Ruby. Ruby scoots her chair a few inches away from him.

Yeah, that constant annoyance seems very sibling-ish.

Except that those two are *not* like siblings in any other way.

Fortunately, there are so many people in the room and they're all talking to one another, so no one else really notices the two of them.

"We just wanted to talk about what's going to happen in the next couple of days," Linnea says, taking charge even though the Crown Prince and Princess are right here.

"I was thinking it would be great if you guys could stay for a while," she says to me and Cian. "Having Cian, Fiona, and especially Declan all back on the island is wonderful. And this way we could make all of this into a huge celebration. It would go a long way in calming and reassuring the citizens that Diarmuid is healthy and on the mend."

"What kind of celebration?" Cian asks.

"Well as much as Declan will probably disagree, I do think that we need to announce his marriage to Astrid. We can also announce Torin's ascension to the throne and schedule the official coronation before all the grandchildren leave the island." She leans in, her eyes sparkling with excitement. "And if we could introduce Scarlet as Cian's betrothed, it would give everyone plenty of exciting happy news to concentrate on versus the king's health. It would also make *him* so happy."

"So you think we should officially do the coronation sooner versus later?" Torin says.

"No question," Linnea says. "For the people. But also for Diarmuid. It would mean so much to him to be a part of it."

Even I pick up the fact that Diarmuid turning over the crown is much different, and obviously better, than him dying and Torin inheriting the crown that way.

"The people seeing him crowning you would be good for everyone. When he was crowned after his father's death, it was so sad and it took the people time to really come around." She looks around. "My grandmother told me," she says. "And I've read about it."

I see Torin and Abigail link hands and Abi give him a squeeze. She leans into his shoulder, clearly offering support.

"Well, I have a request," Torin says. His eyes are on me and Cian now.

"Anything we can do," Cian says.

"Would you consider having the king bless your marriage?" Torin asks. "Once he turns the crown over, he could do it ceremonially, of course. But it wouldn't be the same. While it would be an honor for it to be one of my first official acts, I think it would be nice that Diarmuid would have blessed all four of his grandchildren's marriages."

My heart thuds against my ribs. Marriage. Wedding. The king.

This is all getting official.

But I feel Cian squeeze my leg and I take a breath and I just *know*… this is what I want. All of it.

"It's just a blessing?" I ask. "I thought he performed Declan and Astrid's wedding."

Torin nods. "Yes. He can do that. A lot like a judge. Both Fiona and I chose to also have a representative from the church. Our grandfather was there and offered the family's blessing though."

Cian shifts underneath me, the hand that's on my leg squeezing again. "Scarlett and I—"

"Oh, well, let's do that," I say. "Let's have the king do the whole thing like he did for Declan and Astrid."

I know that Cian is about to say that he wants to give me more time or that we're not quite ready. But the truth is, I am. And I know he is. We're going to get married. And if this is something meaningful to his family, to his grandfather, there's no reason to wait.

Cian's hand tightens on my leg. "Scarlett."

I look down at him and give him a smile. "Will you marry me?"

His eyes are filled with a myriad of emotions. Love is absolutely front and center. But possessiveness, heat, relief, and overwhelming happiness are all very clear.

"Anything you want, Scarlett. Always."

"You," I say simply. "That's what I want. Always."

His hand squeezes again. Then he looks at Torin and Linnea. "Let's plan a wedding."

Suddenly Mariah is throwing her arms around both of us, and I hear a little sniffle. I hug her tightly and when she pulls back, I see tears tracking down her cheeks.

I lift my hands and wipe them away with my thumbs. "You're happy?" I ask, though I already know the answer.

"So happy. Thank you so much."

"Thank you?" I ask. "For what?"

"I've always wanted a Brian. And this one is amazing." She grins at Cian through her tears.

And his eyes fill as well.

And now I'm crying.

I look over at Ruby and she's crying too.

Even Linnea and Abigail are dabbing at their eyes.

I look down at Cian.

He grins at me. "Magic," he says softly.

Three days later, Declan and Astrid's marriage has been announced, Torin's coronation is planned, and I am standing at the end of the aisle getting ready to walk down the aisle and say I do.

The smaller formal ballroom on the palace's first floor has been transformed for our wedding ceremony. The larger formal ballroom—I'm not sure if there's an *informal* ballroom somewhere—is where we'll host our reception.

I am wearing a dress. It's cream colored, hits me just above the knees, cinches at the waist and flares over my hips. And there's no train or veil. Still...it's a dress.

I'm not wearing boots with it, but the shoes are basic and flat because I do not want to risk turning my ankle in heels.

I'm carrying a little bundle of Forget Me Nots. Cian and I thought those were the most appropriate flowers for us. Not only because of the name but because they are a pretty blue, like the stones in Cian's crown and the tiara I'm wearing on top of my curled and twisted romantic updo. And they remind me of the blue of my prince's eyes.

My mom turns to me with a smile. "I'm so proud of you," she says.

I take a deep breath. "Thank you. And thanks for always being there for me, even after everything I've put you through."

She laughs. "That's what moms do."

I lean in and hug her. "Thanks for flying in here. And walking me down the aisle."

She nods and says, "Flying in for the wedding was a no-brainer. And I'm so glad we've had a couple of days for me to get to know everyone. But I'm not going to walk you down the aisle, Scarlett."

I frown. "What?"

She squeezes my hand. "You are going to walk yourself down the aisle and give yourself to that man. You don't need anyone else to do that for you."

"But..."

"Scarlett, I'm here to support you the way I have through every big choice you've ever made. But you've made those choices yourself. And they've always worked out. You know what you want. Walk down there and marry that man."

My eyes fill with tears. But they're happy tears. I've had a lot of those lately. I nod. "Okay."

She smiles and gives me another hug. "I'm going to go take my seat. I love you."

"I love you too." I watch her go to her seat then I face the front, take a deep breath, and start my walk down the aisle. Myself. To meet my husband.

My daughter and sister stand at the end, my maids of honor.

Henry and Torin stand on Cian's side.

The audience is full of members of Cian's family, including the Olsens and almost all of the Landrys.

My mom is the only one here for me.

And yet, I feel like I'm in the midst of family and friends. Cian's given me a community just like he said he wanted to on my back patio.

Cian watches me walk toward him, our gazes locked on one another.

He looks proud, happy, and very in love.

I hope he can see all of that in my eyes as well.

When I get to the end of the aisle, he seems nearly overwhelmed. He immediately takes my hands and tugs me close.

"You are absolutely everything I never even knew I could dream of," he says, his voice gruff.

I shake my head. This man is unbelievable. "Thank you, Cian. So much."

"For what?"

"For coming after me. For waiting for me. For believing in me. For wanting those nineteen days even after you found out...everything. And then for wanting forever."

He steps even closer, squeezing my hands. "I will always come after you. I will always wait for you. I will always believe in you. And I want the rest of your days."

I feel a tear slip down my cheek, and I blink up at him with a smile. "Ditto. To all of that."

"Well, those sounded like vows to me."

We both turn and look at King Diarmuid. We laugh.

"I'm sorry, Your Majesty," I say. "You can go ahead."

He chuckles. He's been getting stronger every day and he looks healthy and happy today. He smiles at me, his affection clear. I've had some time to talk with the king over the last couple of days and he is a lovely man who loves his family deeply and I think he likes me.

"All I ask is that you love my grandson with all your heart."

I look at Cian. "I can definitely promise that."

"Do you take him as your husband?"

"I do."

"Cian, do you promise to love Scarlett with all your heart?"

"I promise."

"Do you take her as your wife?"

"I absolutely do."

"Then I officially declare you husband and wife," the king proclaims, his voice much stronger than it was when Declan and Astrid became husband and wife. He raises his hand. "Go forth with my blessing."

"Your Majesty," Cian says, his eyes on me. "Unlike Declan, I'd really like to kiss my bride."

Diarmuid chuckles. "Never ask anyone's permission to kiss your wife."

Cian gives me a grin, then cups my face and brings me in for a long, sweet kiss.

Then he says against my mouth for my ears only, "We're definitely making it on the podcast for this."

"We'd better," I tell him. "That's the whole reason I said yes to this."

He nips my bottom lip. "Witch."

I laugh. "Actually, that's *princess* to you now."

He pulls back and grins down at me with possessiveness, pride, and love in his eyes. "Yes, it certainly is."

CHAPTER 38

CIAN

"Oh my God, we're two hours late for dinner!"

Scarlett comes out of the bedroom, redressed in the clothes I stripped off of her two and a half hours ago when we came upstairs to get dressed for dinner. The dinner that started two hours ago and has easily been over for an hour.

Her hair is still wet from the shower we had to take after I got her nice and messy.

"Well, now you know what happens when you refer to yourself as my wife," I tell her unapologetically from the couch in the sitting room, where she ordered me when I wouldn't keep my hands off her as she was trying to do her make-up and get dressed *again*.

She laughs. "I wasn't even saying that *to* you."

I shrug. "Doesn't matter. You being my wife makes me feral."

She smirks as her hand drops away from brushing

through her wet, dark hair. "I noticed the same thing happened when I referred to myself as Princess Scarlett."

Yes, the same thing definitely happens when I'm reminded she's my princess. I growl and get up from the couch. "If you want dinner at all tonight, you'll control your wicked side. At least until we get back up here."

The grin she gives me in return is also completely without apology.

"We have to go to dinner tonight. Everyone let us get out of everything all day yesterday and most of this morning. People are going to wonder if we're still alive up here."

I walk over to her, take the brush from her hand, and turn her to face away from me. I start pulling the brush through the long strands. "The empty dishes we keep setting outside of the room are proof of life."

She laughs and the sound hits me hard, filling my chest with emotion. It's not just lust, but the overwhelming love that I feel for this woman that has intensified now that everything is open and official, and she is freely sharing all of her emotions with me. I had no idea I could feel this way about someone.

"I guess you have a point. Still, I have an impressionable teenage daughter. I need to resurface at some point. Even if we are newlyweds."

I chuckle as I divide her hair into three strands. "If you think your fifteen-year-old doesn't understand what we're doing up here..."

"Do not finish that sentence," she tells me.

I don't. And I understand why that makes her uncomfortable. Mariah is now officially my stepdaughter. She is far too young to know anything about sex. Way too young to date. I don't want her even remotely interested in boys. Or girls, romantically. And I feel a very strong surge of protectiveness go through me at the idea of some stupid teenager showing up at our doorstep, wanting to take her out. There is no chance there is anyone good enough for her out there.

Hope she's okay with being a spinster.

Then again, she's going to be so busy changing the world, that she might not be interested in silly things like romance.

But then I take in the woman before me and think about how much better a person I am with her than I ever was without her. She's my *partner,* not just my lover or even my friend, and I realize I do want *this* for Mariah. I want her to find someone that builds her up and worships her and wants her happiness even more than they want their own.

Scarlett reaches back to feel what I'm doing with her hair.

"Hey, don't mess with it," I tell her.

"Are you French braiding my hair?" she asks, surprise in her tone.

"It's still wet. This is probably easier and will take less time than if we wait for you to dry it," I say, finishing the braid and reaching for her wrist. I know she has an elastic band there. I pull it from her wrist and wrap it around the end of her hair.

She turns to face me. "You know how to French braid hair?"

"That's nothing. I can do a lot better than that. I have been doing princess hair since Saoirse's got long enough to put in a barrette. Don't insult me."

Scarlett's lips curve into a bright smile that I swear I will never get tired of seeing.

"I guess I didn't think of that. You helped with her hair?"

"Fiona's too," I tell her, mock insulted.

"Well, that is very handy to know, Your Highness." She gives me a tiny bow.

I growl. "You know what calling me Your Highness does to me too, wife "

She holds a hand up and starts backing away from me. "No, no, we're not starting this. We need to go down and eat dinner."

I stop advancing but give her a warning look.

Then she gives me a flirty grin. "But if I say anything like that during dinner, I probably deserve to be spanked for it later."

I growl again and take a step forward, wrap my hand around the braid I just created, tip her head back, and say, "I am so fucking in love with you. "

Her eyes are dancing as she looks up at me. "Ditto. And your hair styling skills are very good to know about."

I lean in and drag my lips down the column of her neck. "Is that right? You want me to do your hair more often?"

"Yes, I do, actually. Very hot," she murmurs. "And you know, it will be handy if there are ever any other little princesses around."

I lift my head quickly. Is she talking about nieces? Or Mariah? She's not really *little*. Or granddaughters someday? Or maybe...little princesses she and I make?

I open my mouth to respond when I hear a knock on the door and our doorknob rattle.

Scarlett's head comes up and her gaze flies to the door. "I thought you said no one would interrupt us."

I let her go with a little sigh. We are *very* late for dinner. "There was one exception I gave them," I say, referring to the palace staff and our friends that I instructed to leave us alone until I said otherwise—instructions that have miraculously kept the hallway clear for the past day and a half since our wedding.

"What exception?" she asks as I cross to the door.

"Mariah."

Scarlett's expression softens. I shrug. "Of course she's the exception."

But as I reach to open the door, I hear voices in the hallway and I pause.

Mariah and Saoirse are on the other side.

"You shouldn't bother them," Saoirse says. "They just got married. They want to be alone. After my mom married Knox, I stayed over at the other house with Torin and Cian and everyone for like three days."

I grin at Scarlett. She's not exaggerating.

"I have to talk to her," Mariah says. "They've been in there forever. They totally missed dinner." She sounds exasperated. "After I show them this, they can go back in there and I won't bother them anymore."

"Okay, I'm just saying, this is normal. They'll come out eventually."

"But my mom will really want to know about this," Mariah says. "This is *huge*."

Scarlett and I exchange a look.

I point to the doorknob and lift a brow.

Scarlett nods.

I swing the door open.

It startles the girls. "Oh my God, Cian!" Saoirse gasps.

"You guys, you're not going to believe what happened!" Mariah exclaims as she immediately comes into the room.

Saoirse is typing on her phone as she follows Mariah to the sofa.

"We were just coming down for dinner," Scarlett tells them.

The girls look at each other and then look at us. "Dinner was over an hour ago."

Yeah, I'd called it. We're probably going to need to get food brought up again.

The girls plop onto the sofa right next to one another.

"So what happened?" Scarlett asks, dropping onto the cushion next to Mariah.

"You know how Leah texted me yesterday?" Mariah asks.

Predictably, the podcast had covered the fact that Scarlett and I got married. And all the other royal family news. Including that I was now a stepfather to a fifteen-year-old girl named Mariah.

Not long after, Leah Lawton, of all people, had texted Mariah a wide-eyed emoji, a crown emoji, an hallelujah hands emoji, and a heart-eyes emoji.

Mariah had been shocked. She had also taken it as a pseudo apology.

"Of course," Scarlett says. It had been huge news in our family, obviously.

"Well, Greta sent me this from a little bit ago."

I round the back of the couch and lean over so I can also watch the video Mariah is showing Scarlett on her phone.

It only takes me two seconds to recognize the lunchroom at Emerald High School.

The video is of Leah walking into the room...and being booed.

She stops, looks around as if confused, and then a girl in their class named Skyler stands up and calls out, "Mariah was telling the truth this whole time! *You're* the liar!"

Leah looks shocked, then embarrassed. She gets very red in the face, but then straightens her spine, and says, "I know! I was wrong, okay?"

But there's more boo-ing and eventually Leah flounces out of the lunchroom followed by her two best friends.

Greta is obviously the one recording the event because she turns the phone around to show her face and mouths, *holy shit*. Then laughs, blows a kiss to the camera, and says, "I miss you, Princess Mariah!"

Mariah stops the video and looks up at her mother, then up at me. "Can you believe *that*?"

Scarlett's eyes are wide, but she smiles. "You deserve that."

Mariah sighs. "I know. But after Leah texted me yesterday, now I kind of feel bad for her."

I put my hand on top of her head. "Imagine how great it will be when you get back to school and you can show everyone that you've forgiven her and you can both just move on from this."

"Yeah. I guess I can make this better for her," Mariah says thoughtfully.

"Exactly. You have the power to make this hard on Leah or show everyone what grace and forgiveness looks like," Scarlett says. "I don't think anyone would blame you if you wanted to make her face what she did, but I know you'll do the right thing."

Mariah is still clearly mulling that over. "Oh, well, just so you know, something similar happened to Hannah," Mariah says.

Scarlett sits up a little straighter. "What?"

"Yep. She went to the café with her friends, and someone there said something about how now everyone knows that you really did date a prince and were telling the truth and she should be ashamed of how she talked about you."

Scarlett looks at me. "Oh. That's…"

"Great," I say. "You both deserve to have the town know the truth."

Scarlett nods her head. "Yeah. I guess. I just wish…"

I put my hand on her head now. "You'll handle it. This is a great chance for you to show them all who you really are now. Just like you wanted."

I wish they'd suffer even more for the lies and nastiness, but I know that's not very generous of me. Scarlett will do the right thing and be a bigger person.

She's awesome that way.

"Oh, and tell them the other thing," Saoirse says. "Then we need to take the selfie that we're going to send. "

"What other thing? What selfie?" I ask my niece.

"The podcast wants to interview us. And they want us to send a photo of us together," Saoirse replies.

"That's great."

These two are going to be a force to be reckoned with together. But the podcast would be really fun for them. I look at Scarlett, though. It's her call. I'm the stepdad. This is new. I don't get to make big decisions about these kinds of things involving Mariah.

Scarlett looks up at me. "Can we trust them? I mean the podcast women?"

"For sure," I say. "We can also go with the girls. Or maybe, better yet, send Linnea with them."

Scarlett nods quickly. "That would be fantastic. I know Linnea will protect them from any inappropriate questions or topics of conversation."

"Of course I will," Linnea says, breezing through our doorway with Jonah right behind her.

"She told me to let her know if I saw you guys out of the room," Saoirse says. "I texted her because I figured this kind of counted."

I round the couch and sink down onto the cushion next to Scarlett. I reach for her hand, threading our fingers together. We are probably going to be here for a while.

Fifteen minutes later, Henry arrives, looking confused as if he's been searching for everyone. "Didn't think we'd be welcome across this threshold for a few more days," he says.

"Welcome is a strong word," I tell him.

No one in the room seems at all offended by that.

"I was just filling them in on the trip to Portland to open up the new moms' community there," Linnea says. "And telling them how excited Christopher is to have us come to New York and open one. He'd like to sit down and meet. He has some great input on some good locations."

Apparently Linnea is hoping to have Declan and Astrid involved with the Portland site, and Christopher Waite, one of the senators from New York, involved with the one there.

"Of course he is," Jonah says, his hand moving from the back of the loveseat where he and Linnea are sitting to the back of her neck in a very possessive though almost second-nature gesture.

I know that Christopher had some interest in Linnea in the past and that she actually went on a date with him when she and Jonah were in Washington, DC, just a few months ago.

That could be interesting.

"*Anyway*," Linnea says. "The trips are all planned. There are a couple of interviews I think would be interesting for you as well, but we can check on those as we go. And I love the idea of talking to the podcast. In fact, I'm going to pitch to them having Mariah come back after we've gone around the country and opened some of these homes. I'm sure they would love to have a young woman's perspective on this kind of work."

Mariah sits up straighter. "That would be really neat."

Linnea smiles at her. "You're going to be so great at all of this. As an ambassador for the royal family, but also for all of the wonderful things your mom and Cian are doing."

Mariah looks over at us, almost as if she's stunned.

"As much as you want to do," I assure her. "Your call."

Saoirse leans over and nudges Mariah with an elbow. "It gets easier as you go along."

My chest feels tight as I look around this room. This is exactly what I wanted to give my girls. A family, a community, a place where others would see how amazing they are and where they could really shine. This feels so damned good.

"Where is Ruby?" Henry asks me underneath the rest of the conversation.

I look at him with surprise. Typically, he knows everything that's going on around the palace and on the island. "She left. Last night actually. She texted Scarlett when she landed in Ohio this morning."

He scowls. "She left?"

"You didn't think she was going to stay with us indefinitely, did you?"

Looking at his face right now, I realize that he kind of did. Or that she'd be with us until we went back to Emerald. Or maybe he just hadn't really thought it through at all.

"She wanted to get back," I say. "She has a life in Ohio. She had to get back to work. She's got a house. Friends. She can't travel around the US with us."

He's still scowling. "Why not? You could support her."

"That's not the issue."

"Then what? A bartending job she does only out of

necessity in a town where she lives only because Scarlett wanted to move back there? Emerald was never Ruby's plan."

I glance at Scarlett but she's listening to Linnea and Mariah talk.

I lower my voice and lean closer to my best friend. "Well, I don't know what to tell you, Henry. She came in and said her goodbyes. I arranged the plane. She texted Scarlett when she got home." I study him for a moment. "I take it she didn't say goodbye to you?"

He blows out a breath. "No."

"Maybe that's for the best?" I ask.

He doesn't say anything for several seconds, but finally, he gives me a single nod. "Yeah, maybe."

Just then Scarlett's phone rings.

"Sorry," she apologizes, pulling the phone from her pocket. She glances at the screen and frowns, then looks at me. "It's Ruby."

"Take it," I say. "It's fine." This is hardly a formal meeting.

Besides, Linnea is in charge. That's really all any of us need to know. We'll go where she tells us to, when she tells us to, and everything will turn out great.

Scarlett stands and takes a few steps away from the group, lifting her phone to her ear.

I watch her, feeling my neck muscles tighten as I observe her body language.

"Something's wrong," Henry says, clearly reading the same thing.

Scarlett comes back over to the couch. "We might have to rearrange our trips a little bit."

"What is it?" Henry asks, his tone sharp.

"We just need to go back to Ohio. Or I do. Maybe you can go on without me," she says to me.

I frown. "No way. Why do you have to go back?" I stand. "Is Ruby all right?"

"Yes. Kind of. She's...taking someone in."

Henry is on his feet now too. "What the fuck does that mean?"

She looks at both of us then glances around the room. Everyone is listening. But this is our family. They would find out eventually anyway. And we might need some of their resources.

"You can tell everyone," I assure her. "They're all here for you and for Ruby."

Scarlett's shoulders relax a bit at that.

"So you know that Ruby was with me when I faced down our father in the café," she says.

I nod.

"And Ruby's also been making noise about the church and city refusing grant money to help support single moms."

I nod again.

"Well, she's on some shit lists for that, but she's also being lauded as inspiring to others."

I look at Henry. He's staring at Scarlett.

"So, a woman who knows Ruby from the bar has decided to leave her abusive husband and reached out to Ruby for help. Ruby invited her and her young son to come stay at our house until the woman can get her legal stuff in order and figure out a plan."

"No," Henry says firmly.

Scarlett frowns up at him. "She's not asking for permission, Henry. From me or you. She was just informing me."

"Why do you need to go home then?" Henry asks, his tone challenging.

Scarlett shrugs. "I know the guy. We went to high school with him. He's definitely not a good person. I am afraid he's not going to let his wife and son leave peacefully. And I'm afraid he's going to blame Ruby directly."

"So she's not safe," Henry says.

Scarlett grimaces. "That's what I'm worried about."

"Then I'll go."

We both stare at Henry.

"You're going to go to Emerald? And you'll do what? Protect Ruby?" Scarlett asks.

"Yes." Henry looks around the room. "I'm trained for this, for fuck's sake. She couldn't have better protection. It makes perfect sense."

"Except that she doesn't want to see you anymore," Scarlett points out.

"This isn't about that. She needs to be safe. We both know we're not going to talk her out of doing this. So I need to be there to make sure she's all right."

"But—" Scarlett starts.

"Even if you did go, you will not be as good at protecting her as I will," Henry says. "And if you and Mariah go home, there are two more people for this asshole to threaten and potentially hurt."

My gut tightens at that.

"You two stay away until we get this woman and her kid settled. I'll be there to be sure they're okay. And Ruby, of course."

"It makes sense, Scarlett," I say.

She frowns. "What about Cian?" Scarlett asks Henry. "I thought you always had to be with him."

Well, there is that.

"He's got you now," Henry says.

Scarlett stares at him. "What?"

"You can keep him from doing anything stupid."

"I..." She looks from him to me, then back to him. "I was thinking more of the keeping him from being assassinated thing."

"He can't be anywhere safer than here in Cara," Henry says. "And when you go to the US, Jonah will be with you." Henry turns to Linnea and Jonah. "Right?"

Linnea nods. "Right."

Jonah looks at his wife and then at Henry, "Yeah. Right." Clearly this is news to Jonah, but he's rolling with it.

Henry turns back to us. "So he'll have a babysitter and a bodyguard with him."

"Hey," I protest.

They all look at me expectantly.

Then I shake my head. "No, never mind. That sounds good."

"I'll call you from Emerald." Henry turns and strides from the room without another word.

Scarlett looks at me. "So he's just going to go?"

"Yep."

"And I don't have a say in it?"

"Oh, definitely not."

"Do *you* have a say in it...Your Highness?"

I growl and lean in to kiss her.

She giggles and leans back. "Well, do you?"

"Do I what?" I don't remember what she asked me before calling me *Your Highness*. She never should have called me that while on her knees in the flower garden. Forever that's going to result in an instant erection.

"Ever tell Henry what to do," she says. "Since you're basically his boss."

Jonah and Linnea both snort at that. I think I even hear Saoirse giggle softly.

"Oh, I'm not Henry's boss. And no, I don't do that."

Scarlett laughs. "I'm shocked to hear that."

"I have *tried* it in the past," I admit. "And a couple of times he's gone along with it. Specifically to prove the point that he's always right. I gave it up four years ago when I was in the ER waiting to get stitches and he was assuring the first-year intern that I didn't need any numbing."

She smiles, then sighs. "So Henry's going to Emerald. Where it will be just him and Ruby."

"Yep."

"Ruby's going to kill me for that."

"Nah, Jonah won't let her," I tell her with a grin. Then I lean in and kiss her. "Let's give Ruby and Henry some space. Let's go to Portland, then New York, and we'll…see how things are in Emerald then."

She looks at me with wide eyes. "Wait…Cian O'Grady, are you playing matchmaker?"

"Maybe? Henry will be *a lot* easier to live with for the rest of our lives if he and Ruby can work this out. But… if it *doesn't* go well, I'm not interested in being there with Ruby and Henry if they're *not* getting along. I say we stay away until they're madly in love or until this woman and her abusive asshole husband are taken care of and Henry doesn't feel worked up about protecting the woman he can't have."

Her eyes are wide, but she nods. "Yeah, you have a point."

Then she leans closer and says, "I'm so glad we worked out all of *our* issues. I'm so lucky to be your *wife*."

That's it. "Okay, everyone out. My wife and I need to eat dinner."

I need to feed my woman so I can take her back to bed. She'll need the calories.

Everyone laughs and gets up, heading for the door. I take Scarlett's hand and tug her up from the couch. I start to follow the group out of the room, but I feel Scarlett pulling me back.

I look at her. "What's going on?"

"Bye, girls! Love you, Mariah!" she calls.

"Bye, Mom! Love you too!"

Then they're all gone, the door shutting behind them.

"I was just thinking," she says. "Could we have dinner brought up? Since we missed it anyway?"

"Sure. But why?"

She slides her arms around my neck and presses close, kissing my throat. My cock immediately begins to respond. "It's just... you're right. The "my wife" thing is really hot."

I grin down at her as I slide my hands up her back to her hair. I pull the ponytail holder free, wrap it around my wrist, and start to unbraid her hair. "Yes, it is, Princess. Yes, it fucking is."

"So..." She kisses along my jaw as I pull my fingers through her hair. "Maybe we can wait a little bit to call down for food too, Your Highness?"

I bend and sweep her into my arms. She gives a sweet little gasp then giggles as I carry her into the bedroom.

"Yes, but..." I stop next to the bed and let her slide down my body. "I believe it's *my husband* to you now."

She gives me that smile that will forever reach into my chest and wrap around my heart as she pulls me down onto the bed with her. "Yes, it certainly is, my husband."

Thank you so much for reading Cian and Scarlett's story!
I hope you loved Rags to Royals!

Want more from Cian and Scarlett (and Mariah)? **I've got a BONUS EPILOGUE for you right HERE!**
bit.ly/Rags-to-Royals-Epilogue

*Wondering about **Astrid and Declan**?*
*Don't worry! There's more to come! Want to see what's going on with them right now? They show up again in Astrid's brother Alex's book, **Just Don't Call It Love** (and then…there will be more!)*

*And YES, **Henry and Ruby** are up next in Recklessly Rogue!*

This woman is why I've actively avoided falling in love.

Though it's never really been a temptation before.

Flirtation and seduction sure. But love? No.

My time, my attention, my loyalty, protection, and heart are already spoken for.
I've dedicated my life to a prince. It was just a job for only about a month. Then he became my best friend, and his family became my family. I would put my life on the line for any them without question.

I don't have room for anyone else.

But this woman...
the one I met accidentally,
the one I walked away from when I first felt the stirrings of something more,
the one I didn't *stay* away from like I should have,
the one I'm now living with so I can protect her because her heart is bigger than her common sense...

She's going to ruin everything.

And I think I'm going to let her.

And the best place to find out all the news about that (including title and cover reveal, release date, and more!) is right here!
bit.ly/Keep-In-Touch-Erin
(be sure you get those dashes and capital letters in there :))

And this is your personal invitation to my Facebook group, Erin Nicholas's Super Fans where you can get first looks, behind the scenes peeks, and daily fun with fellow romance lovers (including me!)!

CONNECTED BOOKS FROM ERIN NICHOLAS

All of these can be read as stand-alones, even though they are part of interconnected series! Jump in anywhere and enjoy!

Want to know more about Torin's sister Fiona, his brother Cian, and their bodyguards, including Henry and Colin?

Check out **Kiss My Giraffe** (a grumpy-sunshine, princess-in-hiding, small town rom com!) and **Better Safe Than Safari** (a bodyguard-rockstar, curvy-girl, steamy rom com)**!**

Find all of these and so much more at www. ErinNicholas.com!

About Erin

Erin Nicholas is the New York Times and USA Today bestselling author of over sixty sexy contemporary romances. She's known for her blue-collar book boyfriends and big, boisterous found families in small towns. Her stories have been described as toe-curling, enchanting, steamy and fun. She loves to write about reluctant heroes, imperfect heroines and happily ever afters.

She lives in the Midwest with her husband who only wants to read the sex scenes in her books, her kids who will never read the sex scenes in her books, and family and friends who say they're shocked by the sex scenes in her books (yeah, right!).

Find her and all her books at
www.ErinNicholas.com

And find her on Facebook, BookBub, and Instagram!

Copyright 2024 Erin Nicholas

All rights reserved.

No part of this book may be reproduced in any form or by any electronic or mechanical means, including information storage and retrieval systems, without written permission from the author, except for the use of brief quotations in a book review.

This book is a work of fiction. Names, characters, places, and incidents are either products of the author's imagination or are used factiously, and any resemblance to actual persons, living or dead, business establishments, events, or locales is coincidental.

Editor: Lindsey Faber

Cover design: Qamber Designs

Digital ISBN: 9979-8-9908220-2-3

Paperback ISBN: 979-8-9908220-4-7

Special Edition ISBN: 979-8-9908220-5-4